Something Down There

By

Nancy Widrew

Other works by Nancy Widrew

"Tchotchke Lessions" published in Dark Fire Fiction

"Losing It" published in SNM Horror Magazine

"To Dance With The Bogeyman" published in Absent Willow Review

The short story "Losing It" was in SNM's print horror anthology, Bonded By Blood IV, because it was voted one of the best for the year 2011 by their editors. (The Horror Zine, another webzine, gave the anthology good reviews but not specifically my story.) Also all of these magazines (except for Dark Fire Fiction) are no longer publishing.

Something Down There

By

Nancy Widrew

azure
spider
publications

This is a work of fiction. All the characters and events portrayed in this book are either products of the author's imagination or are used fictiously.

Something Down There.
Copyright ©2017 by Nancy Widrew
Cover by Circecorp
Published by Azure Spider Publications LLC
1051 NE Pepperwood
Grants Pass, OR 97526

www.azurespiderpublications.com

Library of Congress Control Number: 2017951754

ISBN: 978-0-9974621-9-7
ISBN: 978-0-9994071-0-3ebook

First Edition November 2017

Printed in the United States of America

This book is dedicated to my mother, Molly, who loved to read and write.

Acknowledgments:

I'd like to thank my husband, Ray, for his love and support. Without his knowledge of computers this wouldn't have been possible. I'd also like to thank the people at Azure Spider Publications for their help in polishing this story.

Chapter 1

Fall, 1977

Nearly one mile beneath the earth's surface, candles cast abstract patterns on the backs of nine people huddled together. The wind whipped the sooty air, causing flames to flash and sketch skewed halos across the participants' heads. Someone groaned, others sighed, a testament to the evening's grueling debate. Only their leader remained focused, smoothed over differences, preventing hurtful words or actions from spinning off into permanent wounds.

"I'm willing to go over the issue again," he said, "even though I doubt further discussion is necessary."

A female spoke up. "I don't like any of this. Maybe we should just admit defeat."

The leader turned to her, his creased forehead and steely demeanor barely visible in the amber glow; still, she felt his cool appraisal, and more significantly his release of animal pheromone, bending her to his will. She shrank back.

"There'll be no admission of defeat," he said. "No giving up. Sometimes we have to make hard choices. Risk everything if necessary." His voice was calm but with a serrated edge, since he had learned years ago that he could get more with subtle intimidation, using tricks as simple as flared nostrils. Of course, if more was needed, threats remained a viable option.

Another man spoke up. "I've made my decision," he said with a wink toward the leader, "and I'm ready to vote. We've been going round and round for the past month. I think we should just get this over with."

"I'm ready too," said the leader. "But"—he held up a finger—"with one stipulation. Due to the subject matter, I don't want to use secret ballots like we usually do. This must be a unanimous decision. I need to know we're in this together." He looked at each member. "Agreed?"

There was fidgeting, murmurs, grunts, but finally nods of approval all around.

"Good. Then let's do it. Everyone knows my position. We've covered the pros and cons down to the last detail. So if you trust me, believe in me, you'll follow my recommendation. Now those in favor, raise your hands."

Immediately, five hands shot up, then two others, and, after a protracted pause, an eighth. Only a half-smile appeared on the leader's face since one more affirmation was needed to ensure complete triumph. He narrowed his eyes to envelop the sole dissident, a plain-looking woman known for her stubbornness. "Mary, Mary, Mary," he said, repeating her name with a shake of his head. Taken aback at being the lone holdout, the woman felt a catch in her throat followed by an acrid taste on her tongue, prompting second thoughts. Like a helium balloon, her hand soared into the air.

"That's better," said the leader, staring at the troublemaker with a laser beam's intensity. Springing to his feet, he rose on his toes, adding not only height but the illusion of strength. "The motion is approved," he said, chest out, smiling ear to ear. "And now, my friends, my dear, dear friends—I bid you a pleasant night with pleasant dreams."

#

Worlds away in Baltimore, Maryland, Karen Dryer wished her husband dead. Until they'd met, she had never heard of caving or spelunking, as he called it. He urged her to go. "Absolutely not," she said, tossing aside his latest speleology magazine as if it were yesterday's smelly underwear. "I have no intention of entering a black, muddy pit with rotting bones, bugs, and who knows what."

Fearing marital warfare, Jeremy reached for her hand. "You've got it all wrong, Karen. You'll have one of the best days of your life. Guaranteed."

Knowing a spiel when she heard one, Karen looked up, studying the ceiling. Still she wavered and finally after pleas of "I'd do it for you" and "I'm only asking you try this once," she'd given in to his wishes; being married only eight months, she still wanted to please.

But now, peering through the open slats in the Venetian blind, she regretted her decision. Before her loomed night's shrouded expanse, devoid of all familiarities that make life pleasurable during the day, and against her will an image took shape: a bleak rendering of a shallow mound bled into an unmarked grave with her below, a nobody so easily forgotten that it scarcely mattered she had ever lived at all.

"I hate you," she hissed to Jeremy's outline, lying leaden beside her. Then, guilt-ridden, she took a cleansing breath. Feeling better, she threw off the covers and toddled on Raggedy-Ann knees to the bathroom.

The water from the showerhead massaged her skin with its dancing fingers, but as she scrubbed away yesterday's grime, she realized the futility of her routine, knowing she'd soon be up to her elbows in muck. Shrugging off the deduction, she grabbed a towel, drying herself from top to bottom, the downward curve of her mouth a testament to dysmorphophobia, a distortion in body image.

This distortion, a cognitive blip, prevented her from seeing the obvious: an attractive woman responsible for many a double take from passersby. Instead she fixated on minor imperfections, like her demitasse-sized breasts, and for a moment she considered buying a lacy pushup with padding. "No," she muttered, knowing that wouldn't solve the problem. Disheartened, she squinched her nose above compressed lips while adjusting her bra with a snap.

After putting on the extra layer of clothes that Jeremy suggested, she started out the door as he brushed past. With eyes half-closed and wearing nothing more than a T-shirt, he reached for the sink to support his barely awake body. For the hundredth time, Karen questioned how he could be so casual with his nakedness while she retained a hefty dose of modesty.

Looking up at him, she smiled a good morning.

"Whose idea was this anyway?" he asked, slurring his words.

Her jaw tightened. "You know perfectly well who."

"Sorry, babe. Just kidding." He bent down and planted a kiss on the top of her head.

She stared at his face: handsome, almost perfectly so, with hero-like looks and a cleft in his chin as if molded by some genetic demigod. "I thought *I* was supposed to be the pretty one," she'd often joke. Now realizing she'd meant every word, she turned away, disappointed, as if she'd been handed second prize at the fair.

Once again, she started out the door.

"Don't forget the coffee," he called after her.

#

Using a fat, black marker, Karen drew an X across October 15 on the calendar. With a new year creeping up, she crossed her fingers, wishing for a better one. She put the percolator on the stove and sat down to wait for the brown bubbles to appear. Furrows etched her brow. *If only Carl and Joan hadn't canceled.*

Carl worked with Jeremy at the *Baltimore Beehive,* an alternative weekly. Having both been hired the previous spring—Carl as a photographer and Jeremy covering local news—they'd soon become friends, particularly when they discovered their mutual interest in caves. Carl, however, was the expert, introducing Jeremy and other employees to spectacular caverns in West Virginia, and this time the wives were joining them.

Unfortunately, Carl called the night before. Between coughs and shotgun sneezes, he spelled out the obvious, leaving Karen steaming, not at Carl but at Jeremy.

"We'll go by ourselves," Jeremy had said. "Remember, you promised."

Angered by his brazen arm-twisting, she spat out a string of curse words, triggering Jeremy to strike back with his own nasty zings. This was followed by his-and-her shouts, slammed doors, and worst of all, a pained silence lasting hours.

Finally they'd made up with Karen capitulating, admitting a promise is a promise. Still, she held out hope for one last approach—a candid conversation—and with nothing to lose, she braced herself for the showdown.

Alone in the kitchen, Karen clasped her hands in a white-knuckled grip. Feeling her fingers grow tingly, she pulled them apart, waving them pell-mell like an elephant flaps its ears. "Damn!" she yelled as she knocked over the sugar container, causing the table to tilt. After adjusting its misaligned leg, she cleaned up the mess and poured herself a cup of coffee. Once again, she sat down to wait.

"Everything all right?" asked Jeremy, walking in moments later. "I heard something fall."

"It was nothing," she said, pausing to lift the mug to her mouth. "But, uhh … since you asked … no, everything's not all right. I'd still rather wait until Carl and Joan are better." She forced a smile. "Even that third couple canceled."

"That's 'cause they're also sick. But we're fine. Look, we've been planning this for weeks, and I know what I'm doing. Besides, you've been down before."

"Yes, but that was a commercial cave, and we were part of a group. I don't like the idea of just the two of us fifty feet below. And what about that rule you told me about? 'Never go below without three people, minimum.' I haven't felt so scared since—"

Jeremy interrupted, finishing her sentence. "Since the day you almost stepped on a snake. And then it only turned out to be a common garter." He held back a laugh, but his mouth zigzagged with the elasticity of a rubber band. Using a napkin, he attempted to hide his mocking smile. Unfortunately for him, Karen caught the ploy.

"Don't you dare make fun of me," she said. "You think I'm blind? I saw that patronizing smirk."

Jeremy blanched under the remains of his summer tan. "I'm sorry," he said.

Karen, no longer in a forgiving mood, said, "I'll bet you're sorry. Screw my promise. You can kiss today goodbye. I'm going back to bed."

Jeremy's shoulders slumped at his blunder. He closed his eyes, thinking. "I don't blame you, Karen, but if you give me another chance, I'll change my behavior. Tell you what … tomorrow I'll fill in for Joan at those movies you've been raving about. The ones with the tap dancing and goofy dialogue. I have a feeling she'll be too sick to go anywhere."

"Really? You'll do that? I love those old movies. They're classics."

"Well, classics or not, they're torture for me, but if it makes you happy, I'll go. In fact, let's call it a date—a real date, like before we were married. Maybe we can eat out afterwards. You've been wanting to try that Mexican place. And as for today"—Jeremy shrugged—"it's your choice." While pausing to let her think and hopefully reconsider, he washed his mug and hers, moving his hands back and forth, up and down, with flamboyant Liberace-like gestures to make sure she noticed. "Hey you know what?" he said, glancing sideways. "I've got an idea. We'll go to a different cave. Dinky Cave. It's so easy that the three-person rule won't apply. You've nothing to be scared of. I swear."

By this time Karen barely heard, already ensconced in a bubble with the 1940s Brazilian bombshell, Carmen Miranda, known for wiggling her hips like a hybrid hula-belly dancer. As Carmen coyly trilled "Lady in the Tutti-Frutti Hat," Karen, still in her chair, hummed and shimmied to the catchy number, risqué for its day, with scantily clad women waving six-foot bananas. She moved her upper torso so enthusiastically that even her small breasts jiggled. Taking that as a favorable sign, Jeremy chuckled as Karen cocked her head and nodded.

#

Although they took Karen's car, Jeremy did the driving, allowing her to rest and, hopefully, unwind during the two-hour-plus trip to the cave he had selected in the Shenandoah Valley. With the highway a boring array of signs advertising gas, food, and lodging, Karen set the radio dial to easy-listening music. Tapping her foot to a snare drum's backbeat, she pictured long-past bucolic summers where cows grazed and goats nibbled, but her chain-saw tooth-grinding testified failure.

The main problem, she realized, went beyond the cave. Ever since they had left New Hampshire, just six months before, she had struggled with that damned black cloud floating above her head. While she felt happy for Jeremy's good fortune, her personal sacrifices—particularly the relinquishment of her job—had coalesced into a non-healing scab, and although she had prepared herself for difficulties, she'd never imagined anything like this. It seemed that every high school English teacher in the United States had also moved to Maryland, and her ability to maintain an optimistic outlook had quickly dimmed.

"Something wrong?" asked Jeremy, noticing her half-chewed nail.

"Nothing," she lied. "Just tired." Actually she was afraid to speak, afraid of what she might say, particularly after last night's major battle and this morning's minor one. If only she didn't feel like a dupe, always giving in, making the concessions; still, that was the price she paid for love and love mattered, dammit. Besides, she had acknowledged before they were married that Jeremy had the more forceful personality. Or maybe she just loved him more than he loved her.

Absentmindedly, she spat out the tip of the nail she'd been nibbling, leaving a jagged edge.

#

They stopped for breakfast just over the border at a gray clapboard structure serving as both restaurant and country store where locals could eat, purchase small items, and, most importantly, gossip about the goings on in the lives of their neighbors. A sign on the road read *KATE'S PLACE* and depicted a cheery woman holding a coffee pot. Jeremy held the door for Karen to walk through and the smoky smell of bacon hit her like a slap to the face. Karen's mouth watered.

A brusque, sleepy-eyed hostess, obviously not Kate, led them to a booth with red vinyl seats and a standard Formica table screwed to the floor. The seat was lumpy with duct tape running across the middle to cover a tear. Karen shifted her weight, trying to get comfortable. There was no point in asking to be moved since morning business was brisk.

Their waitress's name was Betty, made clear by the plastic tag pinned to the front of her uniform. She raised her arm to direct their attention to a glass coffee pot that looked like a natural extension of her hand. When Karen and Jeremy nodded, she flipped over the cups already seated in their saucers and poured. "Be back in a couple of minutes with menus," she said, "unless you want the house special; it's our best deal."

"What's that?" asked Jeremy.

"OJ and coffee. Two eggs, two bacon, two sausage, home fries or grits, and toast."

Jeremy said, "Can I have beans instead of fries or grits?"

Betty put down the pot, removed the pencil from behind her ear, and licked the point. "You mean baked beans?"

"That's right," said Jeremy.

The waitress squinted and looked at Karen for an explanation. "I'd prefer beans too," she said.

Betty jerked her head back and twisted her mouth. "Okay," she said, writing it in her pad with an underscore. "To each his own, I suppose." She hitched her shoulders and walked off to have a good laugh with the cook and the rest of the staff.

Karen pressed an elbow against the table and rested her chin in her palm. "I guess she's never been to New England."

"Yeah, I miss it too, but next spring I'll have two weeks of vacation saved up. We can go back, visit friends and family, eat at the *Red Arrow* every morning if you like."

"Really?" said Karen.

Before Jeremy could respond, two plates were plopped down on the table. "Be back in a sec with your b-e-a-n-s," said Betty. She dragged out the last word as if it held some sort of contaminant. Nevertheless, two bowls promptly arrived. "It's kinda liquidy so I didn't put it on the same plates with your eggs. I also brought extra spoons in case you prefer them to forks for your b-e-a-n-s."

"Appreciate that," said Jeremy.

She left after pouring more coffee, and Jeremy took a taste of the sweet, lumpy mixture in its familiar brown sauce. He licked his lips and began to sing, "'Beans, beans, the musical fruit.'"

Karen joined in: "'The more you eat them the more you toot.'"

They both grinned, snickered, then guffawed, causing nearby patrons—more curious than annoyed—to turn in their direction.

Jeremy reached for his wife's hand, relieved to see her more animated with her mouth an upturned crescent moon, exposing two front teeth, slightly gapped.

Jeremy always found this a charming attribute, amusing too, although he was careful to never mention it.

"Karen," he said, "if you don't want to go, if you want to turn around and go home, I'm okay with it. Really! I won't be mad."

Karen raised her eyebrows. "I wish you'd said that yesterday when Carl called, but we've come this far so we may as well continue. Who knows? Maybe I'll even enjoy myself."

Jeremy tipped his head, smiling with his eyes. "I love you," he said. "You're the best. I'm some lucky guy."

Karen took a bite of toast, swallowing it along with a lump in her throat. "I love you too," she whispered. And as had happened many times before, she wondered what he saw in her.

#

"Wake up, sleepy-head. We're almost there."

Karen grunted, stifling a yawn. Sitting up straight, she turned her face to the window. Despite the sunny sky, a pattering of rain splashed across the windshield, and the contrast reminded her of something she had heard many years before on a sixth-grade outing.

"This phenomenon is a sun shower," Mrs. Frankel had pontificated, "and it means something exceptional is about to happen." *Maybe old Mrs. Frankel wasn't crazy after all,* Karen reflected, imagining the forthcoming day with its plunge into the unknown.

A sudden swerve and Karen found herself tilting sideways. "Watch out!" she screamed, bracing her arms for impact. Despite the seatbelt, she hit her shoulder against the door.

"Shit!" Jeremy snapped, turning to Karen as he cut the engine. "Sorry about that. I guess I was driving too fast with the rain. You okay?"

"I suppose," she said, her voice rising an octave as if she were unsure. "Why'd you turn onto this two-bit road, anyway? Is this the place?"

Jeremy nodded. "Yep," he said. "This is it, and it looks like we're not alone." His thumb and forefinger formed a gun which pointed toward an unoccupied car with Pennsylvania license plates, the source of his displeasure.

Springing out of their subcompact, Jeremy did a 360 loop around a sporty coupe station wagon. "Well, at least they have good taste in cars."

Cars, like caves, were not high on Karen's list of interests and she offered no response; on the other hand, she felt relieved that they wouldn't be alone after their descent.

When she didn't rush out, Jeremy tapped on the window and waved his hand backwards in a beckoning sweep. "Hurry up," he called. "It's not getting any earlier."

Karen climbed out, zipping up her fall jacket with its faux fur lining.

"You won't need to wear that," said Jeremy, trying not to sound patronizing. "It stays warm below, all year long. You know. Natural insulation."

Karen shrugged. She unzipped the jacket and tossed it into the back seat and then followed Jeremy to a hole at the base of a hill.

"That's the entrance," he said, pointing to a small opening camouflaged behind shadows of weeds and rocks.

Her shoulders sagged while her mouth formed a circle of disbelief as she bent down to take a better look. "You've got to be kidding. That's barely a foot high. I'll never fit through."

"You will," he insisted, "and don't worry. It gets bigger inside. You'll be able to stand at first—hunched over, that is—and then we have to crawl a bit." His dark eyes flashed like the sun's rays skimming a crystal clear lake, conveying not only his enthusiasm but his satisfaction at being the person in charge.

"Help me pull our gear out of the car, and try not to break the carbide lamps on the helmets," he warned.

After bringing their backpacks and hats to the mouth of the cave, Jeremy went under and through in one deft movement. Karen pushed everything in to him from her side. "I'll be right with you," she said. "I have one final thing to do."

She spun on her knees and rose. As if trying to freeze the moment, she stared at the world, from scrub and dirt to panoramic sky, taking pleasure in its familiarities. Even with its problems, she felt reluctant to trade them for the mysteries below.

With autumn's tableaux spread before her, fixed to perfection like a touristy postcard, she was suddenly aware of the legacy that was hers; yet despite the beauty, she couldn't help but be reminded that this was a season of endings. Earth would continue on its orbit, soon making such delights a mere memory, and there was something sad about memories, even pleasant ones.

Feeling a sudden chill, she tugged down her shirtsleeves, wishing for something warm to drink. *A cup of cocoa would be nice,* she thought, picturing her mother making it from scratch. *If only I had it now!*

Turning back to the cave, she clenched her jaw to stop her clattering teeth. "Well here goes nothing." Her words were prophetic. In trying to imitate the same swift maneuver as her husband, she hit the top of her head and wound up with dirt falling on her face. "Son of a bitch!" she yelled at the top of her lungs. Having few outlets, she loved to curse. Although she saw it as a shortcoming, she did it anyway since it never failed to bring relief.

Jeremy ignored her outburst but solicitously wiped her cheeks with a handkerchief. "Look," he said. "Just try to enjoy yourself. Pretend you're on a geological dig. You liked the dinosaur bones at the natural history museum, remember? But tell you what. Besides tomorrow's movies, next weekend is your turn. We'll do whatever you want. Maybe I can even take Friday off. How's that?"

Karen twirled a finger in the air. "Woohoo!" she said, thinking of a warm beach with a White Russian in her hand. "It's a deal. But don't forget, that means *anything.*"

Jeremy's laugh held a mischievous ring as if he were playing with her. "Uh-oh," he said. "I'm regretting it already."

They put on their hard-hats with the lamps attached to the front. In addition, each had a flashlight. In their pockets they had candles and matches. Jeremy's backpack held an emergency kit, rope, and a few other necessities. Karen's held food.

They stood inside a narrow tunnel, but after walking a short distance, the ceiling began to drop, gradually at first, then suddenly. They both got down on their hands and knees, and when that proved unworkable, their bellies like snakes.

Karen inhaled mud and gravel into her nose and mouth. She tried spitting out the grime, but her efforts failed and her teeth crunched on something hard. Using her hand, she began picking out pieces one by one, but that took too long and she found herself falling behind.

Glancing at the barren gray surroundings, she thought, *What am I doing here?* A growing fear of the tunnel collapsing took hold in her mind, and again she imagined a lingering death with her screams going nowhere. She called out to her husband for reassurance. "I thought you said this was an easy cave." Her quavering voice echoed back in her ears.

From somewhere she heard, "Be patient. We're almost there."

Almost? she thought. Too soon would be a gift, and as for "there" she had no idea what he meant.

She wiggled along, feeling tiny rocks scrape her palms, tear at her nails, and wished she had taken precautions. Why hadn't Jeremy suggested gloves and knee pads? She remembered the nail polish, "Spicy Rose," she had purchased for an upcoming job interview and glanced down at her fingertips, filthy and abraded. *Ugh!* The last thing she'd want would be to call attention to them now.

A common earwig with rounded pincers scrambled inches from her nose and provided the final straw. On the verge of screaming she'd had enough, she heard Jeremy cry out a few feet ahead. "There's the end. See? Just like I said. Piece of cake. Was I right or was I right?" Karen clamped her mouth shut, almost biting her tongue. Then, picturing his head under water as bubbles rose to the surface, she let out a sigh and relaxed.

Chapter 2

The tunnel opened room-size. Karen rose, glad to be able to stand to her full height, and turned her neck and shoulders in soothing circles. Assuming the worst was over, she examined her clothes with resignation. They were filthy, of course, but that was minor compared to the material, now damp and bristly against her skin. She shook her head in disgust.

They walked until they came to a ledge. Looking down, she felt her stomach rise into her chest. "Are you nuts?" she cried.

Jeremy's eyes narrowed into determined slits. "Listen," he said, "you've come this far. Think of this place as a virtual playground. Would I bring you here if I considered it dangerous? Where are your balls?" He slapped his thighs, laughing at his joke.

Karen didn't even pretend to be amused and watched deadpan as he tied a rope to a boulder near the ledge with a bowline and stopper's knot. "We really don't need this," he explained, pointing to the rope. "There's a path along the wall over to your right. We'll use it to climb back up. It's just more fun jumping down. Watch me."

Using identical knots, he fastened the other end of the rope around his chest, adjusting it until it fit comfortably under his armpits. "You know how it's done," he said. Begrudgingly, Karen grumbled a *yes* since he had demonstrated the technique numerous times over the previous week until she had mastered it. Now he pulled hard on the rope, testing its grip on the boulder. Satisfied, he inched his way off on a slight incline, counting to twenty as he walked. "See? No problem." Suddenly, he jumped from the ledge with a loud "Yahoo," swung into a pendulum arc, and landed gently on the ground. Untying the rope from his chest, he looked toward Karen, her light a solitary beacon against the dark. "Okay. It's your turn. Pull it up."

Standing at the edge, Karen's mouth slackened as she stared off into the void, realizing what she had to do. Gripped by a sense of disbelief, she froze in place.

If not for a sudden flood of resentment, causing the nerves of her spine to tingle, she would have broken down, but imagining her hands around Jeremy's neck prevented her from losing control, not only of her mind but of her bladder.

Pretending the rope was his neck, she squeezed hard as she hoisted it up, tightening her grip with each pull before securing the end to her body. She tested its grip on the boulder as Jeremy had done, and then, knees shaking, slid down the passageway, her back toward the wall. After counting off twenty paces, she took a deep breath, let out a silent scream, and jumped. With the air rushing past her, she felt as if she were flying and blinked with wonder and surprise, sorry that the experience ended so quickly.

"I did it!" she screamed. "I did it!" Laughing and crying at the same time, she reached up and wiped tears from her face, embarrassed by her outward display.

"I knew you could do it," said Jeremy as he planted a kiss on the tip of her runny nose. Looking up at his eyes, she let hers linger there, moved by the love and respect reflected back. As a result, she forgot her anger and pressed her body against his. After her breathing returned to normal, she looked around, startled by what she saw—an exquisitely sublime uncharted world. Feeling blood pulse through her veins, she acknowledged a sense of pride at being one of the chosen few to see this subterranean wonderland and could understand, for the first time, why people risked their lives to reach the tops of mountains or the depths of the ocean or even the far reaches of space.

"I know I shouldn't forgive you so easily," she said, "but as usual I can't seem to stop myself. Besides—it really is beautiful here."

The walls of the large, cathedral-like room were moist and contained a small smattering of glistening, crystalline deposits that called to her. In response, she reached out and touched an overhang, noting the sparkling droplets from the ongoing seepage. Her fingertips shimmered under her helmet's light.

Turning to her husband, she asked, "Why is it wet here?"

With a tour guide's precision, he explained, "This type of rock is sedimentary, carried here by wind or water hundreds of millions of years ago. It's mostly limestone. You brush your teeth with it."

Karen smirked in disbelief.

"I'm serious," he said, his voice rising on the wave of a laugh. "It originally formed on the ocean floor, by the pressing together of marine life."

"'Marine life'?" she repeated.

"That's right. You know ... tiny sea creatures, shells, and coral. It's their deposits that help make all the oddly shaped things you see." He pointed to the bizarre-looking formations, hanging from the ceiling and growing up from the floor.

"Stalactites and stalagmites," she stated, almost raising her hand as if answering a teacher's question. "But I can never remember which is which."

Jeremy smiled, not only happy to help, but relieved by her sudden interest. "Stalactites grow from the ceiling down and stalagmites from the ground up. Remember the *c* in stalactites and the *g* in stalagmites: ceiling, ground."

He reached over to touch a column but stopped himself, afraid of disturbing it. Despite his half-dozen trips to caverns, his sense of wonderment hadn't diminished. He could never get over the fact that it took thousands of years for such formations to add one additional inch. What lay before him was the history of the world, and he momentarily held his breath in reverence.

"What are you thinking?" asked Karen, noticing him becoming quiet, lost in thought.

"Of the Manhattan skyline, actually. It's funny … Remember our trip there last year?" He turned his face around, his lamp's beam casting small yellow suns on the wall each time he shifted position. "Well, now I feel the same awe, like we're in some upside-down city, only this one's built by God or, at least, something omnipotent."

"I think I understand what you mean."

"Hey," he said, taking advantage of her upward shift in mood. "How about we do a little exploring? Last time I was here, Carl and I looked for traces of an underground river."

Karen flinched.

"Don't worry," said Jeremy with a playful jab to her chin. "All we found were puddles. Although some of the back walls appeared to have water marks higher up."

"I'd just as soon stay away from there," said Karen. "I've heard of caves flooding quite suddenly."

Jeremy spoke in a clipped professorial tone. "Not this time of year. Maybe in the spring when everything melts and you have runoffs. Anyway, it hasn't rained much this fall."

"Still, I'd just as soon stay away."

Wisely, Jeremy dropped the subject and they continued arm in arm, examining every crevice and wrinkle as Jeremy pointed out the names of various formations. "Those are called curtains," he said. "Looks like our living room. Whaddayathink?"

Karen shrugged one shoulder, thinking they looked more like egg cartons with their tiny rows of conical cups between the folds.

"And those hollow tubes over there are called soda straws. See how they're not tapered at their ends; no wider than a drop of water."

"This place is full of curiosities," said Karen. Her wide-open eyes as large as soup bowls revealed just how intrigued she was.

Jeremy, having not given up on that river, dared to suggest that they explore separately, and this way he could move at his own pace. He assured her that every passageway off the cathedral room circled back. "You can't possibly get lost."

"Okay," she relented. "But only if we stay within hearing distance of each other."

"You got it," he said.

Karen called out his name every few minutes, and after walking hunched over through two narrow tunnels—and seeing nothing but mud for her effort—she sat down on the ground back in the cathedral room to take a break, satisfied that Jeremy was nearby. The beam from her lamp ensconced her in the safety of a golden moon, and she breathed out a peaceful "Om" thinking, *I'm starting to like this place. It's like being part of the infinite.* Then ... *I feel so small* ... and her mind, once again, took a turn for the worse.

Hearing the sound of multiple footsteps and rocks being kicked caused her to rise to her feet. Heart pumping double-time, she turned to see her husband approach with three people. The laughter, amid soft voices and calm, friendly faces, put her at ease. *Oh, yeah,* she reminded herself, *must be the people from the car.*

Jeremy made the introductions. After meeting this trio of fellow explorers, he had forgotten about the river. Now he went up to Karen and draped an arm around her shoulder. "This is my wife, Karen. Karen, this is Sara and George and their son, Keith."

George and Sara were a middle-aged couple, respectable-looking but with a touch of the nonconformist. George reminded Karen of a former college professor, with his full red beard and pince-nez glasses. Sara, thin yet muscular, seemed the athletic type, and Karen surmised that they were here at her request. Their son, in well-worn jeans, hair tied back in a ponytail, pretended to be bored with his surroundings, except for Karen's chest; he couldn't keep his eyes from straying where they didn't belong.

Karen forced herself not to laugh. She couldn't imagine what he found so fascinating about her two measly protuberances, hidden under layers of clothes, no less. Even Jeremy joked that they were not her finest attribute. "Fortunately, I'm an ass man," he would often say when they were in bed together, gripping a soft handful.

"Hello," she said, turning from the parents to the son. Caught in the act, Keith dropped his eyes to his shirt tails. To spare him further embarrassment, Karen focused on Sara. "You must belong to the car we saw outside."

"That's right," said the older woman. "We drove down for the day from Pittsburgh. This is my second time here in Dinky Cave. George told me that's what the locals dubbed it. He went to high school nearby. Anyhow, it may be small, but it sure is pretty—and fun, too, don't you think?"

"I was just considering that," said Karen, with a nod toward Jeremy. "But I have to confess that I'm not really the outdoor type, although we really are completely indoors, aren't we?"

Sara's face crinkled into a wide grin. While it resulted in tiny cracks along her eyes and deepened her smile lines, it somehow made her look ten years younger. "That's true, of course, but I can't think of a better way to spend a day, although I'm not ashamed to admit that my first few times caving kept me up the night before. Right, George?"

Her husband nodded. "Yeah, and your knees would shake on the way to the car. But, don't forget, this was originally your idea."

"But now we all love the sport. Here we own the world. Even Keith likes it. Right, Keith?" She reached out and squeezed his shoulder.

Keith ignored his mother. "I'm hungry," he said. "Can we eat now." His words were more a statement than a question.

Sara winked at Karen. "See? Just like I said. Well, I guess this is as good a time as any for lunch. Care to join us?"

Neither Karen nor Jeremy was hungry after eating a big breakfast, but being a part of this small human family fostered a sense of camaraderie and obligation.

"How about we all pull over a boulder," said George. He emptied his backpack of food before shoving it under his butt as a makeshift seat. "It's a little cold below, if you know what I mean," he added.

The others did likewise.

Karen's appetite picked up with the array of food from both families spread out on a plastic tarp: sandwiches, fruit, home-made trail mix, and chocolate chip cookies—Sara's specialty. Jeremy, whose appetite was easily triggered, had no trouble making room. There was plenty to go around since everyone shared from the communal pool.

Taking a large thermos of coffee, Sara offered some to the younger couple.

"Thanks, but we brought some too," said Karen. "It's my only addiction— well, that and chocolate chip cookies." She eyed them guiltily and reached for a second, thinking about those extra five pounds she wanted to lose. *Screw it. Women are supposed to have curves.* She let the sweet taste sit on her tongue for a few seconds, then sighed and blissfully chomped away.

After pouring some milk into a paper cup, Jeremy offered it to Keith. The young man snorted as if insulted and said, "I stopped drinking that years ago."

Sara rolled her eyes discreetly.

Conversation turned typical, centering on jobs and family. George, it turned out, worked as an electrician. *So much for stereotypes,* thought Karen as she erased college professor from her mental list.

Sara, like Karen, was a teacher.

"Phys-ed," she said, lowering her voice.

Karen often wondered why physical education majors seemed defensive about their career choice. With two left feet, she had a healthy respect for people who possessed a semblance of athletic grace. In fact, teachers as a whole were given a bad rap, she decided, recalling the words: *"Those who can't do teach, and those who can't teach, teach gym."* She couldn't quite place where she had heard this—a movie perhaps?—but vowed to toss it into her personal trash can for quotes best forgotten.

"I teach English," said Karen. "At least I used to. When we moved from New Hampshire last spring, I had to give up my job. It hurt. I can't deny it, but Jeremy was given such a good opportunity in Baltimore. Still, I had no idea the market would be flooded. It seems there are fifty applicants for every opening."

Sara leaned in toward Karen. "I know just what you're going through. When I wanted to return to work, I had the same problem."

Karen's eyebrows shot up. "What did you do?"

"I subbed. Besides bringing home a paycheck, I made connections."

"'Connections'?" she parroted.

Sara shook her head, amused by the younger woman's naivety. "Of course. Everyone knows it's not what you know, but who you know."

"I suppose there's something to that," acknowledged Karen, pressing an index finger to her mouth, "and anyway, subbing would be a lot better than sitting home alone. Thanks. It's a good idea."

"My pleasure, and I'd be interested in learning how you make out. Say, why don't we exchange phone numbers?"

"I'd like that," said Karen, "and if you're ever near Maryland, I hope you'll look us up."

Sara and George exchanged glances. "As a matter of fact," said Sara, "we were planning a trip to Washington, D.C. next spring. Ever been there? It's just a hop, skip, and a jump from you. Maybe we can meet and take in the sights together. I've always wanted to see the cherry blossoms."

Keith smirked, causing his mouth to pucker like a crooked seam. "Count me out. I'm not into cherry blossoms."

"But we can also visit Georgetown University when we're there," said George. "It's time you started looking at colleges."

With a shrug of indifference, Keith said, "I suppose so."

Karen borrowed a pen and small notebook from Jeremy, who never went anywhere without them. Being a reporter, he considered them part of his anatomy.

After Sara had scribbled her number inside, Karen wrote hers on a separate sheet, and, as an afterthought, added Jeremy's work number on another page. She tore them off and handed them to Sara, who immediately transferred them to her pants pocket.

Karen, normally shy, hesitated before speaking. "Then we have tentative plans for Washington and cherry blossoms?"

Sara returned the question with an affirmation. "I'd say it's more a definite date. I'll look forward to it."

George stood up, cracked each knee in turn, before raising his hands above his head for a luxurious stretch. "Sara, my love. I think it's time we got going."

"I think so too. We've done enough exploring for one day." She turned toward her new friends and explained, "We've been here since early morning, and we have a long drive home."

Karen's lips tightened into a thin line. Not wanting anyone to notice her disappointment, she bent down and began gathering the remains of their lunch, throwing it into a paper bag. "I hate when people leave their trash behind," she said, keeping her face lowered.

"I know what you mean," seconded Sara, scrambling on her knees to help. "I saw a couple of beer and soda cans lying about, even a condom. It's downright sacrilegious in a place like this, although I know the local kids use this cave as a hangout. George used to be one of them."

George nodded reluctantly, the color on his face deepening. "That was years ago," he said. "Should I tell everyone how you passed geometry in junior high?" Sara and George looked at each other with Cheshire cat grins, then burst out laughing at the same time. Still chuckling, George extended his right hand to Karen and Jeremy for a friendly goodbye as well as to change the subject.

Sara, more affectionate by nature, gave Karen and Jeremy hugs, saying, "We'll be in touch."

All five walked to the rocky path along the wall leading back to the outside world. George pointed to the rope still dangling from the boulder above. "I see you took a shortcut down."

Jeremy's sideways smile seemed more like the smirk of a mischievous boy caught cheating at school. "I thought Karen would enjoy the thrill of flying. But we'll be following your example on our way up."

"It was fun going down that way," Karen admitted, "but once was enough."

The young couple watched as the threesome started up single file. George, the last to ascend, turned his head around and stopped. "Oh, by the way, did you check out the waterfall?"

Jeremy's ears perked up immediately. "I didn't know there was one. Where is it?"

"Just follow that passageway I pointed out earlier. The one with the cigarette butt stuck in the wall. Then take a right at the second—no, let's see—third offshoot. The first one is little more than a crevice and the second comes to a dead end. The third is the largest so you can't miss it. It's worth checking out." He continued on with a wave of his hand.

Karen's forehead formed ridges as she watched her new friends leave, knowing she'd have to imitate their maneuvers soon enough. After turning around a bend, the threesome disappeared for a few seconds. When they were back in view, everyone smiled and waved again. Soon the path became trickier but the climbers were adept, managing the handholds and footholds in the spiky-toothed boulders with proficiency. Karen reached up to rub her temple, now beginning to throb, and she wondered whether Jeremy had packed any aspirin.

Before she could ask, she heard Sara calling from above. "We're up. See you next spring." Her voice trailed off until it sounded little more than a murmur.

Karen could only see the lights from their headlamps, but knowing they were safe, she began to relax. Then, glancing down at her feet, she noticed a slip of paper and bent down to pick it up. Written on it was Jeremy's work number. Apparently it had fallen out of Sara's pants. *Damn,* she thought. *Oh well, at least they have our home number and we have theirs.* She folded the paper and placed it inside her pocket.

Jeremy tapped her shoulder. "You ready?" he said, eyes bulging like snowballs. "Let's find it."

"Find what?" said Karen, knowing full well what he meant.

Seeming to sense her reluctance, Jeremy unhitched his backpack, reached inside and pulled out a ball of string. "There," he said. "You can't accuse me of not being careful. When we get to the passageway, the one with the cigarette butt, I'll put this loose end"—he held it up for her to see—"under a heavy rock and unwind as we walk. We'll be all set."

Karen took a deep breath, puffing out her bangs as she exhaled. She knew he would look for the falls with or without her, and she didn't want to be left alone. Reluctantly, she followed.

The string, shadowing dutifully behind, offered Karen a tangible connection to the world but provided little release from her growing concern. Jeremy, to Karen's relief, was mindful of her feelings, and grabbed her hand with a comforting pat. Together they continued, paying careful attention to George's instructions.

"This must be the first offshoot," said Jeremy, pointing to a crevice in the wall too narrow to squeeze through. They walked beyond the second, the dead end, adjusting their bodies to the height of the ceiling and the sharp bend in the tunnel. Karen, however, began to feel claustrophobic, and though their lamps provided ample lighting nearby, distant shapes grew huge and demonic with components resembling misshapen heads and limbs. Swallowing fear, Karen felt like calling out for her mother but instead heard herself say, "I don't like this. I want to go back."

His arm around her waist, Jeremy leaned in, whispering, "You hear that?"

Karen stood still, cupped a hand around her ear. Yes, she heard it too—a tapping, then a deep thumping like the pizzicato from a bass fiddle being plucked with a finger.

They walked on, following the call of the down-flow, and as they approached the third offshoot, it grew to a rumble as if glad to have someone hear its timeless peal, a coloratura of runs, trills, and polyphonic vocalizations.

The falls was not what she'd expected, but far from disappointing. The water, instead of gushing from a towering overhang, seeped between rocky layers, increasing in volume on its descent until it was greater at the base than the top. Yet its steady and subtle performance allowed her to see the lightly colored stones underneath, shaded as a bride by her veil.

Karen put her hands under the water, forming a cup, and raised it to her lips. "It's delicious," she said. Then thinking she'd made a mistake said, "I guess I was thirsty. Is it all right?"

After Jeremy assured her that the water, filtering through rocks on its decent, was safe to drink, she helped herself to more. Drops dripped down her face. She didn't bother to wipe them off.

The water drained into a shallow pool perhaps twenty feet across and then onward before finally seeping into the ground and becoming no more than a puddle.

Karen looked around her and said, "It really is lovely and I'm glad we came, but I'm ready to go home." Her eyebrows shot upward and two parallel lines deepened between them as Jeremy began to strip off his clothes.

"W-what are you doing?" she shrieked, not believing her eyes.

"What does it look like? Come on. Loosen up for a change and join me."

Loosen up? she thought. *What's he talking about? Am I really an old fuddy-duddy?* With a determined I'll-show-you look, she stripped off her clothes, flinging shirt, pants, everything on the ground, and jumped into the pool beside Jeremy.

The ice cold water caused goose bumps to appear on her flesh and her nipples to stand at attention like two toy soldiers. Jeremy circled her inside his arms, passing on his warmth. She proceeded in kind by reaching up and drawing his head down to nuzzle her neck. The thought of making love passed through them both, but looking at the rocks and mud amidst the cold water made them both reconsider.

With a trace of a kiss still on her lips, Karen slipped from his arms and the moment faded. "We can continue this later at home," she said, her voice low and suggestive.

"Whatever you want. You've been great today, Karen. You never fail to surprise me. I'm proud of you."

They stepped out of the water, letting the air dry their bodies.

Karen froze. "What was that?"

"What was what?"

"I heard something. It sounded like voices."

"I didn't hear anything."

Karen frowned as she scrambled back into her clothes, suddenly aware of her nakedness.

After picking up their belongings, they made their way back, following the string, until they were in the main section of the cave. They checked to make sure they weren't leaving anything behind; satisfied, they walked over to the path along the wall, the same one Sara, George, and Keith had used less than an hour ago.

Jeremy adjusted his carbide lamp, searching with his eyes. "Funny," he said, the corners of his mouth drooping like sleeves from an oversized sweater. "I don't see our rope hanging down."

Karen, for a second, thought he was joking. Then, bewildered, she walked to where it was supposed to be. She stared at the spot unable to believe it wasn't there, somehow hoping her concentration would force it to reappear.

"I don't understand," she said, pacing back and forth. "Even if it had fallen, it would still be here."

"It must be some bad practical joke," said Jeremy. "But who would do such a thing?"

The idea of their new friends, Sara and George, committing such an act was inconceivable. Perhaps their son, Keith? *Yes, he seemed the type, insolent and ready for mischief.* Karen had had such boys in class before. And who else could it be, anyway?

Jeremy's lips pulled back in anger, baring his teeth at the transgression. "Well, at least we don't need it to get out of here. Still—"

#

Not long after they'd already stopped to fill up the tank and use the restrooms, Keith announced, "I gotta take a crap."

George gripped the wheel. "You gotta what? What kind of talk is that, young man? Someone should wash your mouth out with soap."

Sara burst out laughing as if she were watching her favorite sitcom. "What's wrong with you, George? You think he's a little kid? Besides, you use worse language all the time."

George's lips spread into a lopsided grin. "Yeah, I do, don't I? Oh well. Can you wait till we get home, Keith? We stopped less than an hour ago, and we only have another thirty miles left."

"Don't think so, Dad. This time it's real business."

"All right, I get your drift." Steering the car to the outer lane, George shifted to second gear and drove off the exit ramp. Within minutes he found the bright orange roof of a Howard Johnson's and pulled into the parking lot. Keith rushed out while George pocketed his keys and Sara fussed with her purse.

"I'm not very hungry," said Sara, "but I could use a drink."

"Me too," said George. "Counter okay?"

"Sure."

The restaurant was warm, and Sara draped her jacket over an unoccupied stool.

"Just two cokes," said George as a waitress in a white paper cap approached. "Should we order one for Keith?"

"No. He may want something else."

"So what do you think? Did you enjoy the day?" George leaned forward as the waitress placed his drink before him.

"Yes," said Sara, "but next time I'm ready for something more challenging." She peeled the paper from a straw, placed it in her soda and took a sip. Immediately she began to sneeze.

"Bubbles again?" asked George.

"Yep. Went right up both nostrils." She took two napkins from the dispenser, honked, wiped, and placed the dirty napkins in her pocket before finishing her drink.

"I may as well use the bathroom as long as we're here. See you in a minute." She walked down the corridor, passing the men's room, where Keith, his back against the wall, was zoning out on a joint. Sara swore under her breath as the sweet, smoky smell, which she recognized from years past, wafted by.

"Dammit, Keith," she barked through the small crack between the door and jamb. "I know what you're doing. No wonder your grades are plummeting. How do you expect to get into college?" She rattled the handle, but it was locked. "Wait till I tell your father. And you can forget about using the car tomorrow." She let out a "Grrrr."

After entering the ladies' she emptied the contents of her pocket, inadvertently throwing out the second sheet with Karen and Jeremy's home number mixed in with the dirty napkins. Straightaway, she realized her mistake and considered going through the trash. "No way," she said, still distracted and fuming over Keith's smoking dope. By the time she got home, she had already forgotten about her new friends. She had more pressing issues on her mind.

Chapter 3

Karen felt it first: that prickly, bone-chilling, ice-on-the-neck sensation when you're certain you're being watched. Standing still, eyes and ears on alert, she heard a soft giggle followed by a series of clicks like the striking of castanets. She turned in the direction of the sound to see a man and woman approaching.

Karen moved closer to her husband as he clenched his fists, drawing them up and back.

"Is this yours?" the man asked, holding on to their rope. "I'm sorry. I thought it belonged to the family that left earlier. People are always leaving things behind, you know. Oh, excuse me for not introducing myself. I'm Abraham, but everyone calls me Rahm. This is Rachel." He extended his right hand.

Jeremy relaxed his fingers and reached out to shake the offered hand. The man had a strong grip which wasn't surprising considering the well-defined muscles and cordlike veins running down his pale, taut arms.

The man's features were hard to make out due to a shadow falling across his face and his full, light-colored beard. Karen, however, sensed a person with an acute intelligence and strong personality. He was of medium height, but the muscularity of his upper body made him appear taller. She felt unable to pinpoint his age, but judging from his voice and physique, Karen guessed anywhere from thirty to early forties.

The woman was small, almost tiny, yet her wiry build along with unusually thick calves suggested that of a predatory animal capable of moving an incredible distance in seconds.

Their clothes, ill-fitting, inappropriate attire, hung loosely at the shoulders and hips, and Karen wondered how they managed to keep their core temperature regulated. While it was far from cold in the cave, it wasn't tropical either.

Strangest of all was the focus of their eyes. With a dip of their heads, they avoided looking at anyone or anything directly; instead, they gazed with an off-centered slant as if they were blind. *But,* thought Karen, *that's impossible; they move too easily to be blind.*

Intuitively, Karen sensed something wrong and circled her body with her arms in defense.

Rahm handed the rope back to Jeremy. "Take it," he said, speaking in a deep, authoritative voice as if he were used to giving instructions. "We weren't stealing. We just like to keep the place tidy."

Karen looked to Jeremy for reassurance, but he, too, seemed to sense the bizarre nature of the encounter. He squeezed his eyes, causing tiny crow's-feet to form toward both temples while Karen wiped cold sweat from her forehead. Forcing herself, Karen took a step forward. "I don't understand. Are you locals? Are you paid to keep the place clean?"

The odd couple exchanged a coy glance before throwing back their heads and laughing.

"Yes and no," said Rahm. "I suppose you can call us locals. That's accurate enough. But no, we aren't paid to clean up. It's just with all the junk people leave behind, this cave would be unlivable in no time. Besides, some of the stuff's useful."

"I still don't understand," said Jeremy. "What do you mean by 'unlivable'?"

"Just that," said Rachel. "You see, the cave is our home." This was the first time she'd spoken and her low-pitched, droning tones sounded more robotic than human.

Rahm interrupted. "I think I'd better explain. Rachel's telling the truth. We really do live here. Just much lower down." He swung his finger like a plane in free fall and smiled, as if amused by the couple's confusion. "You didn't know there were lower levels, did you?" Answering his own question, he said, "No, of course not. No one knows."

Jeremy ran his hand across his face. "You're kidding." When he saw they were serious, his eyes opened wide, exposing the whites, top and bottom. "But why? That's insane. Don't the two of you get bored? Lonely? And hasn't anyone tried to find you?"

Rahm inched closer. "Actually, there are eleven of us. Nine adults, two children. We live here because we want to." Reversing his crash-landing finger toward the surface above, he said, "None of us left much of anything behind. Not possessions, nor close family or friends, so I doubt we've been missed. And no one knows we're here. That is, until you."

The yellow glow from Karen's helmet shone directly on Rahm's face. He blinked in response as if it burned. Recovering, he ran his eyes along the S of her form before lingering on her hips for a protracted moment.

Karen recoiled and leaned against the wall for support. She stared at Jeremy, now looking spellbound, and immediately understood why. How many times had he had told her how he pictured his name above an exclusive article featured on page one? And this craziness offered him a perfect shot at success.

"Do you suppose," he said, "that I could interview you? All of you, I mean. I work for a small newspaper. It would make a sensational story. I don't have to say where the cave is."

Rahm's pleasant expression transformed to granite: firm, stoic, and unreadable. "I don't see why not. What do you think, Rachel?"

"It's okay with me," she said, her face as rigid as her companion's.

Karen turned to Jeremy, her voice dim and shaky. "I want to go home. Right now. We've been down here for hours, and I'm tired."

"Please, Karen," pleaded Jeremy, his voice rising louder, higher. "Do you know what this could mean? It's the story of the year—the decade. I may never get another chance like this."

"No!"

"I promise I'll never ask you for anything again. Please!"

Sensing his desperation, Karen found herself vacillating. Since she knew how much he wanted to advance in his career and deal in hard news, she offered a trade-off. "All right," she said, "but only if we fly to Bermuda next Friday for a long weekend. Remember you said we'd do whatever I want, and that's what I want."

Relieved, Jeremy exhaled a slow, deep breath as the muscles in his jaw relaxed. "It'll be expensive, but okay. A deal's a deal."

"Good," said Rahm, "and now that that's settled, why don't we get started. Umm, one more thing … at some point, I'll ask you to turn off your lamps. As you said, you wouldn't tell anyone where to find us. Still, we have to take precautions. Also, I suggest you put all your valuables in your backpacks. You don't want to lose anything." On Rahm's face, a twist to the mouth grew larger, but he subtly hid it with a cough and a clearing of the throat.

Before Karen could respond, Jeremy spoke up. "Of course," he said, stuffing his wallet, rope, and flashlight into his backpack. "No problem. Oh, by the way, what was that clicking sound you made?"

"Clicking sound? We'll explain it later. All in good time."

They started out, Rahm leading the way. Jeremy breathed hard with excitement while Karen did likewise with fear. Rachel, trailing behind, smiled broadly, a secret on her lips which she made no effort to hide.

Single file, they walked back toward the waterfall, stopping at that same second offshoot, the dead end. Karen's senses, now on edge, felt the fall's vibrations and heard its ancient voice, as if some enlightened sage were speaking inside her head. But before she could intuit the message, Rahm spoke.

"I'm afraid I'll have to ask you to turn off your lamps now. Everyone thinks this offshoot goes nowhere, but that's as far from the truth as possible. This holds the key."

Karen could feel her blood coursing through her veins, but imagining Bermuda just one week away, she did as instructed. Still, the absolute blackness of this sucked-empty zone took her by surprise, sending her brain spinning. All around her was nothing but a landscape of vapor and vacuous space. She began to sway, feel disoriented. Hearing noises in the distance, she asked, "What's going on? Are there others here?"

Rahm sidelined her question. "No need for you to be concerned. Everything's under control."

Control? Who? What? Karen stood still. Refused to move. "I want to go back. I want to go back right now!" She began to yell while her seemingly disjointed arms flailed at her sides.

"Stop!" barked Rahm as if commanding a military unit, and the unknown noise immediately ceased. Karen's barrage, however, continued. Rachel stepped forward.

"I assure you that you're safe. Rahm would never let anything bad happen to you."

"And I wouldn't either," said Jeremy. "We'll be talking about this day to our grandchildren."

Exasperated, Karen threw up her arms. "Okay already. You win. But I'd better not regret this or you'll be sorry."

"You won't be sorry, Karen. This is gonna be great! The best day of our lives. You'll see."

With Karen's tantrum at an end, the small group moved on. Rahm prodded Karen forward, firmly yet attentively. Each time the ceiling dropped, he'd place his palm on top of her head so that she'd stoop lower. Karen felt the walls brush against her. As they continued, he'd move his hand to her arm, her hip, and then back to her head, signaling when she should bend, turn, or get down on all fours. At one point, Karen sat on the bare ground, insisting she needed a break. Rahm acquiesced but only for a few minutes, before pulling her up and onward.

His words steady, adamant, and evoking the confidence that comes with power, he said, "It gets tricky here, so pay attention." He shifted her sideways, placing her arms at her sides, explaining, "You'll need to wiggle some at the hip. Don't worry. You won't get stuck. Just take a breath, let it out. Now hold it."

She heard scraping sounds as he went first. He reached back, linking his fingers with hers, and pulled her to safety. "The next crevice is even tighter," he warned, but with a sculptor's precision, he molded her, helped her twist her body so that she slid through the sliver-sized space like well-greased toast buttered on both sides.

They crawled through a narrow hole, and she exhaled again to make herself smaller. Once on the other side, she could stand tall and breathe normally. She circled her neck, stretching in relief, but stopped, certain now of the presence of someone else. She listened as objects were shoved aside—large objects, boulders perhaps. They creaked and grated, one against the other, and she smelled something musty, foul, followed by a male voice groaning with effort. Every nerve in her body screamed, *Take me back, take me back,* followed by her angry "Damn you, Jeremy," not even realizing she had spoken out loud.

Rahm laid his hand on her shoulder, his fingers squeezing gently. "Don't be afraid," he said. The click-clicks resumed.

He led her on, steering her down—always down to a lower level. The comfort from his physical touch resulted in a feeling of gratitude. A few times she felt an urge to turn on her lamp, but like a child afraid of disobeying her parent, she refrained. *What if he leaves me here?* she thought. Instead, she kept her hands pointed outward, searching, probing like a blind person in unfamiliar territory and in need of protection.

In the distance, Karen heard Jeremy yell "Shit!" With all the turns, the shifting, the sliding in and out, she had no idea whether he was ahead of her or behind, but one thing she presumed: he had injured himself. Unlike her, Jeremy usually used that one measly word for anything unpleasant, and since there were no further outbursts, Karen concluded it was a minor bump or abrasion. Rachel wasn't being as careful with him as Rahm was with her. Unconsciously, she smiled at the thought.

Rahm's hand on her elbow signaled a halt, while another person (probably the same from before) crept up beside her. She felt his breath upon her face, hot and dank, but only Rahm spoke. "You'll have to trust me from this point. I'm going to put you in a full body harness. You'll feel like you're sitting in a chair. I'm also going to take your helmet. That's for your own good so you won't be tempted to turn on the light. Believe me, you'll be grateful. With your permission, I'm going to tie a scarf around your eyes. I know you can't see in the dark, but I guarantee you'll feel more secure with it on. When you reach the bottom, I'll take it off."

"Permission? Scarf? Like hell! And what do you mean you'll get there before I do?"

Rahm laughed. "After years of living here, I'm like a mountain goat or an acrobat with no need for a net."

"But what about me? I'm scared."

Rahm patted her arm. "No need. You're perfectly safe."

Before she could protest further, expert fingers strapped her in at the waist, chest, and hip; knots were tied and yanked across her body. She prayed they were secure. "There," said Rahm. "All set. Now listen closely. If you hit the cave wall, don't panic. Just push off with your feet or hands. I'll be right by."

"Wait!" she screamed. "I don't like this. I changed my mind. Let me off, damn you! Stop …!" It was too late. Hearing a crank being turned, followed by a whirring noise, she was lifted off the ground, rotated, and gradually lowered into empty space, far beyond any zip code.

She felt pressure against her chest, dead weight, and her breathing increased as if she were running while her teeth chattered a dirge for the doomed. Instinctively she reached up to turn on her lamp, forgetting it wasn't there.

Despite her fear, she did remember to kick off when her knees or backside brushed the wall as she spun in the air on her endless descent. "Dear God," she heard herself say over and over until it became a mantra, a chant, a hymn. And then, once again, just like her initial jump off the ledge that very morning, she was flying, escaping her worries, leaving frustrations behind. She felt the wind kiss her face, and she swung her feet like a child on a swing. Then suddenly the chair apparatus stopped with a jolt, hovering somewhere, nowhere, while still turning in circles, making her dizzy.

The parachute descent resumed, but only inches at a time, causing her to bounce with each movement. A steely clamp grasped her ankle and her muscles tightened, then froze until she realized it was a human hand. Slowly, carefully, she felt herself pulled downward. When her feet finally touched rock-hard, blessed ground, she gasped in fear, wonder, and relief.

He was there. Rahm. He removed the scarf and helped her from the harness. With both of her knees now unstable hinges, she grabbed his shoulder for support. Hearing faint voices reverberating in the labyrinth, she asked, "Is that Jeremy? Rachel?"

He brushed off her question, saying, "You did very well."

Although still sightless, she sensed people watching her, judging her as if she were a trophy. She heard a trickle of water and wondered if they were near a stream, but felt reluctant to ask. Again her hand went up to her head to turn on her absconded lamp. She let it fall to her thigh, useless.

And then she saw something moving. Drops of water, perhaps? No. Whatever she saw, it moved side to side, flickering. Candles, she realized, upon turning toward Rahm. She blanched at his enigmatic expression, set in a ruggedly handsome face, outlined by the soft ethereal light.

"Welcome to Second Chance City," he said. "Home."

Chapter 4

Carl slammed the front door with his foot. His monster-sized "Achoo" hit the air at ninety miles per hour, making him sound like a cheerleader for the common cold.

"Thank God you're back," said Joan, echoing his mini explosion with one of her own.

He placed a plastic bag on the coffee table. "I picked up some decongestant, lozenges, and four boxes of tissues. That should hold us for now."

"What about cough suppressant?" asked Joan.

"I thought about that, but I read it's good to bring up all the crap in your throat. Anyway, I'll go out later if you want. Oh, by the way, I stopped at Jeremy and Karen's house."

Joan pulled the cover down from her face. "How come?"

"I was in the area and his muddy sneakers have been in my car for a month. Jeremy finally took my advice and got himself a pair of real climbing boots. Figures, they weren't home, so I left the sneaks outside the door. No one's going to steal a pair of cruddy old shoes."

Joan made a face. "Yeah, but now other tenants will know they're out. Oh well, it's a safe building, and they should be home soon enough. Didn't you say they were going biking or hiking today? I can't remember which."

Carl shrugged.

"You sure they wouldn't go caving by themselves?"

"Naw, Jeremy can't be that dumb."

"Well, in any case, you just reminded me that I have to call Karen later about the movies tomorrow. I think I should pass. I doubt I'll be well enough, and besides, I don't want her to catch what I've got." She began to cough and grabbed for the lozenges. "Oh, good. Cherry."

#

Rahm kept her helmet, explaining that the glare from the spotlight would hurt everyone's eyes so she had to make do with the subdued lighting from the candles and hurricane lanterns spread about. Jeremy, who had arrived minutes before, had finished questioning Rachel, taking notes with schoolboy enthusiasm, and then left to probe the underground lake one level below. Karen bristled, thinking this was the man who had promised "to love and to cherish." *What a crock!* Now, with the possibility of fame and fortune waving its glorious flag, he had walked off, leaving her alone and vulnerable, a solitary figure unsure where to turn.

Forcing herself, Karen lifted one foot then the other with a "Whew" on her breath as if surprised they still worked. She crossed an intersection of sorts, two paths forming a right angle, and entered what appeared to be the living room, lit with overhead torches in addition to the lanterns. The walls sparkled with lustrous white crystals reflecting light in all directions. She turned her face up where giant stalagmites rose like steeples, ornate and layered with castle-like turrets before disappearing into misty cave clouds.

One large section, decorated with delicate sheets of flowstone, formed ripples and folds along the wall, translucent near the top but taking on a rosy hue as it worked its way down, before fading like a streak from a painter's brush. But what surprised her even more was the amount of furniture on hand, although basic and worn. The contrast between that and the cave's natural wonders left her disjointed. She sucked in her lower lip.

A large rug, ravaged from the steady accumulation of grime, had slivers of green poking through to reveal its original color. Surrounding it were three shabby couches and four equally worn chairs. Bare wooden planks and rows of milk crates, stacked one on top of the other, were used to hold card and board games. The supply of books was impressive. It would have filled a wall in her apartment.

Stalagmites and stalactites, almost in a line, separated the living room from the dining room nearby, with its large wooden table. She walked over. On closer inspection, she could see that the table consisted of two ordinary doors placed side by side atop four sawhorses. Circling it were plain aluminum fold-up chairs, beginning to rust.

Having gotten her bearings, she turned to the others, who seemed mesmerized by her mere existence, staring at her as if she had two heads. *Screw you,* she thought, crossing her arms as she tried convincing herself that this would turn out just peachy: Jeremy getting his big story—his lucky break—and she her trip to Bermuda, dining on guinea-chick lobster.

The adults wandered off, unnerved by her aggressive posturing, but left behind two children. Both had odd, filmy eyes with red, dilated blood vessels running through the sclera. Like Rahm and Rachel, they also had gazes tracking at the periphery, then moving slowly inward. Wondering whether they might be blind, Karen raised her hand above her head, and they both moved their eyes correctly, answering her question.

"Why did you do that?" the smaller of the two asked. He appeared to be three and a half, perhaps four, with white hair down to his shoulders. At first Karen mistook him for a girl, but on closer inspection, along with taking in those streaks of dirt running down his face and under his pointy nose, she corrected herself.

Embarrassed, she hesitated. "I was wondering if you could see."

"We see like bats," he answered. "That's what Mommy says."

"Actually," interrupted the older boy, "Jon is kind of blind. He can see shadows and detect movement, but that's about all; still, he can find anything faster than anyone else. As for me, I see pretty good, but not as good as I used to. I'm starting to find things almost as quickly as Jon though. How well can you see?"

"Usually fine, although in this light it's more difficult."

The two boys came closer, and Karen narrowed her own eyes into slits. The china-whiteness of the older boy's face unnerved her, but the nearly translucent skin of the younger one caused a visceral reaction. She thought she could see the blood pulsing beneath, but told herself she must be imagining it. Still, she felt a wave of nausea and looked away.

"You sick?" asked Jon.

Taking a deep breath, Karen looked again. She immediately regretted it. Not only could she see his blood, bright red along with a deeper, almost purple shade coursing through veins and capillaries, she could make out the outline of his skull. "I think I'd better sit down," she said.

"Come with me," said the older boy. "To my bedroom. You can sit there and rest too, 'cause it's quieter. When I turn twelve next year, I'm getting my very own room. That's what Rahm says. Now I have to share." He led her down a passageway while Jon ran off in search of more playful pursuits.

"This is Suburbia," the boy said with a sweep of his arm.

"Suburbia?"

"Uh-huh. That's what we call it—the place where people sleep. The main area—the living room, dining room, and kitchen—is 'Downtown.' At least, that's what the grownups call it. I call it 'The Ballroom' 'cause it's got diamonds."

"Diamonds?"

"Well, not real ones. Just sparkly things in the walls."

"Yes, I noticed," said Karen. "It's beautiful."

The boy beamed like a proud host with his worldly goods on display and stuck out his right hand for Karen to shake. "My name is Randy. What's yours?"

"Karen."

"Nice to meet you," he said, pushing a sheet across a rod to reveal a heavyset thirty-something woman. "Mom, this is Karen, my new friend." The woman, sitting cross-legged on a mattress covered by a chewed-up woolen blanket, was looking down at her lap, but shifted sideways to make room for her "guest." Then seeming to remember something from long ago, she reconsidered and said, "I can get you a folding chair if you'd rather—"

"No, that's okay," said Karen, lowering herself to the mattress while taking in the simple furnishings: two more mattresses, arranged asymmetrically to fit between stalagmites; seven crates containing personal items; a portable coat rack, sagging in the middle, which held miscellaneous clothes.

Karen bent forward, pushing in on her stomach with both fists. Feeling the nausea lift, she turned toward the stranger beside her, whose skin, although pale, was normal—thank goodness.

"I'm Janet," said the woman. Despite the slack flesh on both sides of her lower jaw, her face showed small, even features, remnants of the pretty young girl she had once been. Now, however, she appeared as faded as the blanket her large rump rested on. Her dirty blond hair hung limp and stringy.

"I see you've met my son Randy," she said. She turned her head in the same lopsided manner as the others, studying Karen with new interest. "You all right?" she asked, noticing Karen unconsciously massaging her stomach.

"I'm better now. Thank you."

"Randy, why don't you get Karen some water?" the woman said anyway. Then, curling a clump of hair around a finger, she whispered, "Rahm find you?"

"Yes and no," said Karen. "We sort of found each other."

"That man ... the cute one ... he your husband?"

Karen shrugged, surmising she meant Jeremy, who'd been flitting about like a kid chasing a ball.

"Sure is nice-looking. Haven't seen too many lately." The small laugh, coming from deep in her throat, held the suggestion of a cry. "My husband, Tom—been dead two years now."

Karen looked down at her feet. "I'm sorry," she said.

"Don't be. I'm glad. He's buried over there." Raising a fleshy arm, she pointed off into the distance.

Karen followed the outstretched arm, grateful to see Jeremy walking toward them to rescue her from an uncomfortable moment. His words and voice, effervescent and growing louder, filled the empty space with a blast of enthusiasm.

"I've just got the interview of the year," he blurted out. "Did you know there's a whole society down here? The lake is huge. I wouldn't have believed it if I didn't see it myself. Rahm's practically a king—a god. There's even three people buried here."

"Three?" said Karen, jerking her head back, her slack-mouthed expression between a question and a scowl.

Janet nodded. "In addition to my husband, there's Eugene and Louise. They were married before coming here. Happy marriage, best I could tell, but bad karma rained down, killing all three together. Imagine that!" She hiccupped a plaint as if she couldn't believe it were true. "Now there's only one married couple left—Mary and Brian. Mary's religious, believes in sin and all that. Otherwise she'd have dumped him down the toilet long ago. Hates his guts."

"That so?" said Karen, eyeballing Jeremy. "Well, marriage is sacred, at least to me. But those people that died ... How? What happened?"

Janet tensed and began to stutter. "I-I ..."

Sensing trouble, Jeremy broke in. Afraid Janet might clam up and end the interview, he shot his wife a warning before turning back to Janet. "Maybe you could just fill us in on everyone's background. Why'd you all come here? In case Karen didn't mention it, I'm writing an article for a newspaper."

Janet relaxed and, obviously enjoying the attention, the words flew from her mouth. "A newspaper? You don't say." She stretched her legs and settled into a comfortable position. "We're a bit of everything, I suppose. You know—this and that. Rahm says we shouldn't dwell on the past. That it isn't healthy, and I suppose he knows best; still, some things are hard to forget. Don't you think?"

"Yes, certainly," said Karen, recalling all she'd left behind when moving to Baltimore.

Janet smiled, flattered to have someone agree with her. "What's important is keeping busy and we all do our share—that is, everyone except Helene. She's from a stinking rich family: best schools, best everything. Spoiled rotten, if you ask me."

"Why'd she come?"

"David, I suppose. He's her screwed-up boyfriend, and I don't like him much either. Too strange for my taste, if you know what I mean." She raised an eyebrow, casting what she presumed to be a meaningful look. "But with you here today, things will change fast." She hurried on before innuendos could take root. "Let's see. There's Rachel and Rahm, of course. I suppose you'd like to know about them."

"Yes, please," said Jeremy. Poised for something sensational, he flipped his memo pad to a clean page, but his hopes for an earth-shattering expose soon sank like flotsam.

"Hmm," said Janet. "Now that I think about it, I know very little." Her eyes opened at the revelation, and she turned to Jeremy, who mimicked her response. "All I can tell you is Rachel's from out west. Belonged to some wacky cult. She often sprouts off about meditation and other transcendental stuff. I don't pay too much attention to her.

"As for Rahm"—she threaded her fingers and twiddled her thumbs—"I know even less. He did serve in Vietnam with Norman. He's one of the other men here. Anyway, Rahm doesn't like to talk about himself. That's not even his real name—not Rahm, not Abraham."

"Did he commit a crime?" asked Jeremy, still hoping for some hidden nugget. "Is that why he changed it?"

"It's possible, but you'd have to ask him yourself. I sure won't! Now, let's see. That leaves just Lily. She and Norman share a room. I like them okay. Lily's straight from the Bible Belt. Church Sundays, evenings too. She says she's a nonbeliever now, but that's just a crock. She still gets uptight on the subject of sex. That doesn't keep her from having it, though."

"So Lily and Norman are a couple," said Karen.

Janet raised her hand, palm down, slightly rocking it. "Sort of," she said. "Lily's indifferent, but Norman worships her. I don't know how he wound up here since he's a big-city boy. From Brooklyn, originally. His momma raised him with fire and brimstone—or so he tells us—but now he's a skeptic, like Lily. At least they have that in common."

"What about you?" said Jeremy.

"Me?" Janet shrugged as if surprised to be asked. "I'm from Nebraska. Mom was a housewife. Dad a salesman. Traveled a lot. One sister, one dog. See? Nothing special." She dug her heel into the ground as if expecting to hit some infallible truth. When nothing significant appeared, she said, "I'm no longer sure what I believe except for the fertility gods, of course."

"The what?" said Jeremy.

"The fertility gods!" she repeated, raising her voice as if he were both deaf and addlebrained. She pulled out a necklace from under her shirt, a piece of rock with an irregular shape dangling from a thin cord. She rubbed it. "For good luck," she said. "But so far the gods haven't listened too closely—at least not to the others. I'm the lucky one; they listened to me."

"You mean Randy?" said Jeremy.

"Yes, and Jon too."

Karen's eyes rounded like matching bowling balls. "I didn't realize Jon's also your son. That they're brothers."

"Actually," explained Janet, "I think they're half-brothers. Randy was born in a hospital in Charleston. He was six when we came here. My dead husband's his father. I'm not sure who Jon's father is. He does resemble Rahm though, don't you think?"

"But your husband would have still been alive," said Karen, furrowing her brow.

Noting her reaction, Janet lowered her head in a placating bow. "You see, it's very difficult to get pregnant here. We don't know why. Maybe it's toxins in the air or the water. There's tons of minerals in this place—calcite in particular. Or maybe it's just the will of the gods." She automatically rubbed her necklace again. "But whatever the problem, Jon's the only child who's been conceived and born below. Our fertility room is in the same passageway leading to the cemetery."

"There's a—a fertility room?"

"That's right. In the beginning, it was for privacy, more or less, but now it's to ensure that rituals are properly followed. At Rachel's insistence."

"What rituals?"

Having apparently slipped beyond her comfort zone, Janet avoided Jeremy's eyes. "At mid-cycle, the women drop everything to be with the gods. Rachel offers the blessings, chants prayers, and lights the incense. Then the men come to fulfill their obligation. Nothing seems to help though, and everyone's feeling the strain, since without children we'll die out. I'm okay since I have my boys, but I often hear others cry out in their sleep. Right now Helene's there, and I suspect that's why I haven't seen Brian and Norman today."

Jeremy tried not to snicker. Still, unable to resist, he said, "Maybe I should give it a shot, for the sake of on-the-job-experience, of course."

After thumbing her nose at his wisecrack, Karen shifted the conversation back to that troubling question—the one Janet couldn't or wouldn't answer. "I hope

I'm not being pushy," she said, "but the people that died … Were they also infertile? Sick? Is there some connection?"

Janet swallowed, gulped air. "Oh no. Nothing like that. You see, there was an accident. A terrible accident." She opened her mouth to say more, but as if sensing a menacing presence along with a warning, she closed it, tightening her lips in a seal.

Karen, misinterpreting Janet's behavior, reached over and patted her knee. "I didn't mean to upset you," she said. Then hearing the scuff of a shoe, she turned to see Rahm staring down, appraising the situation with a chess champion's strategic skill.

"Forgive me," he said, addressing the young couple. "I've been a poor host, but there were pressing matters to address. Anyway, it looks like you've managed without me—thanks to Janet here. Now, ready for that tour I promised?"

His words and tone sounded more like a command than a question, spurring Karen and Jeremy to rise and follow behind. Janet remained as they found her—sitting, dreaming, ruminating alone with her thoughts.

Chapter 5

With the help of strategically placed torches, the cave blazed like a cosmopolitan city at nightfall. "We've lit them for you," said Rahm, pointing to a flaming light above. "Normally we only have a few going—often none at all since we find they're not really necessary. See the wool on the end? Makes a great wick. Burns nice and slow."

Karen expressed a need for a bathroom, making that their first stop. A raised, bare-bones structure resting on wooden planks showcased the obvious. Holes, cut into the pine, allowed for human waste to fall into a trench below, and water, seeping from a nearby crevice, served as faucets. Rahm pointed out a cabinet with soap and toilet paper, and then moved away to allow for privacy. Hating latrines, Karen gritted her teeth, afraid of falling in, and swore to never complain about cleaning her bathroom again.

They circled back along minor passageways, the equivalent of side streets in a town. By the time they reemerged in the communal area, both Karen and Jeremy had lost all sense of direction. Taking hold of their elbows, Rahm led them to a pit, dug into the ground, surrounded by cinder blocks with a metal grid across the top. Brown, fibrous matter—"Peat," he explained— burned with a red-blue flame, heating a Dutch oven hanging above. While Rahm's nose twitched in delight, the couple recoiled when Rahm disclosed that the simmering meal was his favorite: salamander and worm stew.

Sick of the sights, the smells, Karen moved on to the pantry where unfinished pine boards, separated by bricks, stocked a wide assortment of non-perishable foods in cans and plastic containers. Farther off, crates and shelves held bedding and household items. She wandered among coat racks where pants, shirts, and jackets hung in graduated sizes for children and adults. The amount was impressive.

Rahm explained it had taken years to amass the supplies, lowering them in dumbwaiters and scaffolds, or in some cases merely allowing them to fall from cliffs. Then, when the last item had been checked off, the group's diehards had thrown an all-night bender in a grungy neighborhood bar, knowing they had reached their goal and there'd be no turning back for anyone.

Rahm scratched an ear as if delaying a confession. "While I wish it were different, we're still not totally free from the outside world. I, along with one of the others, go above when critical supplies run low."

Jeremy noted the disclosure, and asked how often, but before Rahm could reply two men approached, exchanging good-hearted back-slapping like boys in a locker room. Rahm made cursory introductions.

Both men were tall with full beards. The older, Brian, was stocky and almost completely bald. His stomach poked through the space between his shirt and pants whenever he raised his hands, which was often since he made wide flailing gestures when he spoke. His voice, loud and pressured, permeated the surroundings and bounced off the walls like peals of a gong.

The other man, Norman, seemed his opposite: slim, pensive, quiet, but beneath his bushy mustache eyebrows, his dark stare appraised the new couple as if they were running for some best-in-show competition.

Karen's hand rose to her throat.

Prudently, Rahm said, "Let's move on. We've only one more place to see."

As the threesome headed off, Karen turned to see Brian and Norman nudging each other with pointy elbows. Feeling their eyes on her body, she fastened the top button on her shirt.

They scaled an incline with Rahm in the lead, his presence being the couple's sole link to the safety of the outside world. Karen, aware of her dependence, swallowed fear as she scrambled between boulders, all the while paying careful attention to directives. Jeremy, however, remained too excited to pace himself. He stumbled and cursed as jagged edges braised his shin.

As the smoky fragrance of incense entered her nostrils, Karen tugged on Rahm's sleeve. "Is this the fertility area? Janet mentioned something about incense." From farther back in the darkness, a breathy "Hello" rang out a welcome, answering her question.

Rahm lit a candelabrum set on a small table, and Karen and Jeremy were able to make out a young woman lying across a mattress. Plump, cottony pillows were strewn about. The woman's attire, a transparent nightgown with a plunging neckline, made the outline of her body a visual feast: chestnut-colored hair coiled down her back; her breasts, twin mounds with two erect points, asked to be kissed; and her thighs, soft and round, signaled an invitation for love.

Oddly, she didn't seem surprised to see strangers. Looking from Rahm to Jeremy, she said, "Have you come for a turn?"

Still able to appreciate the uniqueness of the situation, Rahm smirked. "Not just now, Helene."

Running a hand seductively down her body, she said, "That's all right. My time is just about over." Then, nonchalantly, she asked, "Who are your friends?"

After making the introductions, Rahm explained they were unexpected guests.

"'Guests,'" she sniggered. Immediately she realized her misstep and covered it with a giggle. She fondled the necklace around her neck—similar to Janet's—and gathered her possessions: two small clay statues, a man and a woman, both naked. Then, drawing herself up to her full height—almost eye level with Jeremy—she walked off, dismissing them all with a wave of her hand.

Karen wasn't sure what to make of this striking creature, wondering if she had merely glimpsed a facade. Perhaps underneath that flawless exterior lay her namesake Helene, a mythological Amazon warrior. Then again, perhaps she was only an object of desire, as Janet had insinuated.

Karen could see Jeremy sharing her confusion as he stared, mouth agape. The fact that Helene was exceptionally pretty had just added to the effect of her blatant offer. Questioning whether love was part of the vocabulary in this odd community, Karen laughed, thinking she was more of a prude than she'd realized.

Rahm lit other candelabra and the newcomers set about exploring this purported revered area. Toward the center stood an altar with small stones and books of sacred writing on top. Nearby, the joining of a stalagmite and a stalactite formed a thick column. Karen and Jeremy had difficulty keeping their expressions serious when they focused on the pillar's chiseled-out depiction of the group's supreme god, Tloc.

Tloc appeared to be a larger yet similar version of a statue they had seen earlier among Rachel's possessions. He stood fully exposed with a face surrounded by a decorative headdress. Small crystalline rocks had been placed in the eye sockets, and the arms were folded at chest level as if declaring his preeminence and insistence on adoration. Here, too, the main embellishment was the exaggerated size of his phallus.

Karen had no desire to insult her host, yet her crinkled eyes held amusement. To stave off a faux pas, she joined Jeremy at a second column showcasing the nearly completed goddess, a mate for Tloc. Like Tloc, she stood, arms at chest level, but those folded extremities gave way to a swollen belly. Karen, despite her best effort, tittered behind compressed lips. "I'm sorry," she said, noting the deepening flush on Rahm's face.

As the tribe's leader, Rahm was accustomed to shouldering most problems with backbone, but it was obvious this touchy matter proved challenging. To compensate, he stood erect, elbows back, jaw jutting forward. "I heard you and Janet talking about our bad luck," he said to the couple.

Karen and Jeremy squirmed.

"It's funny," he continued. "Our bodies have adapted to all conditions here in the cave except procreation. Some members thought adding a goddess might help. As you can see, she's a work in progress, but with Rachel's skill, I'm sure she'll be lovely. And don't feel embarrassed on my account. I know what you're thinking." He stared at the ground, then faced them head on. "None of this was my idea, but what's the harm? Having deities appeases the members. Gives them hope."

Jeremy spoke up. "But you're not a believer, are you? This is nonsense."

Rahm threw up his hands. "Does it matter what I believe? What's religion, anyway, but a source of strength for its followers? Gives them a purpose for living and an excuse when things go wrong. I expect it's no different for you."

Karen offered a half-smile, having no argument with Rahm's premise, even though the idea of worshiping a clump of rock seemed ridiculous. She tensed, however, when Jeremy gnashed his teeth, intuiting his displeasure at the defacement of cave formations. As a precaution, she whispered in his ear, then relaxed when he shoved his fists into his pockets—insurance against knocking down the Golden Calves.

"You may not agree with our theology and behavior," said Rahm, looking at Jeremy, "but you have to understand this is our home. I hope when you write your article, you'll do it with respect."

Jeremy, remembering why he was here, uncurled his fingers. "Of course," he said, letting his hands fall from his pockets. "I shouldn't judge."

Rahm picked up a candelabrum and pointed out some drawings carved into the cave's wall. "This is Rachel's work."

Karen walked up, nose inches from the limestone canvas for a better view. The drawings, showcasing a timeline, ran from left to right. Most of the earlier ones were done in stick figures, but she noted improvement as Rachel's talents had progressed over the years. "How interesting," she said, adding the trite phrase from her lexicon of half-truths.

She ran a finger along the latter images, each with multiple colors of browns, reds, purples, and yellows. These figures were etched deeper into the wall, giving them three dimensions and helping her recognize the people portrayed. A stout Brian and a doughy Janet, depicted together in a sexual pose, drove Karen to the brink of a laugh. Immediately she tensed her jaw.

"How did you decide on a name for your god?" she asked. "Tloc? Did I pronounce it right?"

"Rachel named him. I think it's similar to an Aztec god, and only she says it right. But you did pretty good. We haven't come up with a name for the goddess yet. I suspect Rachel will think of something." He smiled. "In case you haven't noticed, she's the boss."

A token boss, thought Karen. Then, "How did you get the paint?"

"Rachel made it. She ground up mineral deposits from rocks and mixed them with fat from the animals that occasionally wander in. We eat them, of course. Nothing's wasted here. But we don't kill for pleasure; only for food. Or"—he cocked his head—"when absolutely necessary."

"Right. Sure," mumbled Jeremy, missing the nuance, his attention suddenly sidelined.

"Something wrong?" asked Karen, noticing him patting his shirt pocket."

"Yeah," he said. "What happened to my pen? You know, my lucky pen. I gave it to you when we exchanged numbers with Sara and George."

"Did you? I thought you gave me a Bic. Anyway, I gave it back."

"Uhh. You sure that was a Bic?"

"I think so, but to tell you the truth, I didn't pay much attention. It was dark and you always carry Bics. Anyway, whichever pen it was, it's probably in your backpack."

"I hope so," he said, puffing his cheeks before expelling the air. "Yeah, I guess you're right. Must be there." Reassured, he pulled out a replacement clipped to his pocket flap and returned to the pictures.

Since every image had to do with intercourse, the task proved simple enough. As he circled about, scribbling notes and making cartoon depictions, he touched a drawing, the last in the row. Inadvertently his fingernail flicked the earthen wall, splitting the image in half. He gasped at his blunder and extended an immediate apology.

Rahm's face tightened, but he remained polite. "No problem. It's gypsum. Easy to repair."

Jeremy wiped his brow with the back of his hand and blinked back relief. "Phew," he said, casting a surreptitious and calculating glance at his watch.

Karen caught the gesture and did likewise to her wrist. "I didn't realize it was so late," she said. "Listen, thanks for the tour. This had been a remarkable day, but it's time for us to leave."

"Oh," said Rahm. "I thought you were staying for dinner."

"I don't think so. Salamander and worms are not one of my favorite dishes."

Rahm smiled automatically, as if it were part of a well-rehearsed speech. "We can easily fry you some salvelinus fortinalis."

Karen screwed up her face. "Sounds disgusting."

"Actually, it's fresh brook trout and very delicious. They live in the lake. Also," continued Rahm, "I was hoping you'd stay a little longer and tell us what's happening in the outside world. Most of the members haven't been above in years. It would be such a treat, especially for the children."

Jeremy, still searching for a catchy angle to begin his article, paused to reconsider and decided breaking bread with this loopy bunch might be just the solution he was looking for. Turning toward Karen, a no already on her lips, he parried with a silent but unmistakable *please*.

"I suppose one more hour can't hurt," she acceded, "and you"—she switched her attention to Rahm—"you did say trout."

Suddenly, a scream followed by a scuffle diverted their attention.

"Rachel ... you lying bitch!"

"Uh-oh," said Rahm. "That's Mary. Maybe I'd better look." Before he could lift a foot, a woman bolted down the passageway, shouting obscenities, her fingers rounded like claws.

"Oomph!" yelped Mary, grimacing with pain as Rachel turned and surprised her pursuer with a headbutt. Although caught off guard, Mary still managed to grab a handful of hair and pull the smaller woman to the ground. Mary, however, lacked

Rachel's split-second reflexes. Before she saw it coming, Rachel had Mary pinned with her thighs and landed a punch to her cheek, clipping the side of her nose.

"Aren't you going to do something?" asked Jeremy.

"Nope," said Rahm. "As you can see, Rachel can handle herself despite her size and Mary's a pain in the ass. Besides, she'll give up in a minute. She has no taste for violence."

As predicted, Mary scrambled backwards, pushing with her legs and mewing like a sick child. She turned toward Karen and snorted contemptuously, running her eyes over the younger, prettier—and, worse: *healthier*—version of herself. Karen blanched and twisted a corner of her sweater, unsettled by the display. Finally, reason seemed to overtake jealousy and Mary cried out, "I tried. I really did." Then, stumbling to her feet, she licked the blood off her upper lip and ran to the safety of her room.

Rachel, still remaining, shot Rahm an I-told-you-so glance before heading off with the unwanted bonus of a tiny bald spot, gleaming in the torchlight.

Jeremy scratched his head.

"Sorry you had to witness that," said Rahm, "but you'll see, our Mary will be smiling and apologetic in no time."

Karen grabbed Rahm by the forearm. "What were they fighting about? And what did Mary mean by 'I tried'? She was looking at *me*."

"Mary's emotions run hot and cold, and I've given up trying to fix or understand her. Sometimes she just needs to vent. Anyway, she was talking to me, not you. She just doesn't like her assignment for the week. That's all it is, I assure you."

Karen pulled away, troubled by an ice-water sensation on her neck and tingling down her spine. Most of all, she chafed at Rahm's words, finding them far from assuring. Jeremy, on the contrary, smirked like a wise-ass chauvinist and shared a man-to-man, all-knowing grin with Rahm.

Chapter 6

The threesome arrived back at the common area where a few members were putting the finishing touches on meal preparation. The others sat or stood nonchalantly, chatting in measured tones, attempting to act casual. Karen knew they were talking about her. Jeremy too, of course. She didn't mind; it was only natural, yet she noted a flaw in their demeanor. All the adults smiled but immediately looked away, appearing fidgety and anxious, eyes cast downward. Karen rested her chin on the steeple of her forefingers and wondered why they seemed so solemn, despite their smiles. *No, that's not right,* she corrected herself. *They look guilty, like a child who's done something wrong. But what could be wrong?*

Rahm whispered something into Janet's ear, and she immediately rushed back to the kitchen. He gestured for Karen and Jeremy to join him at the table. He sat between them.

"I asked Janet to fry up some fresh fish. She's a good cook and I'm sure you'll be pleased, but I'd appreciate it if you make it a point to tell her. She's prone to depression, and I'm concerned. But now, I'd like you both to meet our family."

Rahm nodded his head and everyone flocked over. Karen wondered how those standing off to the side had noticed. *Did they feel a vibration of some sort?* She bit her tongue, deciding not to ask.

With the exception of Janet and the boys, they all sat down and said their hellos to the newcomers, their lips pulled back as if posing for a class picture.

"These nice folks are joining us for dinner," said Rahm. "Jeremy's a reporter and is doing a story on our lives in the cave, so let's all try and make a good impression. And this beautiful woman," he added with a wink, "is his wife, Karen. Since they've already met some of you, let's start with those who haven't been formally introduced. You, Mary?"

Mary, as Rahm had predicted, had already calmed down, even going so far as to put on a clean change of clothes. In addition, all traces of blood were gone. What remained was a grim-faced woman, with ho-hum, forgettable features, looking out of place among this outlandish bunch. Despite her mundane appearance, Karen wondered why Jeremy continued to stare. *Was he imagining her naked in the fertility area?*

What a crazy thought, she said to herself. Hiding her discomfort behind a pasted-on smile, Karen felt a sense of unease.

Apparently the feeling was shared. "Nice to meet you," said Mary, her monotone a dead giveaway to a lie.

David, unlike Mary, was welcoming. His boy-next-door looks (if next door meant a penthouse or a thirty-room mansion) just added to his appeal. With thick, sandy hair and a smile both innocent and suggestive, he appeared a close counterpart to his bedmate, Helene. He was also the only clean-shaven male in the group. Somehow in these surroundings it seemed out of place, and Karen wondered if it was a case of vanity or something else. Likewise, she thought it astounding that there appeared no anger or jealously in David's attitude toward his partner, who sat beside him and had so willingly offered herself to any man just that day.

David rose and with a slight bow toward the new arrivals, said, "Delighted to meet you both."

Karen smiled back, unconsciously fluffing out her hair, flattered by his walking up beside her to kiss her hand, but she noticed his eyes lingering on her husband longer than her.

Jeremy returned the greeting as enthusiastically as it was given, either oblivious or indifferent to any indiscretion.

Karen exchanged pleasantries with Lily, who put her at ease with her low-key demeanor. Seemingly bright and not much older than Karen herself, she had symmetrical features in an oval face. Sitting there in jeans and an oversized sweatshirt, she looked a vision of femininity, without the blatant sexiness of Helene. Still, the hint of a rounded hip, along with a glimpse of cleavage when she bent over, suggested a low smoldering fire.

Janet walked in with an oversized bowl brimming with salamander and worms. The smell hit Karen like an unflushed toilet. She grimaced and repeated to herself, *I will not get sick, I will not get sick*. The two boys helped their mother, scrambling back and forth from the kitchen. Karen kept her eyes down so she wouldn't have to look at the food or Jon's face.

Janet handed Karen a specially prepared plate with trout. "I hope you enjoy the fish," she said. Large platters were passed down the table from person to person. Rice and mushrooms helped fill out the offerings. Karen found she had little appetite.

Rahm was quick to point out that everyone took turns, men and women alike, in all the chores, including preparing the food, serving it, and cleaning up afterwards.

"I guess," said Jeremy, "the feminist revolution has penetrated down here too." He tried not to choke when he laughed and swallowed at the same time.

"We brought it with us," said Lily. "We all do our fair share, although we try to make allowances so people can contribute in ways they prefer. For instance, Janet likes to cook, and I like gathering the mushrooms."

"'Gathering the mushrooms'?" said Jeremy.

"That's right," said Lily. "They grow wild in the peat, down by the lake. The boys found them one day and came back after gorging on them. At first we worried they'd get sick. You know, poisoned. When they didn't, naturally we were relieved. We started cultivating new crops to increase the yield and save the wild ones for official functions or special occasions."

Rachel put down her fork, looked up, eyes glistening in the candlelight. "This cave is extraordinary. Beyond extraordinary. It's magical."

Karen tipped her head sideways, confused. "But even mushrooms need some sunlight."

"Maybe they're some kind of hybrid?" offered Brian. "Have you noticed how warm it is in this cave? About ten degrees higher than what you'd expect. Maybe that's why they grow. Whatever the reason, we think of them as a gift." He stabbed another with his fork.

"What about the rice?" said Jeremy, scooping up a mouthful of the puffy grain.

Randy, eager to be part of the adult conversation, spoke up. "We've tons of rice. We buy it above, then store it in containers in the pantry. It keeps forever. Rahm says I'm almost old enough to go with him on a shopping trip. It'll be my first time." He looked toward Rahm and began to stutter. "Y-you didn't forget or ch-change your mind, did you?"

Rahm reached across and tousled the boy's cornstalk-colored hair. "Have I ever lied to you?" he said. As Mary subtly raised an eyebrow, Randy beamed with the love reserved for a father.

And why not? thought Karen. *His real father's dead. It's nice Rahm takes an interest.*

Jeremy broke her train of thought with a question she had wanted to ask, but pushed aside, considering it rude. For once she felt grateful for his doggedness, and zeroed in on the exchange.

"I don't mean to offend," said Jeremy, resting both elbows on the table. "But I couldn't help noticing how you look at us funny. Sort of sideways."

Karen squirmed as the tribe's members appeared to collectively hold their breaths. Finally, Rahm cleared his throat, then plunged ahead with the answer.

"Living in the dark is slowly destroying our eyesight," he began. "Objects, faces, and colors get blurry, especially for Jon. But our peripheral vision remains strong. That's why we tip our heads."

Horrified, Karen asked, "Have you considered seeing a doctor?"

Rachel's response of "Puh-leeze" caused Karen to immediately back off. Rahm, on the other hand, remained forthright, hiding nothing. "At the beginning we panicked. None of us had considered the possibility of near-blindness." He shook his head. "I know, seems stupid, but fortunately we found a way to compensate—a solution far superior to eyesight."

"And what's that?" said Jeremy, eager to hear more.

Like a conspirator, Rahm pushed his chair closer. "Echolocation," he said, articulating the syllables as if they were distinct words.

The couple turned to each other and lifted their shoulders, puzzled.

"It works like sonar," said Rahm. "We've trained our voices to find the right pitch and frequency—too high for you to hear, except for the click-clicks at the starting point. We use suction from our tongues against the roofs of our mouths and go up the scale. I can tell when I'm approaching the right level because my teeth start to vibrate. When I've reached that triggering phase, my voice bounces off objects and the returning signals—or echoes I get—produce images in my brain."

Karen's mouth opened in disbelief while Jeremy countered with "Sounds amazing."

"Would you like to see how it's done?"

Rahm, eyes closed, lips parted, tapped his tongue against his palate, loud and slow to demonstrate the technique. He moved the tip of his tongue father back and the tapping increased, the pitch soared, resulting in a tingle on Karen's neck. She fought the urge to scratch the affected spot, now itching like a bite from a bug. Rahm's tongue began to flutter and the sound seemed to grow less intense until it disappeared into an inaudible range.

He looked at the astonished faces of his guests. "Of course, we do it so quickly that you'd barely notice. Would you like to give it a try?"

Jeremy jumped at the chance. When his voice rose, warbling like an adolescent, he gave up, embarrassed, and laughed with the others.

"Nice try," said Rahm, "but maybe you'd better have more food instead."

"What about you?" said Rahm, turning to Karen. "Want to try?"

She shook her head *no* but asked how they thought up the idea.

"Good question. It came from the bats."

"The *what?*"

Rahm placed a placating hand on her back, high up where it met the arch of her neck. "It's okay," he said. "They live in another section of the cave. They fly out at night through their own passageway. Actually, they're very useful creatures since they eat insects by the thousands, and we collect their guano for fertilizer. All that crazy, scary stuff about them getting in your hair—no need to worry. We leave them alone and they do likewise."

"But it was actually Jon who taught us the method," said Janet, smiling down at her son. "He's got some kind of natural instinct. I don't understand it, but he watches those creatures like they speak the same language." As Janet gazed at his face with a mother's love, Karen risked a peek—fearful not only of his appearance but his potential. *Could he do more? Read minds, perhaps?*

"You have every right to be proud," said Rahm. "Of Jon, of Randy, and yourself." He turned to Jeremy, sitting to his right, and gave him a slight nudge with his elbow.

Like a restaurant critic in receipt of a bribe, Jeremy praised her cooking, from side dishes to entrees—even the grotesque samples he hadn't tried—just as he planned to do in his article.

Not used to compliments, Janet's eyelids fluttered as if a speck of dirt lodged inside, and her pale skin turned shiny pink.

"Would you like to try the salamander too?" asked Jon. "Or the worms? I helped."

Jeremy covered his mouth, attempting to hide a look of revulsion. "I'm afraid I ate too much trout. Couldn't eat another bite of anything." He changed his mind when Janet placed a small bowl in front of him.

"What's this?" he asked, peering at the tiny, round, plum-colored objects that smelled like vanilla.

"They're berries," said Janet. "They're another of our little miracles. They grow in bushes near the lake. See the color? It's one of the few things in the cave that remains so bright, and what's more, the shade deepens or lightens every few months. We think it reflects their vitamin content. It certainly changes the flavor. Right now they're both sweet and tart. Try some."

Jeremy popped a fistful into his mouth. He ran his tongue across his teeth now stained purplish. "They're good," he said, scooping up the last few with his fingertips.

Rahm pushed back his chair and rose. The light from the candles sculpted his face, enveloping it within a sultry shadow that emphasized his strong features and high forehead. Speaking to everyone, he said, "Since Janet and the boys are on kitchen duty today, why don't the rest of us settle in the living room where it's more comfortable?" Then, smiling down at the newcomers, he added, "You've been asking questions all day. I hope you won't mind reciprocating."

As the others walked off, Karen volunteered to help with the cleanup, recalling her mother's advice on good manners. Janet graciously shooed her away, insisting she join her husband.

Karen took a seat beside Jeremy on one of the couches, the two lanterns casting a soothing glow in the cavernous space. She ran her hands across the fabric, feeling an abundance of grit, and imagined herself soaking in a hot tub, washing away her cares along with the palpable dirt below her nails and on her skin. She sank deeper. Rubbing her half-closed eyes with her knuckles, she said, "We have to leave soon. I can hardly stay awake."

Jeremy pulled her close as the flickering flames washed away all lingering protestations. Her head against his shoulder, Karen fell into a well-needed sleep.

#

With his wife content, Jeremy turned to the surrounding rapt faces. "I guess I'll let her doze for a while. We've been up since early morning." Stroking the stubble on his face, Jeremy began going over local and international news, medical achievements, Hollywood scandals and gossip. From their spellbound expressions, it was obvious that some had pangs of homesickness and maybe regret over what they had left behind.

Jon, having had his fill of cleaning, ran to Mary and plopped down on her lap, a thumb in his mouth. Since the boy had never been above, Jeremy did his best to describe an assortment of what he would find: trees with branches, large and small, interconnecting like tendrils of hair; leaves waving at a hazy sky where pillows of dark, puffy clouds threatened rain; snow, six feet deep or a mere dusting like rice on the pavement; sunshine; grass; and on and on. The concept of color was impossible for the boy to grasp, as was the purr of a kitten.

"What's a kitten?"

"A furry animal with four legs and a tail."

"Fur? A tail? Wow!"

The questions were endless. Patiently, Jeremy got through them all. That top leaders from fifteen countries had recently signed a nuclear non-proliferation pact, sent the adults into reels of laughter.

"Well, at least we're safe in the cave," said Helene. The taut muscles around her mouth spoke of contempt for the world above.

Jeremy tilted his head. "Who told you that?"

Helene looked at Rahm.

"I never said we were completely safe. Just safer. The rock provides some protection from radioactive fallout, but if there's ever a full-scale attack, we may be doomed anyway. Still, I'd rather take my chances below." He turned his face up and smirked. "Here we have a chance."

Jeremy wasn't surprised by the significance of the nuclear issue. He had come across it so often in his line of work that he expected it to crop up under any circumstance.

What did surprise him, however, was the clamor for personal information. Rachel, especially, pried into his life as if he were some A-list celebrity, even going so far as to ask if he ever fathered a child.

"No," he answered, noting her contemptuous pout as if she were personally offended.

Rahm took a different approach using more tactical questions. "Does anyone know you're here? Family? Friends?"

Jeremy squinched his eyes. "Why do you ask?"

"What if you had an accident? Isn't it wise to let others know your plans?"

"Yeah, you're right, of course. And I meant to, only everything happened so fast. You see, our friends got sick and we switched caves. But come to think of it, there was another family here. We met them purely by chance. Shared lunch together."

"So no one—that is, no one from back home—knows where you are."

Jeremy tensed, then laughed it off as overexcitement and exhaustion, compounded by the anomaly of being the interviewee rather than the interviewer. "I-I guess that's true, but fortunately everything turned out great. Soon I'll be in the newsroom, with a helluva story to write." He stopped to check his watch. "Oh, shit. It's nearly twelve." Although he tried fighting it, a mammoth-sized yawn engulfed his face. He turned to Karen and wanted nothing more than to join her in sleep; in spite of that, he said, "Today has been a once-in-a-lifetime experience. I wish I had another week, but, unfortunately, I'm a working man."

"It's been our pleasure, believe me," said Rahm, "but may I suggest you stay the night? The roads around here are difficult in the dark. You're likely to get lost if you're not familiar with the area."

Jeremy paused and scratched his nose. "I understand. Still, we'd better be on our way."

"But look at your wife." Rahm gestured toward the sleeping figure. "She's totally zonked out. It's difficult enough getting back up under the best of circumstances. Even after we hoist her up the cliff, she'll still need to climb. One bad move and you could break a leg."

Jeremy's head dropped, sinking between his shoulders. With a nod toward Karen, lying in blissful serenity, he determined it would be the equivalent of a sin to wake her. "Okay, you're right again, and besides, I'm half asleep myself. Well, as long as you don't mind—"

"Mind? We'd be delighted."

Blankets were immediately brought over. Jeremy went to the kitchen. A small stream of water trickled from the earthen wall. He filled a cup and swished the liquid in his mouth. It was a poor substitute for brushing, but it would have to do. He walked to the toilet, carrying a lantern, and relieved himself. Finishing that, he went back to the living room and listened to Karen purring beneath the blanket someone had laid across her. Lowering it slightly, he gazed at her lovely face, so vulnerable in the candlelight.

Then it hit him like a punch in the gut. He gasped, felt chilled, and ran both hands down his cheeks, realizing he was totally dependent on these people, these strange, half-crazed, screwed-up baboons. Swaying forwards and back as if he'd been drugged, he slumped into a chair. "Shit!" he groaned. Without someone showing him the way up, he was trapped like a circus animal, allowed out only to perform. But perform what? Dead fish, he knew, were more entertaining than he was; he recalled a high-school recital which had earned him a "Kick Me" sign. "This is nuts," he said to Karen's sleeping figure.

Unable to confront the possibility of any catastrophic ramifications, he erased the thought from his mind, told himself he was exaggerating, being paranoid, and replaced his concerns with a new one: *What will Karen think when she wakes in the morning and sees we're still here?* For the first time, he felt guilty for forcing this upon her. *I'll make it up to her,* he swore to himself. He lay down on a nearby couch and closed his eyes, grateful as sleep overtook his exhausted body.

#

Carl snuggled under the quilt in his comfy bed, a calico kitten curling next to him. "Are they home yet?" he called to Joan, downstairs in the kitchen fixing tea with honey.

"No. I've phoned countless times and it's almost midnight. You don't suppose they went caving by themselves and something happened?"

"Nah," said Carl as he reached for a tissue. "Jeremy knows the rule: you never go below without at least three people." He reached for another tissue. "Jeremy sounded disappointed all right, about postponing the trip, but he understood. He said he and Karen'll wait till we're better. Who knows, maybe they went to a disco."

"A disco?" Joan walked to the foot of the stairs, one hand on the banister, one holding her tea. "Are you crazy? Jeremy hates anything with dancing as much as you do. That's why I was supposed to go to those musicals with Karen."

"Well, whatever it is can wait for tomorrow. You coming to bed?"

"Not yet. I think I'll watch TV a bit. My head feels swollen and I'm drowning in snot."

"Me too, but I'm going to sleep. At least, I'm going to try. I'm bushed."

"Okay. I'll be up later. Sleep well. Love you."

"Goodnight. Feel better. Love you too."

Chapter 7

On bare feet, she moved closer to them. After listening to their even breathing, she reached for their backpacks without stirring the air. In silence, she slunk back to her quarters.

"Did you get everything?" he asked.

"Yes. Over here." She pulled the backpacks across her body, opened the zippers and dumped out the contents. Conscious of her mission, she replaced all the useless material—flashlights; a leftover sandwich; knee crawlers still in their original packages—and kept strictly to business. "Here it is," she sang out, smiling in triumph.

Rahm wrapped his fingers around a set of keys. "I can start the car without them, but this will save time."

Rachel muttered an inattentive "Uh-huh" as she searched through their wallets. "Just your usual junk," she snarled. "Credit cards, insurance cards. Not even good for fertilizer."

Picking up a plastic-coated card, Rahm turned it over. "Identification for his job at the newspaper. Says *Baltimore Beehive*. Ever hear of it?"

"No, but then I've never spent much time in Baltimore. Anyway, Jeremy said it was fairly new; had a small readership."

"Then I doubt they'll be missed by too many people."

"You don't suppose their friends—whatever their names were—could cause any problems? And what about that family, the couple with the teenage son that was here earlier? Did you recognize the man? You're originally from this area too."

Rahm sat back, stroking his beard. "Nope. Never met him before. Even if we went to the same schools, he's at least a decade older than me. And anyway, they live in Pittsburgh now. They'll probably never hear about missing persons. As for their friends ... didn't Jeremy say they think he went to a movie or a different cave, one in the opposite direction? So don't worry. Even if the authorities wind up searching here, they won't find anything. We couldn't have planned this better. For a reporter, Jeremy sure is dumb."

"It's ego," said Rachel. "Stupid ego. Just hold out a chance for fame and fortune, and people forget all the good sense they've been taught."

"Yeah, that too." Rahm handed Jeremy's ID back to Rachel. They exchanged a brief look, but long enough to read each other's thoughts. Neither had any doubt about what they were doing. "I'm leaving now," he said. "I'll see you in the morning."

"Be careful. So much depends on this." She kissed him fully on the lips as if sealing a pact.

While Rachel returned the backpacks, Rahm made his way out of the cave. He had nearly a mile to climb, but with the expertise of a hoofed animal accustomed to living in mountainous conditions, he conquered each challenge.

He leaped twenty feet at a time, his suction-cup fingers grasping the limestone, sealing it with sticky secretions. "Click-click, click-click," he exhaled as he continued onward, an unmatched human machine, proud of his skill.

If there had been an outsider present, witnessing this spectacle, he'd have though he had lost his mind and seen some mythical flying creature.

But this was real! And although Rahm's eyesight was poor, the ultrasonic squeal coming from his mouth provided a sixth sense superior to any other. Without a doubt, he was an evolutionary marvel.

As he got closer to the mouth of the cave, however, and moonlight began to filter through, he closed his eyes. The light cast unfamiliar shadows, resulting in a moment of disorientation, and after crawling through the same tunnel that Karen and Jeremy had earlier, he donned a pair of sunglasses. Standing outside, he paused to breathe in the fresh air. It felt strange, and, yes, wonderful. He had to admit, painful as it was, that he did miss the feel of the crisp autumn breeze on his face and the sounds of night creatures foraging for food. But this was no time to be nostalgic; he had to be back by sunrise.

He walked to the car, unlocked the door, and got in. Not wanting to draw any unnecessary attention while he sat behind a wheel, he put his sunglasses in his pocket. Although it had been some time since he last drove, he felt comfortable with the prospect. Good eyesight, he reminded himself, was not necessary. Turning on the ignition, he parted his lips to emit his supernatural call, a paragon of direction.

He remembered the way and wasn't surprised to find himself almost alone; only an ear-popping clunker—its muffler obviously broken—trailed father back. He slowed down, letting it pass. Few people were aware of this road, old and unpaved, but being a local he knew of its existence, and just as he'd presumed, time hadn't changed it much. It took longer than expected to drive the thirty miles, since he didn't want to risk a flat. He could have brought the car to their safe-house, owned by Norman, but that would have been riskier since it involved driving on a main road with traffic, and besides, this car was past its prime and they didn't need another.

He slowed down; almost there. Squinting his eyes, he looked through the windshield toward the sky, guessing it was between two and three o'clock. He'd have to hurry.

A minute later, he arrived at an old wooden bridge, or more precisely, "Junkyard Bridge." Yes, it was still there, a relic from the past, broken boards and all. Driving onto the structure, he stopped at mid-point, held his breath, afraid it might collapse. Fortunately it remained stable, although the rotting timbers screamed in protest. He turned the car's wheel, climbed out, and pushed hard. It went over with one long heave. As he listened to the splash, he bit his bottom lip, relieved that the first part of his mission was complete. All the same, his gut churned with acid. What he was doing was necessary, yet it brought him no pleasure. With total self-discipline, however, coming from detailed preparation for this crucial and unprecedented event, he forced all negativity aside.

He crossed grasslands where parched weeds climbed up to his knees and tickled his legs through pants worn nearly bare. He cut through a graveyard without fear of moldering bodies or diabolical spirits. Finally, reaching the highway, he walked up the ramp. No cars coming. If he were lucky he'd get a lift at least part-way, but if necessary he'd run the whole distance. He began with a trot, speeding up like the Thoroughbred, perfectly attuned for speed and agility. Feeling the adrenaline flowing through his veins, he felt invincible, an Olympian enjoying the challenge.

#

The two teenagers busily engaged along the bank, adjacent to the bridge, abruptly stopped.

"Did you hear that?"

"It's nothing," said the boy, unfastening her bra. "Don't pay any attention."

"What was it?" she insisted.

"It's just a car being junked. That's the second one this week."

"What do you mean?"

"Don't you know? People junk their old cars here. That's how this place got its name."

She paused and put a finger to her lips, thinking. "How do you know this is the second one this week?"

"W-well, I was here with G-Gary the other night."

Immediately, she pulled away, adjusting her clothes. "Don't you lie to me again, you lousy stinker. You mean Lisa."

Joey grabbed for her, but she was too quick, and all he got for his effort was a handful of air. "She doesn't mean anything to me, Jo Ellen. Honest. Come back … please … please … Oh, shit!"

#

He had just cleared the five-mile mark when he felt the vibration of an approaching car. He stuck out his thumb. A few cars had already passed, and while he enjoyed the feel of his legs in motion, attuned to the pumping of his heart, he knew he should try hitching a ride. What if he fell and twisted an ankle? Better not take a chance. He slowed down and luckily a pickup pulled over and stopped.

An old man with a younger one half hidden behind the brim of a baseball cap peered out the window. The younger one rolled it down and pointed a shotgun at Rahm's face.

"Where you go'n'?"

Keeping his face slack, Rahm answered, "To Britton. My ma's sick."

"Where you from?"

"Creston Falls."

The man nodded and lowered the firearm. "We can take you as far as Little Dale if you don't mind ridin' in the back. No more room up front."

"I'd sure appreciate it. My ma's gonna go any time now." He hopped into the back, pushing aside boxes, wheels, a car battery, rakes, and hoes. He found a blanket, spread it out and lay down. The night was clear with a full moon and stars eager to flaunt their splendor. Even his weak eyes could appreciate the show they were putting on. Again he felt a sense of melancholy well up in his throat for his former home, but he knew it was just the awe of a tourist, and he allowed himself the luxury of a cat nap.

As the truck came to a sharp stop, his body shuddered, awakening him. Parting his lips, he put forth his characteristic cry and felt the vehicle pull up to a solid structure. He knew from the smell it was a restaurant even before he saw the blurry neon sign blinking *Good Eats Diner*, inviting travelers to come on in, eat, and, most importantly, spend their money.

He jumped off the truck as the two men got out of the cab. The old man smiled, revealing toothless gums, and rubbed his day-old stubble. "Join us for coffee?"

"Don't think so. I'd better be on my way."

"Sorry we can't take you further."

"That's okay. Thanks for the lift."

He was making excellent time, better than he'd hoped for, and decided to take it easy and enjoy himself. Walking at a leisurely pace, he took in all the things around him: the smell of decaying leaves and auto exhaust; the feel of the earth beneath his feet; and the choral symphony of birds, welcoming the new day in the trees above. Tipping his head up, he saw a black cloud spreading out, swirling in all directions, and he clicked his tongue in response. As he'd suspected, it wasn't a cloud, after all, but a colony of bats, perhaps his bats, enjoying their daily meal of tasty live insects.

This is it, he thought. *Our moment of reckoning.* Confident in that certainty, he arrived at the mouth of the cave with time to spare and sat down to watch the sunrise. While he had enjoyed this glorious spectacle numerous times when he'd lived above, he now felt an obligation to see it through. "Who knows?" he said out loud. "This may be my last time ever." Despite the help from his sunglasses, he had to watch with his customary sideways glance as the morning sky gave birth to a dazzling display, a heavenly landscape spewing streaks of fire. It reminded him of the walls below where mineral deposits created a spectrum of colors, albeit more subdued. He took a breath and exhaled a thank you for a successfully completed mission, and with an absolute appreciation for his hidden home, he crawled inside to begin the journey down to his secret, infertile oasis.

#

Lightly brushing Rachel's lips with his own, he murmured, "It's done. Everything went perfectly."

In response to that rather chaste kiss, Rachel kissed back with open eyes, all senses on alert, as if she'd been expecting trouble. "What took you so long? I hardly slept. Did you stop to watch the damned sunrise or something?" Not waiting for answers, she added, "Fortunately they're still asleep. I just checked."

Rahm traced a finger across her cheek, and lay down beside her. Yes, he cared about her—loved her in his way—and though it would be nice to prove it, it would ask too much from his overworked body. And besides, there was still one huge hurdle to overcome. Before changing his mind, he sat back up. The forthcoming day would test his powers as leader to its limit. There hadn't been a crisis like this since that bastard, Tom, died. Reaching down to his innermost core, where his passion for life gave him a decided edge, he sucked in a swell of air, expanded his chest, and gathered the strength for the final task. Turning to Rachel, he asked, "You ready?" When she mumbled a *yes*, he said, "Then let's begin."

Like soldiers on a mission, they walked in sync, lighting the torches and the candles left out from the night before. The others in the tribe were still in bed, but from their rustling bodies, Rahm knew they, too, were awake, waiting for his signal.

Rahm looked down at the sleeping figures of Karen and Jeremy, still drained from the preceding day's physical and emotional toll. He leaned in, close to Karen's ear, suspecting she would be more startled than her husband, and in an even, reassuring voice said, "Good morning. You fell asleep. Everything's all right."

She opened one eye, then the other, and sprang to her feet with a yelp.

The sudden noise and motion awakened Jeremy, and he rushed to her side, certain she'd be in a foul mood. He tried placating her. "It's true," he said, kneading his intertwined fingers. His face was flushed, but not from sleep. Sky-high guilt resulted in him keeping up the useless banter. "You looked so exhausted, honey, I didn't want to wake you. We spent the night here."

Karen ran her tongue across her lips as anger replaced confusion. "You didn't want to wake me? What a crock of shit!" Spit flew from her mouth. "You probably planned this and wanted to spend the night here. Well, I've had enough of this cave of horrors. Let's get our stuff and go."

As she began gathering their belongings, Rahm reached over, grabbed hold of her body. She tried pulling away, but his grip was firm. "I suggest you eat something first. You'll need energy for the climb."

"Rachel," he yelled, though she was standing nearby. "Get some granola for our guests." To Karen, he said, "It's good. We make it ourselves."

"I don't give a rat's ass about your precious granola. We'll go to a restaurant. I just want to get out."

Rahm moved his hands to her shoulders, forcing her to face him. "Please. Try to calm down. It's very early and there's no restaurants around. Not for miles."

"He's right," said Jeremy, sotto voce as if afraid to speak. "Besides, I'm starved, and I could use some coffee."

With no door to slam, Karen kicked the couch. "Screw your coffee. Can't we ever get out of this place?"

Jeremy took a step back, afraid she'd hit him. He'd never seen her so angry. "We'll leave after breakfast. Not a moment later. I promise."

"Should I tell you what I think of your promises?"

Rachel, with the help of Janet, whose hands were shaking from the commotion, brought over two trays. They quickly walked off, leaving Karen and Jeremy alone to eat in silence.

I'm sorry," said Jeremy. "I can't wait to leave either. I've had enough of this gloomy gray shithole, and I've had enough of caves for years, perhaps forever. I want to see the sun again."

Karen pecked at her granola. It was passable at first, but the powdered milk tasted anemic, leaving a sourness on her tongue, and the aftertaste from the fruit-flavored breakfast drink was chemical. She took a sip of the lukewarm coffee and handed the rest to Jeremy. He thanked her with his words while his eyes begged forgiveness.

As Jeremy drank his second cup, Karen began, once again, to gather their belongings. After a moment, she cocked her head, replacing her scowl with a quizzical look.

"Something wrong?" asked Jeremy.

"My car keys. I can't find them." She turned both backpacks upside down, shook them, and then searched through the side pockets.

"We probably left them in the ignition. Don't worry. I brought an extra set. See?" Reaching into his pants pocket, he drew out a small leather case attached to a silver chain and dangled it before her eyes.

Karen grabbed it from his hand and looked it over as if she needed to make certain it was real. "I know I took the damned keys from the car," she said. All the same, she felt a moment of relief at having a new set in her possession. That relief, however, ended in a flash.

With a powerful leap to a ledge above, Rahm crossed his arms over his chest like a dictator about to make a pronouncement. "They won't do you any good," he bellowed.

Jeremy swallowed hard, raising a hand to his throat. "W-what do you mean?" he said, reaching out for something to grab onto. Finding nothing, he spread his legs wide, feet flat on the floor, trying to maintain his balance.

Rahm, aware of the significance of this moment and wanting to ensure that it remained stamped in everyone's mind, stood tall, chin out. "While you were sleeping last night, I climbed out and drove your car off a bridge. You will not be allowed to leave."

Karen's hands flew to her face. She began to cry and dropped to one knee. Protectively, Jeremy rushed to her side, encircled her in his arms, and pulled her close. He glared at this insane man, his new enemy, standing above. With hate etched in the dark hollows of his cheeks and in the lines of his furrowed brow, he said, "What do you mean? Why can't we leave? You won't get away with this!"

Rahm, a leader of few but a leader nonetheless, addressed his flock, gathering with solemnity about the pair, now unofficial members of the tribe, even if against their will. All eyes riveted up.

"You can't leave because we need you. That is, we need your baby—the baby you will have, sooner or later. And yes, we will get away with it. You see, the harnesses are gone, and we dismantled the machinery that lowered you down. You will never be able to find your way out. Don't even try. It would be suicidal."

Karen stared at her husband, her jaw dropping in disbelief, as the horror of her predicament bore down with jackhammer force into her brain. Unless she and Jeremy were guided out, they were snared, trapped, condemned, damned. Without the candles, lanterns, or torches they couldn't see the tips of their fingers, and even with their carbide lamps they wouldn't know the way through this puzzling maze with its unknown levels and intricate network.

Jeremy's nails dug into his wife's shoulders. "Dear God," he wailed. "We're doomed, and it's all my fault. Forgive me, Karen. Please!"

She looked at him blankly, then blinked, her breath coming in staccato bursts, piercing her lungs like wounds from a knife. She began to run blindly, crying, "Let me die! Let me die!"

She ran down unfamiliar passageways, reeling haphazardly, until her foot hit an obstruction, tripping her, causing her to tumble to the ground. Lying on the cold, damp earth, she rubbed her throbbing ankle. Instinctively she moved it in circles, relieved it wasn't broken. When the pain lessened, she rose to her knees. Despite her terror, her fingers sought out the object responsible for her fall. Pulling matches from her pocket, she lit one, then another. From the glow, she was able to make out a wooden marker, protruding from an oval mound. *The graveyard,* she thought. She began to tremble. Close by, she found the two other markers, and wait—there was a fourth, slightly smaller than the others. Putting her nose to the inscription and tracing with a forefinger, she made out the words: "Baby Bruso, female stillborn." It was inches from the marker reading: "Louise Bruso, 1949—1975. RIP."

Karen put her hands over her ears and screamed and screamed and screamed.

Chapter 8

He stayed back until the pitiful, hopeless cries ceased; even they pierced his calculating heart. He went to her, squeezing her shoulders as she lay on the ground, face up and deadly quiet. Raising her hand, he deliberately let it go, but it hung in the air with a life of its own. He raised the other, and it, too, hung as if attached to a sleepwalker or a person afflicted with some black-magic curse. Finally, lifting her in his powerful arms, Rahm carried her to her disbelieving husband, a shaken and quivering mass, waiting in his Frankenstein cell, his new underworld home. Jeremy took one look at his wife, seemingly hovering between life and death, and dropped his head with a sob.

#

Upon awakening Sunday morning after a night of coughing fits and mouth breathing, Carl stumbled down the stairs. He found Joan sprawled on the couch, the TV still on and an open magazine on the floor where it had apparently fallen when she'd drifted off. He fixed two cups of instant coffee and went back to the living room and turned off the set. The motion and sudden lack of background noise woke the sleeping beauty, although the line of mucus under her red nose made her look less than ravishing.

"What time is it?" she yawned, wiping her face with a sleeve.

"Quarter past eight." He pushed her favorite blue ceramic mug across the coffee table along with a box of tissues.

Joan sat up and straightened her glasses, sitting askew across her nose. "Thanks," she said, taking a sip.

"I called."

"Called who?" said Joan.

"Karen and Jeremy. I just called their number."

"Oh, shit," said Joan, now fully roused. "They're still not home?"

Carl lowered his eyes and sighed. "No one answered, and I'm not sure what to do."

"Should we call the police?"

"I thought of that, but maybe it's too soon. I don't want to sound the alarm bell for nothing. Maybe we should wait till tomorrow. If Jeremy doesn't show up at work then something is definitely wrong."

"What about their cat?" said Joan.

"Oh yeah, I forgot about Boots. They probably left extra food if they were planning on being away, but I'll go over and get the superintendent to let me in to check."

"You think he'll do that?"

"I think so. I've met him a few times. He lives in the building. Anyway, he'd better. I don't want the cat to starve. You know, just in case."

"You think they went into that cave alone?"

Carl shrugged. "I can't picture Jeremy doing that. Still, you never know."

"Jesus!" said Joan.

"Yeah, you can say that again."

#

"Karen, Karen," he pleaded, cupping her head in his hands. "Please wake up." When she didn't respond, Jeremy stared helplessly at his wife, then accusingly at Lily. "She's been like this since yesterday. This is all your fault. You and the rest of your goddamned kidnapping friends."

"She'll come out of it," said Lily as she shook Karen's immobile body, but the oblivious woman stayed lost in an impenetrable fog. "I've seen this before. She's not asleep and she's not unconscious. She's catatonic."

"She's what?" asked Jeremy, his pupils darkening at the sound of the word.

"Catatonic. I've seen it in people with mental illnesses. Sometimes a catastrophe can cause it too—in otherwise healthy people."

"How do you know so much?" asked Jeremy, his voice a heavy rasp, teeming with hate.

Lily looked away, too shame-faced to meet his eye. "I worked as an aide on a psych ward for a short while. Don't worry. She'll be okay. Here, I brought you some food."

"I'm not hungry."

"But you must be," she insisted. "You haven't eaten since yesterday morning. See? It's only more granola."

"I said I'm not hungry!" His voice rose to a yell.

"Okay, but at least feed your wife. You want her to get better, don't you? Come. I'll help." Apparently much stronger than she appeared, Lily raised the top half of Karen's body, propping it up with pillows. She dipped a spoon into the cereal bowl and brought it to Karen's mouth, which remained closed. When prodding with the spoon proved useless, she pinched Karen's nostrils.

Alarmed, Jeremy swatted her hand. "What are you trying to do? Kill her?"

"Of course not. I'm just getting her to open her mouth. Look."

Instinctively, Karen sucked in a deep breath of air along with the cereal. She began to cough and spit out all she had just taken in. Lily waited for the spasm to stop and tried again. This time it worked without any dire consequences, and Karen ate what was offered. When she'd finished, Lily wiped away the remaining dregs from Karen's face and shirt.

"I'm going now. There's an important meeting I need to attend, but Mary will be back later to check on you both. She's a nurse, you know."

"I know," said Jeremy.

"I'll be back too, if you like."

Jeremy remained silent, but his fingers twitched as he imagined Lily, her pummeled arms turning black and blue, blood dripping from her nose as she begged for his mercy. He could actually see her falling—bruised and traumatized—a frail, slender heap not worthy of compassion. Afraid he might actually do damage, he placed his hands under his thighs and pressed down. *Hurting Lily won't help Karen,* he berated himself.

As her footsteps trailed off down the passageway, he rose to his feet, continuing his contemplation. Lily turned back to stare. Narrowing his eyes, Jeremy could just make out her face, outlined by the overhead torch, and could see himself as she saw him: a half-crazed, pitiable creature. And poor helpless Karen, lying like a piece of dead wood, unable to give or receive comfort. "Damn them all. Scum of the earth." Weeping softly, he had never felt so helpless.

#

"I don't approve," said Mary, muscles stiff, shoulders squared as if she were a prosecutor in a courtroom.

Flicking her long hair from her eyes, Helene interrupted. "Exactly what is it you don't like?"

"We've no right to keep them here against their will."

"You have a point," said Helene, "and I'm not arguing about that. But that's not what I asked. I want to know what you don't like."

"I already told you."

"Don't expect me to swallow that bleeding-heart bullshit. We all know why you're pissed off. You're jealous. You want to be the next to have a baby. Now you're afraid it won't be you."

Mary tried to keep herself in check, but her taut lips and bulging owl eyes betrayed her fury. "That's a lie!" she blurted out. "How dare you speak to me this way?"

"Why not? It's the truth. You're close to forty, and it's time you accept what your chances are." Sucking in her bottom lip to hide a complacent smile, Helene added, "Practically zero."

"I'm thirty-seven. I still have years left," said Mary, "and you, with all your smutty ways, have never conceived. Not even once. At least I did, even though I miscarried."

Helene snickered. "You were probably just late."

Rahm rose to his feet. "This has gone far enough. We're a family here, and it doesn't help if we turn on each other. Karen and Jeremy are now part of our family. Who cares which of you has a baby first or who's the father? All that counts is that we stay together and grow. Now isn't that right?" With a hard stare from his blue-gray eyes, he engulfed them, turned them to compliant disciples, until a semblance of peace was restored.

Once again Helene flicked her hair, an obvious affectation. She smiled with her lips, but her demeanor remained cold. "Of course, right," she said.

Mary continued to sulk.

"I suggest," said Rahm, "that we get back to work, but"—he raised his eyebrows—"with the complication of caring for the recent arrivals, I think it best if we stick with last week's schedule. Are there any objections?" When there were none, he said, "Good. Then let's get going. Oh, except you, Mary. Can I have a word?"

Mary thumped her fist over her heart, ordering it to slow down. Rahm, in acceptance of her unpredictable whims and passive-aggressive behavior, pretended to be oblivious.

"I already asked Lily to take over your duties this week," he said. "I hope that's okay. I'd like you to concentrate on Karen and Jeremy. I hear there are problems. Of course, that was to be expected, but this will give you a chance to brush up on your nursing skills."

He walked off, leaving Mary staring in his direction. *He didn't even wait for an answer*, she reflected. *Just assumed I'd do his bidding*. After cursing in silence, she took a deep breath and felt the familiar pangs of self-pity well up inside. She puffed out her abundant chest and transformed her face into its characteristic hard facade, being astute enough to know that she shouldn't let anyone see her unguarded. Even she agreed that the *real* Mary lacked looks and charm, as her husband so eagerly pointed out. Oh, the bum never said as much; in fact, he never said much at all—not to her, anyway—but his repugnant conduct made it clear as day, each time a woman entered the fertility area. During those periods, he remained on call, first in line, prepared to do his duty. It was so blatant that everyone joked about it. Staunchly, Mary bore the embarrassment, just as she bore every disappointment, of which there were many. But payback time would come, she felt sure of that, and, best of all, it would come soon.

Carl put the receiver to his ear, the tangled cord wrapping around his arm. He placed his finger in the rotary phone's wheel, listening to the swoosh of the dial as it moved clockwise before returning with a click-click-click to finish its connection. His coworkers crowded around, all holding their breath.

On the other end a sonorous voice answered. "Police station. Sergeant Perozzi speaking."

Carl, unable to believe this was happening, spoke softly, almost imperceptibly. "I want to report a missing person. I mean persons. There were two."

"Talk louder," said the officer. "I can barely hear you."

"I want to report two missing persons."

"How long have they been missing?"

"Since Saturday night."

"Well, that's just a day and a half. Are they adults?"

"Yes."

The sergeant sighed. "In most cases these so-called missing persons show up. Took a spur-of-the-moment trip. Had a family emergency."

"You don't understand," said Carl. "I haven't actually spoken to them since Friday. What's more, Jeremy didn't come to work today. He'd never do that without calling. Also, I went to their apartment yesterday and their cat's bowl was nearly empty, their backpacks gone, climbing ropes too. I think they went into a cave. By themselves."

"What makes you think they did that?" asked the officer.

Carl explained the situation and Sergeant Perozzi's manner abruptly changed.

"Perhaps you'd better give me more information, after all."

#

As she'd been doing all week, Mary cleared her throat to announce her presence. "How's my patient today?" she said to Jeremy with a nod toward Karen. While she was concerned about both of them, her primary focus remained Karen, still barely conscious. "Any change?" she asked.

Jeremy didn't speak, merely shook his head.

Mary sighed. "And you. Are you remembering to drink water like I've instructed? You don't want to hurt your kidneys now, do you?"

Jeremy bristled, shot daggers from his eyes.

Mary placed the tray of food on a side table, handing Jeremy a plate which he promptly set aside. "Well, at least you could try it, after all the trouble I went to." In truth, she hadn't gone to much trouble at all. From the cupboard, she'd taken a can of beans and slopped some onto the flatbread that Janet had made earlier that morning, and rolled it up Mexican style.

The brown liquid oozed out, resembling fecal waste, and Jeremy felt a wave of disgust.

"I brought some powdered milk too," she said, pointing to the white, lumpy mix. "You'll get used to it in no time."

Sitting cross-legged on the ground, Mary began spoon-feeding Karen. Jeremy watched as a soupy goop ran from his wife's mouth.

"I want you to know," said Mary, looking at him from over her shoulder, "I'm on your side. It's true I initially agreed to this madness, but Rahm set the agenda and I was browbeaten; besides, I never imagined he would actually follow through. Anyway, at my insistence we voted again, and this time we used secret ballots. Unfortunately, you just missed the mark."

Jeremy's eyebrows shot up. "What do you mean?"

Mary squirmed at the hip, trying to get her thunder thighs into a modicum of comfort. "I gather," she said, "that no one's explained the rules to you yet. We are a democracy, you know. It takes six votes to pass a law. There are nine adults, remember? Actually, six of us did vote in your favor, me included, but Rahm vetoed it. It takes seven votes to override his veto, and I'm afraid we couldn't persuade one more person to switch sides. Since we used secret ballots, I don't know who voted which way, but I can make an educated guess. But don't worry. I'll make sure the issue is taken up again, and besides, there are other ways."

Jeremy, realizing he had an unexpected ally, grabbed hold of Mary's shoulder, his eyes tearing up like a man told that thingamajig on his body wasn't malignant after all. "What ways?" he asked. "Can you lead us out yourself?"

"No. I don't think so. It's been years since I've ventured far from here. By the time I found the way, someone would suspect we were missing. And besides, no one can know I'm helping you. You won't tell anyone, will you?"

"Hell no! Of course not!"

"Good. Then just be patient. Sooner or later something will turn up."

"I hope it's sooner."

Mary sat up straighter, shoulders high, elbows at right angles. "So do I," she said. "So do I."

#

The employees of *The Baltimore Beehive* met in the conference room where a frustrated Carl slammed his hand on the table, catching his pinkie on a sharp edge. One of the account executives pushed over a napkin. Carl wiped up the speck of blood. "I don't understand," he repeated over and over, his voice louder each time. "The police said there was no sign of them in the cave we had originally planned on going to. They even checked a number of other caves in the surrounding area using professional spelunkers. And there's no report of a missing car either. People just don't vanish off the face of the earth."

Jeff, publisher of "The Hive" as staffers dubbed it, was equally perplexed but had other things on his mind. Despite being a trust-fund baby, with money handed down from generations of investment bankers, he took his obligations seriously. He had started the weekly after finishing college, and with his natural business acumen, along with a dose of good luck, the paper was finally turning a profit.

Jeff removed his tie and rubbed his neck, grateful to have it off. He had plans on expanding the paper's distribution and made an effort to dress appropriately when meeting with big-shot community leaders, as he had done earlier that morning. Now he forced himself to concentrate on the present heated conversation.

A woman from classifieds spoke up. "The police said a waitress from some dumpy diner recognized their picture. Apparently she was the last person to see them. So at least we know they got that far. Any chance they could have driven out of West Virginia?"

"Why? They had no reason to do that," said Carl.

Jeff made doodles with his pen. "You know Jeremy a lot better than I do, Carl. Tell me, did he ever mention being a member of a fringe political group—you know, one of those crazy societies, right, left, or otherwise?"

"No. Of course not."

"What about a hippy commune or a religious cult? You know, like the Hare Krishnas."

"No. Absolutely not!"

"Then I just don't know."

"I'll tell you what I think," said Carl, pointing a finger at no one in particular. "I smell a skunk and it stinks." Struck by his own guilt in this imbroglio, he crossed his arms, placing his fists under opposite armpits and pressing down hard, afraid a finger would sneak out and snake dance toward him.

"You may be right," agreed Jeff, glancing at his watch. "Nevertheless, we have to get back to work. You and the rest of the crew can't keep filling in for him. It isn't fair. Look at you, Carl. You've got rings under your eyes. I'll have to find a replacement—temporary, that is—until this whole mess is resolved." Tweaking his words to find the right touch, he added, "You do understand. Don't you?"

Carl took a breath and let it out slowly. "I understand. You have no choice."

"In that case, how about Phil? He's new, but you like him, don't you?"

Carl raised one shoulder in a halfhearted shrug. "I guess so." To himself, he thought, *I'm sorry, Jer ... but we really don't have any choice. I, we—God forgive us—have to move on.*

Chapter 9

Jeremy took on the care of his wife, boosted by the prospect that Mary would somehow deliver them from this hellish dungeon. Hell was precisely how he thought of it, and on those occasions when fear got the upper hand and he could see no way out, he drew up plans to kill himself. Yes, he could do it: jumping from a ledge, hanging from a rope, plunging a knife into his neck—somehow those thoughts also lifted his spirits since he'd welcome death over the loss of his freedom. But what about Karen? Should he kill her too? That question remained unanswered.

Lily and Mary alternated bringing them food and liquids. They were the only people, besides Karen, that Jeremy had seen since he was brought to this area. Not sure how much time had gone by, he was afraid to ask, afraid to wonder why there were no signs of any rescuers. *Someone must be looking by now.* "Must be," he said to his inert wife.

Karen continued to stare through unseeing eyes, and sometimes he envied her ability to blot out the horror and disappear into a self-imposed fog. Other times he felt glad to be alert, so that he'd be prepared for the precise moment when their saviors would arrive. That expectation and Karen's incremental improvements gave him hope. With assistance from Mary, Karen was beginning to walk, although she appeared trancelike and had to be pushed or pulled along.

To keep his sanity, Jeremy played games with himself, imagining he was a prisoner of war, a war about to end. Any minute now he'd hear a joyful *yahoo* and a soldier, filthy from battle with eyes huge as cannonballs, would rush in and announce: *It's over. You're free!* Sometimes Jeremy's side won, sometimes the other. He didn't care because either way they'd let him go. When that vision played out to a happy ending, his body would relax and he'd grab some sleep, dreaming of home, always home.

But his present waking dream vanished as Mary strode in followed closely at her heels by Lily, a small shadow in comparison. Mary, now cold and indifferent, said, "It's been decided that you've been coddled long enough. You'll have to come to the dining room to eat like the rest of us. We'll help you bring Karen."

Her brusqueness seemed to carry a trunkload of broken promises, and he instinctively called out, "Don't touch her."

"Don't be silly," said Mary. "I don't take orders from you." As she reached for Karen, Jeremy pitched forward, scrambling to stop her, and lost his balance in the effort.

"Dammit!" he yelled as his arm and Mary's fell across Karen's face. Immediately, a welt began to blossom under a half-closed eye. The eye trembled, and as if some inner battle were taking place, it forced itself to open.

A hand—Karen's own—rose up in defense. This was followed by a piercing plaint like the yelp of an injured animal. "Oww!" she cried. "Get off me." Looking like a bruised, disheveled orphan straight from a Dickens classic, Karen sat up, unsteady but aware.

Elated at her return from her neither-here-nor-there world, but dreading to fill in the blanks, Jeremy engulfed her with his body, hiding her from their common enemy. He turned his face to the unholy twosome and hissed a no-holds-barred, unequivocal threat. "Leave. Right now. Or else."

Wisely, without argument, they backed off.

Refocusing on Karen, Jeremy could read the fear in her eyes and terror on her parched lips and understood there wasn't much to explain. She hadn't blanked out totally, after all; merely chose not to communicate as her mind and body fine-tuned, recouped, and adjusted. She knew the score, played its dissonant music, sang its ugly, disquieting lyrics. There were some lapses in memory, but he quickly filled them in. Now they were alone once more, but at least they were alone together.

#

Later that evening, Mary returned to her charges, minus Lily. She kept her distance, still wary, not wanting to distress Karen or further antagonize Jeremy. Before either could yell, curse, or lash out physically, she spoke. "This is the last time I'm coming. Tomorrow you'll join the rest of us. But don't be alarmed. I haven't betrayed you. I just had to be careful. Lily may look sweet, but trust me, she'll tell the others if she suspects anything out of line."

The couple stayed silent, but Mary's sensitive hearing and echolocation picked up movement. While Karen remained sitting, Jeremy stood up, hanging on to every word, straining for clues. "If you don't join us tomorrow," she continued, "they'll let you starve since you won't be of any use. I know it's crazy, but you have to pretend, play along—to save yourselves. When the time is right, I'll let you know."

Jeremy finally spoke. Oddly, his sparse words and monotone emphasized his fervid emotions instead of detracting from them. "If you do betray us I'll kill you."

"I won't. I swear." Mary walked off, leaving behind not merely a tray of food but, more importantly, her pledge.

Karen, somewhat confused about Mary's words and motives, asked, "What was that all about? Not betraying us?"

"Remember, I told you? She claims she's on our side."

"But why? What's in it for her?"

Scraping his bottom lip with his teeth, Jeremy admitted, "I don't know. If you ask me, she's got a crack in her skull as deep as a gully. But who cares? All that counts is that we get out of this filthy sinkhole. And we will, Karen. I promise you that." Then speaking more to himself, he went on. "I won't spend my life down here. But," he added, shaking his head, "why haven't they found us? Someone must be looking. Where are they?"

"Oh, my God!" yelled Karen, bolting to her feet, clutching a stalagmite to steady her still wobbly legs.

Jeremy's eyes opened saucer size, and he grabbed hold of her hands. "What is it?" he asked, still worried about her fragile state.

"Don't you see? They're looking, all right. But not here."

"What do you mean?" he said. Then "Oh, no!" He fell against the wall, hit in the gut with a fastball of reality. "You're right. I didn't tell Carl we were switching caves or—holy shit!—spelunking for that matter. I told him we might go to a movie or something. I'm not sure—I'm so mixed up I can't think straight. Still"—he paused and licked his lips—"Carl may have figured it out. He knows how impulsive I can be. I'm so sorry, Karen. I'm such a fool." Head down, he covered his face, speaking in undertones. "That's why those bastards were asking such probing questions. Damn them. They had it all planned." He continued berating himself, moaning, pounding the air with his fists.

"What about our car?" said Karen. "They've got to find our car."

"But Rahm said he drove it off a bridge. Wait," he said, with a flicker of hope. "What about that couple, Sara and George? They saw us here, and they have our phone number."

"You think we'll be in the Pittsburgh papers?"

"I doubt it," said Jeremy. "We're nobody special. In any case, they were going to call us."

"But not until next spring. To see the cherry blossoms."

"Maybe we'll be lucky and they'll want to go to Washington before then. Thank goodness you wrote down my work number, too, in case our home line's disconnected. They're our last hope." Karen flinched at the words "work number" and "last hope." She watched as Jeremy, eyes brimming with tears, slumped to the ground and clawed at the earth as if he could dig his way out. With his attention turned elsewhere, she reached into her pocket and pulled out the paper with Jeremy's number that Sara had inadvertently dropped. Crumbling it, she returned it to her pocket. She didn't have the heart to tell him. Now it was her turn to be brave.

#

The next morning, as instructed, the twosome straggled into the dining room. The community members, already eating, made an effort to be nonchalant. The effort, of course, proved futile as the tension hung in the air like wet paint refusing to dry. Reaching for a glass of juice, Karen carelessly knocked it over. She didn't bother to apologize. Like a servant on duty, Lily jumped to her feet, set it upright, and wiped up the mess.

Finishing breakfast, Jeremy went straight to their quarters while Karen stopped to pull a book from a shelf.

"Why did you bring that back?" he asked upon her return, his voice high-pitched and shaking.

"I need something to do," she explained.

"I don't see how anyone can read under the circumstances, but feel free. Do whatever you want." He threw up his hands to emphasize his disapproval.

Karen lay on the mattress, the book against her elevated knees. She moved the oil lantern closer, the one that Mary had thoughtfully left behind. Its glow cast a bright, steady light, good enough for reading.

Jeremy sat stiff-legged in a rocking chair that he had dragged in from the communal area. He leaned forward and back, setting its bottom arc in motion as he obsessively went over every detail, every last component since their capture, searching for a weak point, anything that could help their cause. Finding nothing, he sank into a sinister mood, alternating between rage and hair-pulling hopelessness, while his nonstop rocking wore two parallel grooves in the earth. In this cruel, monotonous manner, one day followed another until an unaccountable span had gone by, offering no relief.

Ignoring Karen's repeated attempts to break through his state of despair, Jeremy warned her with harsh words and black looks to leave him alone.

Being used to a career with intellectual and physical challenges, Jeremy now chafed at the monotony of his routine. Soon a feeling of unrelenting boredom set in. He pumped his legs faster and faster to the creaking of the chair, as a wretched theme repeated in his mind, burning his ears: *This is my prison and the sentence is life; all that's missing are the bars.*

"Let me help you," cried Karen, "the way you helped me when I couldn't eat or care of myself. I love you."

"No one can help me now," he yelled back, and his frustrations, having no healthy outlet, searched for a scapegoat and found it in her. Everything she did was wrong: little things became huge and even those habits that he had once found endearing were now a source of irritation.

"You're tapping on that damn book again," he said, his voice ululating in a low, jarring growl that caused Karen to startle. "And you look terrible. Your hair is sticking out like a witch's broom."

"You don't look so great yourself," she said in defense. "I barely recognize you. And you smell worse than Boot's litter box."

"Poor Boots," said Jeremy suddenly. "What's to become of him?"

Karen's chin trembled, but she refused to cry. "Boots is with Carl and Joan. I'm sure of it. They won't let anything bad happen to him."

Jeremy, in a rare moment of calm reflection, pictured Boots in his wife's lap, purring contentedly while kneading her with his paws. But then Karen resumed reading. *How dare she!*

Jeremy shook with anger as he stared at Karen, now a symbol of disloyalty, and his eyes narrowed to fierce-looking slits. "You're tapping again!"

"I'm sorry. I forgot." Sinking lower into the mattress, she retreated further into her book.

The sight of her turning a page resulted in a frenzied eruption. With lightning speed, Jeremy reached over and ripped the hated tome from her hands, sending it flying into the blackness beyond. Shaking her head, Karen opened her fingers beseechingly. "Why?" she said. "What did I do?"

Jeremy snarled. "You were humming," he said, his canines, white and pointed, seeming ready to tear her flesh.

"You always liked my humming."

"That was before. Now you'll do what I say, and I say no humming, no tapping, and no reading."

With her self-respect on the line, Karen stood up. "You have no right to tell me what to do. If I want to hum, I'll hum; if I want to tap, I'll tap; and if I want to read, I'll read." Thrusting her chin out defiantly, she stalked off to retrieve her book.

In seconds, he fell upon her. Gripping her with clenched fists, he whipped her about, shaking her so wildly that her head appeared detached from her neck. For a minute he forgot who she was—just a thing, an object—then worse, a scheming, evil entity on a mission to drive him crazy.

"L-let go!" she screamed as she swung her hands, raking his face with ragged nails.

Jeremy's raw, burning wounds, running diagonally across both cheeks spilled blood, further inflaming him, and he shoved her against the wall. Then he straddled her, placing his fingers around her neck and squeezed. Her last gasp of air and terror-stricken eyes made him come to his senses and perceive that this person he was about to strangle was Karen, his wife.

Karen immediately moved away, tripping as the cuff of a pant leg caught on one of the curved bands of the rocking chair. She fell, rolled onto her side and curled into a small heap, whimpering softly. Jeremy stared at her, confused, almost as if he had no idea what had just taken place. Then a look of panic replaced his dull, vacant stare.

Hesitating, he touched her shoulder.

"Stay away," she said, choking back sobs while trying to catch her breath.

"Please," he pleaded, again grasping for her.

Fearful and full of loathing for this unknown monster, this evil brute who had somehow replaced her husband, she pushed herself along the ground until she was out of his reach. She rose and ran without direction before winding up near the pantry where Brian and Rahm were at work, hammering away, repairing a broken shelf. She turned and ran farther down a dark tunnel until Jeremy caught up with her. Rahm and Brian arrived soon after.

From Karen's bulging eyes and Jeremy's bloodstained cheeks, it was obvious to the last-minute interlopers that something ominous had taken place, and Karen, with no other choice, took refuge behind Rahm, who intuitively grasped the problem.

Embarrassed to have witnesses to this shameful affair solely of his making, Jeremy said, "This is between Karen and me. It's no one else's business."

Separating them like a referee at a prizefight, Rahm spoke, his voice heavy with menace. "It's bad for the two of you to sit around all day doing nothing. From now on you'll work like the rest of us. No work, no food. Period."

"You son of a bitch," snarled Jeremy. "You'd really let us die?" For a moment he debated whether to up the ante by taking on the challenge, declaring a hunger strike or physically attacking his nemesis. But after scanning Rahm's well-developed arms, he knew that that would be stupid, and one thing he wasn't was stupid; besides, Brian would jump in, making matters worse.

Rahm remained stoic. Still, he avoided a direct answer to Jeremy's question and returned to his decree. "You know what the jobs are. Now choose."

The air held a malevolent foreboding, heavy as the mountain of stone and earth pressing down from above, but fortunately Rachel appeared in time to overhear the last of the conversation and redirect its menacing implications.

"I can use some help in the mushroom garden today," she said. "It's down near the lake. I just started two new beds."

"I'll help," said Karen, casting one final scowl, one last look of disgust at her husband. She grabbed hold of Rachel's elbow and stomped off beside her.

Jeremy felt the visual dart from Karen's eyes, sending his heartbeat sky-high. *What have I done?* he thought, hanging his head like a condemned criminal at the gallows.

Chapter 10

Despite the language of caves, still new, Karen was learning to negotiate its obstacles. And even though she couldn't see in the tar-colored darkness, her ears picked up a familiar sound: the rippling of water due to a breeze skimming across a liquid surface. "Is that the lake?" she asked. "Jeremy told me about it."

"Yes. That's it," said Rachel, impressed with Karen's auditory perception. "And the garden's just beyond." Within moments she signaled their arrival by squeezing Karen's arm. Next she lit the oil lanterns left in their designated places. The yellow flames' light flooded the cavernous area, opening up a unique panorama of ancient primordial growths.

"What are those paper-cup thingies hanging from the ceiling?" Karen asked. "And those funny cork-screw shapes? They remind me of party streamers."

"They're all helictites," said Rachel. "Rahm says they're very rare. See that one?" She pointed with a finger to a form that looked like antlers on a deer. "Seems to defy gravity, doesn't it? You can read about them yourself if you're interested. You know where the books are kept."

"No, I'm not that interested," said Karen, turning her face away, embarrassed to have exposed her curiosity.

"Well, what I really wanted to show you were the mushroom beds, anyway. They're over here."

Karen followed until they came to six raised mounds of earth and six trenches, each approximately six by one-and-a-half feet, all arranged in rows, side by side.

Karen rubbed her eyes; they were beginning to burn.

Noticing the tears flowing down Karen's face, Rachel said, "It's the guano. Norman usually gathers it. He doesn't mind, and everyone's happy to let him. In any case, it doesn't smell bad once you get used to it."

"Get used to shit?" said Karen, pinching her nose. "I doubt it."

Rachel shrugged, and guided Karen to a heap piled against the wall. She took a long stick and began to turn it over. "This ensures even fermentation."

Karen backed away since it reeked like a room full of decaying bodies. She began to cough. In response, Rachel dipped a rag into a pail of water and handed it to Karen.

"Seriously, in a few days you won't even notice. And in a few weeks, when the fermentation process is complete, it loses its odor completely. Then you know it's ready to line a bed." She pointed to the last two trenches at the end of the row. "I just dug those out yesterday. Lined them with guano myself. Now we wait seven to twelve days. Through natural decomposition, the temperature in there gets very hot—enough to burn your hand. It helps to kill the bugs and bacteria that live in the guano."

Karen groaned and her face flashed a look of revulsion. Rachel tried hiding her amusement behind a surreptitious smile. "When the temperature drops to the mid-eighties, it's ready for mycelium—that's the propagating part of the mushroom. See those two other trenches? They're ready to be fertilized right now."

Karen cocked her head and spoke through the rag pressed against her eyes and hanging to her chin. Like a wave, it billowed with each exhalation. "How do you do that?" she asked.

"Not much to it. It's just a matter of transferring dirt. The mycelium's mixed right in. Come. I'll show you."

Taking two pails from a recess in the wall, she handed one to Karen. They walked over to a bed that was on its last fruiting. "Each bed," said Rachel, "produces several yields that sprout a few weeks apart. As you can see, this one's just about finished. In fact, we ate most of the remaining crop yesterday."

"Uh-huh," said Karen as she glanced at the last of the mushrooms; thin, dried out, wrinkly even. She grabbed a lantern for a closer inspection and something inexplicable stirred in her mind. "They seem to have faces," she said, staring intensely. "Sad faces." Bending over, she heard a hum and gasped. The sound seemed to come from the mushrooms, and she wondered if Rachel had heard it too. Afraid to ask, she sat down on her haunches as Rachel looked on, her lips bulging in annoyance.

As requested, Karen filled the pails, and the two women moved on to the trenches, where Rachel explained how to place the mycelium along the sides. Karen rolled up her sleeves, ready to tackle the job, while Rachel whisked back and forth, refilling the pails. When the task was completed, they advanced to the next phase.

"After three weeks or so, new mycelium grows on the outer face of the beds," she continued. "Then it's ready for limestone." She demonstrated the final steps by carving the limestone from the cave's wall, chopping it into bits, and throwing the pieces onto a bed. She leaned on her shovel, breathing hard. "While it's convenient having your basic ingredients right at your fingertips, the important part is getting the timing right. Unfortunately, it's been trial and error since the growth cycle down here is unique. But if ants can do it, I figured, so could I."

The pupils in Karen's eyes widened like a startled cat's. "Ants?"

"That's right. I read it in one of the books. It said ants began to cultivate mushrooms long before people ever did. They carry the mycelium in their mouths. Fascinating, isn't it?"

As Karen digested the information, Rachel took a pail of water from another recess and carried it to the bed she had just covered with limestone. "I don't want it getting too hot in there," she explained as she poured. "In three to four weeks this will produce its first crop, and it will look like that."

Karen turned in the direction that Rachel faced and walked over to the beds with recent growth. Many little hoary heads poked through. Although they appeared better than the old crop, they still had a squishy, unhealthy feel. Again Karen felt a strange connection to them; they looked like tiny lost life forms, so pale and fragile in their hidden world. Despite that, or perhaps because of it, she said, "I'd like to help here with the mushrooms. Help them to bloom. That is, if it's all right."

"Uh—of course," said Rachel. "There's always work to do here."

Karen heard a note of hesitation in Rachel's voice, but ignored it. It made no difference. She needed something to do or she'd go positively out of her mind. And, furthermore, she didn't have to admire Rachel, didn't have to like her, understand her or anything else for that matter. She merely had to put up with her for the time being. *And I will,* she told herself. *I'll force myself. What choice do I have?*

#

Their eyes met and locked, each scrutinizing the other, probing, sifting for a vantage point. Taking the initiative, Rahm spoke first.

"I know you hate me. Good. Hate can be healthy if used wisely. It takes willpower and determination to survive the transition to life down here, and I want you to survive. There are different roads to survival, and if yours is anger and hatred, then I say fine. Your wife has chosen a different path, but perhaps *chosen* is the wrong word. We use whatever strengths we possess, and what seems weak to you may really be a source of strength."

"I don't need you to explain my wife's behavior to me," said Jeremy, his forehead a sudden highway of parallel lines. "I know her better than you."

Rahm nodded, conceding the point. "You're right, of course. But what remains essential is keeping busy. Within certain constraints, you'll find you have lots of freedom here."

"Every freedom but the one that counts."

"I've no doubt that in time you'll adjust to your situation, but for now I suggest you make yourself useful. See that tunnel behind you? Follow it. You won't get lost. It leads to the salamanders. Bring some back. Mary wants to make a stew tonight. But even more relevant, you'll find them an interesting diversion. They're quite easy to kill. Just strangle them like this." With a snap of his fingers, he gave a quick, skillful, and deadly demonstration.

Neither words nor actions were necessary for Jeremy to figure out what Rahm really meant: behave yourself or else. *All right, you bastard,* he said to himself. *I'll be good, but just for now. Then you'll get yours in spades.*

#

Jeremy entered the tunnel, not because Rahm had told him to, but because the thought of killing a creature, even a small, defenseless one, filled him with glee and caused his pulse to race as if he were climbing a mountain. The passage, worn clean by many footprints, led down toward the lake but in the opposite direction of the mushrooms. He had already been here on his tour of "Second Chance City"— that first day before he'd known anything was wrong, before he'd known hell really existed.

There they were, a slimy mass of putrid primogenial animal, having no right to exist on God's Earth. Hundreds, several inches in length, were crawling on the walls, stalagmites, and stalactites in search of insects. All were ghost white, without eyes, so that they appeared almost faceless. Some were missing a limb or a tail— perhaps due to mutations or the result of cannibalism—while others were eating their own flesh.

With a wave of disgust, Jeremy kicked at the wall, sending them scurrying. Picking one up from the ground, he effortlessly disposed of it by strangling it between his thumb and forefinger. He picked up another and another, repeating the executions until his abhorrence diminished and his diabolical need felt satiated.

Holding one final specimen by its tail, Jeremy let it dangle helplessly before his eyes as he examined it in detail. Its wiggling, a feeble defense in his grip, increased, and it began to squeak like a newborn puppy. Then slowly, by whatever thin thread of animate existence they shared, its desperation seeped into Jeremy's wounded psyche, and with trembling fingers he let it go and watched as it dropped to the ground.

"I'm sorry," he said as it staggered away, half broken. It tried licking its tiny limb, now protruding at an unnatural angle. Confused, it began biting itself, only compounding its misery.

Waves of remorse snaked through Jeremy's veins until, reaching his core, they transformed into a groundswell of empathy. With the shame of blood on his hands, he ground the salamander into the earth, not wanting it to continue suffering. "I'm sorry," he said again, although no one was there to hear.

Sinking to the ground, he lowered his head to his chest, sobbed, wailed long and hard at the magnitude of all he had lost and what he was becoming. Forcing himself, he looked up toward a sky he could no longer see, and made a promise to himself, to Karen. "I won't let them turn me into a monster!" he yelled. Suddenly, all lingering feelings of self-pity drained from his body along with their traces of poison and ensuing depravity. And with that came strength. "I swear that somehow, someday, I'll get even. He deserves that; they all do." With his brow set in furrows of resolution, he made his way back to the others, sans salamanders for dinner, more determined than ever to survive and win.

#

Softly, with tender care, Karen patted down the beds where the new mycelium had been placed as if putting her charges to sleep.

"You did fine," said Rachel.

Karen rose to her feet, suddenly aware of the twisted world she inhabited. She tossed the rag to the ground, but as she did her eyes skimmed over her fingers, now embedded with dirt, the cuticles near the ends forming black, smiling faces, mocking her. She tried wiping them on her soiled pants, but only succeeded in smearing the mess. "I'm filthy," she said, angry at Jeremy, angry at Rachel, the world, herself.

"No problem," said Rachel, attempting to placate the irritated woman, now glaring with accusatory eyes. "It's *clean* dirt. But I suppose this is a good time to show you where we bathe and wash our clothes. Come."

Each holding a pailful of mushrooms for the evening meal, they walked back toward the lake. Rachel lit a candle and a trickle of water appeared underfoot before seeping into the ground.

"Look for that," she said. "A marker. It indicates we're almost there."

"I can tell," said Karen, reminding Rachel that she recognized the rumbling pitter-patter from earlier that day. Now, however, mysterious splashing thumps added harmonic overtones. "What's that slap-slap noise? It sounds like drumbeats."

"You'll see for yourself soon enough, but wait here until I light the lantern farther up." Moments later, Rachel called out, "You can come now, but be careful. The rocks are slippery."

Karen walked down, arms out for balance since there was nothing to hold on to. She stumbled once but quickly caught herself. Then gazing out at the lake, a smoky black basin in the darkness, she squinted at the bizarre flashes of light hitting the surface. "Is that what you were talking about? Some kind of aquatic firefly?"

Rachel shook her head. "Actually they're shrimp. Like most things here, they turned white, but they're powerful swimmers like their cousins above. That's why we hardly eat them; hard to catch. Hey," she said, her voice rising on the crest of a sudden idea. "Would you like to go out on the water? We have a rowboat nearby. The lake is quite pleasant, peaceful even."

Not knowing the depth of the lake and being a mediocre swimmer at best, Karen answered with a resounding *no*.

"As you like," said Rachel. If she felt rebuffed, she didn't give any sign. "But if you change your mind, I'm sure someone would be happy to take you out. There's a large waterfall off a ways. We often fish beneath it. For some reason, the trout like it there. We're lucky to have them. It's rare for trout to live in caves."

"Did you know they were here before you came?"

"Yes. Rahm discovered them on an earlier exploration. That's one of the reasons we chose this area. There's crayfish here too. They're common in caves, but not in this amount or size. They live under stones in the shallow places. But enough of this. You wanted to clean up."

"Right," said Karen, twitching her nose. "I stink."

Rachel held back from affirming the obvious. Instead she pointed out the best place to stand, a runoff farther down where the water pooled into a hollow. "We do laundry there too. We try not to contaminate the main part of the lake because of the fish. I suppose you'd also like fresh clothes."

"That would be nice."

"I'll handle that," said Rachel, taking the lead along the gravelly shoreline. She stopped at a protruding boulder and handed Karen soap and a towel, always left on the same flat surface.

Karen removed her socks and shoes and immersed her feet in the water. "It's freezing," she said, drawing back.

"Another thing you'll get used to. And while you're bathing I'll go back to the storage area. It won't take me long." She click-clicked and ran her eyes over Karen's body, saying, "I'll just have to guess at your size. We are responsible for washing our personal items, by the way. As for the towels and other community property, we take turns."

Once certain she was gone, Karen stripped naked. She waded in up to her ankles, ran the wet, soapy washcloth over her entire body and scrubbed. After repeating the process, she did it twice more without soap. Despite the cold, she unconsciously hummed just as she had back home in the shower. It felt so good to be clean. Then, as her purple-blue lips and body shook like some long-ago Roaring Twenties flapper, she scrambled back to shore and washed her clothes along the shallow edge.

As she was hanging them on the clothesline, she heard the scuff of feet and quickly finished putting the last clothespin in place. Hurrying back to the hollow, she modestly hunched over, and covered her body with her hands.

"I've got the clothes," said Rachel, waving a bag in the air. "I'll come down and leave it on a rock, then wait by the berry bushes. I may as well gather some for tonight while you're dressing. By the way, I passed Jeremy on my way back. He said to tell you he's very, very sorry."

Karen blanched at her husband's name. Still trembling from the cold, she went into the open and grabbed the bag between numb fingers. The prickly nip on her skin had spread to her bones, making her too uncomfortable to fuss over her nakedness or consider Jeremy's apology. Least of her worries were the outfit's clashing colors, aqua blue on top, olive green on the bottom. She was just glad that Rachel had picked a long-sleeved sweatshirt and heavy-weight cotton sweatpants. The pants, a man's medium, sagged to her hips. She tightened the drawstring. The bra was too big, but the panties felt soft. Perhaps they were new, from one of their infrequent shopping trips above. Furiously she rubbed her hands along her arms to warm herself.

"I'm done picking berries," yelled Rachel from off in the distance. "Let me know when you're ready." Her voice, loud enough to wake the dead, signaled her growing impatience.

Realizing she couldn't delay the inevitable—her impending confrontation with Jeremy—Karen yelled back, "One more second." Then, "Okay. I'm ready to go."

#

Jeremy, eyes and ears on alert, waited in the Ballroom. He noticed her before she noticed him. "I want to talk to you," he said, rushing up, overtaking her before she could flee. Grabbing her by the wrist, he tried pulling her along the passageway toward their quarters. Karen yanked her hand free, nodded toward one of the nearby couches, but changed her mind when Jeremy pointed out Lily rummaging through the books. Brian, too, hovered nearby, probably waiting to spy.

"Okay, you're right," she said. "We'll go back to our room."

Jeremy bristled. The hairs on his neck stung like needle pricks. It wasn't their room and never would be, but he let the word pass without comment. Once again he reached for her hand, adding "Please" like a vagabond begging for food. Karen relented and together they walked back, physically connected but alone with their thoughts.

In his eagerness to begin, Jeremy almost tore off the privacy curtain, separating their quarters from the others. Apologizing never came easy to him, but he knew he was clearly in the wrong and ready to take what was coming. He cleared some space on the mattress, helped her down, and began.

"I'm so ashamed," he said, his voice shaky and muted.

Karen leaned forward, straining to hear.

"Forgive me if you can; not only for what I did today, but for bringing you to this god-awful place. I must have been crazy. So full of myself. I have no excuse. I'm responsible for everything."

When she didn't respond, he felt certain she was still furious. He didn't blame her. "I beg you, Karen. Don't hate me. I need you so much. You're all I have." Tears pooled in his sad, dark eyes.

Karen played with a stand of hair to delay a response. "I don't hate you," she said. Speaking louder, she added, "I love you."

The circles underneath Jeremy's eyes deepened as he questioned if she were merely reciting lines out of habit. "Do you really? Could you still? After all I did?"

"Neither you nor I have been ourselves lately." She snickered, her attempt at humor being more pathetic than funny. "Yes, I still love you," she repeated, "but you must swear"—she stopped, closed her eyes, gathering the strength to bring forth the words—"swear that you will never hurt me again."

Jeremy flinched, pulled her closer, smelling the soapy fragrance on her skin. "I swear," he said. "I'd rather cut off my arms first. I'm totally mortified by what I did. And you're right about us not being ourselves. I've been so out of control that I no longer recognize myself, and I know it's worsened everything. I've got to keep myself together if we're going to escape."

"Then let's remember"—she stroked his cheek with the back of her hand—"who the true enemy is."

Jeremy felt so relieved by her statement that he shifted his legs and straddled them around her hips. Letting go of her defenses, she snuggled her head against his neck.

"God, I'm glad you said that. I was a little afraid you were getting used to it here."

Karen's head swung back, and she opened her eyes in disbelief. "How could you even consider such a thing?"

Not wanting to start another disagreement, he fashioned his words as gently as possible. "It's the way you've been acting since you came out of that ... that stupor you were in. You've seemed too willing to accept whatever they dish out."

Karen fumbled with a response. "I've never been much of a fighter," she admitted. "After we met, I let you fight the battles for both of us. It just seemed natural. But these last few days, I've been so scared of losing my mind again, that I've been grasping at anything that seemed familiar or soothing: a book or even a kindness from Rachel. It's because I'm so afraid, that I'm doing anything, everything, to hold on. I've even been reduced to playing games with myself, pretending we're on vacation or at home working in the garden. Isn't that silly? We don't even have a garden." Her mouth twitched as she spoke, and she quickly looked away, but not before Jeremy saw the pain in her eyes.

"I've been doing the same thing," he laughed. "Well, not a garden exactly, but I've been both a prisoner of war and a pitcher for the Red Sox." It was the first time he'd laughed since the kidnapping.

Encouraged, Karen raised her face. "There is one thing you can be sure of. I want to get out of here every last bit as much as you."

"Good," he said, clutching her shoulders, and as his eyes received and reflected the love between them, he added a pledge. "We will get out, Karen. I'm certain of that. Sticking together, we'll find a way."

Chapter 11

Like an unwelcome trip to the dentist, Karen and Jeremy wanted no part of the community meeting about to begin. Fortunately, Mary offered to fill them in later, and as they stomped off, she fixed her eyes, along with her attention, on Brian.

From the time of his arrival, Brian had taken it upon himself to keep track of the days, months, and years, along with special events such as birthdays and holidays, listing them on the hand-made calendars he kept near his bed. When Rahm came upon an occasional newspaper from one of his weekly scouting expeditions to the upper level of the cave, Brian always double-checked his dates. Happily, he had never made a mistake and over time eased into the role of Minute Keeper. He never saw this as an unwelcome task but an affirmation of his self-worth.

Preferring to stand rather than sit, Brian sucked in his sloppy belly and adjusted his pants. He held his notes a short distance from his eyes, then moved them closer, and closer still. He grunted at the significance. After scanning the first few lines, he turned toward his wife, who snorted contemptuously. Brian snorted back even louder and then began his summation, which sounded more like a rant with an accusatory punch. "Due to the unforeseen complications surrounding our newest ... umm ... comrades, our official meetings have been way off schedule. Then, to make matters worse, Mary wasted everyone's time by insisting we let them go. To placate her, we took up the issue. Even held it to a vote. But was she satisfied? No. She followed up by trying to overturn Rahm's veto. Well, we know how that turned out."

"It's not fair!" screamed Mary. "My side had the majority."

"It is fair," countered her husband. "You needed seven votes and you couldn't get them. We can't change the rules to suit every whim. You of all people should appreciate that."

"All right," she said, "then I propose we vote again. Today."

"That's crazy," said Brian. "Admit it. Your side lost."

Mary huffed and looked around, searching for a savior. When none came, she refrained from her usual effort to cover her disgust. *You lecher,* she thought, glaring at Brian. *I know why you want them here. No. Not them. Her! You can't wait to get your slimy paws on her in the fertility area. But just you wait, you sickening curdle of blubber. You'll never touch her. Never! I'll see to that.* As one corner of her mouth edged up in a half-smile, she made a promise to herself to foil his plans, whatever it took, and again she scanned the faces, hoping someone would second her motion.

Help came where she least expected it. "I have to agree with Mary," said David, his voice crystal clear, rising over the surrounding murmurs as he articulated each word with the precision of a plucked violin string. "We have no right to hold them here. It puts us in the same category as thieves and murderers. I'm sorry I ever agreed to this."

Thank God, thought Mary, making a mental tally of supporters and detractors.

"Furthermore," continued David, "it's not against any rules I'm aware of to vote on an issue multiple times." He paused to see if anyone disagreed. When no one did, he said, "I second the motion that we vote on this again."

Immediately Rahm sprang to his feet, his shadow casting a tall, misshapen silhouette on the wall. Like naughty children caught off guard, each one of the members squirmed. David and Brian took their seats. "I have no objection to voting on the issue again and again, if necessary. But first I insist on speaking."

He took a sip of water and cleared his throat. "Bringing them here, forcing them to stay has been difficult on all of us. But let me remind you, we voted unanimously in favor of this act and now we each have to bear the responsibility. Just because it turned out more complicated than we imagined, doesn't mean we were wrong or should change our minds. Our reason remains as grave as ever: the survival of our tribe.

"I may not be a history professor," he continued, "but I know that sometimes a few have to be sacrificed for the greater good, and what greater good is there than our survival? Of course, there's a practical reason too: if we let them go, they may return—only this time with the authorities. Think about it—the possibility of life behind bars. Oh, we could try to run or relocate, move everything immediately, but do you realize what that would entail? It would be impossible." He paused, waiting for his words to sink in. When blood-drained faces regarded him, he added the finishing stroke.

"There is something else you should know—the most important reason of all." Rocking on the balls of his feet, he looked from one member to the next. "It has been ordained."

Oh crap, thought Mary, quickly unraveling his ploy. Fighting back, she fashioned a sealed-tight mental wall, preventing his passion from polluting her mind. The others, however, were not as strong, and Rahm's persuasive force proved as fierce as a chokehold.

Helene gasped at his words. "What do you mean 'ordained'? By whom? Tloc?"

Rahm bowed his head and, after a protracted pause, looked upward, face luminous. "Yes," he said. "Tloc spoke to me. Assured me we are on the right track."

The simultaneous intake of air within the group told Mary that Rahm's strategy proved a success. *There goes the ballgame,* she said to herself. *He's won, at least for the time being.*

Although she both loved and admired Rahm's ingenuity, she resented his increasing hold over the members' minds. *How stupid they all are. How weak. Following a person just by the force of his personality. Fertility god, my eye. I was born a Christian, not an idiot.*

The voting took place and as predicted, Mary's side, and consequently Karen and Jeremy's, lost; in fact, the count was now down to three in their favor and six against. "Only three miserable votes," she mumbled. Despite the loss, Mary thrust her jaw forward, squaring it with determination.

Later that evening, she filled the captives in on the tally. "I'm sorry," she said. "Rahm pulled a gorilla out of a hat."

While neither Karen nor Jeremy was surprised, they both took it hard, especially Jeremy. "Is there any alcohol in the pantry?" he asked.

"No," said Mary, alarm registering in the deepening lines beside the corners of her mouth. "Some of our members had drinking problems before coming here. Drug problems too. Bear with me, Jeremy," she said, resting her hand on his thigh for a protracted moment. "I have more tricks to play. It just gets more complicated now."

#

Having trouble sleeping, Karen rose early and made herself a cup of tea. She nibbled on bread and jam, then set some aside for Jeremy, knowing he would soon be up. Today she swore to make it her business to gather information on the group's members, looking for weaknesses in character to use to her and Jeremy's advantage.

One by one, the members filed into the dining room with Brian last, his face a smiling, full moon. "Guess what?" he said, waving his arms. "I just checked my calculations, and while I don't mean to brag, I'm right again."

Everyone looked up except David, who'd been out of sorts for the past few weeks. He fixed his downturned features on his plate, his food left uneaten. "Right about what? What's the big news?"

"It's Thanksgiving," said Brian. "You know, turkey day. How about that?"

David flapped his elbows, mocking the other's enthusiasm. "Well, gobble, gobble, gobble."

Helene reached over and gave him a cuff on the wrist. He, in turn, glowered at her.

Refusing to be intimidated, she said, "What's your problem, David? Everything bothers you lately."

"Nothing's bothering me. On the contrary, everything's fine. Just fine." Jumping up, he rattled the table, knocking over Karen's teacup. Fortunately the cup was empty.

Karen stared, openmouthed, as David sauntered away. "Maybe someone should check on him," she suggested.

Helene waved her hand as if she were shooing a fly. "No. Not necessary. David just likes an audience and everyone's used to his antics by now."

Lily, taking a sip of coffee from a chipped mug, cast a doubtful look. "I don't know, Helene. He is acting strangely … out of sorts, even for him. Maybe you should go and check. I'll do it if you want."

"David always acts strangely," said Helene. "Or should I say queerly?" She began to laugh, her nose turning red and runny. She wiped it with a napkin. "Take my word for it, Lil. Just ignore him."

"Well, I guess you know best."

"Me? Best? No, that would be Norman."

Karen shifted her attention to Norman, the conversation piquing her curiosity more and more.

"That's over now," he said, gripping the table. He addressed the group, but fixed his eyes on Lily, the one person whose thoughts on this tangled relationship mattered. He sighed when Lily merely shrugged her shoulders.

"Then I guess David's all mine again," said Helene, her voice as sharp as a nail on a wall. "He's about as useful here as an alarm clock, but I suppose I shouldn't complain. I'm no treasure either, and he's better than nothing." As if reconsidering that, she put a finger to her lips and said, "I wonder."

To Karen's surprise, Helene keeled over, with piercing sobs erupting from her mouth. While the others sat stock-still, perhaps afraid to respond and make matters worse, Karen offered a handful of tissues. Finally Helene caught her breath, saying, "What's wrong with me? Aren't I pretty enough?" Then spewing a string of four-lettered obscenities, she ran off in search of David. Despite everything, she loved him.

Poor Helene, thought Karen, seeing the unfortunate nature of her situation: that the man she loved preferred his meals with link sausages. As for dessert, he was willing to take what he could get.

In contrast to Karen's compassion, Brian's smirk spoke good riddance, and with Helene's departure, he reopened the issue that had set off the fireworks.

"It's Thanksgiving, people," he said again. "Who wants to party? And while we're at it, why don't we throw in Christmas and New Year's? They'll both be coming up soon enough. So, whaddayasay? Who's in?"

"I am," said Lily. "We could all use some fun."

"Fun!" bellowed Karen, saying the word as if it were a contagious disease. "What could possibly be fun in this dungeon?"

Janet squawked. "The cave's not a dungeon and we often have fun. Why we could …?" She drummed her fingers on the table, thinking.

"Quit drumming like that," said Rachel. "You sound like the shrimp in the lake."

"That's it," said Janet. "The lake." Flushed with excitement, her eyelids fluttered like sparrow wings. "Why don't we go to the lake, swim in the water? We may not have a turkey, but we can still make today special. Fun!"

"Oh, please, please!" said Randy. "Can we?" He began jumping up and down on his seat while Jon, needing no incentive, joined in by circling the table and hooting at the same time.

Rahm smiled at the boys. "Seems fine to me."

"I'll make a cake," said Mary.

"I'll help too," said Rachel, "as long as the men share in the preparation and cleanup. And I like the lake idea. That way we can make a whole day of it. I'm sure we can all use a break."

"Then it's settled," said Rahm. "So let's get busy."

Assignments were handed out, and everyone went off to their jobs, leaving Karen and Jeremy alone at the table.

"Want to go?" they said at the same time. While they both snickered at the coincidence, Jeremy immediately followed up with, "Does it matter?"

Karen answered, mindful to express herself cautiously. "We might as well. At least it will be something different. Besides, I have some clothes to wash." She emphasized the last sentence, sensing the need for an excuse. Although tit-for-tat accusations and subsequent reprisals had lessened, she took pains not to offend, since feelings remained raw and menacing undercurrents still lingered. "Is there something of yours you'd like me to wash?" she asked.

"I guess I have a few shirts and stuff," he said, "but I don't expect you to do them for me. Let's do everything together."

They walked back to their quarters without need for a light, maneuvering automatically on the now familiar path. That trifling matter stung Karen like a busted blister, and she suspected it irked Jeremy, too, but wisely refrained from mentioning it. After gathering their laundry, they went back to the dining room to wait for the others.

Returning with a stack of old newspapers, Rachel plopped them on to the table and began cutting long strips. "They're for decorations," she told them. "We could use some help." She added a "Thanks" before walking off.

Automatically Karen reached for the scissors and, following Rachel's example, made the strips into chains by looping and taping the pieces together, the same way she'd done for her wedding celebration almost one year ago. She remembered how happy she had been, stringing chains and streamers from room to room at her mother's house. While only a simple task, it had given her immense pleasure, unlike today where it amounted to mindless busy-work.

As the others dashed about, trying to get everything done at the last minute, Karen and Jeremy watched from their solitary outpost. When Rachel announced they were ready, she handed the pair covered platters of food to carry, then stuffed the decorations into a backpack and hoisted it onto her shoulders. Finally, all thirteen started off, staying as close together as possible. For added safety, Randy and Janet carried lanterns while Rachel kept near the newcomers so they wouldn't trip over baby stalagmites—perhaps only 500 years old—which jutted up along the way.

Arriving at the lake, the members immediately began unloading the supplies. Rahm handed out the assignments. Lily took charge of the decorations by hanging the paper chains among the formations. When she was finished, she stepped back to appraise the effect. She smiled, pleased with the results.

"Nice job," said Helene.

Lily looked to Karen. "The credit goes to her. She did most of the work. I'm just putting them up."

Karen's face turned crimson. With Jeremy at her side, she felt edgy about receiving compliments. Fortunately, Helene spoke up, turning the spotlight back on her.

"Why don't we go for a swim?" she yelled for all to hear, eager as ever to flaunt her body. For the sake of the water's purity, they rarely did, but today was one of those exceptions.

"Good idea," seconded Rachel, unfastening the buttons on her shirt and the zipper on her pants. Everyone followed suit—everyone but the two captives, who chose to emphasize their separateness by moving farther back.

Lily, naked from the waist up, approached the couple. Karen paled and stared into space, while Jeremy vainly tried not to gape at the ski-slope mounds with their delicate pink buds.

"Aren't you going to join us?" she asked.

"I'm afraid we didn't bring our bathing suits," said Karen, her acerbity a verbal assault. "We had no idea our little adventure would turn into an extended holiday."

Lily sniggered, pooh-poohing the innuendo. "There's no need for bathing suits. None of us have any. After all," she continued, "there's nothing to hide. Other than a few minor differences, we're basically the same, aren't we?" The last question was directed at Jeremy.

"But it's the differences that count," said Brian, lumbering up to them, completely exposed.

Karen, after briefly glancing at his fleshy body, looked away in disgust and turned to Lily, who, as if responding to a steamy bump-and-grind, began to remove the remainder of her clothes. Brian watched with greedy eyes, while Jeremy, to Karen's horror, licked his lips with unabashed lust.

Lily opened the barrette tying back her silky blond hair so that it fell in one smooth swoop, covering her back to her waist. Tall and slim, with shapely legs that merged with the soft curve of her hips, she swayed like a long-stemmed wildflower, a perfect reflection of her name. Others tried to imitate her natural grace but wound up looking foolish instead.

Feeling a ping of jealousy, Karen squirmed, hoping no one noticed, especially Jeremy.

Actually, all of the tribe's members, except for Brian and Janet, were in good shape due to the hard work necessary for survival. Simple food and physical labor left little room for overindulgence, and even Brian and Janet, despite their widening girth, could bustle about when given reason to rouse themselves from their sedentary inclinations.

As Jeremy continued his bug-eyed stare, Karen's jealous ping grew to a smolder and in retaliation she contemplated removing her own clothes. Now that she had lost those five pounds she'd once deemed impossible, she felt an urge to show off. Immediately, she tucked the thought away, amazed she'd even consider such a thing.

Instead she retreated into the shadows as Jeremy wandered off to the rocks below. Karen, seeing Jeremy among Lily's slavering throng, stumbled into a berry bush, staining her shirt. "Dammit," she yelled.

"You okay?" asked Norman, rushing over.

"I guess," said Karen.

Norman looked back toward the water. "She is lovely, isn't she?"

"Who?" said Karen, although the answer was obvious.

"Lily, of course."

Karen shot back a "Pugh," along with a gust of explosive air.

"You have to understand," said Norman, "she can't help herself. She rarely talks about it, but if you knew her history, you'd understand her unusual needs. Maybe even feel sorry for her."

"I doubt it."

"Don't tell her I told you, but she's not well. Sick even." He tapped his head to further explain what he meant. "You see, her stepfather abused her, physically and perhaps sexually too. She won't say for sure, but I can read the signs. Then to top it off her mother threw her out when she turned eighteen. Some birthday present!"

"So I'm supposed to feel sorry for her? Besides, I thought Helene was the exhibitionist."

"They both are, for different reasons. No, I take that back. It comes down to the same reason: insecurity."

"So now you're a philosopher. At least Helene's not trying to entice other people's husbands. But tell me," she said, shifting her stance to get to the crux, "where did you two meet? Was it love at first sight? Or lust?" Her voice dripped sarcasm, which she made no effort to conceal. Norman, to his credit, overlooked the inflection and threw back his head, chuckling.

"We met in the red-light district of New Orleans, and it *was* love at first sight. Okay, lust too, at least for me. I saw her dancing at a topless bar and found myself hooked. Finally, after two weeks, I mustered the nerve to ask her to dinner. Over drinks she told me she got a kick out of all that X-rated attention. Still craves it, as you can see."

"Well, just tell her to stay away from my husband. Unlike everyone else here, we believe in the sanctity of marriage."

"I'll be sure to remind her. And speaking of Jeremy, here he comes. Sure you won't go for a swim?"

"Positive."

As Norman left to rejoin his friends, Jeremy took his place beside his wife. Karen turned away.

"Don't be upset," he said. "I wasn't trailing Lily. I mean, she's lovely and all, but what I was really up to was scrutinizing the group. Spying, if you will. I've been trying to figure out how nine adults could possible leave everything behind for a life of nothing. And that's the truth!"

Placated, Karen said, "That's exactly what I've been doing."

Jeremy spread his hands in disgust. "Look at them. It's inconceivable. All losers!"

Karen agreed, but the impact of watching them from afar softened her impression as lanterns cast sparkles of confetti on the water's glistening froth.

Laughing and smiling, the members looked like regular folks, teenagers even, tossing a ball at the beach. With the exception of Brian, everyone seemed to naturally accept each other's nakedness, and it was only when bodies touched that eyes flashed and knowing smiles deepened. Even in their innocence, the ancient courting game was played out as it had been over the ages.

When it became Mary's turn to throw the ball, her face lit up, catching Karen's attention. From this new vantage point, Mary appeared not only years younger but free from the malignant burden of a husband she hated. Gamboling there below, so relaxed and spirited, she looked almost pretty. Karen wondered if Jeremy also noticed. Turning in his direction, she blanched to see how much he had changed.

Over the past few weeks, she had noticed spidery lines forming along the outside of his eyes—the product of stress, she presumed. Reaching up, she rubbed the back of his neck. He rolled his shoulders and twisted his head from side to side in response.

"Feels good."

"You always did like that," she said, pleased to render relief. Then offhandedly she added, "Why don't you take it easy today? I know you volunteered to help with the washing, but I don't mind doing it myself. Really."

"Thanks, but it's not fair for you to do all the work."

"It helps when I keep busy," said Karen.

Jeremy gazed at the cavorting group, and reconsidered. "Well, I never was one for laundry, and I don't want to join them either."

"You don't have to. There's a boat nearby. You can take it out onto the lake. There's also a waterfall, a big one, farther off."

"Is there? How do you know?"

"Rachel told me."

Jeremy kissed his wife on the cheek. "In that case, maybe it's not a bad idea. As long as you're sure it's okay."

"I'm sure. Now go. Just be careful of the falls." Giving him a push, she sent him on his way, following along to the bottom of the incline where he faded into the gloom. She looked again and he was gone.

A sudden gust of wind chilled her arms, and she yanked down the sleeves of her pullover, but it had little effect. She began to tremble; what if she'd made a mistake? *He could have an accident, get hurt, and there'll be no one to hear him. He could—no. I won't think about that.* Her obsessive thoughts persisted, culminating in the certainty that she would never see him again. Panicking, she almost screamed for him to come back, but instead stood transfixed, unable to move.

Pictures spun in her head, ugly and macabre, until sanity returned with a *Shut up, Karen. You're being ridiculous.* She went back for their laundry, then made her way down to the hollow, where she scrubbed and scrubbed.

#

Before wading into the water, Jeremy rolled up his pants until they sat securely above his knees. He held the candle high to keep the wick from getting wet. As the flame burned brightly, his body, from the waist down, wound up soaked to the skin. He cursed out loud as the cold hit like a sheet of ice, yet his mind flipped to an image of pleasant family vacations off the coast of Maine. If only he were back in Ogunquit, he thought, allowing himself a moment to reflect. Picturing a long-ago day, he saw a boy playing in the sand with the sun streaking his hair, his mother rubbing baby oil on his nose, not a problem in the world. He shook his head as reality set in and he mumbled words of encouragement. "You can do this," he said, as a vague plan coalesced into one course of action.

After placing the candle securely in the boat's holder, he climbed inside and unhitched the rope. He pushed off with an oar and paddled until he came to the middle of the lake, its deepest point. Then he lifted both oars from the water and secured them in their collars. Taking the candle from its holder, he held it at arm's length, moving it in a semi-circle. The water surrounding the boat was ink black, yet comforting in its stillness. Nonetheless, Jeremy sensed the lake's ghosts growing thirsty and lying in wait. *Good.* With a reckless laugh, he flung the candle into the beckoning, dark refuge, listening as it fizzled before dying.

He leaned back and felt the world shrink as he, too, grew smaller. His head ached from the transformation, and he heard himself say, "Mama," though she had been dead many years. He closed his eyes, content in her arms, blocking out the hurt as she rocked his tiny form in a gentle dance. Immersed in her comfort, he totally relaxed, his mind floating above while his body rested below.

She kissed him over and over with a mother's undying love. Then reluctantly, yet with great care, she laid him down in the boat, now a cradle. *I have to leave,* she said. *Come with me. Mama loves you.*

"Don't go!" he cried. "Don't leave me."

Come, she repeated. *There's no need for fear. Just follow.*

From her arms draped a soft, white blanket, its warmth waiting to envelop him. Flooded with relief, he reached out to grab it, but came away with nothing but air. He tried again with the same result and fell back, defeated, useless. He dropped his head into his lap.

Now he knew he was the only one here, the only sentient being. But at least this was his world, under his control, and he could end it with a simple act. It would be so easy and of no earthly consequence. In fact, it might even be to Karen's benefit. Karen? He smiled, then chortled as he reminded himself that she wasn't real and only existed, along with the others, in his mind. Moments later, she was less than a memory, less than nothing.

He drifted along until he became aware of a thunderous roar ahead and realized he was approaching the falls. He pictured one of monstrous proportions ready to pick him up in its churning turbulence as it traveled on to the infinite. As he gazed up toward an imagined heaven, he beseeched God for guidance, a God he wasn't sure he believed in. Having come to a decision, he said a final goodbye and prepared for the oncoming waves with their frothy crests to carry him to his final destination.

Something felt wrong. A strong vibration shook his body, sucking his soul, stealing his spirit. It was as if a large mythical sea creature were closing in for the kill, ready to feast. Intuitively, Jeremy knew what—no, *who*—it was.

Just below the surface, Rahm grabbed hold of the rope, looped it across his chest, and pulled.

Jeremy did not need to see his eternal enemy to establish his presence, since the current that passed between them was alive with an electric charge, one of a mutually repulsive nature yet strong enough to attract. As Jeremy felt the boat veer in a different direction, his hand gripped an oar, hoping for Rahm's head to emerge so he could strike him with a mortal blow, tearing open his skull, turning the water red.

When they neared the shore, Jeremy could see Karen's pale, anguished face outlined in the lantern's light. His first reaction had been to blame her for this new humiliation, but in finding her so distraught with her fingers clenched to her chest in a prayer-like pyramid, he knew he was being unfair. And furthermore, how could he leave her here alone at their mercy? He climbed from the boat, head down, ashamed, ignoring Rahm who stood staring at him with a look both intense yet indifferent as if he were an object, a thing, solely for his use. Jeremy went up to his wife.

"Don't be mad at me," she begged before he could say anything. "I know I was being silly and obsessive, but I couldn't stop worrying. And after a while when you didn't come back, I asked Rahm to find you. Please don't be mad," she begged again.

He reached out and kissed the tip of her nose. "Mad? Mad that you love me? You're all that matters, and I'd have done the same if you were out there alone. Only I wouldn't have waited so long."

Pressing his chest against Karen's, Jeremy felt her body melt into his. He pulled back a bit to look in her eyes, a mirror to her soul, connoting how grateful she was that her worst fear had proved groundless. When she returned his kiss, he, too, felt grateful. Hand in hand, they climbed the rocks and joined the others already dressed and helping themselves to food. If anyone sensed a near crisis, they didn't let on. Karen and Jeremy took their plates and moved off by themselves to a clearing. A few feet above, their laundry hung on a line where it clapped in the breeze like an annoying bark from a dog.

#

After returning to the common area later that evening, the tribe sat around the dining room table snacking on leftovers. As members toasted each other with a "Happy Thanksgiving," Karen swallowed misery while Jeremy remained mute, his normally intelligent face uncomprehending and drained of life. Pushing back his plate, he walked off to the small piece of ground that had become his own, stooping like a swaybacked horse worked far beyond its prime.

Karen's voice cracked. "Don't you see what you're doing to him? You're killing him. And me too. I beg you. Let us go."

Everyone looked away, up, down, anywhere but at her, as if she held a mirror to their shame.

"You'll never get a baby from us. Never! Don't you realize that? It's been six weeks since we've been here, and we haven't made love once. There's no reason to hold us any longer."

Rahm's head shot up, his narrowed eyes spearing her with a flash of insight.

She stared back, pleading, beseeching, hoping for an empathetic response. All she got for her effort was silence. Rahm kept the mystery behind his insight, along with its looming solution, as cloaked as the seeds inside a forbidden fruit.

"Bastard!" she screamed. "All of you." Seething with fury, she threw the contents of her glass at Rahm. As he calmly wiped the liquid from his shirt, she uttered a cry of triumph and stunned herself by gesticulating with her middle finger. Taking pride in her defiance, she went back to comfort her heartsick husband.

She found him lying on the mattress with the blanket pulled over his head. Sensing he was awake, she climbed inside, forming an *s*-shape behind him, and reached up to stroke his hair. Turning to face her, he kissed her deeply, but it was a kiss of desperation, not love. They lay awake for hours, bodies entwined but barely moving, before drifting off to a restless but well-needed sleep.

Chapter 12

Carl and Joan shared the same spot in Dinky Cave that Karen and Jeremy had two months ago. Alongside them, Phil, Jeremy's replacement, and his girlfriend, Patty, were finishing their lunches. Carl took a cookie from a bag, passing the rest along.

"Thanks for bringing us here," said Phil, food spraying from his mouth. "I'd like to take one more look at the waterfall before we leave. That is, if you don't mind. Anyone care to join me?" Patty, adoration written in her moon-struck eyes, jumped up.

Joan scowled as the couple walked out of earshot. Like new lovers everywhere, the twosome held hands. "I can't believe he just left his wife. Poor Wendy! Imagine, they've only been married three years and have a two-year-old. It's disgusting."

Carl sighed, raised and lowered his shoulders, and shook his head. "It came as a complete surprise to everyone, but apparently the affair's been going on for some time. Just shows you never can tell."

"Well, you'd better not pull that crap on me."

"No chance," said Carl. "I'm a till-death-do-us-part kind of guy. Hey," he said, suddenly startled, "what's that?"

"What's what?" As Joan turned her head, her helmet's lamp picked up movement along the far wall. "You're right. I do see something and, uh, I hear something too."

From out of nowhere, Rachel and Rahm appeared as if molded from mist. Their faces held beatific expressions, intending to relax and mesmerize any strangers they should happen upon.

"Hope we didn't scare you," said Rahm. "We didn't mean to sneak up like that." He gestured to Rachel, knowing her five-foot, ninety-five-pound frame made her look harmless. He pushed her forward. "This is my scouting partner, Rachel. I'm Rahm." Dressed more conservatively than usual, both in boots, jeans, and cotton shirts, their appearance didn't register alarm, but Rahm's disheveled beard and hippie-like long hair struck a chord in Joan.

"We thought we were alone here," she said. "We didn't see another car." She exhaled slowly as her pulse returned to normal.

Rahm went into his well-rehearsed routine about living nearby and cleaning the trash left by local teenagers from weekend romps. He paused and cast his eyes sideways to Rachel with its familiar signal. Before she could respond, however, Phil and Patty reappeared from the waterfall. Phil, as broad as he was tall, showcased an imposing and intimidating figure, especially when he stamped the mud from his boots like a nasty giant in a fairytale. Rachel flinched, but Rahm continued to smile. Carl made the introductions. They all shook hands.

"Beautiful here, isn't it?" said Phil, searching for a commonplace subject, one as mundane as the weather. But Carl had something to ask, something vital, and removed a picture from his wallet. He passed it to Rahm. "You don't recognize these people, do you?" he asked.

Rahm looked closely, turning the picture in his hand. He shook his head. "Sorry. Never seen them." Rachel leaned over, giving the picture a cursory glance, followed by a definitive, "No."

Carl sighed. "You sure? They disappeared months back. We think they went to a different cave south of here, but we still have hope. At the very least, we'd like to find their ... their b-bodies." His voice cracked and dropped to a whisper as he said that forbidden word, having only broached the possibility the day before. "Well, thanks anyway," he added. Turning to his caving buddies, he said, "Guess it's time we got going."

The foursome gathered up their belongings. Carl made a show of picking up every last piece of debris. The last thing he'd want is to be accused of not respecting the spelunkers' code of conduct.

Rachel and Rahm accompanied the day-trippers to the passageway along the wall. "Sorry about your friends," said Rachel. "You can be sure we'll inform the authorities if we see or hear anything." With a final handshake and a wave of her arm, she added, "Have a safe trip home." When the group was farther up and behind a bend, she spoke to Rahm, cupping her fingers around her mouth. "Phew, that was a close call."

Rahm shrugged. "Not really. I wasn't going to suggest anything even before that muscle-bound specimen appeared. Okay, maybe I considered it for a minute, but it's just as well. We have enough problems with Karen and Jeremy. Of course, when Mr. Universe did show up, well, it was out of the question. But we did learn something important." With the small group out of range, he spoke in a normal pitch. "People are still looking for them. Who'd have thought after all this time?"

"Doesn't matter," said Rachel. "They're done with this cave. Hey look," she said, scraping the ground with the toe of her shoe. "They left a bunch of change. We can always use money instead of the typical junk people leave behind." She got down on her hands and knees and began gathering nickels, dimes, and quarters. "It never fails. People are such slobs."

#

"What do you make of those two?" asked Joan as she fastened her seatbelt in the car.

"Seemed weird to me," said Carl, "but then all people around here have their heads on backwards. Damned crazy hillbillies."

"More like a case of their heads up their asses. You know—cerebral rectalitis." Phil laughed at his joke, along with everyone else.

"Did you notice their eyes?" said Patty. "Like they had some kind of weird disorder. My mom's eyes wandered when she got glaucoma." "Aren't they too young for that?" asked Joan.

Carl shrugged. "Don't know, but whatever it is, it's not our problem. Unless they're hiding something."

"You think they are?" said Joan.

"Why would they?" said Carl, considering it. "No, it wouldn't make sense, and I'm beginning to think this is the end." He sniffed and blew his nose in the tissue Joan handed him. Then, feeling the strain from dashed hopes, he turned on the radio to help him unwind. They rode the rest of the way with barely a word spoken.

Nearing Baltimore, Carl dropped Patty off first at her parents' house. She was in her senior year at the University of Maryland and still lived at home, commuting to school. She thanked Carl and Joan for the best adventure of her life, and they both had to admit she seemed nice enough, but when she gave Phil a long, noisy kiss in the back seat, they both rolled their eyes in unison.

"You going back to the rooming house?" asked Carl, when Patty was gone.

"Yeah," said Phil. He spent half the week in the suburbs, trying to work things out with Wendy, and the other half in a run-down dwelling on the outskirts of the city.

"I know it's none of my business," said Carl, pulling up to the rooming house, "but it won't help your marriage if you keep seeing Patty."

Phil puffed his cheeks and exhaled with a whoosh. "I know. I just need some time to figure it out." He grabbed his backpack, dragging it along the seat. "See you Monday, Carl," he said, smiling wanly—a man with a heavy load, only the burden was not as it appeared. To Joan, he tipped an imaginary cap and said the standard, "Nice seeing you again."

Phil took out his key and let himself in, climbing to the second floor. The table lamp with its square-shaped shade had been left on all day, revealing dirty walls in need of a new coat of paint. Phil didn't care. He flung his backpack on the unmade bed and immediately began rummaging through, searching for his discovery. Finding it, he held the pen up to the light: an A.T. Cross 10K gold ballpoint. He had noticed its shiny end peeking from a rock near the waterfall and had covered it with his foot. After waiting until Patty turned her back, he'd surreptitiously placed this golden bonanza inside his bag's outer flap. And now, holding his breath as if he were underwater, he looked closely and read the initials: J. M. D.—Jeremy Martin Dryer—engraved on the barrel. So he and Karen had been to Dinky Cave, after all.

Phil had a similar pen, except his was silver, a gift from his parents upon college graduation. He had noticed and admired Jeremy's pen, clipped to his shirt pocket, right before his disappearance. And now here it was, with its haunting request: tell someone—Carl, the authorities, anyone! Without doubt, that would be the proper thing to do. On the other hand, Jeremy and Karen were likely dead. Lost in the cave, they would have starved to death, but in the improbable chance some miracle occurred (and he had a feeling those screwball hillbillies knew more than they'd let on), maybe he should keep his mouth shut; he liked his job. Of course, it was a temporary promotion until Jeremy returned. Only Jeremy was not going to return. Not ever!

Chapter 13

Karen felt glad to be back with her mushrooms. Even one day away left her uneasy. There was something about being in charge of this small, fragile world with its helpless organic dependents that filled her with a sense of purpose, and more than ever she needed that now.

The work week ran from Monday to Sunday without any days off. Although complaints were voiced in private, no one challenged the rule. Over time Karen, too, acquiesced, having come to understand that tasks needed to be done daily to ensure survival, and at her request the responsibility of the garden fell on her shoulders. Additional help was provided with members rotating weekly, a problem in itself given that each person's personality required compromise and adjustment.

This matter came to a head with David's arrival. Since his Thanksgiving Day blowup, his behavior had grown worse, odd even, and Karen felt afraid to be alone in his presence. Like a matted hairball, her stomach seized and congealed as he entered her garden grotto. Thankfully, her fears proved groundless; in fact, having him with her was like having no one at all. Neither disturbed the other, and they went about their business with solemn tranquility, which soon settled at a comfortable plateau.

Like cloistered monks, it became a game for them to communicate with meaningful looks and hand gestures, and by mid-week David's foul mood seemed to lift. He handled his chores humming Broadway tunes, occasionally dancing in circles, arms out, holding an imaginary partner. Karen smiled and applauded, knowing she had played a role in his recovery.

By Sunday, the last day of his rotation, Karen had come to comprehend his touchy predicament. He couldn't help who he was any more than a thirsty person could help craving water. Sensing she sympathized, he took her hand and kissed it, causing her to almost forget her "vow" of silence. Fortunately she remembered before speaking his name and joined him, instead, in humming and dancing to "Waltzing Matilda," the mushrooms their only audience.

It was only later that evening that Karen grasped the subtle changes in her behavior, and as the magnitude of that realization drained the blood from her face, it reminded her to refocus on her priorities.

The next morning, alone in the kitchen, she ate a cold breakfast of cereal, not bothering to enter the dining room where assignments were being handed out. Whomever Rahm assigned as her helper seemed irrelevant; she'd find out soon enough, anyway.

Nearing lunchtime, Helene sauntered into Karen's garden refuge. Despite her tardiness, Karen smiled, anticipating the possibility of pleasant girl talk. It didn't take long, however, for Karen to wish David were back since Helene's lazy habits along with her ceaseless babble resulted in a challenge beyond her capability. By midweek, Karen had reached her limit, and on the verge of telling Helene to shut up, she remembered her primary goal. Tactfully, as if she were speaking to parents at an open house, she redirected the conversation along useful lines, beginning innocently enough.

"When David was here last week, he barely spoke at all, while you are a person of"—she paused to think—"uncommon verbal ability. How do you manage to stay together?"

Helene batted her eyes, mistaking Karen's words for a compliment. "Old habits make for strange bedfellows. We're actually very compatible. He doesn't bother me, and I don't bother him."

"Sounds like true love," said Karen, unsure whether to smile or look grave.

Helene solved that problem with a whimsical quip. "As a matter of fact, I did love him once. Still do, I suppose." She lowered her voice and looked around, double-checking to make sure they were alone. "In fact, I loved him so much that I followed him down to this zombie mausoleum."

Karen's ears perked up. "I didn't realize you felt that way. I assumed you wanted to come."

"I did, but just to be with him. Anyway, that was years ago, so it no longer matters. Here I am and here I'll stay, unless—" Caught off guard, she immediately changed the subject and shook her head like a wet dog trying to dry off. "Have I told you yet what it's like to fuck Rahm or Norman or even that lecher Brian for that matter?"

Holding her mid-section from the effects of a belly laugh, she began what was tantamount to a lesson, not leaving out a single detail. Karen found herself laughing too, while looking for any pearls of information to use to her advantage.

With all barriers broken down, Helene spent the remainder of the week filing Karen in on the tribe's intimate relationships. While she hardly lifted a finger workwise, her mouth proved a useful tool. It was obvious Helene was trying to shock her, but Karen managed to dig nuggets from the trash.

"Rahm's missing part of his heel," she said. "A war injury. He uses an insert in one of his shoes to compensate."

"Really?" said Karen, refraining from jumping up and down at that useful information. Instead she managed to file it away in her mind with an underscore and three exclamation points.

"And there's rumors of an above-ground house, a safe-house," said Helene, "possibly owned by Norman." That information alone sent flashing signals to Karen's brain like a stop sign in the desert.

By the end of her rotation, Karen had to admit that her time with Helene had proved valuable indeed. She'd learned about the strengths, weaknesses, and conflicts of the members. Mary's intense desire to become the next mother could be a source of subterfuge, and the petty jealousies among the members could easily be used against them, but what struck her most was the possibility of deceit. According to Helene, Norman had voted to keep her and Jeremy prisoners, not set them free as he'd once claimed when they were alone. With the risk of misinformation, confusion, and lies, deciding whom to trust would be impossible.

That evening, as in all others, Karen filled Jeremy in on every detail, large or small. His mood had picked up since their time at the lake, and he found the news of Rahm's handicap particularly delightful. "We'll be able to use that for sure," he said. "Don't you see? We can steal his shoes."

"I thought of that too," said Karen, "and who knows what Norman will tell me? I think he'll be coming tomorrow. I feel like a spy."

"That's exactly what you are, so be smart about it, which means play dumb."

Like members of a secret club, they shared a high five. Then, to further salute their progress, Jeremy proposed a toast and poured water from the pitcher he stored near their bed. "Remember back in New Hampshire how I called our state motto corny? Well, now I think otherwise." Raising his glass, he sat up straight, threw back his shoulders, and said, "Live Free or Die." Karen did likewise, adding, "To General John Stark, my hero. May he lead us to victory." They clinked glasses and drank.

#

Norman was busy chopping limestone when Karen arrived at the garden. "I woke up hours ago," he explained. "I hope you don't mind my starting without you. I'm not made to sit still."

Karen smiled. *Friendly Norman, helpful Norman. No doubt about that.* With multiple talents, he was the go-to guy, always doing something: building furniture, replacing shelves, adding cupboards. But what about duplicity? Karen looked into his clever face—clever like a fox? Or just plain smart? Could he be persuaded to help her and Jeremy or was Helene correct? She told herself to be careful. *Push, but not quickly or obviously.*

Up till then, Karen had either brought lunch with her or had gone back to the dining room and eaten there. Norman insisted on preparing a small feast for them both. Late in the morning, he'd head to the kitchen and whip up a basketful of surprises. Then he'd carry it back to the garden where they'd take a long break. In addition to the lanterns, he'd light a scented candle as if they were at a fancy restaurant.

"You're spoiling me," said Karen, sniffing the air while chomping on a mushroom stir fry wrapped inside a crepe.

"I like spoiling people I like."

Karen bit off a crusty edge. "Why do you like me?"

"Because you're sweet, thoughtful, and"—he lowered his eyes—"beautiful. Look, I know you've been dealt a hard blow. And while I can't change what's happened, I'd like to make your life easier."

Karen swallowed, put down her plate, and placed her hand on his shoulder. "There is something you can do. You can start by being honest, answering questions. Every time I ask one of the others, they brush me off."

"About what?"

"A number of things. The people in the cemetery, for starters. Tom, Louise, Eugene. I read their names on their markers. I want to know how they died."

Norman winced. "You have a right to know, I suppose. But take my advice. You're better off not knowing. It's an ugly story."

"I don't care," she insisted. "Tell me."

Norman circled his head until he heard a crack, then crossed his legs and leaned back. "Okay," he said, closing his eyes, forcing himself to peer into the worst days of the tribe's collective past. "I'll begin with Tom, Janet's husband. After Jon's birth, he began to behave ..." He groped for the right word, but his tongue felt thick. "I'm, I'm sorry," he said. "It's still upsetting even after all this time. I regret that I didn't pay more attention. Maybe there was something I could have done, but I, like everyone else, assumed Tom would be thrilled to have the first child born here. Of course, he may not have been Jon's biological father, but that didn't matter. Right? He was the symbolic father and given all due respect. "I have to admit, though, he wasn't much of a father, even to Randy, who Janet swears is his biological son. Tom all but ignored both boys."

"Must have been hard for Randy," said Karen. "Adjusting to a baby and having a father who didn't care."

Norman shook his head up and down. "We made sure to give Randy lots of attention, and as you can see he's a great kid. But for Tom, things got worse real quick. He took up with Louise outside the fertility area, even though she and Eugene claimed to have a solid marriage.

Karen raised her eyebrows.

"Oh, don't look so shocked," he said. "There nothing unusual about having affairs, even here. Only the timing was bad. And Eugene? Well, he didn't care since he was involved with Helene."

Karen stopped him with a pointed finger. "Wait," she said. "Didn't you just say Louise and Eugene were happily married? This is getting complicated."

Norman laughed but his face darkened with a warning: "Pay attention, 'cause it gets worse." Karen withdrew her finger, signaling him to continue.

"To everyone's shock, Louise announced she was pregnant. Naturally, we were wild with excitement—two kids in a short time, but you should have seen Eugene. I never saw anyone so happy, practically bouncing on the tips of his toes, and from what Louise said it's unlikely he even fathered the child. But oddly, the only one who cared about that triviality was lover-boy, Tom. He insisted he was the *real* father, said he loved Louise. But, if you ask me, it was crazy love because he totally abandoned Janet and the boys. Demanded Louise move in with him.

"By then Louise had had enough. Told him he was out of his mind. That she didn't love him. Never had." Norman paused, glanced at Karen, who sat eyes ablaze, transfixed, caught up in the drama.

"And then what?" she prodded.

Norman took a breath and set his face in a stoic mask. "The situation appeared to get better at first. Tom, to all appearances, accepted the inevitable, and life returned to normal. Well, sort of. He never did go back to Janet, but that didn't bother her any. She sang to the rafters how tickled she felt to see the SOB go. Called him an "asshole," pardon my French.

"Then about four months later, just before dinner, Tom began screaming, parading back and forth, ranting, pulling at his hair. He told Louise she'd better move in with him or he'd kill her. Yes, he actually used those words. She ran to get Eugene and in the meantime we tried calming him down. When they came back, Tom was on his knees bawling his heart out. It was pathetic. I don't recall ever seeing a man—or a woman even—acting like that." He bit his lip as he relived the experience.

"Anyway, Tom finally did calm down and begged Louise to forgive him, insisting he didn't mean to threaten her. Louise said she'd accept his apology if he'd promise to leave her alone, and who knows? Maybe it would have ended there if Eugene hadn't butted in. But by then he, too, was worked up." Norman swallowed a sip of water and wiped his mouth before continuing. "So next Eugene grabbed Tom by his shirt, pulled him to his feet, and told him to stay away from his wife. Said he'd been a lousy father to Jon and Randy and he wasn't going to let it happen again. I can't help but think maybe that was the final blow.

"At any rate, Tom walked away without saying another word, as if nothing unusual had happened, and I thought—prayed—that that was the end of it. And it was the end in a way, but not how I'd hoped." He turned to Karen, who stared back like an onlooker to a highway mishap, confusion and dread in her eyes.

"I still hear those screams when I'm trying to fall asleep. The gasps, the death rattle in Eugene's throat." Unconsciously, he covered his ears with his hands. "Fortunately Louise never knew what hit her. Tom crushed her skull with the first strike, but Eugene was a large man and fought back. Of course, the contest wasn't fair since Tom used a rock. The first blow probably stunned him, the second did irreparable damage, and the third was lethal; he died before we could do much."

Norman, overwhelmed, almost stopped at that point, but it felt good to talk about the tragedy. No one else wanted to, and he needed to wash off his ensuing guilt. "Rahm chased after Tom as he tried to make his way out of the cave. He knew the route. Rahm told us later what happened. There was a fight, a fair one according to Rahm. Tom was much bigger but not in great shape and had ten years on Rahm. He slipped and fell to his death, or, who knows, maybe it was suicide. Anyway, no great loss. Look what he did!"

Karen felt certain Norman had left out an essential point, but being too keyed up, she let it pass. Sensing her angst, Norman hurried on, determined to finish so he'd never have to expound again. "Rahm dragged the body back. Janet wanted to dump it into the guano and let the bugs feast, but Rahm would have none of that. He buried Tom himself—dug the hole and placed him in it. He even insisted we have a ceremony, the same as we did for Louise and Eugene."

With a shake of his legs, Norman indicated he was finished. Karen, however, bordering on obsession, had one final question. "But why the separate burial mound for the baby? After all, it wasn't born yet."

Now it was Norman's turn to squirm. Shielding his mouth as if hiding an evil secret, he said, "Mary felt we should attempt to save its life. With her medical training, she volunteered to do it."

Karen blanched. "You don't have to explain further. I understand."

Norman's lips flared with a "Phew," relieved to skip over the grisly details. He did see fit to add that the baby never had a chance. "Too small. Too premature. It never took a breath and mercifully didn't suffer."

"That's quite a story," said Karen. "Still, I understand how Tom, or anyone for that matter, can lose their mind in this place."

Norman, whose eyes hadn't deteriorated like the others, shot Karen a perceptive glance, discerning she had chosen those particular words as a rebuke. Recovering his composure, he knew better than to get angry or defensive. "It's impossible to tell who'll adjust and who won't to any major change, here or otherwise. It may sound peculiar," he said, "but it's fortunate that all of us in the original group considered ourselves failures with nothing to lose and so much to gain."

"Seems to me," said Karen, "that you've gained very little. Just a dark hole with no sky, no stars, not even a skyscraper."

"No, you're wrong!" he said. His voice shook like an itinerant preacher speaking God's truth, spreading salvation. "Look around you. We do have skyscrapers, natural ones, massive ones, tens of thousands of years old. The stalagmite you're leaning against is far more majestic than any of your so-called skyscrapers. We have flowers and stars too." He stood up and held the lantern high over his head, aiming its light toward the ceiling. "See the anthodites?" Karen followed the direction of his arm. White crystal needles bulged and protruded, twinkling like brilliant jewels in a cloudless night. As Karen moved her head, they formed patterns like bits of glass from a toy kaleidoscope, reminding her of snowflakes, each one unique.

Karen parted her mouth to ask a question, but Norman rushed ahead to make a final point. "What we've gained is miraculous: the opportunity to build a new civilization, blessed by the gift of a second chance. If we were in the far reaches of space it would be no less significant." His eyes shined with the fervor of conviction. "All those people up there, those downtrodden souls living on the surface, how many make a difference? Any difference? How many are happy? I certainly wasn't."

"Oh? Why not?"

Norman snickered, revealing two dimples, one on each side of his face, just above his beard. Despite his Shirley Temple look, the bitterness in his laugh rang clear as a firehouse bell. "I was," he said, "the black sheep of the family."

Confused, Karen squinched her cheeks, her skin creasing like a Shar-Pei's.

"I'm serious," he said. "You see, my mother was white, my father black. I didn't get to know his side of the family until I was older, but my mother's … well, they never really accepted me. Not completely, anyway."

"But you don't even look black. Not that it would matter, anyway." Realizing her words sounded trite, she turned her head, afraid he'd notice her reddening complexion.

"It's funny," said Norman. "Many years ago a classmate asked if I could change one thing about myself, what would it be. I told him I'd get rid of these stupid dimples, but that was a lie. I knew what I wanted, and what was worse, so did he."

Karen remained silent, ruffled by his candor, but Norman recovered and his voice softened with longing. "You know what? Now that the cave's drained me of my color, I actually miss it. And don't tell anyone this, but sometimes I dream of spending a whole day above, just sitting in a park or shopping for food and sampling every damned thing from appetizers to desserts."

Sensing a timely opportunity, Karen grabbed it before it faded into the barrens of the cave's apocalyptic landscape. "So you do have regrets. Can't say I'm surprised. Listen, Norman, if you have any thoughts of returning, you'd be astonished by the changes. Why, in the last few years, amazing possibilities have opened up for women, and for minorities too. Did you know there's a black mayor in Washington, D.C.? Name's Walter Washington."

Norman snorted. "Forgive me, Karen, and please understand, I'm not making fun of you. It's just that you're so naïve. But I'm afraid I may have given you the wrong impression. I don't want you to think I dropped out because I was running away. Well, okay, maybe that was part of it, but mostly I was running toward. Like I said before, we're crusaders down here. Pioneers."

"Oh," she said, her bottom lip thrust forward in a pout. "And you still feel that way?"

"You know, nothing's ever as good or as bad as you imagine. But to answer your question, yes. Even today I see myself forging into the unknown, breaking down barriers, solving mysteries. I do have one regret, though."

"And what's that?"

Norman sucked in his cheeks and his dimples deepened. "I never imagined after all these years I'd still be sleeping in little more than a cubbyhole. I thought I'd have my own house by now. I even picked the perfect spot by the lake."

Karen started. "You're joking, of course."

"No," he said. "I'm serious. Oh, nothing fancy, mind you. Just a small, practical structure, but big enough for the wife and kids I hoped for. Somehow that wasn't my destiny, I guess." He exhaled with a sigh. "Yet even with that disappointment, I've never doubted my initial decision. Not for a moment."

"Tell me," said Karen, "is homosexuality part of your new frontier?" Immediately she felt like kicking herself. It wasn't her business to judge, especially after all she inferred about tolerance.

Norman clenched his jaw, and the smile left his mouth.

"I'm sorry," said Karen. "I had no right to ask."

"It doesn't matter. What happened between me and David was of no consequence, at least to me. I'm afraid he took it more seriously, but he'll get over it."

"You don't have to explain," Karen insisted.

Norman shrugged. "I don't mind. Tell me, have you ever been on an ocean liner? On a cruise?"

"No," said Karen.

"I was once. Too much food, too much sun. My point is that too much of anything can get boring. Even in Vietnam there were days where we just sat around spinning our wheels, waiting for the damned action to begin. After a while you need to get up and fire a gun, scratch that damned itch in the center of your back, the one you can't reach. To get relief, you rub against a wall. David was a wall. Nothing more." Norman closed his eyes. When he reopened them, they were red.

"Something wrong?" asked Karen.

His face relaxed. "I was just wondering … How come it always seems that the person you love doesn't love you?"

"Are you referring to David or someone else?"

"Both, I suppose. I know you're aware of my feelings toward Lily. I keep hoping that one day she'll wake up, look over at me lying beside her and realize how much she loves me. But who am I kidding? If I were to die today, she'd probably not notice till tomorrow. Still, I can't do without her." He turned toward Karen. "You're lucky," he said. "To love someone who loves you back."

Lucky was the last thing Karen felt, but before she could answer, he sprang to his feet. "I'm ready to get back to work. What would you like me to do? I want to leave here with everything on schedule and running smoothly by the end of the week."

Karen, touched by his thoughtfulness, said, "Lily's a fool." As for Norman himself, she found taking his pulse proved more of a challenge. She reached for his arm, offered with a chivalrous spin of the wrist, and allowed him to help her up. But was he friend or foe? Both, she decided, as if such a thing were possible.

#

That night, Karen and Jeremy pooled their information. Afraid she might be forgetting something, he prodded her again and again. "Think carefully, even if it seems trivial. You never know what may come in handy later."

Karen dissected every last detail, major and minor, including her reservations regarding Norman's forthrightness. Finally Jeremy felt satisfied. Then it was his turn.

He had spent the last few days fishing for trout. Although thoughts of suicide had left his mind since the day at the lake, Rahm, as a precaution, had sent Randy to accompany him. Prudently, he'd selected the youngster, feeling he would be less of an irritant. So Randy, under the pretext of friendship, stuck to Jeremy like gum on a shoe. Jeremy didn't mind. In fact, he too had a motive and decided to cultivate their relationship. "If I can get the boy to like me, confide in me, we may learn secrets. Who knows? Maybe he'll even lead us out."

"Lead us out?" said Karen. "Now that's a crazy thought. In any case, whatever you do, make sure he isn't emotionally scarred. He's only a child."

"A child!" exclaimed Jeremy, immediately lowering his voice, cognizant there may be people close by, listening in. "This is no time for virtue. This is war."

#

Waving a steak knife at his sister, Phil hissed, "This is war."

"Oh, don't be so dramatic," said Margaret, wiping her mouth with a cloth napkin. "I've been down that road. Matthew, too." She turned to her husband, an attorney, who specialized in anything that increased his family's bankroll and funded luxurious vacations as well as their second home in Martha's Vineyard.

Phil resented his brother-in-law's success. In addition to fancy houses, his cars were upscale, his watches expensive. On the other hand, he did grill a good steak and, besides, he needed his advice.

"I tried to make it work. Really!" said Phil. "Gave it my best shot. Even went to marital counseling, but it's over, and the bitch won't give up."

Margaret stared at Phil, explosives flaring from her eyes. "Don't use that sexist language with me, baby brother. You played a huge role in this mess."

"Okay, you're right," he conceded. "And rub it in while you're at it, but I've tried to reason with her and she won't consider a no-fault divorce."

Cries and shouts from an upstairs bedroom immediately put the discussion on hold. Margaret looked at her husband. "Yours, mine, or ours?" The shrill voice of a young girl, screaming, "It's my toy!" provided the answer. "Ours!" said Margaret, taking off in the direction of the commotion.

"How can you stand that racket?" said Phil. "Five kids. Sheesh! One drives me nuts."

"I like kids," said Matthew. "In fact, we're thinking of having another."

Phil gaped in openmouthed wonder. "To each his own, I suppose. Anyway, getting back to my problem, do you have any great lawyerly advice for me?"

Matthew's disdain for Phil rose higher than an overflowing bathtub, but he crossed his arms and put on a professional face. "You know, there is an advantage with a *fault*-based divorce. You won't have to wait a year; besides, you gave her more than enough grounds."

"I don't care about the stupid year. Look, I don't plan on getting remarried tomorrow. I just don't want any bad publicity. I'm fairly new in town, and my career's taking off. I have to be careful."

"What makes you think you're so important that you have to be concerned about bad publicity? You only work at a small newspaper; the one with the silly name: Baltimore Bees."

"That's *Beehive*," said Phil, taking a long sip of wine while smoldering at the put-down.

Matthew, knowing he'd scored a point, smiled openly, and with that advantage in plain view, offered a morsel. "I think I can solve your problem, Phil. It comes down to biology. For most women kids are their number one concern, and you obviously don't like them. That's your solution, your bargaining chip."

Phil rubbed his face. "Hmm," he said. "When I was at the house yesterday she just assumed I'd fight for joint custody. That's the last thing I want. I'd like to see the kid, of course. At least once in a while."

Matthew gawked, his eyes round like a bullfrog's.

Phil smiled snidely, immune to the contempt on his brother-in-law's face. He resumed eating and poured himself a second glass of wine. "So that's the key, my golden ticket." He raised his glass in a mock toast. "Thanks bro," he said, swallowing the pricy Cabernet Sauvignon in noisy gulps. Matthew turned away in disgust.

#

A scraping noise caused Karen to awaken. She sat up, fully alert, searching the darkness for danger, having the distinct impression someone was watching her. "Who's there?" she asked, pulling the covers higher.

"It's only me," said a small voice. "Randy."

Karen released a long drawn-out breath. "What are you doing here?"

"Looking for Jeremy. We're supposed to go fishing."

"Is it morning already?" She lit a candle and checked her watch. "Is it really this late? Damn. I overslept." She rose, flinging the blanket back to the mattress. Her clothes were already on. As usual, there had been no reason to take them off. "Did you try the bathroom? He's probably there."

Before Randy could answer, Jeremy appeared holding a lantern, his mouth brimming with a self-satisfied smile.

"Where have you been?" said Karen, speaking in even tones in an attempt to hide her anxiety.

"Out for a walk." He gave a small nod in Randy's direction, indicating she not question him further. Karen caught the look and understood. Whatever the reason, it would have to wait until later.

Jeremy ruffled the boy's hair, surprised to note those additional inches, the unmistakable shift from child to adolescent almost overnight. "Ready to go?"

"Uh-huh," said Randy, "and guess what? I already packed our breakfast and lunch. Well, Mom did it mostly, but I helped." Despite the admission, he stood tall and straight, holding the bag out before him.

"Good," said Jeremy. "I'd rather be with you than with the others." Turning toward Karen, he added, "Except for you, of course." He gave her an obligatory peck on the cheek before heading off with Randy to the lake.

With the route now familiar, Jeremy easily avoided the pitfalls, especially in those places where one misstep could have deadly repercussions. Although his senses weren't as adaptable as Karen's, his expanding knowledge of the cave aided him in sharpening his survival skills. With a mental list of obstacles to overcome, he symbolically checked off adjusting to darkness.

Jeremy rolled up his pants and waded into the chilled water. As usual, he steeled his jaw from the momentary shock before climbing into the boat and lighting the candle left in its holder. Randy stripped off both top and bottom clothes and climbed in beside Jeremy, who was now shivering from a sudden draft carrying an icy-wet spray.

Teeth clucking hen-like, Jeremy stuttered, "H-how come you never get cold?"

"I don't know. I just don't." He began rowing.

Jeremy reached out. "Hand me the food. M-maybe it will help."

Randy passed over the bag and Jeremy scoured through. He clutched a thermos. "I hope it's coffee." Thankfully it was, and as the hot liquid passed through his body, the trembling subsided and he got down to business. Taking an earthworm from a small box, Jeremy ably baited the hook on the tip of the fishing rod and cast off with a straight overhead motion. The rod was heavy, cheap but strong, and it had taken him a while to adjust to its feel. Although he made steady progress, Jeremy had to admit that Randy's instincts in knowing where the fish would be added to their success.

"Stay close to the banks," suggested Randy. "It's still early and the fish are hungry."

Jeremy had already learned that that was where the trout caught their morning breakfast of insects and crayfish.

"Next," said Randy, "we can try behind the rocks and in the riffles."

"You mean ripples."

"No, riffles. Those are shallows where the feeding's good."

"You certainly know your trout," Jeremy said in a deliberate attempt to win the boy's affection. "How did you learn so much?"

"Rahm taught me. He's taught me everything I know, besides my mom, of course."

"I see," said Jeremy. "And did he—" Feeling a tug on the line, Jeremy stopped in mid-sentence and shifted his attention. Randy leaned forward, tongue clicking, focused. As Jeremy reeled in the fish, Randy got the landing net in position. When the boy sensed the time was right, he lowered the net into the water just ahead of the fish, which simply fell in head first.

"I got it," said Randy, beaming in victory. He placed the net in the boat with the fish splashing wildly inside, further wetting them both.

Randy's smile abruptly drooped. "It looks pretty small. I think I'd better throw it back."

"That's all right," said Jeremy. "We've still got the day ahead of us."

Randy calmed down. "That's true. Besides, I can always catch crayfish."

Jeremy didn't like the taste of crayfish, the miniature, lobster-looking crustaceans, but he was impressed by how easily Randy caught them with his bare hands from under the rocks that lined the lake.

While Randy removed the hook from the fish's mouth, Jeremy studied him from the corner of his eye. Tentatively, waiting for the right moment, he asked, "Ever think about going above ground?"

Randy's whole face lit up as if he'd been handed an unexpected treasure. "Rahm's supposed to take me soon. When we need to replenish our supplies."

"I meant live up there. You know, permanently."

"Gee. I never thought of that. I like it here enough, I guess, even though I only have stupid Jon to play with."

"Well, if you lived above, there'd be kids your age to play with, do things with like eating ice cream, going to school, Disney World."

"I know what school is, and I miss ice cream. But what's Disney World?"

Jeremy raised a knowing eyebrow, certain he had stumbled upon a loose end. "Tell you what. I'll teach you about my home above if you teach me about yours. Deal?"

"Deal," said Randy, matching Jeremy's smile.

"Good. Let's shake on it."

The man and the youngster shook hands. Jeremy, pleased by his subterfuge, silently congratulated himself, determined to be the main beneficiary in this sober, high-stakes game.

Chapter 14

Karen sat on the "throne" in the Ballroom. Even though stuffing was starting to show through the padded arms, it remained the most comfortable, most sought-after chair. As an added bonus, it reclined on demand and a footrest popped in and out if the handle was pushed-pulled, a favorite game of Jon's.

Karen fixed the position to upright, her back rigid, while her ears strained for hints, rumors, anything noteworthy. After some self-directed pep talks, she had upped the notch in her determination to escape, but hearing only useless babble, she cursed through her teeth and collected her belongings to leave for the garden. At the last moment, Brian pulled on her sleeve, informing her of a change in plans. "Lily can't join you this week," he told her. "She's gone to the fertility area. Rahm's arranged for someone else to fill in."

Karen scowled, not caring if he took it personally. "Whatever," she said before hurrying off, rattled by the smug look on his face.

She was happy to find herself alone with her fungal friends. Those few solitary minutes provided a boost to get her through the day. Since childhood, she'd rarely felt the need for prayer, but now she lowered her head, folded her hands, praying for the strength to do the impossible and secure her ultimate goal. In the meantime, she asked for a day's worth of serenity along with a request that Lily's replacement not be Brian. With that act complete, she felt renewed, and as she moved among the rows, she took in the product of her labor. The mushrooms, she saw, were thriving as if grateful for her care; she sat back, smiling with satisfaction.

Hearing the approach of footsteps, she swiveled her head, impatient to see who the stand-in would be. When Rahm wandered in, she was taken aback, not so much by his presence but by her reaction. Her breath came faster and her pulse began to race. *Dammit*, she thought, dismayed by her response, hoping it didn't show.

"I gather Brian's told you about Lily?" he said, his muscled calves and thighs outlined against the thin material of his pants. "She'll be busy for the next few days." His tone held a lilt of amusement. "You don't mind my coming in her place, do you? I've been curious about the changes here; the mushrooms have never tasted better."

Karen picked a piece of lint from her sweater, avoiding his eye. "I haven't been doing anything in particular. It's just as Rachel said. All in the timing."

"Rachel said you talk to them."

Karen's face drained of color. "Only as a joke. I haven't lost my mind."

"Then you must have a green thumb." He sat down beside her and picked up her hand, closely examining the short, cushiony digit. "Ah, just as I guessed. Green."

Flustered, she pulled back her hand, but her mouth trembled at the corners. She had acknowledged, months before, how attractive Rahm was, but that fact alone didn't scare her. The real basis of her problem was more complicated and had only recently entered her consciousness.

Ever since her father's abandonment when she was a child, she had been seeking a substitute—a strong masculine figure to take his place and protect her. She had found that in Jeremy, but now their absurd circumstance had caused a shift, altering their relationship. The need, however, still remained, ever rapacious and ready to soak up its nourishment; she would have to be careful.

At her suggestion, they walked to the lake to replenish the pails with water. "Mushrooms get thirsty too," she explained. Karen told him where and how much to pour on the beds. They added limestone and mycelium wherever necessary and then weeded the garden of defectives not coming in to her standards. Afterwards they harvested the ripe ones for that evening's dinner.

Over the next few days they practiced the same routine, with Karen giving orders and Rahm following. While Karen appreciated his acceptance of her leadership role, she took care to be respectful, not trusting his intentions.

By midweek, however, when she had grown more comfortable in his presence, Rahm, with his hidden agenda, switched tactics and proposed they take a break, relax a bit. Karen, immediately on guard, bristled.

"You've no reason to worry," he said. "I was only thinking of showing you echolocation again. I'm sure you can do it."

"What makes you think I can, or even want to?" she responded.

"The way you deal with the mushrooms. You already have ESP."

"I most certainly do not. I don't believe in that psychic mumbo-jumbo."

"I'm not referring to telepathy or the supernatural; just using your brain beyond the regular channels of perception. Come on! You've seen how the rest of us do it. Anyway, I think you'll find it useful."

That final word struck a chord and Karen reconsidered. "All right," she said. "Show me how."

Rahm nodded, smiling faintly. "Why don't you have something to drink first? To help you unwind. Look at you. You're as tense as a jackrabbit." He opened a thermos and offered her tea, then helped himself to a cup.

Karen took a sip and made a face. "What's the vinegary taste?"

"It's just the mushrooms, the special ones that grow in the peat. Don't worry. They're not poisonous; on the contrary, brewing the stems triggers a nice soothing effect. Rachel gathered some this morning and steeped them in hot water. If you don't like it, don't drink it."

"No, I guess it's okay. I'm just not used to"—she sniffed—"tree bark." She finished her drink and handed the cup back to Rahm.

"Ready? Good. Then let's begin." Facing her, he crossed his legs, indicating for her to do likewise. "Before we get down to basics, let your head roll around, then your shoulders. Yes. That's good. Now close your eyes and let your thoughts drift to peaceful surroundings."

Karen did as told. Slowly, steadily, seamlessly, her mind cleared of dark shadows, replaced by an endless stretch of pearly white sand—a 360-degree panorama with living, breathing glints, holding insights of seasoned truths.

While the knowledge pierced her boundaries of reason, she now felt grateful to be among the select, those chosen to experience this once-in-a-lifetime phenomenon, and as she ran her fingers through the granular material she became aware of a missing piece, a vital one.

She had to find it. Nothing else mattered. Digging with her hands, she pushed away all extraneous substance until she hit a chest—a treasure chest of sorts. Brushing away the last of the sand, she opened the lid and heard a whooshing sound like the breaking of a seal.

The chest, while empty, sucked her inside, and she spun through a vortex yet felt no fear, due to a soothing, beelike buzz. The soft drumming rose to a familiar click-click before fading away, and she tumbled out before a wall of frosted glass holding back a sea of foam.

The peaks rose and fell, became crested waves, striking the barrier with ancient, blue-green currents. She heard the drone of the ocean, felt its spray on her face, and smelled the salt air. She heard the clicking again, this time coming from inside her head, but continued to stare as the wall began to vibrate and bulge at its center.

A crack appeared, and it looked as if it might break. She heard a voice—her own—high and shrill. The crack deepened and she had the sensation that she had experienced this all before—a familiar yet unidentifiable taste on her tongue. She licked her lips and everything stopped dead, and she grudgingly found herself wrenched back to where she had begun.

He stroked her arm. "You did very well, just as I expected. Tomorrow we'll try again."

She looked at him, her brow tight with confusion. "Where am I? That other place—it seemed so real. What happened?"

"You'll know soon enough. Until tomorrow then." He brushed her cheek with a single finger, and walked off without another word.

#

Karen avoided mention of echolocation to Jeremy, and, pleading a headache, walked to the supply area for aspirin. On the way back, she acknowledged that guilt had struck a chord, and until she reasoned everything out, she'd keep any conflicts to herself.

Unable to sleep, she rode out her inner battle, going over the previous day's experience, assuring herself, as Rahm had suggested, that possessing this skill might prove useful. But the second reason, the real reason, grated like an ill-fitting shoe: she wanted the knowledge for its own sake and therefore had accepted the challenge.

The next morning she rushed to the garden, eager to finish her chores and move on to her lesson; consequently, she was glad to see Rahm, already there, bustling about, ready to begin.

Once again, she spun off to an otherworldly domain, a shimmering palace with stalagmite trees bearing crystalline fruit. Above her were upside-down glaciers, huge white stalactites breathing answers. She reached up, attempting to touch the largest glacier, a perfect isosceles triangle with a flower of ice on its down-pointed tip. Its height, however, necessitated another means of communion. She began warbling a wind-chime trill and exhaled a breath, warm and misty. The vapor rose in a helix, spraying the ice flower, causing it to melt. Droplets of truth dripped on her face. Her tongue, snakelike, slipped from her mouth to taste the answers, but like the day before, when victory inched a heartbeat away, she was abruptly brought back to her steely, dark surroundings. She hung her head.

"You mustn't be discouraged," said Rahm. "It takes time and patience, and you have both."

Karen raised her head, her voice rebelling against his words. "I want to try again. Right now!"

He laughed at her defiance. "No," he insisted. "It takes too much energy. You need to recoup."

"All right," she said, pouting with resentment, knowing he wouldn't change his mind. "But the least you could do is answer a question."

"If I'm able."

"Tell me," she said, "why did you kill Tom?"

"Who told you that?"

"Norman said he fell, but I don't believe him. I think you pushed him."

He moved closer, his eyes narrowing into reptilian slits. "I prefer not talking about it." Karen's scowl burned hot on his skin, and he reconsidered. "Even if I had killed him—and I'm not saying I did—he deserved to die, but I didn't murder him. There was a fight. He fell. Too bad!"

"You don't sound sorry."

"Should I? What Tom did to Louise and Eugene was atrocious, bashing in their heads in their sleep. He was a coward. And while I have no regret over any of my actions, believe me, nothing comes easy."

"But why no trial?" she admonished. "He deserved that. Everyone does."

Rahm scoffed, curled one corner of his mouth. "We weren't prepared for a trial and have no time for such foolery. Besides, it would only have torn us apart.

Tom got more justice than he gave his victims." He opened his hands and stared down at them. "I never asked to be the group's leader," he went on, "but I'm the only one willing to take the responsibility."

Karen paused, her knuckles digging into the hollow of her cheek. "Has anyone else ever tried?"

"Every year on March twenty-first, we celebrate the vernal equinox. It's also the anniversary of our arrival, so that's when we hold elections. I'm the only candidate who's ever been nominated, and I've always been reelected—unanimously. No one else has been willing to run."

"Then anyone could be a candidate?"

"Anyone who's a member of our tribe."

"I see," she said, weighing his words. "And how does one become a member?"

Rahm paused, then pinched the bridge of his nose. "That's never come up. I suppose by simply stating your wish to join us and pledging allegiance."

Karen filed away the information, smart enough not to press him further, but after a brief silence, she said, "There is one last question I've wanted to ask."

Rahm tilted his head. "You're certainly full of questions today. I guess there's time for one more. Fire away."

"Why did you come here?"

Rahm's lips tightened before loosening on an exhalation. "I don't like to speak about myself, but today I'll make an exception. For you! But I'm afraid you'll be disappointed. Like everyone else here, I didn't fit into so-called normal society."

"I was hoping for something more specific," said Karen.

"Okay, I've nothing to hide." His voice dropped a degree as he began. "I grew up in a small town not far from here. While this part of West Virginia is my home, I always felt like an outsider. My parents originally came to this state in the early '40s at the request of John Lewis. Ever hear of him?"

"No," said Karen. "Should I have?"

"I suppose not, although in his day he was a big shot, on the front pages of every newspaper. He was president of the United Mine Workers and the Congress of Industrial Organizations. Anyway, my father was a union organizer and a friend of Lewis. Lewis liked him, was grooming him for a leadership role. Then when the captive-mines dispute broke out, Lewis asked my dad to come and stir the miners up further."

Karen held up a hand. "What do you mean 'captive-mines'?"

"Those were the mines owned by the steel companies back then. The conflict surrounded opening union shops for the workers. Naturally it wasn't in the interest of the owners to allow them to operate. Strikes broke out all across the coal belt in support of the cause.

"The shit hit the fan in '41 and unfortunately it rained on my father. He was shot and killed when he went to picket outside the Frick coke plant in Edenborn, Pennsylvania, one month before Pearl Harbor and four months before my birth. My mother never recovered. Years later I learned she'd been having a difficult pregnancy and now on top of that she'd had to deal with his loss. Her doctor warned her about traveling back north while she was pregnant. Said she was too weak. Then, by the time I was born, she decided to stay."

"Why?" asked Karen.

"Partly out of revenge, I suspect, and partly because she had started to lose her mind. Lewis was unable to come to the funeral. It was during wartime, and he was involved in intense negotiations. He did send a representative, though, but my mother never forgave him. As far as the local folk, well, you could count the number who showed up on one hand. At least, that's what my mother loved to say, and she said it plenty. I suppose lots of people were suffering then, dying too, so what was one more? And besides, it wasn't easy to lose a day's pay.

"So she decided to stay and make everyone feel guilty. Unfortunately, no one did and she became the local crazy lady, the town joke. The union took care of us financially. It wasn't much, but we scraped by. Out of necessity, I became a loner, since it was impossible to bring anyone home. With my mom ranting half the time, I had to rely on myself.

"I couldn't wait to grow up and leave this state. College was out of the question; I barely finished high school—hated to study. So I bummed around before the draft caught up with me. I joined the Marines. It wasn't out of political conviction, believe me. It just seemed like the only thing left to do. When they shipped me off to Vietnam in '65, I didn't care. I'd run out of places to see and had nothing to look forward to."

Karen lowered her eyes. "Helene mentioned you were wounded."

"Did she? Well, it's true. I was in one of the first combat units to go ashore in Da Nang. We were supposed to guard the Air Force base there and scout out the Viet Cong in the surrounding territory. I was there for less than a month when I was out on patrol with some buddies. Somehow—I'm still not sure—a soldier stepped on a booby trap. One of ours, I think. It killed him instantly and seven others. I fell—of course, thrown is more like it—on top of Norman. That's right," he said. "*Our* Norman! That's how we became friends. I saved his life, or at least that's what he insists since I pushed him when I fell. But to tell you the truth, it was out of my hands. The blast sent me flying like I'd been hit by an exploding truck. A metal fragment missed his head by inches, another ripped through my left heel." He pulled off his shoe and sock to show her. A chuck of the bottom of his foot was missing, the surrounding skin calloused and scarred.

Karen grimaced and pulled back instinctively as she looked at the mutilated limb. "Does it hurt?" she asked.

"Not anymore. It did at first. Hell, I don't know what I'd have done without morphine. I spent a couple months at Walter Reed. Had two surgeries. I have a special insert in my shoe so I can walk without limping."

"I see," she said, shielding her face to hide her smug smile.

"Afterwards, I was sent to a VA hospital in Martinsberg, West Virginia. That's where I met Rachel. She was working as an aide in the physical therapy department."

"Really?" said Karen, vainly trying to picture Rachel in a crisp, white uniform.

"When my foot improved, we moved in together. She was only seventeen but already married to a guy who enjoyed beating her up. He tracked her down, and I had the pleasure of busting his nose. To be honest, I did lots more damage than that, and we had no choice but to leave town."

"Is that why you changed your name?"

Rahm grinned. "I'm aware of the rumor. Abraham is my middle name. Rahm is for short. I like it better than my first name."

"And what's that?"

"Gilbert."

Karen placed a hand over her mouth. "Are you serious?"

"I'm afraid so. My mother couldn't bear to name me after my father, so I was named after a dead uncle. And now I'm counting on you to keep that bit of trivia a secret." Karen joined him in laughter before they both settled down.

"So what happened next?"

"Rachel and I … we tried to make a go of it in the conventional way. I pumped gas, she worked in a nursing home, but we both weren't cut out for nine-to-five living. One day, half in jest, I told her about this crazy notion I had to leave everything behind and live in a cave. She took me seriously. I couldn't believe it. But, apparently, she felt as sick of the world as I did.

"We moved back to this county, and Rachel took a job at one of the local hospitals while I spent my time scouting out caves. Finding this lower section was sheer luck. Who'd have thought Dinky Cave held a secret?"

Karen pressed her lips together. *An ugly secret.*

"Talk about providence," said Rahm. "Rachel and I had just gotten a phone when guess who called? Norman! Turns out he now lived here too. Owned a house. I told him my idea and you know what? He didn't think I was crazy either.

"We both contacted old 'Nam buddies. You'd be surprised how many had trouble adjusting, and over time we also found drifters, dissenters, all sorts of rejects who wanted a fresh start. Sure, the numbers whittled down, but that's good 'cause finally we had our core group of true believers. And over a two-year period we planned, lugged building materials, furniture, other essential stuff, until we crossed that final barrier and moved in."

Karen cracked a finger. "You should have turned this into a book instead of losing your mind."

"I assure you I'm sane," said Rahm, dismissing the slur. "Anyway, my spelling stinks. Now, what about you?"

"Not much to tell. I'm just a girl from your typical American family—parents divorced, one brother. I met Jeremy at college." She looked at Rahm for a protracted moment and came to a wary halt.

Rahm broke the silence. "I said a hell of a lot today, didn't I? I'm not sure I like it." He smiled at her, but underneath his droll grin stood a look of savagery which seemed to say: *Now that I've told you everything, you're mine.* Karen's forehead burned as if it were branded with his name; panicking, she rubbed the alleged blot, attempting to hide any evidence, real or imagined.

"I've got to go now," he said, chuckling softly at her angst. "I promised Mary and Helene I'd help settle some dispute. Those two are always at it."

Karen watched him walk away, head held high, a man pleased with his fate. Once again she sat alone with her mushrooms. Heart racing, she leaned over and put her ear way down, touching one on its cap. "Tell me," she said, turning left and right, checking that no human was present to listen in. Satisfied, she continued. "What's to become of me?" When she didn't get an answer, she crumbled, wailing so queerly she sounded like a warped LP that had baked in the sun.

A sudden clamor caused Karen to jerk sideways. Another female, voice loud and sharp, roared into the void, adding to the surrounding tumult. "You're helpless, helpless, helpless," the intruder said. "Helpless and alone."

Karen, recognizing the voice as her own, screamed, rousing her fungal menagerie. Alarmed, they rushed to her defense.

"You're not helpless," they said in unison. "And certainly not alone. You have us."

"Thank you," she said, extending both arms to take them in, hold them close. "You're my angels, my blessings, my saviors. But how will I survive?"

The response came quickly: young ones that had just poked through the dirt that morning bowed their tiny caps with an offer of sacrifice. Obligingly, she popped them into her mouth, swallowing them whole. Then, leaning back, she closed her eyes and sailed off to wonderland, along with her faithful crew of magic mushrooms. When she returned to her room later that day, she bubbled with newfound energy, fortified like a well-fed cat.

#

This time Karen's fully detailed account of Rahm's injury electrified Jeremy. "There it is again. His Achilles' heel! His kiss of death. There must be a way we can use it." He ran his hand across his mouth, thinking. "Also there's one other matter to keep in mind."

"What's that?" said Karen.

"Tom was able to kill two people while they were sleeping. That's when everyone's most vulnerable."

"You're not planning on killing anyone, are you?"

"I won't rule anything out, not even that."

Jeremy's pronouncement made Karen chose her words carefully. She held back her suspicions regarding Tom's so-called accident. Instead she said, "Don't even think about killing. You're no murderer. Besides, I have a better idea." She squared her shoulders, preparing for a fierce objection. "I think we should become members."

"What?" he barked, shocked.

"Don't you see?" she countered. "Then we can vote, and not only that, you can challenge Rahm for the leadership."

Jeremy stared at her with dinner-plate eyes. "Me? That's insane!"

"Maybe so, but sooner or later something's bound to pay off, and with you in control, you can set new precedent, change opinions. By the way, I forgot to ask … the other morning when Randy came to go fishing—where were you?"

A devious grin spread on his twitching lips. "Exploring. And not only that. I've gone more than once. I just lay a trail of string behind me to keep from getting lost. On my way back, I roll it up again. Oh, one other thing." He paused as if waiting to hear the sound of applause. "You must have noticed that funny green glow from the wild mushrooms. I discovered that if I rub them on my skin, it shines like a flashlight. It only lasts a short time; still, it's better than nothing." To demonstrate, he moved his arms from right to left, his fingertips outstretched and pointing like tiny incandescent bulbs.

Karen yelped, thrilled by the news. "Tell me," she said, "what else did you find? Any promising routes heading up?"

"No, nothing yet, but I'm going to keep trying till I succeed."

"What if someone discovers what you're doing?"

"So who cares? What'll they do? Kill me? Hey, want to come with me next time?"

Karen pasted a sloppy kiss on his face. "Yes!" she said. "Of course I do."

"Good. Then let's get some sleep. We'll talk more tomorrow."

"Jeremy," she said, fidgeting in the darkness. "There is one more thing."

He rolled back in her direction.

"It's been so long," she began. "We can't keep going on like this."

The taste in Jeremy's mouth turned bitter. "I'm sorry," he said, the gist of her words ringing in his ears, "but it's out of my control. I don't have the urge."

"But we could try."

"No," he said, stinging her with the finality of his decision. "I won't give them the satisfaction. Now go to sleep."

Karen closed her eyes, but sleep didn't come to her or to him.

#

Karen had just finished turning the guano when she heard him approach. By now she recognized his walk, fast and confident, but with a heavy step on one side followed by a lighter one on the other.

She was feeling more nervous than usual, knowing it was the last day of Rahm's rotation and she still couldn't "see" with her voice. She felt determined to make this the day.

He approached her jauntily, purposely teasing her with a double entendre. "I like fast women," he said, noting both the shovel in her hand and the curve of her hip. "Couldn't wait for me, could you?"

"I was hurrying so we could get down to business." She threw the shovel, missing him by inches to be sure there was no misunderstanding her intentions.

"Sorry, didn't mean to upset you. Look, I'd be happy to start right away, only there's something … a surprise I want to show you first. It won't take long."

"Oh? What's that?"

To make up for his inappropriate quip, he extended his hand like a gentleman, grasping her gently above the elbow. "Come. See for yourself. I promise you won't be disappointed."

He led her down a new path, keeping hold of her arm, so that she wouldn't trip on loose pebbles or ruts. He stopped near a tiny stream where the water formed a shallow pool similar to the one where they did their laundry. After placing a lantern on a flat rock, he took two candles from his pocket and lit them too. The glow from the lights cast yellow beams on the water.

Standing close, he entwined his fingers with hers. "Happy birthday."

"What?" she said, eyes open with surprise as she pulled away, disengaging herself from his grip.

"Brian said it's your birthday. You know how he never forgets a date."

"Is it really? Funny, I haven't kept track." Her words and tone shot forth a note of disdain. He brushed it aside.

"I wanted to give you something nice," he said. "But I couldn't think of anything appropriate. Then I thought of this."

Curious, Karen stepped closer and looked into the water, only inches in depth, noticing glossy white marble-sized beads suspended throughout. Some had sunk toward the bottom where they sat unmoving like a cluster of grapes. "Why, they're pearls," she said, pleased by the discovery. "How did they get here?"

With her words and tone ceding wonder, Rahm steered his answer to complement hers. "They're cave pearls," he said. "They're made of calcite deposits, just like the other formations evolving here, but in this case they grew around a pebble or a piece of sand. Magnificent, aren't they?"

"Yes," she agreed, and before he could stop her, she reached in and drew one out. Immediately, it turned to powder in her palm. "I-I'm sorry," she said. "I didn't realize."

"My fault. I should have warned you." He inched closer, scanning her neck. "A strand of pearls would look lovely on you, but I'm afraid you'll have to appreciate these gems in their natural surroundings."

Karen's lips began trembling and she automatically clenched her jaw to hide any perceived weakness. His words "natural surroundings" struck a chord and she visualized Dorothy tapping her heels, declaring, *"There's no place like home."* How long could she and Jeremy survive in this place full of wonders, yes, but also lightyears from all she knew and loved?

"How about we move on to your lesson?" said Rahm.

Karen agreed, remembering her primary goal. *Focus, focus*, she told herself.

They looked for a dry level space and sat down. This time it took Karen mere seconds to dig through the sand, fall through the treasure chest, and arrive at the palace with its upside-down glaciers.

She didn't stay long. Shivering from the cold, she closed the palace's ice-encrusted door and wandered, lost yet unafraid, shadowed by her sense of purpose, until she arrived at a familiar city with a familiar street. "Why, I'm home," she said, recognizing her apartment building in Baltimore.

She climbed the stairs, her breath coming fast as she took that final step onto the third-floor landing. Realizing she'd misplaced her key, she almost panicked, but fortunately the door flew open on its own accord. Inside, the sealed-tight drapes hid the sun, but she made her way down the darkened hall by feeling with her hands. She found the bedroom, where a cloaked stranger waited. She had expected him. Worn out and famished, she let him lead her to the bed where he fed her delicacies, unfamiliar yet delicious, sweet and sour. She opened her mouth for more.

An orchestra played a slow two-step, and the cloaked stranger said, "May I?" in an invitation to join him in a dance. He didn't wait for an answer, simply held out a hand and drew her up where they cleaved like magnets, forming a whole, like interlocking pieces of a puzzle. The music ebbed to an undertone and she heard a click-click and opened her eyes, stunned to see Rahm, his mouth upon hers. Knees shaking, she dropped to the ground, had a moment of clarity, but the force proved irresistible, and her arms reached out.

"Close your eyes if you wish," she heard him say, "but keep your mouth open. It's the only way."

He pulled off his shirt and placed her head upon it as he began pulling off her clothes. A sax soloist began a bluesy jazz instrumental and she smoldered and slithered as Rahm kissed her neck, shoulders, and each breast in turn, causing her to forget everything but his hands on her, feeling her, stroking her. It had been so long since anyone had aroused her in this way.

Timidly at first, she began to explore his body in turn. It felt both solid and compact, every inch teeming with muscle. His skin felt rough, almost like sandpaper, simultaneously tickling and scratching her hands. Running her fingers over his buttocks, so neat and lean, she became aware of how different he was from her. And she loved the difference.

He licked her tummy, leaving little red love bites, and she groaned with pleasure, spurring him on. He lowered his body upon her, careful not to burden her with his full weight; nevertheless, she momentarily flinched as he pressed his hardness against her. The music shifted, became faster, and she opened her eyes.

Above her a disco ball, with thousands of tiny mirrored facets, spun hypnotically, surrounding her with a light show of flashing, bright rainbow colors. Her body pulsed to the pounding beat of a synthesizer's strings and horns, reverberating off the walls as she writhed to a love-to-love-you female quaver.

Again he admonished, "Keep your mouth open." Not caring or understanding why, she did as told.

She sailed on a boat. A violent gale whipped the small sloop, threatening to tip it over. When finally it did, she fell into the water, which wasn't really water but a slimy, essential ooze made of the basic elements of life. Protozoans merged with starfish, which merged with lizards, and now her. As an ancient sea creature lashed her with its tail, her body contracted with a pleasure she could no longer contain. She sprang up, her back arched at an aberrant angle. She hung like a puppet suspended by wires until she collapsed to the ground, exhausted. Curling on her side, she rubbed her eyes, murmuring, "I just need a minute."

When she came to later, she had no idea how long she'd been asleep. She rose on her elbows, dismayed to find no sign of Rahm, and she wondered if she had imagined it all. Placing a hand on her bare abdomen, she groaned, her nostrils flaring. A trace of his smell had mingled with hers, and she knew it had been real. With the stark implication of what she had done flashing before her, she screamed, "Idiot! Moron! How could I be so stupid?" Picking up a rock, she hurled it into the pool, disturbing the pearls. *Her pearls.* "Fuck them!" she cried.

Hastily she draped a shirt around her body and made her way to the bathing area, where she jumped in without giving a thought to the frigid water. While she scrubbed off the lingering evidence of the morning's activity, she heard a small scratching sound on a rock and turned in its direction. Narrowing her eyes into slits, she still couldn't make out what it was. She opened her mouth. "Click-click." It was only a bug.

#

"How did everything go today?" asked Jeremy later that evening.

"F-fine," said Karen.

"Did you learn anything important? You must have more to say than that."

"I'm sorry," she said. "I'm tired. If you don't mind I'd like to go to sleep." Without waiting for a response, she flicked off her muddy shoes and climbed into bed, burying her head under the pillow.

Jeremy looked down at her, a helpless, anguished creature searching for a semblance of peace and safety. Guilt-ridden, he clutched at his chest as he faced an ugly truth. He'd been so involved in his own struggle, his loss, his pain, that he'd hardly given her a thought. Obviously she too was suffering.

"Karen," he whispered.

She groaned.

"I'm sorry about how I've been behaving. I know I've been ignoring you and I want to fix that right now. I was worried, you see, about you becoming pregnant, but from all indications, it's almost impossible in these surroundings. And besides, you were right—we can't go on like this forever."

Before she could object, he climbed in beside her, smothering her mouth with his. "I love you," he said, causing tears to well up in her eyes and flow toward her ears. Jeremy, mistaking them for symbols of joyful celebration, licked them away, not knowing his own moment of celebration was tinged with the height of deceit.

Chapter 15

Rahm sought out Randy for a private chat, waiting until the day's chores were through. "How's your special assignment going?"

"You mean with Jeremy?" he asked.

Rahm moved his head up and down.

"Good," said Randy. "Just like you said, I'm working undercover."

He moved directly in front and gripped the boy by both shoulders. "I knew I could count on your help, and you know why I asked you to spend time with him?"

Randy squirmed. "I think so."

"You're old enough to understand what he did at the lake?"

"You mean tried to kill himself?"

"Yes. That's what I mean. How's he seem to you?"

"Better, I think. Besides fishing, he asks me lots of question about the cave. We take walks and he tells me about life above. You know, there's a place called Disney World with rides and stuff. And kids go to school too—every day; they learn about history and science. Jeremy says we landed a man on the moon in '69 and there's been more landings since. Is it true?"

"It's true," said Rahm.

"Wow! I'd like to be an astronaut when I grow up. I miss seeing the stars. You still taking me above like you said, right?"

Rahm hesitated. "Of course. When you're old enough."

"I'm old enough now. I'll be twelve soon. Can you take me to Disney World?"

Rahm pressed his forefinger vertically against the midpoint of his mouth. "That costs lots of money," he said. "Hey, you know what, Randy? You don't need to follow Jeremy around so much anymore. In fact, Norman needs help fixing the cabinets. They're falling apart. I'll check when he's going to start. You interested?"

Randy tipped his head. "I guess so, as long as there's time for me to start school. Karen said I should learn to read and she's going to teach me. Math, too. I better go ask her when my first class begins."

Rahm remained behind as Randy ran off. He had an unsettling feeling. Perhaps his plan hadn't worked out the way he had hoped. Then again, maybe it did.

#

Before breakfast and after dinner, Karen and Jeremy investigated the myriad passageways in what seemed an impossible maze. Karen took the lead, lighting the way. She dared not use echolocation, fearing he'd hear the first few clicks and discover her secret. Jeremy followed, struggling to both lay the string and sketch a diagram of their route. So far all attempts had ended in disappointment as one tunnel after another brought them to a dead end or back to their starting point.

"This is damned discouraging," said Jeremy, tearing that evening's sketch in two.

"Don't do that," admonished Karen.

"Why not? Fuck it! It's good for nothing."

"That's not true," said Karen, crinkling her nose. Unlike her, Jeremy rarely used the F-word. "We are making headway. At least we know which ways *not* to go."

Jeremy raised a single eyebrow, a talent he had used as a reporter, thinking that it made him look clever. Now it was just a habit. "Okay, you've got a point." He jammed the paper into his pocket. "I guess my patience is wearing thin. Maybe we should head back."

"It's still early and we haven't tried that tunnel yet."

Jeremy looked in the direction she pointed. "Haven't you had enough punishment for one day?"

Karen persisted. "We may as well try. It's right here."

"Okay, okay," he said. "But I'm sure we're just wasting time in this area. Well, let's get it over with."

Soon they were shuffling sideways in a narrow space with Karen still in the lead. When the tunnel finally widened, the ceiling, as if out for mischief, dropped a foot and Karen and Jeremy both skimmed the tops of their heads. "Slow down," said Jeremy, wiping what he hoped wasn't blood from his scalp. "I'm pooped and my back hurts."

"Mine too," said Karen, "but we do seem to be heading up."

Jeremy stood still, trying to fix his internal compass. "You know, I think you're right."

Karen looked back, wary. "Better not get excited. It's probably nothing."

Despite her warning, they moved faster. When Jeremy walked straight into a column, bumping his nose, he didn't complain. When a rat scampered across Karen's shoe, she didn't scream. *Did it recently come from above?* she wondered.

Lying flat on their bellies like lizards, they wriggled over huge boulders using a swimming-like motion, with arms circling forward as they pushed with their feet. Eventually they found themselves in a large room. Jumping to the ground, they strode about counting the offshoots. "Dammit!" yelled Karen, throwing a rock against the wall. "There are four ways to go and I'm exhausted. What do we do?"

Jeremy caught his breath. "First thing is to keep our cool. That was your advice. Remember? But just think! This is a great find, and it also happened at the right time." He held up the ball of string, now shrunk down to thimble size. "It's probably best if we go back. If we don't, someone's bound to miss us and come looking." He lifted the string again. "This was from our backpack, but I'm sure there's more in the supply area. We can check later." He gave Karen a hug, thrilled by their progress. She beamed in response, both at his display of affection and the possibility of a real discovery.

After retracing their steps, they paused at the end of the tunnel where Jeremy completed the final corrections on his diagram. He turned to his wife. "You can't let anyone see that goofy grin on your face. You look like you discovered America."

"You should see yourself. You'll give everything away without even opening your mouth. I guess we'd both better calm down."

They laughed, letting their excitement drain off, and as a final precaution, Karen bit down on her tongue. "How do I look now?"

"Like you ate a roach."

"Good."

With their expressions fixed at neutral, they strolled through Suburbia and Downtown, continuing on to the supply area, where they found Helene poking through the shelves. "Can't find the fucking tampons," she said.

Karen and Jeremy exchanged glances, mumbled hellos, and went back to their quarters. Jeremy put a finger to his lips, reminding her, "This place is like an echo chamber. We don't want anyone to know our plans."

"Just what are our plans?"

"I've got it all worked out. I'll get up during the night, go back to the supply area, and get the string. Tomorrow you go to the mushroom garden as usual. I'll explore the cave mountain on my own."

"What's the 'cave mountain'?"

"Just a generic term. Everyone uses it for all the passageways leading up, and best of all every last one connects to that supreme place on top: freedom!"

"But I want to come too."

He shook his head. "Won't work. Rachel's your partner this week. If you don't show up in the garden, she'll report back. I can always say I don't feel like working—too depressed or something. They got a taste of my screwy behavior at the lake and won't be suspicious if I momentarily slack off. Tomorrow was supposed to be my last day with Randy. He's starting a new project with Norman. He'll be disappointed, but I'll make up an excuse."

"Why can't we get up early like we usually do?"

"It may take too long. Remember, there are four paths to check out. We'd better play it safe." He smiled in that teasing, lopsided fashion that had first made her fall in love with him. "Don't worry. When I find the way out of this prison, I'll come get you. Just think, Karen: by this time tomorrow, we may be free."

"Please," she said. "Don't say it. Don't even think it. If it happens, I swear I'll go to church every week for the rest of my life, but if it doesn't, well, at least I didn't get my hopes up."

He nodded, kissed her once, then savoring the taste on his lips, kissed her again. As she removed her clothes, he took pleasure in watching. Following suit, he stripped off his own clothes, climbed in beside her, and fell into her waiting arms.

#

Someone smelling of bacon and buttered toast gave her a gentle shake. "Oh, Mom," she said. "It can't be morning already."

"Wake up," said Jeremy. "It's me. You're talking in your sleep."

Karen groaned, rubbed her eyes.

"Look. I got it. The string."

Careful not to show her disappointment as reality set in, she asked, "What time is it?"

"Time to get up. You're running late. You wouldn't believe the mess Helene left—stuff thrown every which way. Norman's sure gonna be pissed. He's such a neatnik, but who cares? I found the string and that's all that counts." He patted the bulge in his pocket.

With Jeremy's help, she heaved her unsteady body to a sitting position and put on the clean change of clothes she had laid out the night before.

"You'd better make an appearance in the dining room. Remember, act natural. I'll stay here until the time is right."

"Aren't you going to get something to eat?"

Jeremy pulled a soggy sandwich from his shirt pocket. "This will do. Remember, tell them I have a stomachache or something."

Karen crossed her fingers and brought them to her lips. Then, reaching over, she marked his cheek with her touch. "Good luck," she said, climbing out of bed as he tumbled in.

Jeremy fell into a light twilight fog, but sprang up upon hearing Randy's approach. He put on an anguished face as he rocked back and forth, clutching his gut. "Sorry kiddo," he groaned, "but I'm not up to it. Be a good boy and catch lots of crayfish."

Randy's face drooped.

"You don't need me," said Jeremy. "You're the best fisherman I've ever seen." Knowing this was to have been their last day together, Jeremy hoped his compliment would neutralize any hard feelings. Then, when he felt certain it was safe to proceed, he placed the two balls of string in his pockets. He left his backpack behind, sprawled across his bed, in case some busybody came by and noticed it missing and surmised he was up to no good. Then, lantern in hand, he slunk off and made his way to where the tunnel branched out, sorry Karen wasn't with him to note his progress. Remembering her Midas touch, he pressed his fingers to his cheek where she had anointed him earlier that morning. Then he took out the second ball of string.

Being methodical, he chose the branch farthest from him, working left to right. He pumped himself up with clichés, certain he'd never succeed on the first try. *Nothing good comes easy.*

He was right. The path, after circling around, exited where the second began. Worse than he'd thought. Now there were only two possibilities left. "Please, please, please," he cried. He resisted the impulse to fall to his knees.

After retrieving his string, he began again. He tried to prepare himself for failure, but after walking an identical number of paces and seeing the pathway continue on unobstructed, he felt a resurgence of hope. "Stay calm," he warned himself, along with an order to slow down and pay attention.

With caution, he planted each foot solidly on the ground, aware each step could lead to potential disaster. Loose stones, a wrong turn, a sudden slip off a ledge, and it would be over. Sweat pooled under his armpits and dripped into his eyes.

When the tunnel kept going, he told himself that it meant nothing. So what if he was heading up? So what if the walls looked a more normal brown instead of the potpourri on the lower levels due to their high mineral content? At any moment, it could end like before with an indifferent finality, leaving him nothing but shattered dreams like the crushed pebbles under his feet.

He slowed down to catch his breath and unbutton his shirt, now totally soaked. He placed the lantern on the ground and extended his arm. "Good God!" he screamed, as his worst fear materialized. The tunnel, though not circling around, came to a comparable fate—a dead end. He pounded the wall with both fists until his knuckles split open. But instead of persisting until he broke a finger (or worse, his whole fist), he stopped. With his thoughts racing a millisecond faster than his hands, he gulped down a swig of foul air. Something else was off. He knew it down to his toes. His toes!

He wiggled them in his shoes, and his thoughts coalesced until the unknown became obvious: the lower half of his body was out of alignment with the upper half as if his feet were trying to walk on, leaving his torso to struggle behind.

He dropped to the ground and saw that—"Dear Jesus!"—the tunnel continued after all. On closer inspection, it looked as if someone had carved out the entranceway by himself. Jeremy ran his finger along the rim. Yes, it felt smooth, too even to have happened naturally. Perhaps it had been a tiny hole once, too small to climb through. Yet someone saw fit to expand it. *Why? Could this be a way out?*

With the possibility of escape before him, he put all answers on hold, and flattened his body on the ground. Arms extended, he squirmed through the foot-long passageway, eating dirt and undulating like a snake with a series of forward thrusts. After exiting, he turned around and reached back to retrieve the lantern, careful not to knock it over. He stood up, grateful the ceiling allowed him to stand to his full height.

As he struggled on, he remembered his mother's advice before she'd died: in the face of adversity, puff yourself up to the size of a truck, a plane, a rocket. You decide what size is needed, she had told him, but whatever you decide, remain coolheaded. You can always break down later, but not when it's time to act.

With that in mind, Jeremy trudged onward, visualizing himself a hero, the last remaining soldier in a lost platoon, until he arrived at a point where longing mixed with reality. The mixture fused, and peaked, forming a pinnacle where he could no longer trust his senses. Light appeared to be infiltrating the cave. Was this the equivalent of a mirage or reality? *Please, please, let it be real!*

He rushed ahead, breathing heavily. In the distance, he could make out an open space with a heaven-sent radiance. Like a quasar in an ancient galaxy, its glint seemed to burst into flame. Being unaccustomed to natural light for so long, he shielded his eyes as a wail of joy escaped his lips.

He laughed and cried, rolled in the dirt, rose and flapped his arms as if he expected them to lift him and carry him away. For a second, he contemplated forgetting about Karen—just run off where he was safe and free—but he could never do that.

Dizzy from hyperventilating, he staggered as the walls and ceiling swirled before him. Pinpoints wavered, but as a cohesive unit in a choreographed display. The tiny dancers pulsed, seemed alive, but of course they couldn't be. Certain he was having visual hallucinations, he blinked, wiped the film from his eyes, and concentrated. Then he heard it: intermittently at first, then a city of sounds, some soft and rustling, others high-pitched and chirping. Unsure what it was, he remained still as the acoustics swelled into a crescendo. At the same time, he became aware of a familiar odor, pungent and foul. *Like shit*, he thought, taking another sniff. *Definitely, like shit.*

The sight, the sound, the smell … *What was it Rahm said months ago?* Months that now seemed like years. Jeremy, using his mind, filled in the blanks. *Of course. Bats. Guano.*

Thousands, perhaps millions, were packed together like peas in a can, but more noteworthy was the merciful hole he could see farther off where they left the cave on their nightly hunt for insects. His stomach pitched at the thought of passing beneath them, but he told himself they were harmless, even shy creatures with a misunderstood reputation; besides, they were his saviors and he should be grateful. They would lead him and Karen out.

He ran his eyes from the floor to the ceiling. There appeared to be only one feasible way up, but one was quite enough. He licked his lips and headed off to check it out, but froze statue-like as his feet began to stick to the ground. Looking down, he saw brown muddy goo under his shoes. Pulling a rag from his pocket, he reached down to clean them off.

"I wouldn't bother if I were you."

He recognized the voice; he'd know it anywhere.

"I'm afraid this is not the answer to your dreams," said a poker-faced Rahm, emerging like some evil ghost creature from the reaches of hell. His lilting tone made clear his amusement at the situation's unfolding absurdity. "If you look closely, you'll see it's impossible for you to get out this way."

Jeremy, still reeling from the shock, stood speechless as Rahm continued. "You were about to touch the guano. If you walk out another ten feet, you'll be in a sea of filth with all kinds of live bugs—worms, maggots, cockroaches, spiders—crawling in your mouth. Years ago scientists came in from above to study the bats. That time's over and now no one comes. And, by the way, don't bother with that fourth offshoot. Just like this one, it'll lead to a disappointing end. Of course, this finale's far worse—a stinking, suffocating, gruesome way to die."

Jeremy stared at the world outside, within his reach yet so far away. Nothing mattered, and the tenuous connections that had held him together gave way in an instant. Beyond desperation, he swung out toward Rahm and was surprised to find he had connected by hearing the thud of bone hitting bone. A triumphant "Ha" had barely escaped his mouth when he felt the air forced from his lungs by a series of expertly placed blows to the trunk of his body. His head spun around and he clutched his chest and midsection before staggering to the ground. Rahm, after satisfying himself that his opponent's injuries weren't serious, left at once, having the decency to let him suffer in private.

#

Karen finished with the mushrooms and began walking back to wait for Jeremy's return. With each step, her joy increased until it pooled in her chest like the swell of the sea. Then, drawing the curtain around her and Jeremy's room, she totally dropped her guard and drifted off to that warm beach he had promised to take her to in exchange for coming to this godforsaken hole in the ground. As she was about to sip her White Russian, she heard his approach, unexpectedly wobbly and unstable, one leg dragging behind the other. The glass vanished from her hand, along with its contents of vodka, cream, and sweet, frost-nipped liqueur.

The dark rings under Jeremy's dead eyes spoke volumes, yet he felt compelled to recount all the details, from his first gleam of success to his ultimate state of despair.

Karen rose, howled in anger. "It isn't fair to have come so close! I hate Rahm. I hate them all. Are you sure it's impossible to escape that way?"

Jeremy nodded, tears streaking his face.

"Still, I want to look. Take me there."

"I don't want to go back."

"Then I'll go by myself."

"What for? It's hopeless."

"Because I need to see for myself," said Karen. "To make it real. But also because I want to see the sun again." Karen reached for her husband, to give and receive consolation, but before she could touch him, he collapsed onto the mattress, whimpering out loud.

"Tomorrow," he said. "We'll go tomorrow. Right now I have to rest." Quivering like a feverish child, he pulled up his knees till they almost touched his chin. Karen remained close by, dry-heaving, no longer able to help him or even herself. Finally fatigue overpowered sorrow, and she toppled sideways onto the cold ground, letting the earth mix with her own tears.

The next day, as promised, Jeremy led her up the now hateful course without bothering to use the string; he no longer cared about nor feared getting lost. From the smell, Karen knew when they were getting close. Working with guano every day, she'd grown accustomed to its odor, as Rachel had predicted. All the same, here, in such concentrated amounts, she felt her throat close in protest and a wheeze escape her mouth.

Jeremy had already warned her to shield her eyes from the light, but as she opened them with the expectation of seeing fiery orange streaks, she looked at him in puzzlement. "Where's that sunlight you mentioned? All I see is a gray smudge."

Jeremy stared, the lines near his mouth deepening. "What are you talking about? Can't you see it?" His jaw dropped as he grasped that she couldn't.

"Oh, Jeremy!" she screamed as the realization hit her too. "I'm going blind."

He held her to his chest to offer the small measure of comfort he still possessed for the giving. Then, together, they cried in grief, in rage, and in horror for the death of deliverance.

Chapter 16

For Karen's sake, Jeremy kept going, but just barely. He still explored but only on those occasions when guilt pushed through. Rahm, aware of his prisoner's chronic depression, once again sent Randy to accompany him out on the lake, but Jeremy, a picture of defeat, no longer attempted to pry information from the boy.

Karen, too, tottered at the precipice of despair, made worse as images of unfinished shapes with tail-like appendages took hold of her dreams. Although she could no longer remember them in the morning, they left her drained as if she had dragged a thousand-pound secret on her back. As a result, she often arrived late at the garden.

Yet more troubling was the queasy prickliness in her stomach. Each day became more difficult than the one before. She struggled to keep food down. The thought of getting sick in a place without modern medical facilities frightened her and she tried telling herself it was just nerves, but a seed of anxiety, growing like a tumor, stroked her intuition.

After a period of constant nausea, she noticed additional changes: her breasts, her two measly protuberances, began to enlarge and feel tender. Her face took on a fuller, almost puffy shape. Fortunately, Jeremy was too disheartened to notice.

Unable to put it off a moment longer, Karen snuck into Brian's quarters when he was busily feasting on seconds after a day of good fishing. She found the latest calendar he'd spoken about on top of the minutes from the last community meeting. She counted the days. She counted again. *Dammit! A full two weeks late.*

She'd been late before, but never two weeks. *It can't be*, she told herself, running her hands over her abdomen, rock hard from her daily physical labor. For a moment, she felt a measure of consolation. *I'm sure I'll get my period today or tomorrow.* Instead her nausea increased.

Mere days later, she awoke with an urgent need to vomit. She knew she wouldn't make it to the toilet and struggled a few feet from the bed where the contents of her stomach erupted with projectile spasms.

Jeremy, hearing her mews and groans, sat up and rushed to her side. "What's going on?"

"I'm sorry," cried Karen, wiping her mouth on her shirt. "Oh, Jeremy. What am I going to do? What are *we* going to do?"

"What are you talking about? Are you sick?"

"Yes," she said. "Sick and pregnant. Oh my God. Oh my God. What's to become of us now?"

#

Joan had just returned from her doctor's appointment to find Carl hungry as usual and sitting at the table, nibbling on last night's leftovers.

"The rabbit died," she said, turning off the TV so he'd be sure to hear her announcement.

Carl scrunched his face, annoyed and confused. "Hey, put it back on. The Bruins are playing. They're about to give the score. And what are you talking about?"

"I'm pregnant!"

Carl dropped his spoon into his bowl of soup; a spot splashed on his shirt, but he barely noticed. He looked at her as if she had just fallen from the sky and sprouted three eyes. "You kidding?"

"No," she said, suddenly afraid. "We planned this, after all."

Carl pressed his fists against his cheeks so hard they stung. "Jeez Louise!" he said. "I can't believe it happened so fast."

"I guess we hit the jackpot at the get-go. You're not sorry, are you?"

"I don't know. I mean, no. Of course not. I'm just surprised, that's all. In fact, flabbergasted is more like it." Looking at her face, now bearing worry lines along her mouth, Carl went to her, drew her up, and took her in his arms. "It's great, Joan. Really! I just can't believe it. I mean, you don't look pregnant."

Joan laughed with relief. "I guess I'm just a little bit pregnant," she said, repeating that oft-used joke as she pushed her palm against her flat belly.

"Hey," he said. "Did they really have to kill a rabbit?"

"No," she said. "All the little cottontails are fine, and so am I. In fact, the doctor said I'm healthy as a horse."

"Wow," he said. "Imagine me a father! Who would have guessed?" Carl turned the radio on, moving the dial until he found the perfect song. With Billy Joel singing, "Just The Way You Are," he twirled her around the room.

#

Time stopped. Someone coughed and shuffled in the distance. As Jeremy's head slumped against the stone wall, the corners of his mouth drooped into folds of anguish and disbelief. "That's impossible. At least, *almost* impossible. Tell me you're joking."

"I wish I was."

"Karen, are you sure?" He watched her dry-heave, leaving traces of half-digested food on her mouth. There was no need to ask again. "Well, that's just great;

it's just what we need." Lowering his face, he pressed his fingers against his temples. When he spoke again, his words and tone shifted, becoming clear and calm. "I suppose we both knew this could happen, even though the odds seemed slim. But if you really are pregnant, we have no choice but to accept it. There's not much we can do about it, is there?"

Karen sat silently. She thumbed through a book and then tossed it away. She picked up another and did the same. Finally she gathered her nerve and asked for clarification. "What do you mean by 'not much'?"

Jeremy answered, without any further hesitation, surprising himself with his position and resolve. "Abortion would be out of the question down here. No one would do it, and if anything went wrong ... No! I won't even think about it. And besides"—he reached over and placed a hand on her belly—"if you're pregnant, it's our child in there. *My child*. I couldn't hurt it, and I'm sure, after thinking it over, you couldn't either."

"But Jeremy," she said, forgetting to lower her voice as she wailed with frustration, "the timing! And not only that. Don't you see? We've fallen into their trap."

Jeremy ground his teeth. "I know and, damn it, that's the worst part. But it's beyond our control, and anyway, there's a plus side to this."

"Plus side? You've got to be kidding!"

"I never thought much about fatherhood before," he said. "I figured some day in the future. Way off in the future. But now I have a purpose again. Don't you see? For the past few weeks I've been a dead man. Nothing mattered. Now I have a reason to live, and a reason to get us out of here. And I will, Karen. I won't let my baby be born into captivity."

Hearing a harsh laugh, Jeremy stopped, caution written in the deepening horizontal lines across his brow. Karen grabbed his shoulder, and they both realized their mistake—speaking too loudly, too openly—and turned in the direction of the eavesdropper.

"What makes you think it's your baby, Jeremy?" said a female voice. He knew immediately whose voice and waited for Mary to creep in from the shadows.

Fixing her predatory, birdlike eyes on Karen, Mary said, "Tell him. Tell him what you did." The veins in Mary's temple stood out, blue and pulsating under her skin. The ferocity behind her pulled-back lips exposed her gums, fiery and red, revealing hatred—an about-to-explode-hatred.

"What's this about?" said Jeremy, shaking his head.

"I-I," said Karen.

Mary guffawed. "Can't tell him, can you? Well, I will and gladly." She flicked her tongue, spewing forth bullets disguised as words which hit their target right on the mark. "You betrayed us all. Me. Jeremy. Even yourself. I could overlook your betrayal if not for your supreme stupidity, although I suppose Jeremy will have to make his own choice. But what I can't forgive is that you're having his baby. *His!*" Her fevered eyes shifted from Karen to Jeremy.

Jeremy's skin burned, and he kneaded the back of his neck. "What's she talking about, Karen?"

Karen opened her mouth, but nothing came out.

Mary immediately cleared up the confusion. "I'll tell you. I'll tell you everything. It's Rahm! Rahm's baby!"

Torn and bloodied from Mary's caustic tongue, Karen stumbled backward, barely recognizable as if her whole body, from top to bottom, had been exchanged with someone else's. Others, hearing the commotion, crowded around.

"I was supposed to be next!" Mary screamed. "How could you? Now they'll never let you go. Never! It's all your fault!"

Jeremy went to his wounded wife. "Tell me she's lying. Please! And not with Rahm. Tell me she's lying."

Karen crouched down, head brushing knees, keening as if she were at a funeral.

"She can't tell you that," said Mary, "because it's true. I was there when it happened, over by the lake. I saw everything. Their silly games. Their flirtation. I saw it all."

Jeremy's open, beseeching hands rounded into threatening hooks. Rahm and Brian stood nearby, ready to jump in if necessary.

"Do it!" begged Karen. "Go ahead. Kill me."

Instead his expression shifted from love to hate before fixing into a rigid mold that said *I never knew you.*

Karen shrank inward, cowering like a guilty person about to be sentenced. The last thing she remembered was Jeremy walking off without another word. *He'll never be back*, she told herself. "God help me. What have I done?"

#

Jeremy collapsed into folds like the pleated remains of a car totaled in a deadly accident. Although he had only gone a short distance, he fell to the ground, weak and disjointed, unable to breathe. Memories of his life with Karen flashed before his eyes. He knew he should cry, rave, do something to rid himself of the fury pulsing throughout his body; instead he sat there, immobilized by grief, the victim of a bad joke, pretending to go along with the mockery to spare himself further shame.

I should have done it, he thought. *Killed her. First her, then me.* Realizing it wasn't too late, his mouth shifted perversely, one side going up, the other down, while his mind, with the help of willing fingers, considered the best way to proceed: strangling or stabbing. He imagined them both. Strangling, he decided; he'd watch her face as she succumbed.

He lay still for hours, obsessing, until crazed with madness and feeling less than human, he crawled, then stumbled upright, along a passageway. Hearing movement, he realized he was no longer alone. "Who's there?" he said.

Lily struck a match, lighting a candelabrum. "I'm sorry," she said. "Don't you know where you are?"

Jeremy sneered at the two fertility gods: the larger male one and the recently completed female with its stone adornment hanging from its neck. Together they were symbols of an ugly act which spoke of the worst type of duplicity. He got up to leave, but Lily's questions stopped him. "Wait," she said. "Is something wrong? I heard yelling before. Can I help?"

"Can you teach me to fly? Can you save my soul? No, of course not, but sure, you can help. Why not?"

He let his eyes roam over her form before resting on the small, triangular mound under her flimsy nightdress. "You want to be useful? Take off that silly gown and lie still."

"But—"

"And shut up while you're at it."

"There's no need to be rude. It's just that I thought—I mean, what about your wife? Norman warned me."

"Wife! I have no wife."

Lily opened her mouth, then closed it. She crossed her arms and yanked the little bit of fluff that passed for covering over her head. Only a thin cord with an irregularly shaped rock remained on her body.

Jeremy reached out and touched the hateful symbol lying against her skin. He twisted the figurine, causing the cord to cut into Lily's flesh.

"Stop it!" she screamed, but Jeremy persisted, oblivious to her cries. He continued to twist and pull until Lily raked her nails across his hand. He finally let go but grabbed her arms, pinning them behind her back. She swiveled at the waist and freed herself. Flailing pell-mell, she found his hair, pulled hard, coming away with a few strands. Jeremy yelled. She spat at his face, and he spat back, pushing her down.

Lily looked up and stopped fighting. "Who are you?" she screamed. "You're just like the others. Bastards!"

Jeremy flinched, pulled back, unable to make sense of what was happening.

In the mayhem, Lily grabbed her nightdress and fled.

Now alone in this hateful, decadent spot, Jeremy wrapped himself in his arms, trembling like a fledgling cast from its nest. He pounded his head with his fists until all thoughts, all feelings were blocked from his mind. Finally, overcome with exhaustion, his head bobbed back and forth and he fell into a restless sleep.

By morning all the candles had burned out.

#

Mary stood guard, waiting for Jeremy to open his eyes. She relit the wicks and her face appeared softened and unlined in the flames' mellow glow. Surprisingly, there was concern written in the set of her mouth and the slump of her shoulders.

"I don't know what took place between you and Lily," she said, "but she won't come back while you're here. You'll have to leave; the men are waiting."

Jeremy snickered and grunted. "Big fucking deal."

Mary overlooked his foul language and disposition, saying, "I've set up a new place for you. I've already moved your belongings. I hope that's okay."

Before he could answer, her nostrils twitched and she placed a hand across his mouth. "Shh. Rachel's coming. It's time for her hocus-pocus. By the way, I hear she's planning ongoing services in the chapel on Sundays."

"Chapel? Where's that?"

"At the end of the trail. Shh. Here she comes."

Rachel arrived carrying a cheesy white substance, its pungent smell filling the room. She placed the bowl on the altar and, bowing low, spoke to the gods, asking forgiveness for not thinking of this offering sooner. With her task complete, she acknowledged Mary and Jeremy. "It's royal jelly," she explained. "Queen bees use it to lay eggs. Rahm brought it back from his last trip. Came straight from a bee farm. We'll add it to the food for the ovulating women. By the way," she said, looking at Mary. "Can I have your ring?"

Mary touched the red stone on the fourth finger of her right hand. "You can but you may not," she said with a snort. "Besides, what do you want it for?"

"Rubies are good for fertility. We can add it to the altar." She opened her palm, thrusting it at Mary as if expecting immediate compliance.

"You nuts or something?" said Mary. "You most certainly may not have it."

The corners of Rachel's lips turned downward. "You always were selfish, only thinking of yourself." She yanked off her own ring. "It's an emerald. Opens hearts, not wombs, but I guess it will have to do."

She placed the ring among the other amulets on the altar and picked up one of the sacred books. She began to read.

"'And he will love thee, and bless thee, and multiply thee: he will also bless the fruit of thy womb.

"'Thou shalt be blessed above all people: there shall not be male or female barren among you, or among your cattle.'"

"Cattle?" said Jeremy, inching closer to Mary. "What is she talking about?"

Mary scoffed, mocking Rachel from behind. Still, she took care to speak in a whisper. "She's a flip-flopper when it comes to religion. Also a fanatic, but worse, a hypocrite. Come on. Let's go."

"Where?" he asked.

"Don't worry. I prepared a place for us both."

"What do you mean 'both'?"

"You'll see. Follow me."

Mary led him to a small space hidden behind a huge column, which provided a measure of privacy. On the ground were two twin mattresses, pushed together. His few possessions, packed into a few boxes, rested on one.

Jeremy's mouth formed the shape of the letter O, his brow furrowed, and his eyebrows rose like twin peaks. "What the hell's going on?"

Mary wiped her sweaty palms on her pants. "You need a place to stay and so do I."

"What are you talking about? You're married to Brian."

Mary kept her voice flat. Only her trembling fingers, hidden behind her back, divulged an honest assessment of her feelings. "The man's a beast, and I've only stayed with him all these years because I took a vow: 'until death do us part.' But you know what? In some cultures you merely have to declare you're divorced and it's official. Therefore, I make you my witness." She stretched her neck, straightened her shoulders, and stuck out her chin. "I'm divorced!" she said with proud defiance. Immediately she felt a wave of relief, adding a silent prayer of gratitude for her newfound release from bondage.

To Jeremy she said, "I'm sure you hate me for telling you about Karen and Rahm. But I'm a believer in truth. My upbringing, I guess. And I know I'm nothing to look at compared to Karen, but I'm offering myself to you as a friend or"—she lowered her eyes—"a lover. It's up to you, but whatever you choose there's one thing you can count on: I'll never let you down. You see, I also know what it's like to be disappointed by those we love. Those we trust. Anyway … I'm sorry about Karen."

"Don't apologize. I'm glad you told me. Still, she's the only woman I ever truly loved. But strangely enough, now I feel nothing. Like she never existed."

"I know what you're saying," said Mary. "Brian was different, too, years ago. He called me his goddess when we first married. Even told me I was beautiful. Imagine that!" She avoided Jeremy's face, afraid he would laugh.

"It's okay, Mary. I'll stay here with you. That is, if you'll keep your promise to help me escape."

Mary's pulse raced at his touch. "I will," she said. "Count on it. I'm a man of my word."

Jeremy, standing almost a head taller than she, said, "No way you're a man. I'm fully aware of that fact."

Mary turned lobster red. Her knees started to buckle. If he had not been holding on to her, she would have sunk to the ground, just as she had years ago when watching "Elvis the Pelvis" gyrating on the Ed Sullivan show.

As Jeremy took her in his arms, Mary felt the solid muscles of his chest pressing against her soft, generous breasts. He pulled her tighter until she could barely breathe, but the sensation was delightful, sending hot and cold currents throughout her body. Mary gasped.

#

Following a sleepless night, Karen decided she could no longer remain in the area she and Jeremy had shared as husband and wife. Despite the knifelike pounding in her head, she piled her belongings on top of her mattress and dragged it to the mushroom garden. After several more trips the job was done, and she returned for a final look.

Except for dirt, rocks, and useless rubbish, all that remained were painful reminders, and she wiped the raw skin under her eyes, burning from the flow of tears. Doubling over in grief, she sat on the bare earth and ran her hand along its cold surface. Her fingertips brushed against something hard; something smooth, round, and familiar. "No, not that!" she wailed. Her eyes narrowed as she rose to her knees, searching carefully. She found it and clutched it to her heart. *How could he?* she asked herself. *How could he throw it away as if it meant nothing?*

Her fingers tightened around the simple gold band as she pictured herself selecting it from a tray of matching his-and-hers sets just over one year ago. She sat down again, screaming obscenities to the uncaring emptiness. With her moans at fever pitch, she didn't hear Norman's approach.

She started, then collapsed as he pulled her toward him. "He'll forgive you," he said. "You'll see. He just needs time."

Karen sobbed, then blew her nose into the tissue Norman offered. "No," she said. "If it had been anyone but Rahm, maybe. But now I'm all alone."

"No you're not. You have me." He circled her with a protective arm. "Any time you need to talk, day or night, you know where I am."

Karen placed her head on his shoulder. "I won't forget. You're the only friend I have."

But she had misspoken, and after he had left and the shock had begun to subside, she remembered her mushrooms. Although not friends in the usual sense, they were friends nonetheless. Not only were they steady, loyal companions, they gave her a reason to go on, a lifeline to cling to.

She got up from the ground and brushed off her clothes. Removing her own ring, she placed it alongside Jeremy's—together again if only on a rudimentary level—inside her palm. She kissed them both, symbols of eternal love, and wrapped them in a clean rag, tucking them safely inside her pocket. With a final glance, she blinked away the last of her tears and left for her new quarters, her boggy nook, where the mushrooms, her fungal family, were waiting. Work would now be her sole salvation.

Chapter 17

Brian beamed, proud to be chosen to preside over this once-a-year election, but after banging the rock on the table and getting nothing but indifference and disrespect, he bristled in anger. People continued talking, laughing, playfully poking each other as if his role were merely a joke. Exasperated, he climbed on a chair, waved his arms, and yelled, "Shut up!" This time his efforts proved fruitful, and his eyes popped owl-like, astonished by the quiet faces suddenly staring up at him.

"That's better," he said, climbing down, his tone a mix of satisfaction and admonishment. "And now, let's get down to business. As you know, today is March twenty-first and as we do yearly, we vote for the best candidate to take the reins, ensure our future, and lead us down the right path." He turned to Rahm, who met his gaze with a smile of approval.

"There will be one slight change this year. Since I'm chairing the meeting, David has volunteered to take on the duty of Minute Keeper and will also summarize my notes from our last community meeting. Since we covered some significant issues, please pay close attention. David—"

David walked to the head of the table, flashing his best "on-air" smile. Only his eyes betrayed a glitch. Over the past few months, his vision had steadily diminished so that he now required the use of a magnifying glass to read the small print. Hiding his embarrassment behind a show of authority, he addressed the group.

"At our last meeting we discussed Helene's idea to stagger the work hours. It was voted down. Sorry, Helene," he sniggered, making light of her "Humph."

"On a happier note, we did vote in favor of Karen and Jeremy becoming members of our community with all rights and privileges thereof. Although their requests came separately and took us by surprise, the yeas were unanimous for both. I want to again take the opportunity of welcoming them into our group. Now we are up to eleven adults." His voice rose to a crescendo. "Isn't that great?"

After a round of applause, David took his seat.

"Thank you, David," said Brian with a patronizing wave of his hand. He was about to announce they begin the main event when he noticed Karen staring at Jeremy, who was sitting on the opposite end of the table. He, in turn, seemed to regard her as if she were a piece of furniture. Brian simultaneously chuckled and scratched his head. *Why the hell did they want to become members, anyway? Doesn't make sense.*

He knew they no longer spoke to one another, no longer lived together, yet he perceived something funny—a conspiracy perhaps? In fact, he and Rahm had discussed such a possibility earlier. And Mary? He wouldn't be surprised if she were involved in some type of stunt. Then, noticing teardrops on Karen's cheeks, he switched his musings to one of a more personal nature: Karen's rejection of his advances. *Ha!* he said to himself. *How does it feel to be the object of contempt? Hope it burns like a hot potato.* His upturned lips spread wider, until a double click from Rahm forced him to return to the meeting's primary business.

Picking up a stack of papers, he passed it down the table. Although they'd been doing this the same way each year, he felt obliged to go over the procedure, for the benefit of the inductees. "Elections are won by simple majority," he explained, "and on the sheet before you is the list of candidates. There's also two columns, one marked *yes*, the other *no*. Just check the box of your choice."

"Excuse me," said Karen.

Brian frowned. "Is something wrong? Did you forget how to read?"

"Of course not. It's just that you said 'candidates,' and there's only one name on the ballot. Where I come from, we call that a dictatorship."

Brian dropped the remaining papers on the table. "I just explained. You have a choice of voting yes or no. As for the number of candidates, no one else wants to run."

"I want to run," said Jeremy.

"Wha-at?" said Brian, his voice cracking and turning the word into two syllables.

"I said I want to run."

"But you just became a member."

Jeremy looked around. "Is that against the rules?"

Rahm rose with a prepared answer. "There's no rule preventing new members from running for office. In fact, I look forward to competition. Go on," he said, sizing Jeremy up like a political opponent before a packed house. "Tell us your platform."

Jeremy licked his lips. "I-I haven't had time to prepare."

"Too bad," said Rahm. "Then you'll have to wait till next year."

"Wait a minute," said Mary, her voice ringing high above the others. "I think we should make an exception and postpone the election. After all, what's one week? In fact, I suggest we make it two."

Rahm balled his fists and then raised his voice to match hers. "One week, two weeks. That's not the point. We all know what Jeremy's real intentions are."

Janet, who rarely expressed an opinion, interjected. "How can we be sure without hearing him speak?"

"So who's stopping him?" said Rahm. "Not me. Come on, Jeremy. Speak up. We're all waiting."

Jeremy leaned forward, clearing his throat to gain a few seconds. "I propose," he began. "I propose. Uhh ... dammit ... I need more time."

Like a lawyer defending a client, Mary sprang to her feet. "I move we delay the vote for two weeks." Then before anyone could stop her, she added, "Do I hear a second?"

"I second the motion," said Karen.

Helene raised her hand. "I second the second."

Rahm's back stiffened, but his demeanor remained calm. "All right," he said. "I won't fight any of you on this. Two weeks it is. Meeting adjourned."

As the members staggered off, Brian stayed behind to address Rahm. Believing himself to be Rahm's number one supporter, he waited for an explanation.

"I could have vetoed the motion," said Rahm obligingly, "but I thought it best not to. Better to get this challenge over with soon, destroy it at its inception, rather than let it drag on and fester for the next twelve months. Besides, a little excitement might be good for everyone."

Brian nodded. "I see your point. At least, I think I do. Still, you know you can always count on me."

#

Jeremy spent the next two weeks attempting to form a valid policy. He took it seriously, jotting down ideas, then moments later crossing them off and replacing them with others. He hoped for something novel, an inspiration, even a miracle to earn him a flat-out victory. Despite the effort he put into the task, he couldn't come up with anything substantial. He turned to Mary, always faithful and eager to help.

"Remember what Helene wanted?" she suggested. "To stagger the work hours? And I wouldn't mind having a day off every week either."

Jeremy wrote down the words but wasn't satisfied. He wanted more than practical advice. He needed a supercharged brainstorm to inspire the voters, but unable to conjure up that just-right magical lure, he turned into a sugar-dripping political aspirant, offering false promises and being as nice to everyone as possible, excepting Karen, of course.

He helped Janet wash the community towels at the shoreline; he helped Helene when it was her turn with the dinner dishes; and when David pulled a muscle, he brought him breakfast in bed. If there had been a baby around, he would have kissed it too.

But after days of these shenanigans, he decided to stop, afraid others would see it for the pandering it was.

Fighting the specter of loss and despair, he told himself what he really needed was to get his point across. But what point? He had arrived back at the beginning.

When David asked him over rehydrated powdered eggs what he could do that Rahm couldn't, he told him to wait for his speech. Jeremy gave the identical answer to a foursome engaged in a game of pinochle, since all he'd managed so far were worthless ideas scribbled on paper.

Then before he knew it Election Day arrived, spurring last-minute bustling with little to show. Adding to that, the sight of Brian flitting about as if he were passing out campaign fliers caused Jeremy to succumb to a case of nerves. His body felt weighted, shooting pains pierced his chest, and, worst of all, he couldn't catch his breath. After telling Mary he was having a heart attack, she noted the sweat on his brow. Placing her fingers on his wrist, she felt his pulse, racing and irregular.

"No, you're not dying," she assured him as she kissed his mouth and massaged his neck. "It's a panic attack. You're hyperventilating. Just breathe in and out to a count of five each."

After following her advice, he dropped to his knees in a prayerful plea for guidance. To his surprise, the combination helped, and with a final self-directed word of encouragement, he regained his composure; at least, enough to fool the unknowing.

As they walked together down the passageway, Mary squeezed his hand, reminding him that he was smarter than all the dummies in the tribe, present company excepted. Jeremy laughed, releasing the last of his pent-up tension. With his newfound confidence, he thrust out his chest, ready for battle—that is, until he saw the members, sitting around the table, all with eager, anticipatory faces as they waited for his arrival and long-overdue speech.

Brian didn't attempt to hide his scorn as he resumed his position as chairman. "So, what have you come up with, Jeremy? I hope it's more than pie-in-the-sky promises."

Jeremy once again stood before the group. Feeling like a student who hadn't done his homework, he almost began with "My fellow members," but decided it sounded stale and, worse, phony. He looked at Mary with her thumbs-up sign and made a decision to just begin and forget about introductory statements.

"If I were leader," he said, "we'd stagger the work hours." Encouraged by Helene's smile he continued to item two. "We'd also have a six-day work week." More smiles. "I also recommend—umm, I also think ..." He stopped and blanked out, the same way he had the previous time. In desperation, he pulled his half-written speech from his pocket. Seeing that item three was crossed off, he dropped his head in defeat. "Shit," he mumbled, knowing there was no use in pretending. He had nothing to offer, nothing worth saying, and he threw the paper to the ground.

Mary fisted both hands, pushing tighter, tighter. He could feel her prodding him on as she met his eyes with a don't-give-up plea.

Jeremy took a breath. "Listen," he said. "I can't pretend to have my opponent's knowledge of caves or know any of you as well as he does. But there's one thing I do know. It was obvious to me from the first."

Lily spoke next. Still seething from their time in the fertility area, her voice hissed like steam from a radiator. "And what's that?" she said.

"If you'll allow me," said Jeremy, taking care to be extra polite, "I'll do my best to explain." Then turning to Mary, he performed a two-fingered salute, signaling he was ready to give it one final try.

"All of you came here with a vision," he said. "Freedom from the bullshit needed to survive in the world above. But you've allowed that vision to die. You handed it over—your independence—to Rahm. You say you can choose your jobs, but it's not true. You ask his permission for everything, from changing your assignments to resolving quarrels, to even holding a stupid Thanksgiving party."

He looked at Janet. "Why do you ask him what to cook for dinner? Can't you decide such a simple thing yourself?"

He looked at Brian. "When Rahm refused your request to join him on one of his trips above, you accepted it without complaint."

He looked at them all. "You're not helpless, certainly not simple-minded, so this didn't happen overnight. This process was insidious, took time, but you all got lazy and let it take place. Rahm's a dictator. He may be a benevolent one, but he's a dictator nonetheless."

He paused for a moment to skim the startled faces, the dropped chins, the raised eyebrows, especially Rahm's. "If I were leader," he said, his palms digging into the table so hard his fingertips turned white, "I'd hold daily meetings, and have an anonymous suggestion box so you wouldn't feel afraid to express your feelings. Yes, I've seen the hesitation on your faces, heard the trembling in your voices. If I were leader," he repeated, "I'd include you in the details of community life to make sure you knew your opinions are valued. After all, isn't that why you came here? Above you were nobody. Here, at least, be somebody. Count for something." Jeremy swallowed hard and took his seat, satisfied that he had gotten his point across. But would it be enough?

He looked over at Rahm, who shifted in his chair. Jeremy caught the deflection, a nervous movement, but there was no time to gloat. Using his intellect, he tried getting into Rahm's head to read his thoughts. Would Rahm feel threatened by the challenge? Of course he would. But more importantly, how would he deal with it? What lengths would he go to to neutralize his opponent? Jeremy suspected he'd do anything and everything—whatever it took. Winning was all that mattered and nothing would be off limits.

Rahm was smart. Jeremy knew that. Maybe not book smart, but intrinsically smart, and down here that counted far more than an A plus grade-point average from some Ivy League university. He had heard stories of Rahm's past as a fighter, both military-wise and street-wise, a warrior with cunning instincts. But now he, Jeremy, had stood up and faced him on his territory, in front of people who had only known one leader since their arrival. Whatever happened, he had nothing to be ashamed of.

After Brian made the official introduction, Rahm took his place before his comrades. "We've been through so much together," he began. "We've seen our wishes, our hopes, evolve from fantasy to reality. I don't think I ever told you how proud I am of you—of all of you. Despite what my opponent says, we live in a place where we shape our own destiny. There are no faceless officials thousands of miles away, telling us what to do. The food we eat—we catch it or grow it ourselves. Our daily tasks, we do them from start to finish. We rely on no one but ourselves. Look around you. Look at the person sitting next to you. Go on! Do it!" Faces turned at the order.

"We're a family here. How many people cared about you when you lived above? If this isn't the Promised Land then I don't know what is. And if we have to sacrifice a little bit of our individuality, what better reason is there than the good of the whole? But what remains paramount is that we've done this together. You and me. And to think," he said, his words and voice transitioning to a warning, as chilly as ice down one's back. "Think how it all began—

"You, Mary. Remember how I found you?"

Mary flinched.

"I've never brought it up before, never told anyone, but you've forced my hand." With his eyes on her face, he clicked twice. She immediately looked away. "Without me, Mary, you'd be at the bottom of some insignificant river. A decomposed corpse, buried within a tomb of black, choppy water. No one would have found you, Mary. How could you so easily forget that? I didn't forget.

"When I saw you at that bridge, leaning over the railing as cars sped by, not one person cared enough to give you a glance or a thought. Except me! I was the only one who cared. I slowed my car, pulled over, and let you cry your heart out. And why, Mary? Because I saw you hurting, felt your pain. I cared. That's why."

As he had done years before, Rahm once again went to Mary and put his hand on her shoulder. He approached her so quietly that she jerked. Reaching up, Mary automatically grasped the hand—*his* hand—softly stroking the curve of her neck, exactly as it had that night.

"Lucky for you," he said, "I happened to be driving by. What could you have possibly been thinking? My poor, poor Mary." He squeezed her shoulder and turned away.

"And you, Lily. You were also lucky. It's not every day that someone is snuck out of a hospital ward." Lily gulped as she crossed both arms over her heart. "Now, there's no need for you to get upset. It's no secret what ward you were on. That you never worked as an aide.

"And then there's David and Helene." Walking over, Rahm looked down at the couple, fidgeting like naughty children. His smile, though generous, appeared pulled back by a vise, making it look more like a grimace. "We all know about the drugs, but should I tell everyone how you two earned a living before Rachel and I took you in?"

"You should be grateful," yelled Brian, wagging a finger at Helene, who had taken part in delaying the election.

"Thank you, Brian, but that's not necessary. I'm sure she is grateful. I'm sure they all are."

"I am," said Lily. "I haven't forgotten all you've done. You saved my life."

"Like a messiah," added Rachel.

As Rahm's face flashed in triumph, his eyes became unreadable, darkening like craters despite the lanterns. "There is one more thing I want to add. You already know the quality of my leadership. Jeremy's ability remains an unknown. He himself admitted that. And furthermore, don't ever forget that what's best for our community is my primary goal. Jeremy's first priority is himself. He doesn't care about you despite what he says. We know what he wants." Rahm pounded a fist on the table to emphasize his next words. "I'd lay my life on the line for you, for each of you, for the continuance, the survival of this community. Ask yourself, would Jeremy do the same?" He resumed his place beside Rachel.

Brian wiped the sweat from his forehead. Flustered by the challenge to the status quo, he quickly passed out the ballots, hesitating to make sure there were no more objections. When none were forthcoming, he said, "Okay. Let's vote."

"Wait a minute," said Helene, waving her hand in the air. "Jeremy's name isn't on the ballot."

Brian glared at her as if she were the most addlebrained thing to ever cross his path. "Just write in his name. Do I have to spell it for you?" He almost added *stupid*, but stopped himself in time. "These are the same ballots from our last meeting," he said. "Just place Jeremy's name below Rahm's, and check the candidate of your choice."

When all the ballots were folded over to ensure confidentiality, Brian collected them and handed them to Lily, who had volunteered to do the counting. The members sat with pinched faces, waiting for the results.

She checked them once and checked again, her mouth twisting into an asymmetrical line, a mixture of puzzlement and dismay.

"What's wrong?" demanded Brian. "Are you missing a ballot?"

"No, that's not the problem. The winner is Rahm, just as I expected. But"—her voice dropped to a whisper—"by only one vote. The tally is six to five in his favor."

A collective gasp spread around the table. That Rahm would win was all but assured, but that he would win by one vote was astounding and an embarrassment to him and his supporters. Nevertheless, Rahm rose to his feet. Only a slight twitch of an eye gave any indication that he felt anything but pleasure in his victory.

"I want to thank you," he said, "for your faith in once again electing me to the office of leader."

Expecting a speech, all members sat forward in their chairs, eyes wide open. When instead Rahm walked off without another word, they turned to each other, shrugging, staring, deadly quiet. Brian had blanched. Only Jeremy's demeanor revealed satisfaction as he placed his hands behind his neck, crossed his legs, and leaned back.

He'd known he wouldn't win, hadn't had a chance—not after hearing Rahm's speech—but by doing so much better than he'd imagined, his future loomed brighter. He didn't care about the how or the why. He had witnessed enough elections in his career to know there were always intangibles. All that mattered was the closeness of the vote, that he had broken Rahm's grip on the leadership, making change inevitable. The only problem he could foresee was the next election being a full year away, and he had no intention of waiting that long. And why should he? He and Mary would figure something out: cause a brouhaha over a minor infraction or spread lies, if necessary. Whatever it took, he would rifle the community, necessitating a vote of no confidence or, better yet, discover a powerful, ugly secret. He smiled inwardly at the possibilities, but it exploded on his face like a jim-dandy, red-painted clown mouth. From across the table Karen once again tried to catch his attention. As usual, he paid her no mind.

Chapter 18

It was a perfect day for a funeral. Even though thunderclouds posed a threat, they quickly receded, leaving behind a fitting smudge of gray. Of course, it wasn't really a funeral since no bodies were ever found, but a memorial service proposed by Jeremy's coworkers and friends. They had organized the outdoor event to take place at the Unitarian Church in Baltimore when the six-month anniversary of Karen and Jeremy's disappearance came and went. Jeff, the newspaper's publisher, had covered most of the expenses since readership had picked up and he could well afford it. Flower arrangements of roses, azaleas, and lilies, interspersed with fuzzy green lamb's-ear plants, lined the brick walkway to the patio where chairs had been set up under an umbrella of tree branches just beginning to sprout buds. Understandably, family members had declined the invitation since they still had faith that their loved ones would be found.

A small committee, comprising Carl, Joan, Jeff, and Phil, had proposed an informal ceremony where participants could reflect on touching memories or add tasteful jokes to help everyone make sense of their sorrow. As a result, their two missing friends, perhaps gone from this world forever, would never be forgotten. A second service, one they prayed would not be necessary, would be held in another six-month interval, as a final tribute, if the couple still was not found.

After the minister's moving words, Carl reminisced on his personal and professional relationship with "my good buddy Jeremy." When he finished he turned to his wife, who took her place before the sober gathering. Uncomfortable in crowds, Joan blushed as her voice shook and lips trembled. But for Karen's sake, she fought back, praising her friend as if she were still alive.

"I've only known Karen for one year," she said, "but during that time we grew close and I think of her as the sister I never had. We share many things, particularly a fondness for things past: old movies, music, and singers I'm sure you've never heard of. Well, most of you, anyway. Why, just before she disappeared we were planning to see some MGM musicals at the Paradise. If I hadn't come down with that stupid cold I'm sure events would have turned out differently." She turned to her husband, who shook his head solemnly.

"And most of all, we talked of the children we planned to have. Since I'm an only child, I was in a hurry. More of a hurry than Karen. While I always dreamed of a big family, she said two kids would be plenty." Joan patted her belly. "Still, I had hoped we'd share this experience, but the funny thing is I can't help but feel we are. Carl says it's wishful thinking, but I still feel her presence. Maybe it's because we have their cat, Boots. We thought of changing his name, but decided to leave it as is—for the day they return." She wiped her face. "That's right. I haven't given up hope, but in the meantime let's all give thanks for friendship." Eyes glistening like twin stars, she turned to the large photograph of Karen and Jeremy on display.

After Joan rejoined her husband, Phil rose, checked his tie, pushed back his hair, and made his way to the front. "I didn't know Jeremy well," he began. "Only met him a few times, but I've heard so many stories that I feel like I did. And the times we did talk, he was a funny, upbeat guy. And helpful. Not only in giving me writing tips but telling me where I could get the best steak in the city. And then to top it off, I wound up getting his job." To hold back a satisfied grin, he pictured his soon-to-be ex-wife, sitting on the toilet with pink rollers in her hair.

"Since my advancement came at Jeremy's expense, I want to announce that I ordered a plaque with his name to hang in the newsroom. Jeff thinks it's a good idea. And speaking of Jeff, he also wants to say a few words."

Following Jeff's off-the-cuff but sincere tribute, the minister spoke again, announcing it was time for a symbolic gesture. He led them over to a newly planted flowerbed where everyone tossed handfuls of dirt as a sign of renewal. Joan wept silently, loosening a button around her expanding belly.

On his way back to the parking lot, Jeff draped one arm around Carl and the other around Phil. "I want to express my thanks to you, Phil, for putting in those extra hours at the newspaper. I don't know how we'd have managed without you. Have you thought about what I said the other day—about becoming Senior Staff Writer? There'd be a raise, of course."

Phil smiled, showing perfect teeth. "I'd like that," he said. "Especially the part about the raise." His laugh, although artificial, softened the witticism.

"How does ten percent sound?"

"Sounds good to me."

The men shook hands. Phil waved goodbye to Carl and Joan, and mouthed a thank you to Jeff, along with the words, "See you Monday, Chief."

#

Upon opening the door of his Dodge Dart, Phil breathed deeply to take in the new car smell. While far from the Corvette on his wish list, the Dart outshined his beat-up old '67 Plymouth Belvedere. With his livelihood now secure, he could relax about the monthly payments.

The sky had darkened and those threatening thunderclouds suddenly burst forth with a pouring rain and angry wind, whipping his car from side to side as he headed down the street. Disregarding the weather, he allowed his mind to drift for a minute. He tittered at the thought of the changes in his life arriving so quickly, one after another. They said good fortune came in threes, but his was already at four. Besides his job, Wendy had finally agreed to a no-fault divorce; he had exchanged the dumpy rooming house for an apartment in a nice neighborhood on Charles Street; and his girlfriend, Patty, was hot. His wife had never looked so good, even before the baby's birth.

And, thinking of Patty, he checked the time, noting he was running late for their rendezvous. Her parents didn't approve of her seeing an older man, especially one with a child and still not divorced, but so what? They'd come around, and if they didn't, well, who cared? Certainly not him.

Phil drove onto the highway leading to Silver Spring. Teeming with excitement, he hit the gas despite the wind. He turned on the radio, playing one of his favorite songs, "American Pie," and sang along with the chorus: "'And them good ole boys were drinking whiskey 'n rye singin' this'll be the day that I die.'"

Visibility worsened, became murky, and Phil was forced to slow down as he tightened his hands on the wheel. Suddenly, he regretted not fixing the buckle on his seat belt. The ends fit but failed to lock. *I'll bring it to the dealership tomorrow,* he swore to himself. After moving the lever of the windshield wipers to full force, he glanced up at the rear-view mirror and noticed a large white Cadillac, wavering, but still going top speed. As it tried to pass, it clipped the left side of the Dart's bumper with enough force to spring open the unlocked glove compartment where Jeremy's pen now lay. The A.T. Cross ballpoint flew out onto the passenger seat.

Phil blanched at the sight, cursing, and his car went into a skid. Not accustomed to driving in such slick conditions, he slammed on the brakes, sending the car further out of control into a near 180-degree spin before heading up an embankment and hitting a tree, dead on. The Cadillac continued down the highway, along with other cars, all occupants indifferent, not wanting to become involved, or too lazy to bother getting out in the downpour. Finally, after a full five minutes, a car stopped. A man got out and reached through the broken window. He felt for a pulse. Then turning toward his wife, he lifted his hands, palms up, and shrugged.

#

Jo Ellen hadn't been back to Junkyard Bridge since last fall when that two-timing creep, Joey, had pulled a fast one. Her eyes filled like over-watered houseplants, despite ordering herself not to cry. Still, she needed to be here alone, to think.

She took a deep breath and cracked her knuckles. No one had asked her to the junior prom yet, and with time running out, she felt downright sick. The thought of going with her brother (a mere sophomore) sent flip-flops to her stomach. But what other choice did she have? "I hate boys," she said.

A noise in the bushes set her heart racing. She gathered her belongings to rush off, but seeing the tip of a shoe, she froze, almost wetting her pants. A boy stepped into the open. "Oh, it's you," she said, staring at Joey. "You scared me to death."

"Sorry," he said. "I just wanted to talk to you."

"How did you know I was here?"

"I followed you. I thought you noticed."

"Well, I didn't," she said, turning away, not wanting him to see the nervous tic suddenly contorting her mouth. "So what do you want to talk about?"

"I was wondering … if you don't have a date yet for the prom, would you go with me?"

"Aren't you going with Lisa?" She snuck a peek.

"I told you months ago that she means nothing to me. Besides, she's going with someone else. Not that I care!"

Jo Ellen huffed. "I'll have to think about it. I sort of made other plans."

Joey squirmed, causing an old wooden board to squeak. "There's one other thing I wanted to bring up. The other day in civics class when Mr. Brooks passed that article around, you almost raised your hand."

"Yeah. What about it?"

"I was wondering why."

"Because of the two people in the article. You know, the ones that went missing. Wasn't that the same weekend we heard a car go off this bridge?"

"No, they disappeared the following week, but even if it was the same, what's the big deal? There's no connection." He ran his fingers through his hair, causing clumps to stick out like carrot sticks. "Listen, Jo Ellen, if you tell anyone we were here, I'll be in deep shit."

"Why?"

"Remember how I got probation for egging those cars last year? Well, part of the deal was my curfew. If anyone found out I broke it, they can extend my probation or even send me to juvy hall."

Jo Ellen laughed. "So you want me to keep my mouth shut. My, my, my."

"And don't forget, you'll be in trouble too."

"Maybe, maybe not. True, I'm supposed to be home by twelve, but since it was months ago, I doubt my parents would make a fuss."

"Yeah, but there's no point in stirring the pot."

"I guess you're right, and like you said, it probably wasn't even their car. Okay, I won't say a word. Now what was it you asked me about? Something to do with the prom …?"

#

Carl dropped Joan off at the airport for an early flight to Tampa. "Call you tonight," he said. "Say hello to your parents for me."

"I will. You still visiting Phil?"

"Yep. His wife phoned again, said he's doing somewhat better, so he's cleared for surgery later this morning. I want to speak to her and drop off a card."

"He's lucky Wendy took him back. He would have had nowhere to go. Still, she must be nuts."

"She did it for the kid, but I agree."

After kissing Joan goodbye, Carl drove to the hospital. He rode the elevator up to orthopedics, finding a somber Phil with his leg in a splint, held off the bed by an overhead system of pulleys and weights. Wendy whispered that his doctors had delayed operating on his leg until today to check that he didn't have permanent neurological damage. With his confusion and fuzzy memory, they wanted to run tests to help determine if the injury to his brain would heal with time.

"It looks like it will," said Wendy, bending over to speak directly into Carl's ear. "But we won't know for sure for a while. As for the broken femur, we're looking at four months minimum for complete healing."

A nurse came in to give Phil a pre-op sedative and pain medication.

"Mind if I step out a bit?" Wendy asked Carl. "They're not bringing him to the operating room for another half hour, and I could use some coffee."

"Sure. Go ahead. I'll talk to Phil while you're in the cafeteria."

Phil lowered the sheet, revealing oozy, bloodshot eyes. "Is she gone?"

"Yes, but she'll be back soon."

"I sure messed up. All my fault. All my fault."

"Wendy loves you," said Carl. "Thank your lucky stars for that."

As the meds took effect, Phil began to drone on, his words getting slurry, forming a hodgepodge. "My fault. Wendy. All my fault. Jeremy. A.T. Cross. The cave. The waterfall."

"What are you talking about?" said Carl.

"Waterfall. Jeremy. Dinky pen cave."

"Huh? What's that about a pen?"

"A.T. Cross. At the waterfall. Saw it."

"You saw Jeremy's pen? At the waterfall? What happened to it?"

"Gone all gone with the car. Gone, gone, gone. Gonna sleep now. Gonna sleep." His lips flapped like two sheets of paper, placed on a desk near a fan. He began to snore.

"You son of a bitch," swore Carl under his breath, just as Wendy returned with two medical assistants in her wake.

"Time to take you to surgery," said one of the white-coated men.

Carl left without saying good luck or leaving his Get Well Soon card. Steaming, he sat in his car, his mind honing in with a tunnel-vision fixation, as he obsessed over Phil's disclosure. True, Phil was fuzzy-brained, but he had made enough sense to be plausible.

At work, he explained the situation to Jeff. "With the pen gone, no one's going to spend more time or effort at Dinky Cave."

"Why would they?" said Jeff. "Money's tight and they already checked it out."

Carl pressed his thumb into his chin. "Knowing Phil, he'll deny ever seeing the pen, or, thanks to his concussion, forget about it after surgery."

"You're probably right," said Jeff. "Still, it can't hurt to make some phone calls. Use your extension and don't worry about the long-distance charges."

Carl's first call was to the West Virginian detective who'd been involved in the initial investigation. Just as Carl presumed, concrete evidence was necessary to justify sending out another search party.

"Your sick co-worker is probably hallucinating, delusional, or confused," said the detective. "I'm sorry. Call back if you have more to go on."

Carl gnashed his teeth. After a third mug of coffee, he called the chairman of his local speleological society. "I'll check around and get back to you in a couple of hours."

By mid-afternoon, Carl had been put in touch with two brothers from Pocahontas County in West Virginia, who had volunteered to meet him the next day.

"Say, eleven o'clock?"

"Sounds good. And thanks."

With Jeff's blessing he was given the day off.

#

After waking at six a.m., Carl ate a quick breakfast, fed Boots, and left. He drove on autopilot: shift—gas, shift—brake. With each mile, he fine-tuned his course of action: drive straight through to the cave, check inside, and be back in time to call Joan in Florida.

A burning sensation in his bladder signaled the need for a slight modification to his plan. Looking about, he saw a sign for a restaurant just over the border and turned off the road. After using the facilities, he checked his watch, and, having time to spare, thought he might as well get something to eat. *May be my last chance before I hit the cave.*

All the booths were taken so Carl took a seat at the counter.

"Coffee?" asked the waitress.

"Sure," he said.

The waitress poured. "If you're hungry, the house special's our best deal." She pointed to a large menu board hanging on the wall.

For a moment Carl considered ordering baked beans, remembering Jeremy's fondness for them, then laughed since he hated the taste. "Actually, I'll just have an English muffin, lightly buttered."

"No problem," she said, "and if you want, we have free pastries today. All kinds. They're leftovers from Betty's party. You just missed it by one day. Everyone was invited, even customers."

"Betty? Who's Betty?"

"Didn't you see her picture on the door? It's also in the newspaper." She handed him one from the counter. "She was a waitress here. What a character. I'm sure gonna miss her."

"Sorry, I didn't notice. You know, I don't particularly like anything sweet in the morning. I'll just stick with the English muffin. Thanks, anyway."

"More coffee then?"

"Yes, please, it's damn—I mean darn good."

After pouring a second cup, the waitress walked off to place his order.

While waiting, Carl skimmed through the local newspaper. On page two was a grainy picture of Betty in front of the entrance, a sign above reading *KATE'S*

PLACE. She held a coffee pot in one hand and a menu in the other. He shrugged, wondering if Betty could have been the waitress mentioned in the initial investigation, then kicked himself because he'd never bothered to learn her name or that of the restaurant either. *Probably not her and besides, it wouldn't have mattered.* Looking closer at the photo, he chuckled at the corny image of small-town life, almost wishing he'd never left home for Baltimore. *Been nothing but one problem after another.*

After a third refill, he continued the drive, blocking out all thoughts but one: solving the mystery. "And I will, Jeremy," he swore out loud. "No matter what, I'll solve it today." When he arrived two hours later, he was surprised by how quickly time had passed and that he had gnawed a raw spot in his lower lip.

The sun was high in the sky as three teenage boys exited the cave, but still there was no sign of the volunteers. He got out, opened the trunk, and reached inside for his helmet, groaning when he saw its broken carbide lamp. *No big deal.* All he needed was his flashlight and the spare batteries in his glove compartment.

He checked his watch. At a quarter past eleven a car pulled up. A young girl, perhaps sixteen, got out. "Sorry," she said, "There's been a family emergency and no one can come. My cousins tried calling, but you'd already left." She shrugged. "You might as well go in by yourself. If you stick to the main path you should be fine. Everyone knows this is a baby cave."

Carl jangled his keys. "That's great, just great." But after coming this far, there was no way he'd turn back, three-person rule or not. *Anyway, Dinky Cave isn't a real cave,* he told himself. *Like the girl said, it's just a small underground pit that local teens use for orgies.*

During his snake crawl through the tunnel, Carl juggled the flashlight from hand to hand. As a result, he wound up with torn sleeves and a few abrasions on his forearms. The rocky road down to the main section, however, had been further leveled by an increase in foot traffic, making it easy as pie. Although the cigarette butt was long gone, he didn't need it to find his way to the correct passage. "And now on to the waterfall," he said out loud, counting as he passed the first two offshoots.

Upon hearing the music of the cascading water, he mumbled, "Almost there." Since the light from the flashlight's beam only formed a small yellow circle, he came to the falls with a start. In the shallow pool was a child—a naked female child. *What in heavens is she doing here alone?* he wondered. *Maybe she needs help.*

"Hello," he said, approaching cautiously, not wanting to scare her. To Carl's surprise a man's voice rose above the din and returned the greeting. Carl flinched and asked, "Is that your child?"

"That's no child," said the stranger.

Carl adjusted the direction of the beam and the man's features lit up like a blazing Halloween jack-o'-lantern. There was something familiar about him. Carl pressed two fingers from his left hand against his cheek, thinking. "Haven't I seen you before? I know—the last time I was here."

The man nodded. "Rachel and I come about once a week to pick up the trash, look for valuables."

Carl snapped his fingers. "Yep. That's what you said. And your name … it's unusual. Let me think. It's Rahm, right? But you were with a woman."

By now Rachel was out of the water, still undressed and fully exposed. Carl could see her teacup breasts and pubic hair. She was definitely no child, just waiflike. Carl turned away, swallowed.

"Hey Rachel, put some clothes on. You're making this guy uncomfortable."

"Be right there," she said.

Carl heard shuffling, followed by cracking joints, and material rubbing against skin. Then moments later Rachel joined the two men, shirt and pants properly in place.

"I'm sure you've seen a naked woman before," she tittered.

Carl felt his face getting warm and almost apologized. He shrugged it off and stuck to his goal. "Do you remember me? I showed you a picture of my missing friends? It was months ago."

"Oh, yeah, I remember," said Rachel. "But I still haven't seen them."

"Me either," said Rahm. "If either of us did, you can be sure we would have gone straight to the police."

"But here's the thing. I found out they were in this cave. You see, someone found Jeremy's pen. It's one of a kind. I'm afraid it's gone, but maybe he left something else behind. Something I could show the authorities so they'd come back and search again."

Rahm and Rachel exchanged glances.

"It's funny you should mention pens," said Rahm. "I just found something earlier today. It looks like the cap of a Bic." He pulled a piece of blue plastic from his pocket.

"Holy cow! Jeremy always carried Bics too. Where did you find it?"

"Close by. In the offshoot that leads to the dead end. I didn't do a thorough check. Maybe there's more of his stuff. I'll take you there if you like."

"Yes, please," said Carl. "By the way, where's your light? This place is blacker than a thousand nights."

Rahm nodded, opened his palm, and a flashlight seemed to sprout from the air.

"Wait a minute," said Carl, tipping his head forward. "That's not a flashlight. What is it?"

"I call them magic mushrooms. They grow in the cave. Their light works as well as anything artificial. Amazing, isn't it? Wish I had more time to explain, but Rachel and I, we have to leave soon. Doctor's appointment."

"Oh sure," said Carl. "Sorry. Just lead the way. And thanks for your help."

Rahm tipped his head. "My pleasure."

Carl followed the couple down the passageway.

"Here is it," said Rahm, signaling a halt. "The offshoot I told you about. It's a tight fit, but you're nice and slim."

Carl slipped through the opening, mimicking Rahm's sideways shuffle. "Sure is dark," he said. "I think I need to put in fresh batteries. I can barely see."

"We'll be there in a sec," said Rahm. "Then we'll stop." He pointed his glowing fingertips toward an insignificant area along the base of the wall. "It's over there. The spot where I found the cap."

Carl sprang forth like a jackrabbit and leaned over for a closer look. Seeing nothing, he turned his head, his peripheral vision catching Rahm, swinging his right arm before placing him in a chokehold. Carl's eyes bulged, and his blood pressure soared as his mind flashed the climactic answer he'd been searching for, only it came too late—way too late.

Rahm increased the pressure. With his last moments of clarity, Carl felt himself lifted off the ground as Rahm, using his left arm as leverage, pushed inward, placing him in a vise. Helpless, Carl's legs jerked aimlessly, a pitiful squeak escaped from his mouth, and a small sound—the crack of a larynx—indicated it was over.

#

Rahm wiped his hands. "That's that," he said with an easygoing, all-in-a-day's-work smile spreading across his face.

Rachel, in turn, scowled and kicked the body.

"Be respectful," Rahm admonished.

"Just checking to be sure he's dead."

"He's dead, all right."

She nodded. "You ready to go?"

"Almost. Just a couple more things." Rahm pursed his lips, thinking. "I'm tired of the search parties, busy-bodies, and local riffraff that come in all the time. And now others are bound to check up on our friend here."

"You got an idea?"

"Yes, but we'll have to work fast." He looked overhead, saw a crack, no bigger than a scar, and clicked his voice. The crack deepened and a smidgeon of dust appeared.

Rachel's eyes widened. "I get it, but what about the body? Do we leave it here?"

"No. You know how I feel about that. Everyone's entitled to a proper burial. Let's move it out of the way and I'll come back for it later." Looping his arms around what had been Carl, Rahm walked backwards, pulling, while Rachel held the ankles aloft.

The twosome continued down the fake dead-end passageway, stopping at a safe distance. After propping the body against the wall, Rahm walked back, then found the precise pitch to stir up the molecules in the air. Raising his voice to a jackhammer 105 decibels, he sent out a series of clicks. Soon the small crack widened to a gaping wound and then a chasm, as dirt fell, slowly, quickly. Then boom!

The earth-shattering rumble pierced Rahm's and Rachel's ears. Tons of soil and stone—enough to suffocate, crush a skull, break every bone in a body—tumbled down, sealing the entrance to the dead end. But by that time, the twosome was past the danger mark and well on their way home.

#

Jeremy, taking a break, sat in the dining room, snacking on berries. The color and texture had changed to a velvety purple blue, making them exceptionally sweet and reminding him of the cotton candy from his youth. He was about to help himself to a second bowl when he heard an unidentifiable thud close by. It held such force that it sounded like a bullet or a small explosion. *Maybe it is a bullet,* he thought, *one from a rescuer's gun.* His mind flashed to the rescuers he had imagined, dreamed of months back. *Please God, let it be!* Blood pumping, eyes blazing, he ran in the direction of the noise.

On the ground lay a man; a dead man, who had obviously fallen from above. Jeremy walked over, caution in every step. There was blood seeping from the poor man's mouth, nose, eyes—so much blood that it seemed to flow out of every pore. His arms and legs lay willy-nilly, broken in multiple places, and his head twisted sideways, pooling in a sea of crimson.

Yet there was something familiar about this man. Jeremy leaned over and pulled a wallet from a back pocket, scanning the enclosed ID.

"No!" he screamed, his voice so loud and piercing that it echoed through the chambers, clear to Suburbia. He looked up to see Rahm, a bold-faced, defiant Rahm, leaning against a wall as if he were its load-bearing beam.

This was it, the final straw, and Jeremy raised his fists and positioned his body forward to attack, despite knowing it was pointless. But nothing mattered. His life was over.

At the last moment, Mary's and Karen's arms locked around each of his elbows, holding him back.

"Don't do it," said Mary.

"Please," sobbed Karen. "Not Carl, not Carl."

Jeremy struggled to free himself, but Mary, much stronger than she looked, climbed onto Jeremy's back like a parasitic growth. He tried knocking her off, but her weight brought him to his knees.

As Norman and David dragged the body out of the area, Jeremy heard Brian say, "Rachel's driving the car to our safe-house. She said we can use it for spare parts. The police will assume it was stolen, and for once they'll be right." He walked off with a laugh while Lily covered the remaining gore with old newspapers before blotting it with her feet.

Rahm was the last to stay behind, checking minutiae like a seller in a slave market. Before he walked off, Jeremy saw his highly arched eyebrows, twin teepees, framed in an uncompromising face: the face of the King of the Underworld, a son of satanic royalty, a man with no soul.

#

Mary held Jeremy in her arms until his quivering body and piercing moans subsided. She rocked him like a baby, sang lullabies, and cradled his head.

After a while his haphazard words took on meaning. "Poor Carl. Poor, poor Carl. He sacrificed his life for me; I can't let it be in vain. I won't! But none of this makes sense. Where are the search parties, the newspaper articles, and what about my car? Didn't somebody see something? Anything? Am I all but forgotten, except by a few friends?" Minutes went by with more wailing, more protestations, until finally Jeremy uttered a definitive plaint: "I won't be Rahm's sacrificial lamb. I won't! I won't! I'd rather die."

"I understand," said Mary. "And I'm here for you." She kissed his nose, his cheeks, his chin, knowing that the death of Jeremy's friend cinched a second escape attempt. Furthermore, since she loved him, she'd have to do everything in her power to help. His life depended on it. A lump swelled in her throat. How would she live without him?

#

Keith had almost finished skimming section one of *The Pittsburgh Press* when he heard the ding-dong of the bell. Bounding down the stairs, he yelled, "I'm coming. Who is it?"

"It's me," said Zits, avoiding the use of his unfortunate nickname.

"Hi," said Keith, welcoming Zits and his current girlfriend. He gave a cursory greeting to his own spur-of-the-moment date for the night, a nobody he barely knew, then closed the door.

"I brought the grass," said Zits, holding up a small plastic bag with dried leaves. "Grade A Mary Jane. My brother guarantees it."

"Well, let's go upstairs. I don't expect my parents for a while yet, but no point in pushing our luck."

"Don't worry," said Zits. "They're getting drunk same as my folks. I saw them when we picked up Gloria"—he gestured to the new girl. "Her parents are hosting the pool party at their house."

"Actually, it's my mother and stepfather's house, and not a pool party but a house-warming party. But Zits is right about not worrying. There's so much booze, everyone's probably plastered by now. Oh, by the way, my mother said for all my friends to come over tomorrow and use the pool. It's still supposed to be hotter than hell."

"Great," said Keith, looking at her with more interest. *If not for her Groucho Marx nose she might actually have been cute.*

After heading upstairs, Zits sat down at Keith's desk, turning on the green banker's lamp, and took out some rolling paper. He placed a small amount of marijuana in the middle, spreading it out carefully.

"Stop," said Keith, ripping off a page from section two of the newspaper, not caring if it would anger his parents. "My mom has been checking my room lately. I gotta be careful." He centered the "Best Deals in Town" ad below Zits's busy fingers, missing the story on the reverse side about a young couple probably lost in a West Virginia cave months before.

Zits continued rolling, licked the sticky strip, and pinched both ends. "Voila!" he said, handing it to Keith. "I have enough for one more cig."

As Keith passed it to big-nose Gloria, he popped a cassette into his desktop player. His head began bobbing to the soundtrack of *Saturday Night Fever* as his eyes turned glassy. The room began to spin and peace and harmony reigned, along with Kumbaya.

"Where's the bathroom?" asked Gloria, the first to break the spell.

"Down the hall, to your right."

She flipped on the overhead light and paused to study a picture of Keith with his parents, posing before cherry blossoms in Washington, D.C. "I wish my parents would take me there."

"Trust me, it's boring."

"Still, I'd like to go." Minutes later, she returned from the bathroom. "Hey," she said, "anyone else hungry?"

"Yeah, weed makes me hungry too," said Keith, "but hold on a sec. Just a couple more things to do." He balled up the sheet of newspaper from the desk, along with its dusting of unusable marijuana stems. Placing the heap into a metal wastebasket, he struck a match, dropping it into the trash, and opened the window to clear the air. As the paper went up in flames, it wiped out the small picture of Karen and Jeremy, turning them to black soot and white ash, remnants of lives lost.

"So you guys want some ice cream?" asked Keith. "We've got three cartons in the freezer."

"I do," said Zits, "but not just yet. First me and my lady here have other business to attend to." He jumped onto Keith's bed, pulling his girlfriend with him.

Keith looked at Gloria, his face turning crimson but his eyes wide with hope. "You're beautiful," he lied, praying she'd believe him.

"Really? You're kind of cute yourself. Hey, you got a condom?"

Keith mouth dropped as if he couldn't believe his ears. "Sure do," he said, trying to keep his voice steady. "Two, in fact. Extra-large." *Damn*, he thought. *This must be my lucky day.*

Chapter 19

Joan lay in her hospital bed, staring at her flat abdomen. Tears streaked her cheeks. "Just when you think things can't get worse, they do." She spoke to Jeff, sitting across from her in a blue plastic chair.

"I'm so sorry," he said. "I wish there was more I could do."

She trembled. "First Carl. Now the baby. Both dead. I blame myself."

"Please don't. There's no way you could have predicted a cave-in."

"But if I hadn't been in Florida, I would have gone with him."

"He wouldn't have let you," said Jeff, almost adding, *because you were pregnant then*. Fortunately he stopped himself in time. "Anyway, I'm glad you didn't go. You both would have died."

"No, I'm certain that wouldn't have happened. I don't know how I know, but I do. Oh Jeff, nothing makes sense anymore!" She paused to blow her nose, wipe her cheeks. "And you know what else? They may never get his body out of that damn cave. No one is allowed inside. The authorities say it's too unstable to bring in heavy equipment, so it may take years to get to him, and by then there'll be nothing left but dust. The only good thing"—she looked directly into Jeff's eyes— "is that I lost the baby."

Jeff opened his mouth, horrified.

"It's true. You see, Carl was so looking forward to its birth. Now he'll never know what happened. And you know what else? It wasn't the news of Carl's death that caused me to miscarry. The doctor said there were mutations. 'Incompatible with life' were his words." Her lips twitched. "I think I'm cursed. I think we all are. Everyone at the newspaper."

Jeff cocked his head. "Funny, I had the same thought. In fact, I might close it down. I'm generally not a superstitious guy, but all these things going on, they don't add up. But I don't want to burden you with my problems. Not right now."

"Actually, it helps to talk," said Joan. "With Carl gone, I don't have anyone left. Friends that is."

"I'm your friend, Joan. I mean it. You can call me anytime, day or night. And everyone at the newspaper sends their love. Even Wendy asked about you."

Joan's eyes narrowed. "Who's Wendy? Oh, of course, Phil's wife. How are they doing?"

"So-so. Phil's been in physical therapy for weeks, but they just added occupational therapy too. Apparently the damage to his brain is more serious than they thought. Wendy said it's going to be 'wait and see.'"

A nurse poked her head into the room. "The doctor will be here to see you in an hour, Mrs. Johnston."

"Okay," said Joan.

"Do you know when you're being discharged?"

"Today or tomorrow."

"You have a ride home? I heard about your car."

She shook her head sideways, her face crumpling as if it'd been crushed by a train. "Don't worry. I'll just call a cab."

"Don't be ridiculous. I'll pick you up. And you shouldn't be alone when you get out. I'll ask one of the women from the newsroom to stay with you. If they can't, you're welcome to stay with me. My house is huge."

"No. I'll take you up on the ride, but I want to be by myself. I need to deal with this on my own terms."

"Whatever you want." He stood up and kissed the top of her head. "Remember, whatever you want, whatever you need, you just have to ask."

Joan, averse to letting anyone see her lose control, waited for Jeff's footsteps to trail off down the corridor. Feeling certain he'd reached the elevator, she surrendered to the unspeakable grief that had been so unfairly thrust upon her. As her upper body pitched forward, she covered her face with her hands, her mind reeling and her mouth dissolving into a sea of silent screams. *Why? Why? Why?*

#

Karen could tell it was late spring. While there were no signs of croaking frogs, longer daylight hours, or Baltimore orioles with their orange and black plumage, she could tell by the size of her abdomen. She guessed she was approximately five months along, which would make it mid-to-late May.

With quivering fingertips, she ran her hands along her bulging middle, grateful that the members had reacted with reserve to the announcement of her pregnancy months before; not one person had congratulated her—not then, not later. Perhaps they were rattled by Mary's anger or felt embarrassed by the peculiarity of her situation, especially after her fight with Jeremy and his subsequent abandonment. And then, to top it off, had been Carl's horrific death. That, too, remained verboten.

But now things were changing. With the baby thrust before them like a ripening watermelon, the members started to treat her deferentially, with a reverence reserved for heroes and demigods. She'd lost count of how many times she'd been told "Take it easy" and "Don't work so hard." Paying little attention to their admonitions, she kept going at her usual pace without any thought to her health, or the baby's, for that matter. To her it was a mere parasite—a thing—and an unwanted one at that. At least, that's how she had felt until yesterday.

Sitting quietly, with her arms and legs folded pretzel-like, she had sensed it move for the first time. Initially she'd dismissed the tingle as mere rumblings in her stomach, but then it came again, reminding her of monarch butterflies whose soft-petal wings fluttered in her palms on warm summer mornings; except this tiny creature was fluttering inside her, enclosed in her protective womb.

At that moment, all the hate she had felt toward it dissolved, replaced with a type of love she had never experienced before, a protective love more powerful than what she felt for Jeremy. Within her grew a baby, *her* baby, a thriving miracle moving its tiny arms and legs. She wondered what it looked like, and her eyes misted over as she imagined soft, fuzzy peach skin and a red, bow-shaped mouth. She'd die for this marvel, her creation, a perfect fruit on the tree of life.

But then a horrible thought—the same one every mother-to-be ponders: *what if something's wrong?* She froze and clutched her chest, overcome with the realization that she'd been negligent, had not considered adequate nutrition or rest. What if the baby was born deformed and it was her fault? She would never forgive herself; at that moment she vowed to eat properly and let the others do the heavy lifting and digging in the garden. After all, she was pregnant and pregnant women were entitled to a little pampering. In fact, maybe she should consider turning over the reins; tell others her tricks to make the mushrooms taste both meaty and peppery and smell like cinnamon. Then, with extra time on her hands, she could devote more hours to Jon and Randy. As a former teacher, she had been appalled by the laxity, the downright carelessness that the adults showed toward the boys' education.

Karen looked up, surprised to see Randy.

"Sorry," he said. "Didn't mean to startle you. I just want to ask you something."

"What's that?"

"Remember we talked about increasing my school hours?"

"Funny you should ask," said Karen. "I was just thinking about it."

Randy lips formed a lopsided grin. "I've been saving this for a surprise … I've learned the whole alphabet, backwards and forwards. I followed your advice and been studying picture books, on my own. I can sound out the words. Read whole passages. I want to read a novel—*Owls in the Family*. I pulled it from a shelf."

"But the letters are too small. You won't be able to see the small print."

Randy smiled like a child with a new toy. "That's another surprise. When I helped Norman gather the guano weeks back, I found an area that gets natural light, but is still far enough away to avoid the stinky smell. I've been going there every day with a book. It's helped my eyesight."

"Really?" said Karen, delighted by the news. "Maybe it'll help mine too. At the next community meeting, I'll insist they let us increase our time together."

"Good. Now can I ask you one more question?"

"Sure. Anything."

"Where do babies come from?"

Karen gulped. "Huh?"

"I mean, I sort of know. Rahm explained it to me. Norman too, but I'm still confused."

Karen winced and tugged on her shirt as if trying to hide a shameful secret. With her child's questionable bloodline, she preferred keeping the subject of babies off limits. "Maybe you'd better ask your mother if you're confused."

Randy persisted. "What I don't understand is how you got pregnant without going to the fertility area. You never did go, right? Rahm told me to peek inside when grownups went, and I never saw you even once."

Karen eyes bulged, her mouth flew open. "Rahm told you to *what?*"

"He said it would help my education, but to tell you the truth, it made me feel weird so I stopped after a couple months."

Karen sighed. "You don't need a fertility area to get pregnant. The whole idea is absurd. Aboveground there's no such thing."

"I know," said Randy. "I just thought maybe it was different below."

"Well, it's not. And you don't need fertility gods either."

"I don't really believe in fertility gods," said Randy. "Best I can tell, they're just rock. I even asked Jeremy about it, but he got really mad. My mom said it's 'cause he might not be the baby's father. Is that true?"

Karen stuttered. "I-I'm not sure."

"My mom's not sure who Jon's father is either, but I don't care. He's still a pest. You know what he's been doing today?"

"No, what?"

As if on cue, Jon ran by with something moving inside his mouth. Two tiny webbed feet poked out, which thrashed like the limbs of a human baby and hung toward his chin.

Karen raised the lantern higher, shuddering when Jon chomped on the living creature. But worst of all, with a "Pffffttt" from his lips, he spat out the head. Karen screeched. "What the—?"

"It's a toad," said Randy. "They don't normally live in the cave, but once in a while they crawl through the entrance and make it to the lower levels. Jon loves the taste. Hey," he said, shifting his focus, "can I touch your stomach?"

Karen stiffened. "I guess."

Randy pressed down. "Wow. Feels just like my mom's stomach when she was pregnant."

"If you don't mind," said Karen, covering up her unease with a lie, "I really should go. I'm late for the mushrooms."

"Sure. I'm supposed to help Mom clean our room, anyway. But you'll let me know about any changes with school, right?" He ran off, leaving Karen in a state of panic.

Kicking the icky head of the toad aside, she thought, *Could living below turn my child into an unnatural being like Jon?* A slew of grotesque images formed in her brain, sealing her resolve to make peace with Jeremy. After witnessing today's freak show, she vowed to flee this subterranean house of horrors before it was too late. If Jeremy continued to refuse her advances, she'd try her damnedest without him. With her special abilities and a sacred reason to never give up, she'd find a way. For the time being, however, she'd do what she loved: work in the garden and teach.

Still rattled by Jon's nightmarish display, Karen massaged the knots in her neck. As she kneaded, she devised another plan, a secondary one which involved trickery, and, yes, guilt, but was necessary, nonetheless. For the sake of her child, she would abandon her principles. Recalling Jeremy's words, she spoke them out loud like a president or prime minister addressing a nation under attack: "This is war," she declared, stomping the ground. But with no person in the group she could completely trust, her ploy would have to remain top secret.

#

Mary had never felt happier. To love and be loved in return, to feel someone's warm breath against her face, to hear words of endearment in her ear— this was a gift she had thought beyond her reach. But now that it fell within her grasp, she'd become a changed person.

For the first time in her life she felt pretty. Jeremy told her so, so it must be true, and being the object of desire permitted her to shed her old skin and supplant it with a softer, more feminine coat. Gone was her mulish pocketbook mouth, stuffed with resentments, flapping open or snapping shut. Her current style unmasked a startling panache, uplifting and cheerful, exemplifying health, youth, and beauty. Even Rachel and Norman asked her if she had lost weight or changed her hair.

Although flattered by their compliments, Mary's moment of triumph came when she was sitting in the Ballroom, a queen on her throne. Brian walked in, did a double take, and hit a low-hanging stalactite head-on, cracking the tip. She laughed like a tickled child when he apologized to the formation.

"To whom are you speaking?" she quipped. "Don't you look where you're going?"

Again Brian's eyes darted between Mary and the stalactite. "Huh?" he said. "What the hell? Thought I bumped into someone. What's going on?" He pointed to her. "That can't be you."

"But it is me. Mary. The love of your life."

Waving his hand to and fro, Brian fanned his heated face. "But you're beautiful."

Beautiful? No. That went too far. Mary knew she had changed, but beautiful was out of the question. *Still ...* "Must be the lighting in here."

Brian moved closer, mouth agape, then backed away like a subject before royalty. After he was gone, Mary rose and did a pirouette, relishing her satisfaction like a contented housecat. And all this because of Jeremy, her man.

With his help, her foot had easily slid into Cinderella's slipper for a perfect fit. He respected her feelings, her intelligence, and placed her on the proverbial pedestal, making her feel like a real woman.

They made love on a regular basis and the experience always left her dizzy and tingly, unlike her nausea following sex with Brian or her apathy after fulfilling her obligations in the fertility area. She even dared hope that love would be the magic ingredient to cure her infertility. It certainly helped with her longing for Rahm, secured inside a mental strongbox marked with an R, which would have surely dissipated if she hadn't suspected her time with Jeremy was finite. But Carl's unfortunate death and Jeremy's continual exploration of the cave told her an escape attempt was coming. While he had never learned to echolocate, the depth, comingling, and fine-tuning of his five senses added up to more than the sum of their parts.

But even more than Jeremy's skyrocketing skill, Mary's own words, the equivalent of a sacred oath, proved a greater irritant to her serenity, a constant tickle beyond reach of her hand or conscience. While she regretted those words, going back on them would be tantamount to a sin. No, she'd do as she had said, like it or not. Of course, his constant prodding never let her forget.

Early the next morning, with the two of them still in bed, Jeremy again asked, "Have you discovered anything new?"

With his face touching hers, she said, "Nothing definite, but I'm trying."

Jeremy pulled away, turning in the opposite direction. "If I stay here much longer, I'll lose my mind. Rahm's a murderer. He killed my friend. I have to get out of here, and I need you, Mary. Remember your promise."

"I remember and I'm trying. Really, I am." She reached out to him, ran a finger down his back, but his "Uh-huh" response was as empty as a discarded paper bag.

"Look, I'd be lying if I said I want you to go, but I swore an oath." She took a deep breath and forged ahead before she changed her mind because maybe, just maybe, she hadn't been as forthcoming with herself—or Jeremy—as she thought. "There is one thing we can do," she admitted. "Keep a better eye on Randy."

"Why?" he said, turning back, curious, forgiving.

"He went up with Rahm."

"Up? You mean outside the cave?"

"That's right. There's more food in the pantry, and they even bought some baby things for your w—for Karen."

Jeremy rubbed a hand across his mouth, thinking. "I haven't seen much of Randy lately. He doesn't seem too interested in fishing anymore."

"That's because of Karen's school."

"Her school," he echoed mechanically.

"That's right. Didn't you pay attention at the last meeting? She said that the boys' education was 'grievously lacking,' and volunteered to teach them math and reading. She holds classes most days after she's through bossing everyone around in the mushroom garden. I worked there yesterday and it was no picnic. Karen's so obsessed with those stupid puffballs. Everything has to be just so. She even sleeps nearby, in case you haven't heard." Mary almost added: *I don't know what you ever saw in that deceitful bitch*, but wisely decided against it.

"Yeah, I heard about her sleeping arrangements," said Jeremy. "Believe me, it was purely by chance. I don't give a rat's ass what she does or where."

While Mary hoped it were true, she had her doubts, but his next words took her breath away.

"Look, Mary. If I do manage … No! *When* I do leave, why don't you come with me?"

"You mean leave here? With you? I could never do that!"

"Why not? There's nothing for you here."

Mary's narrowed eyes contrasted with Jeremy's dead-on, headlight stare. "You're wrong," she said. "Everything I value is here. This is my home. And besides, I couldn't leave Brian." She lowered her voice so that Jeremy had to strain to hear. "I know you may not understand or agree, but according to God's law we're still married. And so are you—to Karen."

"She means nothing to me," he said in response.

"I wish that were true, but I've heard you murmur her name when you think I'm not around. You can't tell me that you don't feel something. In here." Mary pressed a palm first to her heart, then his. "I've always known—don't ask me how—that your fate is not with me, with us. But before you go, I want you to leave me a gift, one to remember you by; one I swear I'll always treasure." She took his hand and placed it to her abdomen.

Jeremy tensed and pulled his hand away. "You know I have no control over that."

"You don't, but I do." She smiled at the thin line that formed by his tense, puzzled lips, but didn't bother to explain. He was much too practical, too logical, and would have no basis for understanding; she, at least, had the required faith.

While echolocation was not her forte, over the past weeks she had been practicing and improving her proficiency. She had stopped using candles when she moved among the passageways, forcing herself to rely on her voice. And then she'd had a breakthrough, an honest-to-God, lightning-bolt explosion in her head. Why not use the technique to see inside someone's body as well as outside? Why not follow the pulses where they could search out a promising sperm, coax it, and lead it until it latched onto its mate, an egg, waiting to be penetrated?

"Make love to me," she said, speaking so forcefully he dared not refuse.

"You mean right now?"

"Yes. Now," she said, tearing at his clothes.

They rolled, tumbled to the ground as Jeremy jokingly said, "I love aggressive women." Mary fastened her hands around his neck. Still laughing, he bent over and kissed her open mouth while she click-clicked above his range of hearing.

#

Karen placed her latest book on top of a stack near her bed. Despite her worsening eyesight, two lanterns made reading possible, but her fatigue proved too great a challenge. Since the beginning of her pregnancy she'd found herself nodding off at inopportune times, and she was about to blow out the flames when she heard muffled laughter.

That's odd, she told herself, knowing all the members had gone to the lake to bathe and wash their clothes. Karen had pleaded exhaustion and when Rachel offered to do her laundry, she'd accepted the offer with thanks.

Hearing more giggling, followed by a shushing rebuke, Karen sat up straight, craning her neck around a berry bush blocking her view.

Before she could identify the intruders by spoken word or echolocation, she heard multi-voiced shouts of "Surprise!" Karen stifled a sigh and pushed aside the covers as Lily, Rachel, Helene, Mary, and Janet crowded around her, placing packages on the floor.

"What's going on?" she asked.

"A baby shower," said Rachel, pointing out gifts wrapped with pictures of infants cuddling in their mothers' arms.

Karen held her lips in a pout, trying to decide whether acting appreciative or annoyed would work more in her favor. Compromising, she kept her words polite but her tone flat. "How unexpected, but nice. I'm so pleased."

Helene, too self-absorbed to notice the insincerity, flittered about on her knees, touching each box as if it belonged to her. "Go on," she said. "Open the presents. I can't wait to see what you got." She shoved the largest forward.

Karen reached for it, carefully tearing off the paper. Inside were three one-piece playsuits. She held them up, then passed them around to murmurs of "Adorable," "Look how tiny," and "They're all pink."

"That's because it's a girl," said Rachel, referring to Mary's remark regarding the color. "I can tell."

"You don't say," said Mary. She ran the point of her tongue along the inside of her cheek. "Just how can you do that?"

Rachel smiled, meeting the challenge. "I have my ways and, besides, I have influence."

Lily broke in. "She's been praying a lot. To Tloc and Toca. Especially Toca."

Mary tapped her fingers on an unopened box. "I'm afraid all the prayers in the world won't change the baby's sex. That's determined at conception. I know you never went to college, Rachel. Didn't even finish high school, right? But surely you're aware of that."

Concerned the insult would hit a nerve and cause an argument, Janet quickly spoke up. "What difference does it make, whether it's a boy or a girl? As long as it's healthy."

"Healthy's good," agreed Rachel, "but a girl would be—nice."

Karen compressed her lips, knowing just how nice a girl would be; in fact, a girl was essential since the addition of a third boy would not only complicate matters but make them worse. *I wonder,* she thought, *what they'll do if their plans fall apart?* Picturing a little Bobby or Billy, Karen laughed. As she tore the gift wrapping off another box—this time to shreds—Karen laughed louder. Inside was a sweater, also pink.

By the end of the hour, Karen had opened all the gifts amidst squeals of "Ooh" and "Aah" and came away with a complete layette. Though a number of the items were new, thanks to a special trip above, some were secondhand, a contribution from Janet's children. All, however, were clean and neatly folded.

"I hope you don't mind using cloth diapers," said Rachel. "I know it's harder, but disposables would be impossible down here. But you don't have to worry." She focused her eyes in her peculiar fashion, resting them on Karen's prize booty poking through the bottom half of her shirt. "I'll be more than happy to help you take care of little Sheena."

"Little what?" said Karen.

Janet jumped in. "Don't pay any attention to her, Karen. She tried doing the same thing with Jon. You pick whatever name you like. After all, she's your baby."

"I'm well aware of that," said Karen, noting Janet's use of the word *she.* To rub in the possibility of a potential can of worms arriving in a few months, Karen added, "I'm all set with a boy's name, but not a girl's. Sheena, however, is out of the question. It's too—"

"Strange?" said Lily.

"Exactly."

Mary broke in. "I always liked Melissa. That is, if it's a girl."

"No, Lauren is nicer," insisted Helene.

"No, Jennifer."

"Pauline."

Rachel clapped her hands to call for attention. When everyone settled down, she reached inside a brown paper bag and pulled out a stack of glasses, a towel, and a bottle of sparkling wine. "It's Champagne," she said, even though the label revealed a California vintage. Mary shook her head at the common mistake but decided to keep it to herself.

Rachel went on. "Rahm bought it for us. Wasn't that nice?" Tentatively, she pointed the bottle away from the group, wrapped it in the towel, loosened the tab on the wire cage, and eased out the stopper. "Norman showed me how to do this," she explained, "so the cork won't go flying."

Rachel poured the bubbly white liquid to the brim of every glass except Karen's. At Mary's insistence, the star of the show only received a small amount.

"To the baby," said Rachel, raising her drink in a toast.

"To Karen," added Janet.

"To their health."

"To little Sheena."

"Oh, Rachel," scolded Janet.

They all laughed, touched glasses, and drank.

Karen yawned, tapping her mouth with her fingers.

"I think it's time to call it a night," said Mary.

"But it's still early," said Helene, adding, "ouyay areyay uchsay a illkay-oyjay."

"What's that?" said Mary.

"It's Pig Latin."

"I didn't know you spoke a foreign language," said Rachel.

Helene shook her head. "And they call *me* dumb!"

Mary sniggered. "I studied *real* Latin in school. Not the porky kind. Anyway, what does it mean?"

Helene giggled. "It means you're a kill-joy."

"I think you're drunk," said Mary.

"Well, maybe a little."

Mary rose, then pointed to Karen. "Our mother-to-be needs her rest, and we've all had enough fun for one night."

"Party pooper," said Helene, licking the last drop from her glass.

"No, Mary's right," seconded Rachel. "Karen does look tired, and now that I think of it, I am too." Following Mary's lead, Rachel got to her feet. As the others sauntered off, she made a show of gathering up the empty bottle, glasses, and discarded papers. Finally, she turned to leave but not before slipping something into Karen's hand. "Sleep well," she said.

Confused, Karen stared down at a plain white envelope, sealed shut. She ripped it open, pulling out two sheets of paper, one on top of the other, folded into thirds. The scrawl, large and clumsy, nearly illegible, took up all four sides, requiring total concentration, but by placing the letter directly under a lantern and running her right index finger under each word, she read:

Dear Karen,

Excuse my poor handwriting, grammer, and misspellings. School was never a priority. I have been thinking long and hard what to say. I know these past few months have been difficult and you probably hate me, but I feel certain that in time you will understand I did what was necessary and you'll accept your new life here and find happiness in it's simple pleasures.

There is one thing in particular on my mind. Causing me worry. Soon you will be having a baby—my baby. Mary has assured me that your physical health is good, but I am concerned about your emotional well being. I don't think it's good for a pregnant woman to be living alone and feel it would be best if you moved in with me. You would be my wife and recieve all do respect.

You don't have to be concerned with Rachels feelings. She agrees with me and wouldn't mind living by herself. She's thinking about moving into the fertility area anyway, to be it's preistess. It may interest you to know that we are more like brother and sister lately. Please consider this matter carefully. Take your time as necessary but I hope you will see the wisdom in my words. Let me know your decision.

Rahm

Karen let out a shriek, followed by a "fuck you." The veins in her temples pulsed as she tore the pages and envelope into pieces and stubbed them into the dirt with her shoe. As a final measure, she reached down and lit a match to what now amounted to garbage lying in a small heap. She watched the tendrils of smoke rise, smelled the trace of ash as it entered her nostrils, and breathed deeply, taking comfort in the power of choice.

Her moment of satisfaction ended when she heard a sound, followed by the shuffle of feet. She placed her tongue to her palate and began to click. Rahm's outline appeared in her mind, and she knew he had been nearby, watching.

"It's not your baby!" she screamed, shaking her fists in front of her head, daring him to object. "And you're right. I do hate you. You and the rest. All monsters. Go! I'll never accept you."

Karen held her breath, waiting for a verbal response. When none came, she smiled and then snickered in victory when he stomped off.

No, she would not move in with Rahm. Why, even the idea carried a chill, causing the hairs on the back of her neck to rise in protest. To release the tension, she raised both arms for a slow-moving stretch and pictured a meadow abundant with shrubs, wild flowers, and slim stalks of grass. Interspersed among the lush growth were dandelions, some yellow, some white with fluffy heads ready to propagate. She picked one of the latter and whooshed out a wind-song, scattering the seeds for miles. Smiling at the image, she felt lighter on her feet but still recognized the need for something tangible, more solid than a pleasant thought to draw strength from. As her teeth raked her upper lip, she searched for an answer until the perfect one took shape. Pushing aside books and gifts, she found a small white box peeking out from under her mattress.

Opening it slowly to make the moment last, she removed her wedding ring, her simple gold band because that had been all she and Jeremy could afford. But to her its smooth, unbroken surface meant forever, and she placed it back on her finger, sorry she had ever taken it off.

Even though Jeremy had left her helpless and alone in these harsh, underground wilds, she had to admit her less-than-stellar role in the matter. But more importantly, she had noticed him looking at her of late with a hint of remorse buried in two parallel lines, one on each side of his mouth, running down to where they merged with the subtle trembling of his jaw. Although the exchange always lasted mere seconds, it planted a seed of hope that forgiveness was possible for them both.

As she twisted her ring around the fourth finger on her left hand, she made a wish that Jeremy would someday wear his again too.

"I love you," she whispered to his memory. Then, recalling the words she had spoken on their wedding day, she repeated them once again while praying for a second chance. "I give you my heart and my hand, to love and to cherish, through good times and bad, from this day forward, for as long as we both shall live." She wiped the mist from her eyes and blew out the flames from both lanterns, leaving Jeremy's image to blaze like a sunspot against the dark, where it lingered like a kiss on her lips, warming her, protecting her, and sheltering her in the night.

Chapter 20

Rahm slammed the spade with his right heel and ran a rag across his brow. The work was hard, made harder by the fact that he could only use his one good foot. Deciding it was time for a break, he entered the house through the rear door. He splashed ice-cold beer on his neck, then drank the remainder in five gulps. After finishing, he drank another. He used the toilet, flushing it twice, amused by the gurgle of the water disappearing down the sewage pipe, before returning to work.

Through his filmy eyes, protected by dark glasses, the sky looked hazy, but he knew it burned red and hot with the temperature soaring into the high eighties. Cursing the sun, which made his task more difficult, he removed his shirt, allowing sweat to run freely down his chest and back.

He spoke to Norman. "We have no choice. We'll have to get Randy's help if we want to finish turning the soil in time to plant the seeds on schedule. He already knows about this house as well as its location. I've sworn him to secrecy. I'll tell him to keep mum about the garden too. He'll listen to me. By the way, have you noticed how many inches he's shot up this year?"

Norman nodded. "Yeah, he takes after Tom. That is, if Tom really was his father. That man was humungous, but I hope Randy will at least have more sense. Imagine … he's almost twelve years old! Where did the time go?" Norman adjusted the brim on his baseball cap. "You know what?" he continued. "Besides Randy getting his own room, this garden can be part of the whole birthday package: growing fresh vegetables jibes with our trusting him to go above ground. He'll love the challenge and responsibility. He's so eager to be a man and all that shit, but I think he'll also love those sports shoes you and Rachel splurged on. Great idea! For some reason he's jealous … no, wait a minute … he's *obsessed* with Jon's climbing ability. Don't know why since his skills are so good. They're not like Jon's, of course, but no one's are. Still, those shoes may help with any lack of confidence. And speaking of Jon—now *there's* something to worry about. And not just his looks. His freaky behavior."

Rahm pursed his lips. "Yeah, I'm also concerned, but Karen's been helping, teaching him vocabulary and how to count. He actually did four times four using his fingers. Showed me how he does it. The kid's pretty smart, but you're right. We've ignored his needs, and it's messing him up in strange ways. Too much time by himself. I'll ask Karen to work with him more. That is, if she'll speak to me."

"She'll come around," said Norman with a conspiratorial wink before dropping his shovel to enter the house for another cup of coffee. Despite the heat, he needed his fix. While Norman took his break, Rahm questioned why no one had thought of this sooner: growing "real" vegetables, the kind that needed sun. He, Norman and Rachel had picked up the necessary supplies months before on a trip above, but the idea had come from Rachel and she deserved full credit.

Rahm continued the grueling work, making a mental note to speak to Randy later that day to tell him about his new assignment and what was expected. His trust in the boy's judgment grew daily, and just as Rahm had hoped, Randy informed him of Jeremy's nosing around. Yes, Jeremy continued to be a dilemma, and Rahm didn't know how he'd deal with him in the long run, but for now he remained little more than a pain in the ass. As for Randy, the boy was not only strong in body but in mind. He cared for his fellow members because they were family, unlike Jeremy, who didn't give a crap and ran for office for his own selfish reasons.

With that memory once again brought to the forefront, Rahm spat in disgust, droning on to an audience of one how five people had voted against him. Of course, two had been Karen and Jeremy, but even so. As his face clenched in anger, he reasoned that he shouldn't let anything surprise him. There would always be ingrates, and perhaps it was just some half-cocked rebelliousness on the part of those with smaller minds. *Well, maybe it's partly my fault,* he admitted, tugging on his lip with a finger. *Maybe Jeremy does have a point and I've treated them like children. But then, that's how they behave. Weak and indecisive. But Randy's different,* he concluded, feeling certain the boy would be up to the task of handling the load, years from now, when the time came to transfer the reins. Rahm paused, blinked the sweat from his eyes, and took a swig from the water jug on the porch.

"Goldangit!" he swore, picturing his batty mother before him, paddle ready for when he said anything stronger. "This has sure been some year." Since he had first found out about Karen's pregnancy, the distinction between being a mere father and a responsible, caring parent had grown with the expansion of her waist. He had considered, years ago, that he might be Jon's birth father, but the matter had little value one way or the other. Perhaps it had to do with his feelings toward Janet—strictly platonic and an irony considering the circumstance—or perhaps it was because Tom had still been alive and the paternal obligations were handed to him.

This time, however, the experience of reproduction, from conception to, hopefully, a pass-the-cigars *birth-day,* made his head spin with happiness, along with a pint of worry and questions regarding the meaning of life and—dare he think it?—

God. Further shielding his eyes with his hand, he chanced a quick glance at the sun with its eternal flame, and shook his head with awe, praying for the first time in years for the strength to meet the new challenges.

Can it be true? he asked himself. *Karen and Jeremy kaput, finished with each other?* He snickered like a naughty boy, cognizant of his role in their breakup, particularly when Mary disclosed the smutty details during that big scene where Karen had confessed and Jeremy had stalked off. But in the long run all would work out for the best. As for the baby, he felt sure it carried his genes just as he felt sure that its mother would someday share his bed.

Yet despite his positive outlook, Rahm felt unable to keep Jeremy from souring his spirits. He had not tried to stop him from pursuing his explorations, knowing that without hope we all die, and Jeremy might still play a useful part in their future. So for the present, Rahm would settle on watching his antagonist more carefully. There was no way he'd risk teaching him echolocation as he had with Karen, suspecting the skill would help bond her to the group. No, Jeremy was different, and he'd just have to trust that eventually the man would accept the inevitable. If not, other options remained … but there was no reason to consider them now, not with the future so bright.

Rahm leaned his spade against the wall and ran his tongue across his dry mouth. "It's too damn hot," he said, brushing past Norman, now heading down the porch steps as he headed back up.

"I'll stay overnight," said Norman. "I don't climb as fast as you, and this way I can start early before it heats up. It's brutal."

"Good idea," said Rahm. "I'll join you tomorrow, later in the afternoon, and I'll bring Randy." As the screen door slammed behind him, he heard another beer calling his name.

#

Mary's prediction proved correct. While he had not spoken to Karen in months, had barely looked at her, Jeremy didn't—couldn't—stop thinking about her.

He had been out on the boat alone for nearly two hours without paying one moment's attention to catching fish. As a result, the basket remained empty. "Screw this, I'm done," he howled. Reaching for the oars, he headed to shore, his mouth pinched tight like the pulled casing on a drawstring purse.

After tying up the boat, he retrieved his clothes from a nearby stalagmite. It had been months since he had worn anything while fishing since the coldness of the water no longer bothered him. No point in getting even his underwear soaked, he reasoned.

It was an uphill climb from the rowboat's docking point to the mushroom garden. With his split-second reflexes and knees as springy as Spalding Hi-Bounce Balls, he avoided injuring his limbs while scaling over boulders, some higher than shoulder level. The realization that soon he would be able to compete with Rahm on a level neither had foreseen struck him as triumphant, but he would save the crowing for later. His sense of touch had sharpened too, so much that he could discriminate among minerals, from quartz to aragonite, by a single grain of sand. He stood still, his eyes and ears on alert.

There was not even one candle lit in the garden, but he knew he wasn't alone. Only, the person in attendance wasn't Karen but Rachel. He could tell by her fairy-light movements with her feet barely touching the ground, reminding him of astronauts bouncing on the moon. He realized she also sensed his presence. Still, he didn't bother to speak; instead he walked off, leaving her to wonder.

If Karen isn't here, she must be there, "there" being her makeshift classroom closer to the guano pit. Far enough away to avoid the stench (he had heard her say in the common area) but close enough to get some benefit from natural lighting.

Jeremy squirmed at the thought of returning to that godforsaken place. He hadn't been back since the day of their failed escape when Rahm had caught him and pounded his stomach to ground beef; all the same, he had to talk to her, and now.

He remembered the way, the tunnel, the manmade hole, but then, how could he forget? Arriving at the hole, he found it further etched out, probably to accommodate Karen's widening girth, and soon he heard Jon playing by himself among the rocks and formations. Jeremy wasn't surprised since the boy often ran off alone, apparently too young to concentrate for long stretches of time but also because he was … well, weird. Jeremy berated himself for thinking of Jon as a freak, but seeing him as he was—a ghastly figure that faded in and out with his skeleton on display—how could he not? *Still, it's not Jon's fault,* he told himself. *It's theirs. Those assholes!*

Jon smiled as Jeremy approached. "Want to play with me?" he asked, making rows of rocks and stacking them according to size as he counted.

Jeremy was happy to note that the boy was speaking again, thanks no doubt to Karen's help, but he looked away from Jon's vibrating vocal cords so that his revulsion wouldn't register to the poor child.

"Sorry, I've come to speak to Karen. She is here, isn't she?"

"Uh-huh," he replied. "Want me to bring you to her?"

"Okay," he said, although he could easily find the way himself. Holding Jon's hand, he allowed the boy to take the lead. Jeremy's breath quickened as his determination ebbed, and he felt glad for the small hand clasping his.

With the help of lanterns in a semicircle and a trace of sunlight from beyond, Jeremy made out two forms, sitting close together: Karen and Randy.

When he got within a few feet, he noted Karen's face had lost its girlish prettiness. In its place was an older, less innocent version: a little worn, a little frazzled, reminding him of his mother, who'd become overwhelmed at her husband's premature death and had taken her own life soon after, leaving him an orphan in the care of his aunt. Suddenly afraid, Jeremy shuddered. Choking back guilty tears, he went to his wife. He further noted her face had lost all traces of its healthy glow, and again felt the weight of responsibility.

Karen's eyes widened and the book she was holding slipped to the ground. Reflexively, Jeremy bent to pick it up, but noticing his fingers coated with a white, gooey substance, he stopped and held them to his face, befuddlement written in the lines on his brow.

Karen answered his unspoken question, gulping back her own queasy response. "You held Jon's hand," she explained. "His skin, particularly his fingers, has tiny glands that secrete a sticky substance. It's not his fault."

"I just told myself the same thing moments ago," he said. He wiped the guck on his pants legs and once again bent down to retrieve the book. Passing it to her, he felt the pulse on her wrist, fluttering rapidly like a baby bird.

"Your eyes are well enough for books again?" he asked.

"Y-yes," she said. "Since we started coming here, they've gotten better. Randy's are better too." She gestured to the boy, who watched in silence.

Having enough rambling chitchat, Jeremy said, "Listen, Karen. I'd like to get right to the point. You know why I've come, don't you?"

"I'm not sure. What do you want?"

"Ask the boys to leave, and I'll tell you."

Karen turned to Randy. "Here's my watch. Take your brother and be back in fifteen minutes." Jon had already begun to protest, but when Karen explained he could study the watch, he relented.

Having rehearsed his speech earlier, Jeremy forged ahead. "This morning when I was out on the lake, I recalled something you said. I kept repeating it over and over in my mind.

"It was on the day I almost stra-strangled you" he said, kneading his hands. "You said that no matter what happens, to remember who the enemy is. I'm sorry, Karen, but I forgot. And even worse, for a while I thought it was you."

Karen, confusion written in her eyes, asked Jeremy to repeat himself.

"I'm sorry, Karen."

"Don't apologize," she begged. "It's all my fault."

"No. No," he countered. "It's mine."

"But look what I did. Look what I *did*." She crossed her arms around her belly as if trying to hide the evidence.

"I think I understand now. You blamed me for bringing you here. And the worst part is I knew better. How could I let absolute strangers lead us away from the main section? Dumb," he said, shaking his head, "and worse, selfish too. I just had to have my way. *My way*! It's always been like that, hasn't it?" Jeremy winced at the silence. "Jesus," he said. "It must have been easy for Rahm to take advantage of you—you were suffering so much, and Rahm's great at twisting things to his advantage. If I hadn't been so crazy myself, I'd have seen it coming."

"Oh, Jeremy!" she wailed, covering her tear-streaked face with her hands.

He pulled her to him. "Shh," he said, stroking her hair. "It's all right. Everything's gonna be all right. Please, stop crying. It's all right. It's all right."

#

Jeremy wrinkled his nose. "Squash again?" he said.

"Some of us like it," said David, giving Janet a double thumbs-up. "In fact, you've outdone yourself."

"Thank you, David," said Janet, "but the credit goes to Helene. She added the spices."

Jeremy forced himself to take a few bites before pushing back his plate. Ever since he could remember, he'd hated squash. Whether baked, boiled, broiled, or fried, it remained the same: tasteless and slimy and they'd been eating it for five days in a row. Whatever Janet or Helene had done tonight, the results bore no improvement; still a sloppy mess.

About to leave with Karen, Jeremy noticed Mary's penetrating stare, signaling to him from across the table. Although it had been over a month since he had left her to move back in with Karen, he could still read her face with its I-need-to-talk-to-you message. Reluctantly he helped himself to more of the swill to delay leaving the table. "Why don't you start back without me?" he said to Karen. "I'll be along soon."

"You sure you don't mind? I am very tired."

"Go ahead. I'm feeling quite hungry all of a sudden."

Jeremy played with the squash on his plate, taking only tiny bites when necessary. Lily and Rachel were in the fertility area and the men left to do their duty. Rahm was the last to leave after suggesting a hand of bridge later in the evening.

"Not my thing," said Jeremy. Mary shook her head sideways.

Mary waited a few minutes to be certain no one was returning or spying. Standing between two stalagmites, she peeked into the kitchen, checking on Janet who was scraping leftovers from the plates. Next the busy mother handed her younger son a pail, sending him off to gather berries for tomorrow's breakfast. This being Jon's first official duty, he scampered away, his face flashing like party sparklers. Janet turned back to finish the cleanup. Reassured, Mary lowered her head to Jeremy's ear. "Meet me back at *our* place," she whispered. "It's important."

Jeremy counted to sixty, then forced out a thank you to Janet so she'd know he was leaving. With measured steps, he set off, troubled yet hoping for good news. He ran a finger along a now familiar outcropping and purposely flicked off a chunk laden with popped-corn growths. He laughed at his debauchery. But moments later, he noted his shoes growing damp and wiped his eyes as he imagined summer showers in the real world, not this fake devil domain he was forced to inhabit.

Above, life continued as before: people drove to work, children went to school, the sun shined or it poured cats and dogs. But here there was no change of seasons. Nights held no moon or Milky Way, and his only companions were a combination of screwballs and fanatics.

With Carl's death, now a painful fact, and the chance at victory looking bleak, Jeremy had once again started viewing his own demise as a welcome friend. But remembering his pledge to Karen and his mother's words to never give up, he banished the idea from his mind. *Too bad Mom couldn't follow her own advice*, he mused, picturing them together on his eleventh birthday, mere weeks before she'd died.

He found Mary sitting on what had been their bed. All other items—books, knickknacks, shelves, bedside tables—were gone. But why had she left the bed, now a bare mattress? What was the point?

Not knowing what to expect, he approached her cautiously. She had been so angry, lashing out like a typhoon, when he had moved back with Karen. He had tried to explain his obligations, his feelings of guilt, but she wouldn't listen, claiming she wanted no excuses as she flung his few possessions past the flimsy sheet which had served as their door.

Over the following month, he'd repeatedly tried to resume a friendship, but she wanted no part of it. He only hoped she would live up to her word and contact him at some point, and here he stood, hands held flat at his sides, fingers crossed for luck.

"I'm glad you asked to see me," he said, his pulse pounding in his ears as he struggled to set the right tone. "I've wanted to talk to you, but you never gave me the chance."

Her posture remained stiff. "It wasn't necessary."

"Of course it was. I want—need you to understand."

"For whose sake, Jeremy? Yours or mine?"

"For both our sakes. Please, just listen." In response to her foot tapping the ground, he hurried on. "I thought I hated her. I really thought I wanted nothing to do with her. And why?" Without thinking, he rammed both fists against the wall. If it hurt, he gave no indication, although a line of blood appeared across his knuckles. He paid it no mind. "Think of it from my perspective. Just try! If it wasn't for me, Karen wouldn't be in this mess. Don't you see? I can't let her go through this alone. Even if the baby isn't mine, she needs me. I owe her that much."

Mary held back a response, but his eyes misted over, begging for another minute. "I really loved you, Mary. That was real and always will be. But you know as well as I—you said it yourself—we have other commitments. Wrong time, wrong place, as they say. Just tell me all's forgiven. Please, Mary, don't be mad. I'm hanging on by threads. I can't take any more."

He checked his sore fingers, licked off the blood, and wiggled them. Satisfied all was still working, he shielded them behind his body, ashamed.

Mary went to him, *his* Mary again, and took his bruised hands, kissing them. "I could never hate you," she said. "You gave me back my life. I just needed time to adjust."

"And have you?"

Mary sat down, and lovingly ran her eyes across their mattress. "Yes," she said, "and furthermore, I've moved back with Brian. He begged me! It's amazing how nice he is now. He's a changed person, but then so am I; still, I made sure he knows I left this mattress here. It's my insurance policy. I'll never let him take me for granted again."

"Good for you," said Jeremy, lowering himself beside her.

"But I didn't ask you here to thrash out personal business," she said. "Frankly, I'm surprised you're not jumping out of your skin by now."

Jeremy squinted, held his hands up and out as if he were carrying a tureen. "What are you talking about?"

"Our dinner. Didn't you notice something strange?"

"Yeah," he said. "We had squash again and it's worse than I remembered." He watched her watching him through eyes round with bewilderment.

"That's not the point," she said. "Those were vegetables we were eating and they were fresh. Remember, there's no grocery store for miles outside."

"Yeah, so? I know they go up from time to time to shop."

"But not daily, Jeremy. Use your brain. You went to college."

He bit his lip, thinking, then slapped the side of his head. "Of course. Fresh zucchini! It needs sunlight for photosynthesis. That means there's a vegetable garden near an opening. It can't be outside Dinky Cave's main entrance. Didn't you say Rahm destroyed the passageway? It can't be beyond the guano pit either."

"And so …?"

"And so … Hmm, I'll bet the third opening is near that house, that so-called safe-house I've heard rumors about. But that also means it's close enough to get to daily. Oh my God! A third opening means a third exit!" He jumped up and began pacing in tight circles, his mind switching from one option to another before discarding them all. He turned back to Mary; she had never let him down.

Mary squirmed. "I hope I'm not sending you on a wild goose chase, Jeremy, but I need to clear myself of a sin." She looked into his eyes. "The sin of omission. You see, when Brian and I first moved here, we came in a different way from you and Karen. There was a small house in the woods and even though it was isolated, it had a high fence so you couldn't see the hole in the back yard. Norman owned the place. Said it was a gift from his father. Actually, it was little more than a cabin. Not quite a shack, but small, with no central heating. He said he was going to sell the place and use the money for supplies, but there must have been a change of plans 'cause sometimes he goes up and stays overnight. And I've also heard talk of a car."

Jeremy felt a fire in his gut; the tips of his ears burned. "So that's the safe-house. Why didn't you tell me all this before?"

Mary dropped her eyes, embarrassed. "First, I didn't think it mattered. Second, I didn't put two and two together until now. Also, there's no way I could find the route after all this time, but I do remember first climbing down a series of ladders, then crossing some very tricky passageways before coming out near the lake. Anyway, I think I know who can help you."

Jeremy dropped to his knees in front of her, grabbing her shoulders. "Dear Lord, Mary. Who?"

"Randy! Have you been keeping track of his movements like I suggested?"

He dropped his arms. "Not really. There were more important matters to deal with. At least that's what I thought."

Mary smiled. "That's okay. I've been watching. Late this afternoon, I saw him walk into the kitchen with a backpack. It must have had zucchini in it. Freshly picked. I know it wasn't Rahm that picked them because he's been helping Norman and Brian this week. They're digging new trenches for the toilets."

"Then I'll follow him at a distance," said Jeremy, "and find the route."

"No!" said Mary. "Not you. Karen."

Jeremy tipped his head. "Karen? Why Karen? She's having trouble moving, and I know my way around as well as she does."

"I've been watched her too." said Mary. "She moves just fine despite her belly. But the reason is she can echolocate."

"*What*? She never told me that."

Mary smirked. "Can't say I'm surprised. But don't you see? Karen can stay farther back so there's less chance she'll be noticed."

"Okay. I see your point. Then this is it. Maybe that lucky break I've been hoping for." He lay down on the mattress, exhausted.

Mary swallowed. "Jeremy," she said, her voice low and husky. "Don't rush this opportunity. It may be your last one. But there's something else. Well, two things, actually. Hey, are you listening? I wanted to tell you how Tom died. It might be useful."

"Tom?"

"Yes, Tom. You know—Randy's father."

"Oh, yeah. I thought he fell."

"He did, but there's more to the story than that." Mary paused, then took a breath to reconsider the sequence of her agenda. "Maybe I should go to the other matter first. It's more important. We can get to Tom later."

Jeremy started as Mary sprawled across the mattress beside him, laying her hand on his chest. "I know you're back with Karen," she said, fidgeting like a bashful teenager, "but—well, I'm still not pregnant. If we could just try one more time, I'd be forever grateful."

Jeremy's eyebrows rose and came together, almost forming one continuous line. "Mary, my Mary," he said, repeating her name like the chorus in a love song. He brushed her hair, her cheek, and lightly touched her full lips, so different from his wife's thin ones. "You know there isn't anything I wouldn't do for you, and I— I've missed you so." He hesitated for a moment, but that's all it took, and after running his eyes over her lush form, he shook his head and grinned. "Oh, what the hell!"

Chapter 21

Karen leaned forward to place a kiss on Jeremy's taut lips. Something felt off. She knew it down to her bones. Since their reconciliation, his affection toward her seemed spurious, and his moods fluctuated like an elevator jumping between floors. One moment he would say he loved her, and the next he barely said a word.

Karen suspected he had been with Mary the previous evening. While she tried to convince herself their affair was over—that he and Mary were just friends—she found her trust being tested. But that issue faded to less than nothing when he announced they'd soon attempt another escape, and that it would be her responsibility to shadow Randy, who knew the route out.

"Why me?" she asked.

"Because Mary said you can echolocate. That's why. Why didn't you tell me?"

Karen ran her fingers through her straggly hair. "I was afraid you'd feel my willingness to learn had been a sign of capitulation. It wasn't and that's the truth, but I wish I'd been more forthcoming."

"Yes, it would help if you were honest."

"Speaking about honesty—exactly what happened last night? I know where you were. Don't deny it."

Jeremy shrugged. "Mary and I—we just talked."

Karen raised her eyebrows. "Just talked?"

"That's right! And, since you mentioned Mary, you owe her a debt of gratitude. If she didn't tell me you could echolocate, I'd never know, and we'd be screwed."

Touché on that, she thought, knowing that her sixth sense increased their chance for success; still, the one thing that frightened her more than anything else was failure. Suddenly cold, she pulled the blanket tighter. "I'm afraid," she uttered.

"Of course you're afraid. I'm afraid too. Still, this is our best shot so don't mess it up. But right now I gotta meet Norman at the lake to patch up the boat. I don't want to be late and have him become suspicious. We'll talk more tonight."

Karen remained behind, confused and disheartened. Feeling the weight of their life-or-death circumstance, she hunched over like an old woman. "Someone help me," she sighed.

The baby stirred, both deflecting and demanding her attention. She reached down to touch it with a mother's gentle caress. *Do you have dark hair like Jeremy's or mousy-brown like mine?* Then a looming cloud crossed her mind, forcing another question, one she preferred to ignore: *or blond hair like Rahm's?* Her shoulders sagged and her chest folded inward, causing the baby to press against her diaphragm. Redressing the discomfort, she stretched her torso, palms flat on the ground, and took a deep breath to accommodate its position. Who the father was, she decided, no longer mattered. What did matter was the bond she shared with her child, and with only a slip of membrane between them, Karen knew that the bond would never be stronger.

"Are you hungry, little one?" she said. "Mommy will go eat your breakfast for you." She rose, using her hands and knees for leverage, cognizant of the extra weight, and headed toward the kitchen. After downing a bowl of cereal and a big chunk of freshly made bread, she mixed another glass of powdered milk. While careful to drink the full amount, she crinkled her nose, gulping it quickly, having never adjusted to its watery taste.

She checked her watch, still ticking after all these months, unlike Jeremy's which had gotten soaked at the Thanksgiving picnic. *Time to get to work.*

The first item on her agenda was the one she regretted the most: saying goodbye to her mushrooms. After reuniting with Jeremy, she had returned to Suburbia, instead of sleeping among her fungal family.

She walked along the narrow passage, hands out sideways gauging the thick earthen walls which glittered with golden flecks, reminding her of freckles. "Fleckles," she said, pausing to laugh while making a mental note to check a dictionary to see if there was such a word. She flicked off a chunk of the glistening silt and considered wrapping it in tissue for safekeeping—for the day when this place would be no more than a memory. "No," she said, concluding it best to leave all traces behind; instead she exhaled puffs of air against the fleckles in her palm, watching as they dropped to the ground.

She continued with heavy steps, vacillating between fear and uncertainty. As she felt the power of once more becoming master of her fate, her body gained strength and she called out a "Yesss," stretching the word, repeating it as she marched. With her arm and leg muscles contracting and relaxing, flexing and extending, she finished the walk exuberated, like a jogger out for a run, and arrived at the garden before her assigned helpers, Rachel and Helene.

Following her suggestion at the last community meeting, two people regularly assisted, but Rachel often spent the early hours attending to the altar and cleaning up after the night's debauchery, or perhaps mixing a new batch of royal jelly; as for Helene, she was probably in bed.

Karen lit all the lanterns. She hadn't done this in months since she, without realizing it, had adapted to the darkness and found two or even one sufficient. Now, however, she wanted to see the garden the same as she had when Rachel first brought her here, and like the director of a play, she stood back to take in the scene, holding her breath as the lights shimmered off the walls. She looked again and realized it wasn't only the lights shimmering, but also her mushrooms—they glowed like gems and danced with an élan vital, narrowing and stretching their length, insisting on her attention.

Karen began to sway in sync with the fungal dancers, her body turning in half-circles across the room. Feeling dizzy and afraid she might fall, she sat on the ground to witness the rest of this spectacle. For the first time, she understood Rachel's religious fervor, knowing that no one could comprehend her connection to her special friends as they spoke to her in one commanding voice, resonating in her head.

Stay, they said.

"I can't," she answered.

Please, they said. *We love you.*

Karen covered her ears. "I love you too, but I have to go."

No, they hissed, suddenly angry and sending out tiny shock waves to Karen's skin. She ran her hands along her arms, the hairs stiff and fiery.

The mushrooms became alarmed and began to shrink in size, ashamed of their behavior. Still, they weren't about to give up and called in new recruits from the beds below that tried a different tact, rocking and nodding their caps with the offer of initiation. *Join us*, they said, working their spell.

Karen wavered and once again the mushrooms grew tall, until—

"Enough," said Karen, with a steadfast shake of her head.

They huddled among themselves, murmuring words she couldn't understand. Then, caps held high and staring directly at her, they tried one final approach, a play on her sympathy. *We need you*, they begged. *Don't leave us.*

"I have to. I must. But don't worry. Others will care for you."

Defeated, they dropped down to size. *It won't be the same. It won't be the same*
. . .

Karen wiped her cheeks and swallowed the lump in her throat. The effort did little good since she found herself whimpering, but, hearing footsteps, she grew quiet and sent out her voice. Finding its mark, it bounced off a small, solid object. A fraction of that energy returned as an image which she, in turn, interpreted as Rachel. The whole process took less than a second.

Hearing Karen's cry along with seeing the numerous glowing lights just beyond, Rachel stepped up her pace. "Something wrong?" she asked, coming in from dark.

Karen thought quickly. "No. Just pregnancy hormones. I wanted to arrive early. Make sure everything's okay."

"And is it?"

"Uh, yes, although rows five and six look a little dry and we're getting low on guano."

Taking it as a criticism, Rachel scowled, although the attempt made her look more funny than threatening. "Well, if you had to work with Helene, you'd be behind too. Do you know what time she got here yesterday?"

Karen shrugged, and asked the obvious. "What time?"

"Just before lunch. And then as soon as she got one little nail dirty"—she paused to raise a symbolic finger, sticking it in front of Karen's face—"she said she was hungry. She's thoughtless and lazy and makes it harder for everyone else. I'm sick of that woman."

"Have you tried talking to her?"

"Are you kidding? Of course I have. And you can see what good it's done." Rachel threw up her hands in exasperation.

"I'm sorry," said Karen, patting her belly. "I wish I could do more."

Rachel softened. "It's not your fault, and I shouldn't be taking it out on you. Just tell me what else needs to get done."

"Um, beds one and two look like they need mycelium."

"I was gonna do that today."

"I can help with that; there's not much work involved."

"No. Definitely not. There'll be plenty of time for you to help later."

"Okay," said Karen. "In that case, I'll start my lesson plans for the boys, but first I'll have my own talk with Helene."

"You're wasting your time."

"You're probably right, but what the hell. I might as well give it a try." She turned to go but shifted her weight to the other leg and raised a hand to her chin, hesitating. Searching around the cavernous space as if she had lost something, she scanned the mushrooms until she settled on one in particular with a large bulbous head. Karen mumbled, "You do understand, don't you?"

Rachel looked up. "What did you say?"

Karen jumped, her cheeks turning pink. "Sorry. Just talking to myself. Guess I'd better be going." This time she left without stopping.

#

Just as expected, Karen found Helene all by herself, curled up under the covers. David had left earlier to help Rahm and Brian with the new trenches. Although he also had a reputation for self-indulgence, he couldn't compete with Helene. No one could.

Compressing her mouth in a slit of annoyance, Karen reached down and yanked hard on the frayed corner of a blanket. Helene sat up immediately.

"Hey, what's going on?"

"Yes. What's going on? Aren't you supposed to be somewhere else by now?"

Helene grunted, grabbed the blanket, and pulled it up to her neck. "Since when do you make the rules?"

"I don't, but I know what they are: no work, no food. I seem to remember Rahm saying that once. Maybe I'll have a talk with him."

Helene scrambled to her feet, fully naked, her slim body a sharp contrast to Karen's round one. Each looked at the other, taking in the difference.

"Just 'cause you're pregnant, you think you can do whatever you want. Well, I've got news for you, you fat cow." She stuck out her tongue, almost adding a verbal childish taunt, but reconsidered. "You're really not going to tell him, are you?"

Karen, too amused with Helene's antics to stay angry, said, "If I have to I will, but I don't think it'll be necessary. Rachel will probably do it first. Oh, by the way, I assigned you the best job this week: gathering the guano. Norman's too busy to do it. You may get your hands dirty. Too bad!"

Helene curled her fingers, digging her nails into her palms. "Go ahead!" she shrieked. "Laugh at me. They all do. Why should you be different?" She let out a wail, catching Karen off balance.

"I wasn't laughing at you," said Karen, suddenly ashamed. "At least, I didn't think I was."

"I know what they say. I pretend I don't hear, but I do. They all think I'm good for nothing but sex, but I'm not even good for that." Her lips began to quiver as she stared at Karen's belly. "One, two, three and you're pregnant. I-I hate you."

Karen blanched. "I don't even want this baby," she said, no longer sure if it were true. In any case, Helene was crying too hard to hear.

"I got my period this morning," she moaned as if mourning the death of a loved one. "I'm sorry I ever came to this miserable place. If it wasn't for David, I'd try to leave; even *he* doesn't give a shit about me. No one ever has. It's not fair! It's not fair!" Slumping over, she scooped up clothes from a nearby pile and buried her face in them.

Taken aback, Karen sank down beside the troubled woman, who suddenly seemed more of an ally than a foe. "You're right," she agreed. "It's not fair."

Helene looked up, slowly breathed in and out, easing the tension. "What should I do?"

"Keeping busy works best for me."

Helene's mood shifted and she wrapped her arms around Karen's neck, clinging like a helpless child. "I really don't hate you," she said. "And I'm sorry I called you a fat cow."

"I know you didn't mean it," said Karen, returning the hug. "It's too bad we met under these circumstances. Maybe somewhere, someplace else, we could have been friends." She pulled away and impulsively added a kiss to Helene's face. As usual, Helene was too absorbed in her own problems to notice anything amiss, and Karen walked off with a goodbye under her breath, suspecting this would be her first and last heart-to-heart with Helene.

Rattled by Helene's temperamental display, she stopped at her room for a break. *She's such a mass of contradictions,* she mused, *but then I guess we all are, me included.* Finding the insight disturbing, Karen cleared her mind in the same way she smoothed the ground after a lesson with the boys. She had too much to do that morning to dwell on issues without answers.

She checked the time and hurried off, not wanting to keep the boys waiting. After grabbing a large book from a pile near her bed, she placed it inside a satchel, which she had confiscated from a box in the storage area labeled "useful junk." She looped the bag across her chest and headed in the direction of her school.

With the unpleasant task of spinning lies and manipulations now upon her, she forgot to pace herself for the uphill climb and, breathing heavily, stopped to lean against a stalagmite. She gasped when the top broke off and crumbled to the ground. It had been one of the beautiful, twisted kinds with branches running up, down, and sideways, with no thought to gravity. Knowing it would take many thousands of years for it to replace itself, she held her hand over her heart and apologized, but then reminded herself that this world, and all it represented, would soon be a blur.

In the near distance, she could hear Jon, sounding, thankfully, like a normal child playing in a schoolyard. Her face lit up at the significance, proud of the role she had played. His webbed fingers, however, and see-through skin, were permanent, as well as his pointy rat nose, always twitching. Somehow she'd have to warn Janet to keep up the extra attention or risk losing him again. Fortunately, Randy showed no signs of gross metamorphosis.

Both boys ran up to her, excited and eager to please.

"We've been doing just as you told us," said Randy.

Karen knew what he meant. "If you want to read," she had drummed in, "you have to see the small print. That means additional time with natural lighting."

Unfortunately, in Jon's case the improvement was slight. His vision had always been poor, with people and objects appearing in shadows. While the shadows had lifted a little, the results remained unsatisfactory. For Randy, however, his vision had progressed to the point where he could recognize everyone by their faces alone, although the features became fuzzy if he stood more than a few feet away. Sometimes he complained that it was more annoying than when he could barely see at all.

"Things may seem worse before they get better," Karen explained, followed by a handshake and a hug. Randy flinched as his body warmed up, especially down below. Panicking, he pulled away.

"What about me?" said Jon, craving attention as well as assurance. Karen smiled, although the corners of her lips looked as if they were taped in place. "I'm proud of you too" she said, lifting him up and twirling him around. The arteries in Jon's face and neck glowed, pulsing on and off, further lighting up the surroundings. He laughed and clapped his misshapen fingers. Karen laughed too.

"I'm afraid I didn't have time to prepare a lesson plan today. So how about we do something special? Pretend it's a holiday, of sorts. See? I brought your favorite book. Fairy tales."

While Jon let out a whoop and twirled on his heels, Randy remained quiet, watching as Karen lowered herself to the ground, her unzipped hooded sweatshirt spread out below her.

"I'm ... I'm sorry," he stammered. "I forgot to bring the pillows. But it won't happen again 'cause I'll look for some old ones today, right after we get back. We can store them here, along with the writing materials."

"Good idea," said Karen, motioning for the boys to sit down. They took their positions, one to the left of her, one to the right, each pressing in, trying to gain an advantage over the other, as Karen skimmed through the table of contents.

"No pushing," she said, "there's plenty of room." She let each boy pick two stories from the anthology and despite the fact that she had read them all before, both boys, for different reasons, sat quietly, enthralled by the works of the Brothers Grimm.

Randy, his education so lacking, had no idea that these stories were written for younger children and delighted in the tales of good versus evil and faraway places, and Jon, although he couldn't see the pictures in detail, had an imagination capable of sketching the words. When she finished, Jon, of course, asked for more. "Soon," she told him. "First I want to talk to your brother. Why don't you play by yourself near the rocks? When we're finished we'll come get you."

To Karen's relief, he ran off without complaining. She muffled a sigh, telling herself to be careful since the hard part, the deceptive part, was about to begin. She remembered how she had warned Jeremy to keep Randy out of this dirty mess. "He's only a child," she had said, but now she, too, was about to betray his trust. Boosting her resolve with an inner pep talk, she forged ahead but couldn't help noticing Randy's eyes, so trusting and just beginning to reveal a window to the adult he would be.

"I asked Jon to leave," she began, "because I don't want to hurt his feelings. Unlike him, you've had major improvements since you started coming here. Your skin has a healthier tone and your visual acuity is growing in distance and detail. I know how much you want to read grownup books and you've been very patient and cooperative. Your brother's sight, I'm afraid, will never be adequate, but you—you have a chance. A good chance, and I have an idea how we can hurry things along."

"How?" he asked, after taking the book from Karen's lap and holding it near his face. He moved the precious tome closer, then farther away, trying to find the ideal spot to focus on.

Karen had an immediate answer, having rehearsed it in her mind. "I want you to stop using your voice to see. Totally. Even in the dark. I don't mean forever, of course. Just for a while."

Randy sat back, alarmed. "But how will I get around? I'll be blind."

Karen pulled a candle from her pocket. "No, you won't. You'll use this. I want you to depend only on your sight. When this candle burns down, get another from the supply closet. We'll try the experiment for a week and see what happens."

Randy's mouth sagged. He hated the idea, but since he wanted to please Karen as much as he wanted to read, he promised to comply.

"Now, will you do me one other favor? Go fetch your brother." Without waiting for an answer, she lit the candle and placed the remainder of the matches in his pocket.

While he was gone, Karen wiped the sweat from her brow, relieved that she could dispose of the outward manifestation of anxiety so easily. Lying to Randy felt downright evil and soon he would comprehend how she had used him. She only hoped she wouldn't be around to witness his face as it transformed from confusion to sadness and finally to anger as he fathomed her duplicity. *He may even wind up hating me*, she thought, and how could she blame him, knowing this might be the act that turned his childhood innocence to grownup cynicism?

Randy returned with Jon in tow, followed, to Karen's surprise, by Helene. "I brought your lunch," she said, holding up a pail and looking among the faces. "Rachel told me to. She's such a bully. She also said I should stay here until you finish your milk." The last comment was directed toward Karen, who, conscious of all the complications she had encountered in one day, drank it down quickly, not wanting to add to the tangled mess.

After Helene left, Randy made a sour face and placed his tongue between his lips, blowing out the famous Bronx cheer even though he had never heard of it or its other name—the raspberry. "Helene's right," he said. "Rachel's a bully; worse than my mom. I wanted to bring peanut butter and jelly sandwiches today, make them myself, but she wouldn't let me. She said we should save the canned food for emergencies."

"I want pea butter and jell!" screamed Jon.

"That's peanut butter and jelly," corrected Karen, before smiling in sympathy at the two unhappy faces. "You know, as much as I hate to admit it, she does have a point."

"Rachel always has a point. But I'm almost twelve. I can make my own decisions."

"Yes, you can," Karen agreed before taking a bite from one of the sandwiches Helene had left behind. Gagging at the bitter taste, she placed a hand over her mouth while looking between the slices. Inside was an indecipherable brown substance, and she remembered Rachel's comment about eating worms for lunch. She threw the sandwich down where she wouldn't have to see it. Still her mind continued to work. Addressing only Randy, she said, "Next time it's definitely peanut butter and jelly, but tell me ... did Rachel also say not to speak to me about your trips above?"

Randy's eyes opened to the size of ping pong balls, and he crouched down like a cat cornered by a large dog. "That was Rahm, not Rachel. But how did you guess what he said?"

"Just a hunch. Whenever I bring up the subject, you either change it or ignore it. But you don't have to worry. I'm not asking you to choose between me and Rahm. I just need to picture the world again, my world above, and I need your help. It's been so long, I'm afraid I'll forget."

Turning her face up toward an imagined vista, she spoke as if she were reciting a poem, her voice faint as if it came from far away. "It must be beautiful this time of year. People strolling along city streets, going in and out of shops. The smell of flowers. Families picnicking in parks, the grass thick and green."

"What's green?" said Jon.

"A color. The color of nature. I'm sorry," she said. "I forgot that you only see in black and white, but I"—she stopped, alarm registering in the cleft suddenly appearing between her eyebrows. She got up on her knees and reached for a small box, opening it. "Phew," she said, flooded with relief. "I can still see the difference." Fingers trembling, she pulled out the green crayon, aligned between a blue and a red one, and handed it to Jon along with a sheet of paper. With the boy busy scribbling, Karen's eyes reddened and her nose began to run as she remembered *home* and all that it signified: her mother's hair just beginning to turn gray near the temples; her apartment with its mismatched furniture; her silly cat, Boots, aptly named with his white paws; and her Jade "money" plant with its smooth, fleshy water-drop leaves— green.

Randy took a large gulp of air like he was drinking from a cup. "Karen," he said. "There is something I've wanted to tell you. The grownups think I'm too young to understand, but you treat me differently. You listen to me."

Karen patted his knee, encouraging him to continue.

"Everyone thinks I don't realize what's been going on all these months, but I do, and I want you to know that I feel awful about it. But Rahm knows best. Doesn't he?"

Karen spat out a laugh and her face hardened to what it would look like decades into the future. Randy shrank back, alarmed.

"Rahm's a maniac," she said. "A narcissist. An egotistical bastard."

"I don't understand those words," he said, his voice high, quivering. "You still like *us*, don't you? I mean me and Jon?"

"Of course I do," she said, ordering herself to calm down. "This has nothing to do with you and your brother. Unfortunately, that doesn't change my situation. It's still wrong to hold people against their will."

"But Rahm said we had no choice."

"What about *my* choice? He's taken away my freedom. Made me a prisoner."

"But we'd die off without you. Rahm says ..."

Karen took his hand, gave it a squeeze. "Then maybe you shouldn't be down here at all. Maybe you should be above." Karen pointed her index finger up, moving it higher and higher.

Randy sat silently while Jon climbed on Karen's lap. "I don't like school today," he said, wrinkling his brow which had recently grown a fine layer of short white hair. Longer ones, whisker-like, grew on the skin along the outer sides of his eyes. "Can I have another story?"

"It's okay," said Randy. "Go ahead and read to him. I want to go."

"Why?" said Karen. "Is it what I said? None of this is your fault."

"But I'm almost twelve," he repeated, emphasizing the number. "Almost a grownup. Anyway, I need to think."

Karen nodded, satisfied that she had accomplished her goals for the day: Randy questioning Rahm's judgment and his ceasing to use echolocation. As he stood up to leave, Karen almost said, *remember, no cheating*, but before she could speak, he lit the candle. Karen swallowed her misstep behind an exaggerated cough, grateful she had stopped before proving to be another condescending adult.

She assuaged her guilt toward Randy by doting on Jon. Not only did she read another story, but gave him a lesson in shapes.

"How's that?" he asked, holding up the finished product of circles, squares, and triangles he had glued onto a piece of yellowed newspaper using fish offal for paste.

Karen cupped his pointy chin, raising his face. She smiled. He was kind of cute, she decided, once you stopped comparing him to other children. "I like it," she said. "You know, if I were home I'd hang this picture on my refrigerator."

"What's a re-refrigator?"

"Never mind. It's not important. But now we have to go back. I don't know about you, but I'm tired." Karen told him to head off on his own since his method of travel was unequivocally unique. She stood watching as he climbed a wall barefoot, using his gummy hands, toes, and exposed knees. She waved him off, imagining his shoulder blades growing feathers then turning to wings. *Is it possible?* she wondered. She tilted her head, placed a finger to her mouth, and stood there transfixed.

Chapter 22

Karen joined the other women, already engaged in a noisy discussion regarding Randy's upcoming birthday party. "Where are the men?" she asked.

"Too busy with important work to be bothered with a party," said Mary. Everyone in the group laughed.

"Actually," said Rachel, "Rahm and Norman bought a *real* cake. Yellow with chocolate frosting. They did a special shopping trip. It's got preservative so it shouldn't be a problem till Saturday, but we got it down in the root cellar just in case."

Lily scoffed at the word *preservative*.

"Eating cake with preservatives once in a while won't kill you, Lily. Anyway, no one's gonna force you to eat it."

"I'll take a small piece," she said, brushing off the lecture with an ice-cold stare. "But I'm sure Randy will like it. What does he know about preservatives?"

Helene, who was taking notes with a pencil, nibbled on the thin wooden casing surrounding the dull point. Somewhere was a pencil sharpener, but she couldn't remember where and was too lazy and uninterested to bother looking. "How do you spell *preservative*?" she asked.

"Sound it out," said Rachel.

"I bet you can't spell it either," countered Helene.

"Now ladies," said Mary, "try to control yourselves and remember why you're here. Randy's been gloomy lately. Let's make this a party to remember."

Janet's hands flew up to her chest as if it were exposed. "Gloomy? Why's he gloomy?"

"For goodness' sake, Janet," said Rachel. "Do I have to explain everything? You're his mother. Haven't you noticed?"

"Well, uh …" said Janet, fidgeting in her chair while she picked at her nails.

Helene spoke up. "He's not gloomy," she said. "He's horny. For Karen."

Everyone tittered, except Karen, who flinched, recoiled, and ultimately protested at the insinuation. "Don't be ridiculous! He's just a child."

"You can't miss the signs, and you of all people should know better," said Helene. "You're a teacher; you've been around adolescent boys."

Karen squirmed; she did know better and she did notice the signs. She had just chosen to ignore them, having enough on her plate. "Well, it's not natural for him to be around adults so much. There are no boys or girls his age for him to socialize with."

Rachel leaned forward. "I have a secret. Actually, it's no secret 'cause you'll hear more about it at our next community meeting."

All murmuring stopped and everyone turned to her.

"New people will be joining us soon. Remember Sandy and Larry?"

"Oh, yeah," said Mary. "The couple with the twins. They dropped out before making a final commitment. Sandy was the holdback."

About to speak, Rachel's chin rose and jutted forward.

Karen noticed the motion, having always referred to it as an I-told-you-so grin.

"The kids would be, what, seven or eight now?" said Rachel. "Norman's kept in contact with Larry over the years. Apparently, he lost his job, and, well, you know … there are the other usual reasons—life above sucks. So Sandy said yes."

"At least they won't be kidnapped," said Karen.

"Don't you have anything else to talk about besides that?" snipped Rachel.

Karen said, "Fangul," certain Rachel wouldn't be familiar with the Italian slang for "fuck you." Helene, however, was, thanks to her Italian grandmother, and smirking like a smart-alecky teenager, she reached out to exchange a high five with Karen.

"What's going on?" said Rachel, glaring at the co-conspirators. "Are you two making fun of me?"

"Of course not," said Helene, tapping the pencil against her leg. "We were just joking around. Weren't we, Karen? Now let's get back to the party business, before I eat this point."

"Yes," said Mary. "Let's."

After another hour of tiresome party details, trivialities, and humdrum girl-talk, Karen got up to leave without bothering to make excuses or caring what anyone thought.

"Where you going?" asked Rachel.

When she didn't answer, she heard Mary exclaim, "The nerve of her," followed by a chorus of squawks and snorts from the other women. Karen ignored them all.

Entering her room, she found Jeremy prioritizing and strategizing as he awaited her return. Sure of his plan, he didn't ask her advice. "Let's aim for tomorrow," he said. "Our path toward liberation. Look for Randy in the common area, and try not to let him see you following him."

Karen blanched at the bombshell, although she'd known it was coming. "What if I screw up?" she said, shaking like a student before finals.

"You won't. You can do this. You have to."

Karen winced, her body growing cold. "I'll do my best," she said. But would her best be enough? Closing her eyes, she recalled a Biblical story from Sunday school: the parting of the waters, setting the Israelites free. But would *she* be free? Would Jeremy? *If you're out there, God—if you can hear me—please don't let me fail.*

#

Karen's head jerked forward, startling her out of a catnap. As planned, she was in the common room, but finding herself with her eyes closed and sprawled on a couch had not been in the blueprint, and immediately she began clicking despite the two blazing lanterns. The vibrations bounced off David, sitting on a nearby chair with his left hand held at a funny angle in front of his body.

"Oh, no!" she cried. "How long was I out?"

"Not too long. You weren't here when I passed through a short while ago. Something wrong?"

Karen deflected the question and looked at her watch, hiding her self-reproach. But at least David was right. Only half an hour had gone by. "Was that you moaning? What happened to your hand?"

"A little accident. I hit it with a hammer. Mary said I may lose a nail, but nothing's broken, thank goodness."

Karen nodded. "Must hurt a lot."

"My pride most of all, but on the plus side, I won't have to work with Brian tomorrow. I'm afraid I hit him too. His thumb's already swelled up twice its normal size. If it wasn't for Norman hearing him scream, the fat tub would have killed me."

"Fat tub? You didn't call him that, did you?"

"Yeah, I did, but only after he called me a homo. Hey, tit for tat." He spat out a chortle while pushing down on the chair with his good hand. "Well, I'd better get going. Mary said she'll bandage me after she finishes with him."

Karen smiled to herself. Two injured men worked in her favor. She sat up straight, afraid of falling asleep again. Hearing voices, she turned in their direction, but it was only Janet and Lily.

Lily asked the inevitable "How do you feel?"

"Fine," said Karen, sick of the question but careful not to give away her agenda. Playing the role to the hilt, she glanced down at her abdomen, adding, "I'm just a little tired."

"Of course you are," said Janet, "but it won't be much longer."

"Are you worried?" said Lily. "I mean about the delivery?"

Janet raised her palm in a universal stop gesture. "Now don't start her worrying, Lily. Having a baby is perfectly natural. Why I remember—"

Randy entered the common room, his posture and pace determined and eager. In a seamless minute, he said hi to his mother, waved to the women, and walked on.

Karen scrambled to her feet. "I gotta go," she said. The women raised their eyebrows but shifted their attention as Brian slinked in, sporting a splint and a large gauze pad on his thumb.

Karen hurried off, grateful for the diversion. She kept a good twenty paces behind her target, either slowing down or speeding up as needed. After passing through Downtown and Suburbia, Randy paused to light a candle, and the muscles in Karen's lower face relaxed. Still, she worried he might hear her clicking or the scuffling of her feet, but his constant whistling and singing worked in her favor as he ran through the jingles Karen had taught him.

No sooner did he finish one song than he switched to another, and what he lacked in quality he made up for in enthusiasm, especially with his own compositions, a mishmash of words, whoops, and yelps.

Mary's conjecture that the lower level led to an escape route proved correct. Unfortunately, the open space, adjacent to the lake, held little to hide behind, forcing Karen to stay farther back. She sent out a single note on a long exhalation, bringing a continuous stream of images to the fore. While sifting through the information, she prodded Randy with telepathic messages to sing louder. Until recently, she had never been a believer in such phenomena, but the past months had her reconsidering old beliefs.

Randy stopped to skim the shore, and Karen held her breath until he resumed walking. They passed the clotheslines where laundry flapped in the day's breeze; passed the peat where the wild mushrooms cast a neon glow; passed the berry bushes with their fruit hanging in funny, pear-shaped, upside-down clusters, now a shade of deep royal purple.

The knowledge that Randy couldn't see except within his immediate circle of light gave Karen courage and hope. Her mood sank, however, when she arrived at the one place she dreaded more than any other: the shallow pool where she and Rahm had had *intercourse* months before. She purposely thought of it in its technical term because other words or phrases containing 'love' or 'sex' were either an affront or tantamount to a joke.

Although she tried not to, she fixated on the small body of water. Her high-pitched reverberations told her that her "pearls" were still within, floating placidly in their fluid home. Not liking the pictures they roused in her mind, she returned to her objective, and sent out an unbroken tone in search of Randy, horrified to find him gone. She listened carefully for his singing. A faint sound told her he was out there—somewhere.

Karen hurried, turning her head every which way as she clicked. She came to a bend in the passage and ran her hand along the wall's bumpy exterior. When it suddenly disappeared inside a fissure, she stopped. The cleft in the wall formed a keyhole shape, small on the bottom, round on the top. Standing on tiptoe, she poked her head inside the larger area just in time to see the light from Randy's candle disappear above.

Finding herself in a short but narrow vertical chasm, she scratched her head, having no idea how to proceed. Then it came to her.

Months before she had been inside something similar. Of course, she'd been twenty pounds lighter then, but the muscles in her arms and legs were stronger than they had ever been, and, besides, she had no time to think about complications. With her back pressing against one side of this "chimney" and her feet on the other, she applied pressure, pushing her body up. The maneuver, a horizontal walk, was more tiring than difficult, and she stopped midway to relax her muscles. When her legs quivered in response, she cursed, made bargains with long-dead saints, and fumbled onward with silent words of encouragement: *Just a few more feet; I can do it; almost over.*

She came to the top and rolled onto a level of solid ground, covering her mouth when a grunt threatened to escape and expose her presence. She rose, stretched, and took a step, slamming her shin into a small boulder. Once again she repressed a groan while rubbing the sore spot, tingling under her touch. Assured she'd done no major damage, she quickened her pace with a warning to herself to be more careful.

The passageway now switched to a steep upward angle. Karen recognized it as a good sign, yet faltered with the next maneuver. In imitation of Randy, she sank into a crouch as the ceiling dropped. With her fingertips touching the ground for balance, she tried waddling like a duck. At any other time, she would have found this amusing, but laughter didn't come when she immediately fell backwards onto her rump.

Although harder on her knees, she switched to a crawl, grateful for Randy's slow pace. Actually, he had no choice since the candle hindered his progress. Frequent gusts of wind blew it out, necessitating his stopping to relight the wick.

Karen knew he wasn't used to getting by on the candle's feeble light, and worried he'd be tempted to switch to his voice. She panicked when he leaned against a wall and purposely blew out the flame.

She intuited him debating the significance of his promise and realized her future depended on the intangible. She held her breath. When he went on—the candle relit—her shoulders slumped in relief.

Randy arrived at a junction where one path fed into another like a major intersection in a city. With his hand, he felt for a gap overhead. Finding it, he hoisted himself up and through. Karen watched from behind, using all her senses to keep track.

She took a moment to turn around. Since she was not using a string, she checked out each connecting link with an about-face to prevent getting lost. She did this repeatedly, knowing she would be returning from the opposite direction and would have to be able to recognize the signposts from a different perspective. She noted unusual shapes in the formations, and where necessary she scratched nicks with a fingernail or the toe of her shoe.

Imitating Randy, she flexed the muscles in her arms, climbed inside the hole, and headed up the small pocket embedded with rocks and strategically placed notches, making for an easy ascent. Still, not taking anything for granted, she mouthed a thank you while pressing her face to the ground upon arrival, tasting the loose dirt on her tongue. She didn't bother to spit it out; she had swallowed worse and no longer cared.

The next test came too soon. Finding herself on a ledge with her legs dangling freely, she told herself not to panic. It worked, until her imagination soared and she glimpsed her body sprawled out in a bottomless pit, just as she had in her waking dream, the night before her descent into this wretched place many months ago.

She thought of the baby and asked herself why she was risking its life as well as her own. But the moment passed and she ordered herself onward. Standing up, she placed both palms at her side and leaned against the wall until she could feel her spine from her buttocks to her neck, and continued, side-stepping one foot at a time.

Just ahead, Randy reached out and walked off into space. Thinking the worst had happened, Karen's jaw dropped, her body swayed, and she fell to her knees. Then realizing he had merely crossed over to another ledge, she slumped into a small heap until her pulse returned to normal.

Afraid of losing him, she willed her fear into a metaphorical locked box and proceeded to where he had just so effortlessly stepped across. Extending her arms, she too jumped from the ledge, her feet touching ground before she realized they did. She stamped down, savoring the feel and security of solid earth, and whispered words of congratulations to herself. With her head held high, she marched on, a heroine battling to win, battling for survival.

She moved automatically, using the most primitive part of her brain since the jagged rocks, both small and large along this horizontal rim, could poke out an eye or break a bone. If she thought too hard she'd give in to fear or fatigue. Still, she hoped Randy would stop and rest, and as if her thoughts were contagious, he began to slow down before coming to a complete halt.

Although happy for the break, Karen couldn't afford the luxury of filling her lungs to capacity. Randy had stopped singing and any sound might signal her presence. Carefully, she peered around a corner to further assess the situation, watching as he moved the candle from hand to hand, trying to decide where to place it. Then, putting it between his teeth, he headed straight up the perfectly smooth wall as effortlessly as a common cockroach.

Karen blinked in confusion, wondering how he had accomplished this near-impossible feat. Randy had never given any indication of insect-like mutations.

She waited until it was safe and went over to discover the trick. Touching the wall, she felt a pasty substance across its surface, uniform, as if it had been painted on with a roller. Perhaps Jon had been here, leaving behind a residue, or perhaps it was Rahm. She had heard rumors about him too.

Having no choice, she succumbed to her physical needs and sucked in a full tank of air before starting up. The adhesive was strong enough to prevent falling while pliable enough to allow her to climb. At the top was a narrow tunnel that continued uphill at a thirty-degree incline. She walked, attempted to run but couldn't since a steady ache had settled in her arms and legs, and alternated with jolts of searing pain. When a long spasm hit her lower back, she dropped to the ground, helpless. Stifling a moan, she flipped over and lay flat. The spasm ended, but exhaustion won. In addition, her throat burned and she tasted salt on her parched lips.

She desperately needed fluids, but with none available, her eyes closed and her body grabbed the one essential it could: rest. Within seconds, she was floating on a lake and her brother, laughing mischievously, waded over and splashed her face. *Go away or I'll tell Mom,* she told the bratty creature. Ignoring the threat, he did it again. Something registered inside Karen's subconscious brain and she licked her mouth, now surprisingly wet. The miracle awakened her, and she reached up to touch a sprinkling of drops.

Hope restored, she searched for the welcome fissure, knowing it was nearby. She pawed with her fingers and found the spot, opening it further, allowing a stream of precious liquid through. She cupped her hands and drank enough to fill her dream lake, noting the taste of recent rainwater, heavenly and normal. Encouraged by her progress, her eyes brightened, and her mouth curved upward.

Hearing a noise—the clanging, ringing, scraping sound of metal on metal— she rushed forward. Jeremy had mentioned something about ladders: a series of them closer to the top. Just find the first, he had said. While she would have loved to go all the way up, to see the sky, she knew Randy might be heading back with the vegetables by now; might only be a few levels above. She drummed her foot, debating with herself, looked at her watch and blanched. There was no choice; she had to return. It was getting late.

About to leave, she swung at the waist, but the earth, now soaked from the wide-open fissure, had become a sloppy, slippery mess, and her arms flailed out as her feet left the ground. She tumbled sideways, sparing the baby but bruising a hip. While she wasn't seriously hurt, the suddenness of it startled her, and before she could stop herself a scream escaped her lips, followed by a "Dammit!" It was only a quick scream and a single word; still, it was enough.

Randy, just as Karen feared, was on his way back, but worse than she had imagined, he was only one level above, and having tired of singing had heard the hubbub and recognized the voice. In a flash, it had come to him and two and two became four. Furious, he threw the candle down the gaping hole separating the two levels.

Karen, within range of the thud, went to check. Her foot struck the waxy object, and realizing what it was, she gulped repeatedly. She picked it up and rolled it between her fingers, not sure how this unfortunate complication—a mere accident, perhaps?—would affect her and Jeremy's impending getaway. Just how much did Randy suspect? *Please God,* she silently begged, hoping for the best but fearing the worst. *Let everything be okay.* She sent out a series of clicks.

Above, Randy sat, holding his head, the picture of despair.

Chapter 23

Boots, back arched and ready to spring, chased a werewolf, honked like a speckled dodo bird, and swam the Chesapeake Bay while Karen slept and dreamt throughout the night, morning, and afternoon, nursing a headache and sore muscles. Still, she made it to Randy's birthday party. As Janet brought out the cake, everyone clapped and sang an off-key rendition of "Happy Birthday." Karen sat back, watching as Jon, unable to hold back his excitement, jumped up and down, while Randy sat in silence.

Rachel lit the candles. "I put one extra in the center for good luck. That's thirteen in all. And now, young man"—she gestured toward Randy—"take a big breath and blow."

As directed, Randy rose, puffed out his cheeks, and leaned over the cake.

"Stop," said Rachel, freezing the moment. "Don't forget to make a wish."

He tweaked his nose. "I've got nothing to wish for."

"Ridiculous," said Brian. "I heard you got your own bedroom. Congratulations. You're growing up."

The mood around the table grew increasingly somber as Randy's lack of enthusiasm peaked. Karen mouthed a silent thank you to Mary, who stood up in an attempt to turn things around.

Having spoken to Jeremy earlier that day, she was aware of the possible chink in the escape plan. Now there was no telling who knew what. As an immediate diversion, she grabbed the knife from Janet, told her to sit, and began cutting the cake. "You get the first slice," she said to the birthday boy, passing it down the table.

Randy stabbed at the cream-filled layers with his fork and put a bite in his mouth. Karen winced, noting that even a special treat didn't bring on a smile.

After eating less than half his piece, he pushed the remainder to Jon, then stalked off, scowling like an athlete who'd lost the game.

"What's with him?" said Rachel. "He's been like this since he returned with the zucchini yesterday."

She turned to Rahm, sitting somberly, his index finger and thumb tugging his chin, exposing two rows of teeth, bone white and menacing.

"I think I'd better have a word with him," he replied, pushing back his chair.

"No wait," said Karen. She shot Jeremy a piercing look, trusting he'd notice. Having everyone's attention, she said the first thing that came into her head, not caring if it sounded believable. "Jeremy's good with kids, especially adolescents. Let him go."

Karen smiled in relief as Jeremy, apparently catching the drift, took off in pursuit before Rahm or anyone else could stop him.

#

Jeremy checked Randy's room. Not finding him there, he suspected he'd be at his favorite place near the lake where he often went to skim stones. Randy was there, all right, but not skimming stones, merely sitting with arms across his chest, angry at the world. Rock-still, he appeared small, huddled over like a vulnerable child picked on by bullies.

"Go away," said the boy as Jeremy approached.

Jeremy ignored the order and sat down without a word, experience telling him to wait, be patient, and let Randy fill in the silence. *When he's ready, he'll talk,* thought Jeremy, suspecting barraging him with questions and demands would only be counterproductive.

Randy blinked away tears. Embarrassed, he wiped his face, pretending it was dirt. "Everyone uses me," he said. "First Rahm, telling me to spy on you. Then you, pretending to be my friend. And Karen. She's worst of all. She lied to me. Said I should use candles to improve my vision when all she wanted was to find the way out."

"Karen does care about you. I care about you. It's just we're desperate. We're prisoners here!"

Randy put his fingers in his ears. "Rahm warned me about you and Karen. Told me not to trust you."

"Rahm? He's the last person you should trust."

Randy took his fingers from his ears. Jeremy's words had caught his attention, and he sat up straight as if pulled by strings. "What do you mean? At least Rahm never lied to me."

Jeremy shook his head and guffawed. He really did care about the boy and didn't want to see him destroyed, but with his life on the line, disclosure was his only weapon. "You want the truth? Okay, I'll give it to you, but you won't like what you hear."

Randy narrowed his eyes, ready to catch any nuance of deceit.

"Your father didn't fall from the cliff like Rahm said. He was pushed—by Rahm."

Randy stopped breathing, stood up. "You're lying!"

"No, I'm not," said Jeremy, grabbing the boy by his pants and pulling him back down. "I'm sorry, but Mary told me everything. Apparently, it's not the best kept secret. There was a fight, that part is true, but Tom lost and wanted to give up, only Rahm wouldn't have it. He pushed your dad off the cliff, and I think if you confronted Rahm, he wouldn't deny it. You remember Louise and Eugene?"

"Of course," said Randy. "You think I'm stupid? Mom told me the whole story: that my dad left her for Louise."

"Then you know that Louise wanted to go back to her husband and your dad couldn't accept it."

Randy closed his eyes, trying to blot out the vision. "My dad abandoned me, my brother, my mom," he whispered. "Then killed Louise and Eugene in their sleep."

"That's right," said Jeremy. "And Rahm couldn't just let him leave. That's why he pushed Tom—your dad—off that cliff."

Randy considered it. "Since you think you know everything, why wouldn't Rahm just let Dad leave?"

Jeremy sighed, pruned his words till they were whittled down into a semblance of truth. "Revenge, frontier justice, but even more important, he was concerned Tom would spill the beans about this place. Did you know your dad had a drinking problem, years ago, before he came here? Rahm couldn't take a chance. He won't let anyone leave."

"I want to leave," said Randy.

"What?"

"I do," Randy repeated. "I was really mad when I figured out Karen tricked me, but then I got to thinking long and hard. You've both said this place is like a prison. Well, you're right. No one ever asked me if I wanted to come. Just dragged me down. Well, I like it above. I got to ride in a car with Norman recently as one of my birthday presents and it was fun, and I miss having friends."

Sensing a good opening, Jeremy said, "I don't blame you. Every boy should have friends."

Randy nodded. "There was this kid Lenny who lived on my street years back. His mom made the best bologna sandwiches; used lots of mustard. Sometimes Lenny and me—we'd play stickball with the other neighborhood kids in an empty lot. When his dad bought him a cowhide glove, he let me try it. Just me, 'cause he said I was his friend. His *best* friend!"

Randy began to cry. His head fell between his knees and his body shook like a thin branch on a windy day. Jeremy placed his hand on Randy's back, made tiny circles, trying to comfort him.

"I don't want to turn spidery like Jon or Rahm."

Jeremy's mouth snaked down at the corners. "I'm confused," he said. "I know about your brother, but what do you mean about Rahm?"

"His skin also makes sticky stuff. And threads come from his saliva. I've helped him turn them into rope. We mix it with dirt."

"Threads? Rope?" Jeremy tapped his chin, thinking. "I noticed something funny the other day but didn't touch it."

"Probably spider rope. That's what I call it." Randy sucked in his lips. "I'm leaving tonight," he said. "I've made up my mind, and it's not 'cause I'm jealous of Jon's climbing ability like some people think. I just don't want to become a freak like him, and I will if I stay here longer. You can come with me if you want."

Jeremy's jaw dropped like a scaffold with broken cables. "What about your family?"

"My mother won't notice—not much, anyway. In any case, I'm going. And there's no way you'll make it out without me. It's too tricky, too dangerous, but I know a shortcut. I didn't use it yesterday because of the candle, but I will tonight." He paused and turned to Jeremy. "I'm like the Himalayan Sherpas. Ever hear of them?"

"Of course," said Jeremy. "Where did you?"

"From Norman. He told me all about them. And if you want my help, you have to promise to let me live with you and Karen … till I'm older."

"I promise," said Jeremy, meaning it.

Final details were ironed out. Jeremy wanted to hold off one more day, to give Karen more time to recoup, but Randy convinced him that Rahm would catch on if they waited.

"Then tonight's the night," said Jeremy, his jaw clenching and unclenching as he fought to remain composed. "How's two a.m. sound?"

"Sounds good. Everyone will be asleep."

Jeremy reached out with his right hand for Randy to shake.

Randy took it, pumped it up and down to clinch the deal. He beamed.

Jeremy beamed too. *Mission accomplished.*

#

After the others walked off, Karen helped carry the dessert plates back to the kitchen. Suspecting this may be her last opportunity to press upon Janet the importance of giving Jon additional attention, she spoke up.

In a rare show of anger, Janet threw one of the plates, shattering it against a stalagmite resembling a winged totem pole. Startled by her own behavior, she covered her face. "So you think I'm a bad mother?"

"No, not at all. It's just—"

"Just what?"

"Well, for starters, Jon's vocabulary is below average, and he mispronounces half of his words."

"So you think he's stupid?"

Karen quickly shook her head. "Of course not. Quite the contrary. He's got lots of potential and he's doing much better. It's just that he's been left on his own too much."

"So I've neglected him?"

Karen saw that this conversation wasn't heading in the right direction. She paused to think. "I'm not blaming you, Janet. The main problem is that there aren't other kids for him to play with or socialize with. Randy's too old and the adults have chores to do every day. You must have noticed what's happening. That he's … unusual."

"Just what are you driving at?"

Karen's mind raced, searching for the right words, the right tone to bring home her point. Suddenly aware of her own vulnerability, she assured herself she'd be out of this dystopian madhouse soon, hopefully *very* soon. She gathered her nerve. "I think living here is having a deleterious effect on him physically and mentally."

Janet's face turned as purple as a bruise. "What's that big word you used? Deli something. Are you showing off? Think you're better than me?"

"You know I don't. I like Jon. Really, I do, but I'm concerned. He's beginning to look like a-a rodent." She lowered her voice on the last word.

"A *what?*"

"Don't tell me you haven't noticed, Janet. He's got long whiskers growing off the sides of his face and his nails are as pointy as claws. I had to cut off the tips the other day when he sat on my lap. They were cutting my skin, right through my pants."

Janet swallowed. "Rachel said I should watch out for you. That you weren't loyal, were sneaky, a two-timing traitor. And now you're telling me lies, crazy stuff just to scare me."

"Why would I want to do that? I'm just trying to warn you before it's too late. There's still a window of opportunity to turn things around."

Backing up, Janet put more distance between herself and Karen. "I think you have a hidden motive. You'd like to stir up trouble, wouldn't you? Maybe break up my family or help you do something I'd regret. But I won't, and, furthermore, I think you should stay away from Jon. Randy too."

Taken aback, Karen reached out, her eyes pools of sincerity. "He's your son. He has to come first. In another year he'll be too far gone. You mustn't let that happen."

Soundlessly, as if dropped from a cloud, Jon tiptoed in. It was time for him to gather the berries for tomorrow's breakfast. Janet cradled his head against her hip in a protective show of affection.

Jon squirmed and pulled away. "I itch," he said, reaching behind, scratching some indeterminate spot. He lowered his pants to show his mother and both women shriek at the revelation. On his buttocks, an inch above the cleft, grew what looked like a thumb. Karen looked closer and noticed a curl at the end, reminding her of a piglet's tail.

Janet's lips trembled as she finally faced the facts. She stroked her son's face, his sweet, funny, odd, beautiful face. "It's nothing," she said, her voice a bare whisper. "It will go away on its own. Just don't touch it." Reaching up to a shelf, she pulled down the berry pail and handed it to Jon, sending him on his way. Moments later, she looked at Karen with hate in her eyes and the word *bitch* on her tongue.

Karen walked off, afraid she'd made matters worse. It wasn't her problem, she told herself, and took some solace in knowing she had tried.

As she approached her quarters, Karen cringed to see Rahm on the path, waiting for her, blocking the way. He grabbed her arm and yanked her into a recess, his eyes flashing like molten fire from the torch's light above.

"What do you want? Let go of me."

They stood face to face, he holding her shoulders so she couldn't move. "What's going on?" he demanded. "Something's up."

"I don't know what you're talking about."

"I think you do, but if you're not going to tell me, I have other ways to find out. But first, you and I have business to clear up." He moved his hands to her waist, circling them in back, pulling her close. He kissed her mouth, now open, on the verge of a scream.

"How dare you?" she yelled, still pinned, wishing she could slap him. "Haven't you done enough already?"

Like a cunning fox, he looked down, honing in on the budding life between them, proof of the bond they shared. "It's mine," he said. "We'll always be connected through it."

"No! It's not yours. It's Jeremy's."

He leaned in, his breath tickling her ear. "Stop fighting me, Karen. We both know the truth."

Karen wriggled, struggling to free herself.

"It's mine, all right. That's why you're so mad at me. But I see that I failed to fix matters between us. I hope in time you'll understand and forgive me."

"Understand? Forgive? *Never!*" She jammed her elbows against his arms, breaking his hold, and ran to her room. She sat in the rocking chair, allowing its seesaw motion to soothe her rankled nerves. When Jeremy arrived minutes later with news of their imminent departure, Karen smiled in relief, particularly after having witnessed another of Jon's mutations and hearing Jeremy's story of Rahm's ability to make "spider rope."

"And one other thing," said Jeremy. "Randy's coming with us. I hope that's okay. He knows a shortcut."

"It's more than okay, it's great. I was hoping he'd come. Better that than having him expose our plans to Rahm. Would you mind him living with us till he's older?"

"Funny you should ask. Randy and I already discussed it. We'll figure out his living arrangements when we're home—our real home."

They went over the evening's strategy, step by step, in precise detail. With their tactics in place, Jeremy nonchalantly added, "I'd like to say goodbye to Mary. You know, none of this would be possible without her."

Karen nodded, pretending not to care.

"Why don't you rest?" he suggested before heading off. "We have a long night before us."

Karen resumed rocking, but it no longer served as a balm. Something troubling had seeped into her thoughts, something she yearned to repress but could not. Over and over, she tried pushing it back to that place in her mind where the muck of the day is best left forgotten. *After all, Jeremy's business is his, not mine,* she avowed. Yet she couldn't heed her own advice and, heart pounding, she stormed off, propelled to uncover the truth behind his feelings for Mary.

With no sign of him in Suburbia, she checked Downtown and the fertility area. No one there. She began to click and noticed a vague outline before it disappeared down the trail to the chapel, a place she'd seldom gone since she refused to attend Rachel's religious services.

Creeping up, sticking to the shadows, she found Jeremy and Mary standing beside a horseshoe-shaped wreath made of filigreed rock. They stood together, hand in hand, like a bride and groom, surrounded by cave flowers of delicate, woven designs. Above them an anthodite chandelier sparkled with twisted crystalline rocks, some quill-like, some feathery, jutting out in all directions. Karen held her breath to listen.

"I'm pregnant," said Mary, brimming with excitement and bouncing on her toes. "I know I've said this before, as Helene's only been too happy to point out, but this time it's different. I feel it growing. And it's yours! Brian and I ... well, we haven't ... we haven't done anything."

Jeremy grabbed Mary's wrists. "Listen, Mary. You're a nurse. Even I know it's too soon to tell, but regardless, Karen and I are leaving tonight. Why don't you come with us? With me!"

"What?"

"I mean it."

Mary shook her head and cried tears of pain, of impending loss, mixed with joy. She nestled against his chest, overwhelmed. "That's lovely, Jeremy. Lovely but crazy." She wiped her eyes before getting down to the cold facts. "I'm almost a decade older than you," she said. "You may not care about that now, but in time you would. Besides, I've already told you, I can never leave here."

"But I love you."

"And I love you too, but I still can't." Mary reached up and pulled him close. As they shared a passionate kiss, Karen clutched her throat and stifled a sob. The kiss went on and on, and Karen, seeing and hearing more than she could tolerate, zoomed off, stumbling down the passageway, her legs jerky, as if they belonged to someone else. Now weeping openly, she bumped into Brian without bothering to apologize.

"Hey!" he yelled after her. "You didn't say sorry."

Karen kept going and switched to a run, failing to acknowledge his request.

Chapter 24

Karen collapsed in her room, where she managed to pull herself together by repeatedly counting backwards from one hundred. When Jeremy finally returned, he found her as he had left her, still in the rocking chair, but now with features as unreadable as a blank billboard on a highway.

Jeremy bent down and pecked her cheek. "Mary sends her best and wishes us luck." Karen continued to stare ahead. "And look what I got." Reaching into his pocket, Jeremy pulled something out, shining its light in her eyes. "It's our flashlight. I found it in the storage area and the batteries still work. Can you imagine?"

As a delaying tactic, Karen crossed and uncrossed her legs. Unable to decide on a suitable approach, she settled on fixing her face in what she hoped passed for normal. "What about the other flashlight?" she said. "Didn't we have two?"

"Yeah, but I only found one."

"What about the hardhats? Did you see them?"

"I did, but they won't do us any good. The carbide's all spent, and someone crushed the lamps for good measure. But don't worry. The way I feel at this moment, I could fly if I had to. Listen," he said. "We'd better get some rest. In shifts, of course, since we don't have an alarm. Why don't you go first? You look drained." He placed a hand under her chin and tipped her head up to get a better look. "Hey, you okay?"

"Okay as I could be under the circumstances." She closed her eyes and turned her head so that Jeremy couldn't see the single tear running down her cheek. Without another word, she removed her watch, passed it to Jeremy, and climbed into bed, using the blanket as a shield.

"Goodnight," he said. "Sleep well."

She ignored his words, hoping her silence signaled a rebuke. Overwhelmed and exhausted, she drifted away to a black, distant landscape, then sunny skies, and finally peace.

Too soon, Karen felt a tug on her shoulders.

"Wake up," Jeremy said.

Karen groaned. "All right. I'm up. What time is it?"

"After midnight."

"Really? You didn't have to let me sleep this long."

"That's okay. You need it more than I do. Just wake me at 2:00. You won't fall asleep or anything?"

"No chance. I'll be fine." As Jeremy settled in, Karen returned the watch to her wrist, then marched in place to alleviate any kinks in her body. Sensing a weakness around her middle, she used one of Jeremy's long-sleeved sweatshirts to bind her abdomen. She tightened the sleeves. *There, that's better,* she thought, feeling the baby now safely tucked inside.

She waited a half hour before striking a match. Jeremy lay asleep on his side—his favorite position. A strand of hair crossed his face, and she felt tempted to push it away but held back, not wanting to wake him. *He looks so sweet,* she mused, picturing him as he had been when they'd first met, his face relaxed and unlined, basking in the sun on the college quadrangle. Suddenly she felt afraid and dropped the match before the flame singed her fingers.

As if she were watching snippets of home movies, she drummed up replays of life on the outside. Could they actually pick up where they had left off and go on as if nothing had happened? *No. Of course not.* But could they make peace with betrayals from both sides? The baby kicked and she bit down on a nail, something she hadn't done in months. Hearing a noise, she jumped and turned to confront the intruder.

"It's me," said Randy. "I couldn't sleep. Isn't it time yet?"

Karen's face switched from dismay to alarm as she read the dial on her watch: 2:12. "Dear Lord," she said. "I'm late." She promptly woke her husband with a warning to hurry and the news that Randy was here, ready to go. Jeremy felt for his shoes and laced them up while Karen berated herself for her slipup, an error she decided to keep to herself.

Like trespassers, they slunk through the silent chamber with members asleep in their private niches. Karen wondered if there was anyone she'd miss. Maybe Norman, she decided, despite his half-truths, and—oddly enough—even screwy, selfish Helene. Despite all her faults, she had a straightforward honesty that Karen found refreshing.

They were outside Rahm and Rachel's quarters when Jeremy yanked on Karen's arm. "Hold on," he mouthed silently, his face outlined by a nearly burned-out torch nestled in an overhead crevice. His hand held a large rock. Karen's throat tightened as she begged him with a beseeching look not to kill them. Ignoring her plea, he entered his enemies' chamber, pumping the rock up and down, glaring at the sleeping couple. Karen watched from behind, telling herself that despite all his human frailties, Jeremy was not a murderer; still, her eyes flooded with relief when he placed the rock on the ground and exchanged it for Rahm's shoe. Reaching inside, he removed the insert, transferring it to a pocket.

In the passageway, Randy stood trembling, a line of sweat on his forehead as if he were running a fever. Jeremy shook his head sideways to indicate he hadn't followed through with his plan. Randy exhaled.

They passed through the storage area, again in chaos due to another round of Helene's frenzied behavior, making it impossible to step clear of the mess. Farther on, the fertility area presented more of a problem, and Karen sent out a high-pitched note to check if it was in use.

"No one there," she said, along with her thumb and forefinger forming an okay sign.

Jeremy took a moment to pause before the stone statues and snickered. "Stupid dirty idols." He pulled Rahm's insert from his pocket and flung it toward Tloc, congratulating himself with a raised fist when a chunk of the god's headdress fell to the ground.

When they neared the lake, Jeremy turned on the flashlight and moved the metal rod in an arc, searching for his target. Since he had already suggested this to his co-conspirators, all three ran in the direction of the peat with its prize bonus, wild mushrooms. They dropped down, rolling in the damp moss until their bodies were painted with shiny green particles.

"Am I covered enough?" asked Karen, plucking at her clothes. The extra light allowed her to see the smile of approval on her husband's face.

"You're fine," he told her, "but the effect won't last long so we've got to move fast."

Reaching the shore first, Randy stepped forward and pointed. "We'll be taking the rowboat," he said as Karen raised and lowered her shoulders, her optimistic air replaced with one of confusion. "You'll have to trust me from here on." He moved aside to let the twosome climb aboard first. With everyone settled, he began rowing as Karen, clueless, stared from the opposite plank.

Randy continued speaking. "I know you're both aware of the cliff face. That's our destination."

Like a startled turtle, Jeremy's head folded into his neck. "What are you talking about? I've already checked it out. It's too high. Too sheer."

Karen shuddered, realizing her life lay in the hands of a twelve-year-old.

Randy placed the oars in their metal collars. The boat drifted in the black water. "Only three of us know everything: Rahm, Norman, and me. And I swore I wouldn't tell. I guess that makes me a traitor and a liar." He sucked in his lip, swallowed, and began rowing again.

The current helped propel the small craft to the opposite shore. After mooring it, the threesome walked among large formations which Randy called cave trees. The trunks of the "trees" climbed far higher than Jeremy's head and ended in a canopy of angular shapes from the interlocking branches. Fungi grew around the base of each structure in a multitude of colors, so many they would have pleased the pickiest of artists.

"Try not to touch the moldy stuff," said Randy. "It'll give you … you know … diarrhea."

"Great," said Karen, placing her hands in her pockets. Jeremy, holding the flashlight, paid careful attention to where he placed his feet. Minutes later they came to a dead end with a solid wall. Jeremy shined the light, but it disappeared just a few feet above, telling him little. He looked at Randy.

"This is it," the boy said. "The shortcut. Straight up for half a mile."

Karen gasped, struggling not to take her frustrations out on a child, but she had had enough. "Are you crazy?" she said, touching the wall, loose calcite and mud smudging her fingertips.

Randy's face turned cornstarch white. Immediately, Karen regretted her words, knowing how hard he'd been trying to appear brave and adult-like. *But is he just an untested neophyte, all talk and no payoff, afraid of failure and letting others down? Does he actually know what he's doing?*

"Pass me the flashlight," said Randy. "I told you I'd get you up, and I will."

Jeremy took a step, followed by Karen. Randy directed the beam to what looked like a dangling vine and jerked it off the wall, offering it to Jeremy, who twisted and turned it in his hand. "What the hell is this thing?" He gave a yank, but it remained firm yet supple, and strong as cable wire.

"I told you yesterday," said Randy. "Spider rope."

Jeremy squeezed his eyes. "Yeah, but I never expected anything like this." He rubbed his fingers together. "It tickles," he said, peeling the rope from his skin. He passed it to Karen.

"I feel like I'm being stuck with a thousand tiny needles," she said. "Sticky ones."

"But that's the best part," said Randy. "Watch me." Pinching the two ends of the rope together, he performed a quick demonstration. "It may stick to your skin, but it sticks way better to itself."

"Like Velcro," said Jeremy. "This stuff's amazing. I bet you could sell it. Make a fortune."

"What's Velcro?"

Jeremy held up a forefinger. "Remind me tomorrow and I'll show you."

Karen, not as impressed, turned to the practical side. "How's all this going to help us?"

Randy's eyebrows rose, forming two equilateral triangles. "Easy," he said. "Rahm and I have been working on a web. We're almost done. You see, Norman needed a quick way to reach the top on his own. Rahm and I—we can use our hands and feet and be up in no time, but Norman can't do it so fast. And he prefers the long way—the one we used when you followed me." He turned to Karen. She met his eyes, staring right back with dead-on precision, too overwrought by the imminent climb to feel shamed by her subterfuge.

"Anyway, Rahm figured it out. He anchored a spider rope around a boulder at the top. Then we waited, and sure enough the wind blew the loose end across the wall, where it stuck. You know, like with a real spider web. Then Rahm made lots more rope, and I've been helping him secure the connecting links. Another twenty feet and we'd be finished."

"So how do we get to where you left off?" asked Jeremy. "The wall's so dammed slick. No place to grip on to."

"I worked it out," said Randy. "I'll go first to double-check the connections and throw you the dropline."

"The *what?*" shrieked Karen, reprimanding herself for yelling.

"The dropline," he repeated. "You'll see in a minute." Before Karen could press him further, Randy scampered up and away like a squirrel on a tree. Moments later the line appeared: a loose end of spider rope attached to the web above. Randy called out, "Just secure it around your waist, lean out, brace your feet against the wall, and pull with a hand-over-hand motion."

Karen blanched.

"I'll go first," said Jeremy. Following the directions, he made it to the web without any problems. After linking his arms and legs inside the netting, he threw the line to Karen, who groaned with the effort, her muscles still sore from her exertion a mere day and a half earlier.

Both safely up, Karen and Jeremy paused to familiarize themselves with the zigzag pattern of the web as Randy continued the climb.

"We better get going," said Karen, worried about the time.

Jeremy nodded and tucked the flashlight into his pocket for safekeeping. "Dammit," he said. "Now I can barely see a thing."

"Follow the glow from Randy's body," said Karen, "and I'll guide you from here." Click-clicking like a mechanical clock, she called out instructions. "Move your right foot to the left," she said. "No, that's too much. Okay, stop." Then moments later: "Now move your right hand up a few inches. Good. Now take your left foot. Move it a little to the right. No left. Sorry …"

As Jeremy gained confidence he continued, while Karen proceeded at a slower, more cautious speed, pausing to rest when muscles cramped or a moment of panic set in. Wiping her face, she reminded herself to keep it angled up, away from the ground below. Finally level with Jeremy, she patted his hand and the twosome pressed on, making it to the top just past the hour mark. While Karen beamed, Jeremy, unable to believe their success, flung himself to the ground as if it were his lover. Randy, already up, had thoughtfully lit a match.

Karen stared at the boy's face, admiration in her voice. "There's no way, we could have done this without you, and I want you to know that I'm—I mean, Jeremy and I are both grateful."

Randy flushed. "Thanks," he said. "I've been climbing half my life. That's why I'm good. I swear I don't have any mutations. Anyway, we're done with spider ropes and webs. You two ready to move on?"

Jeremy nodded. Karen did likewise, despite the pain in her joints.

"We'll be maneuvering among ledges for a while," Randy warned. To Karen he said, "Since we took a different route today, we're on the far side of the cave mountain. We need to head back toward the ladders."

With Randy in the lead, Karen and Jeremy followed close behind, the flashlight playing a more pivotal role since the benefit from the mushrooms was wearing off. But working as a team, the threesome fashioned a system for long jumps. Before each hurdle, Jeremy gave Karen the flashlight so she could shine it across the abyss where Randy, already on the other side, stood candle in hand. This way Jeremy could gauge the distance between the two points.

Emboldened by their success, they continued full tilt until Karen, feeling her lungs on fire, called for a halt. Jeremy, too, welcomed the break, and the couple stood, gulping air. When Karen's breathing slowed to normal, she reached for Jeremy to return the flashlight. Thinking it was already in his grip, she opened her fingers. It wasn't until she heard a thump, followed by the disappearing light, that she realized her mistake and gasped.

Karen's brain scrambled, rendering her unable to speak. Jeremy, however, wasn't. "You idiot!" he roared, raising his hand as if to smack her. Immediately, Randy stepped between them, allowing time for a question and an ugly image to form in Karen's brain.

"You were going to hit me. You promised you'd never do it again."

"I wasn't. I swear!"

Karen's eyes filled with tears, and her chest heaved in and out.

"You don't believe me?" asked Jeremy.

"It's just that you looked so … no, never mind. I'll take you at your word. But what do we do now? Do we have to go back?"

"Never!" he bellowed. "I'd rather die." Angry again, the veins in his temple bulged like knotted cords, and he reached into his pocket to take out a candle. "There," he said, lighting it, shoving it into her face. "This will have to do." Karen hung her head.

Like couples who've become too familiar, Karen and Jeremy resumed their upward trek in silence. Randy pointed to the next challenge: jumping between ridges with narrow level plateaus at their tops. Karen, immersed with guilt, grabbed the candle and bolted before anyone could stop her, displaying a reckless disregard for her safety. The rushing air snuffed out the flame as she soared in space. "Karen!" she heard Jeremy scream before landing safely. She relit the wick, clicked, and scoured his face now drained of color, causing her to wonder if he had been more concerned for her or for the possible loss of the candle.

In an attempt to heal the rift, Jeremy promptly jumped and went to her side. Tilting her head, he kissed her lips. "Don't ever do that again. I thought you were gone for sure. And I'm sorry for blaming you for dropping the flashlight. It was my fault as much as yours. I love you, Karen."

Karen choked back a cry. "Don't lie to me, Jeremy. You love Mary. I heard you in the chapel."

"No, I love you. Okay, so Mary too, but it's the cave that changed everything. I swear. It does funny things to you."

"Maybe it just caused us to be who we really are."

"That's crazy talk. Don't say that." He pulled her closer.

Karen looked into his eyes, searching for something to hold on to, but all she saw was a blank canvas and pulled away, despondent.

"Let's finish this conversation later," said Jeremy. "What time is it?"

Karen looked at her watch. "Oh my God! It's just after four."

"Jesus!" said Jeremy. "We'd better get going. Rahm and Norman are both early risers."

The small group finished the scaling and jumping without any further mishaps, thanks in part to Randy's good judgment. Earlier he'd had the presence of mind to place extra mushrooms in his pockets, and the threesome passed them around, rubbing them on their hands and fingertips.

"That was smart of you," said Karen, praising his foresight. "How much farther do we have to go?"

Randy pointed to a gray wall, which looked like so many others. "Don't you know where you are?"

Karen looked around. "No. Should I?" Hearing a familiar clang, she turned her face to the ceiling and stared at the very hole where Randy had so recently flung a candle in disgust. "The ladders," she said. "We're close to the ladders. We're near the end."

Jeremy looked up, straining to see.

Randy explained there were four more levels connected with rope ladders having metal rungs. "Regular ladders, not spidery ones," he added. "A few of the steps are rusted and some are missing so you need to be extra careful, but Norman still comes this way often, and remember, I do too, to gather the vegetables."

Karen sighed while Jeremy stared in disbelief, the lines on the outer sides of his eyes wrinkling like tiny birds' feet.

"It's okay," said Randy. "Really!"

"What's holding the ladders up?" asked Jeremy.

"They're bolted at the top of each level. You climb by straddling one edge of a ladder, locking your hands and feet into the rungs. That's the best way. Oh … there's that small vertical chasm to climb first, but it's a piece of cake since Rahm left some spider glue inside. Ready?"

Karen and Jeremy nodded solemnly while Randy, teeming with youthful energy, bounded up the sticky wall. Minutes later he stood waiting, an archetype of vigor, as his compatriots emerged to join him on an even surface with a high ceiling. "See?" he said. "Like I told you. Piece of cake."

Jeremy took a moment to stretch his back. Looking down at his hands, he was dismayed to find the final effect from the mushrooms gone. His mouth sagged, but hearing the iron rungs creak in their worn-out sockets, his face lit up and he began running in their direction as if angels were leading the way. "Hurry up," he yelled to Karen. "You're slowing us down."

Karen steamed at the rebuke. She wanted to scream, *I'm pregnant, you idiot,* but, as usual, shame held her back. Instead she yanked hard on Jeremy's sweatshirt, still binding her middle, and barreled ahead.

Arriving at the first of the four ladders, she looked up, sending out her voice. She bit her lip at its flimsy construction—two vertical ropes about twenty feet long with horizontal bars flapping in the wind. She didn't like what she saw but kept it to herself.

"Here I go," said Randy, after demonstrating the technique at the bottom. To ensure safety, they all understood that only one person would climb at a time. "Rungs five and seven are corroding," he cautioned as he made his way up. "Don't cut your fingers on them. And number twelve is completely missing," he added moments later. Karen and Jeremy yelled back up, acknowledging that they had heard.

With the candle in his pocket, Jeremy started his ascent, mumbling a prayer of thanks for his enhanced sense of touch.

Karen, clicking feverishly, offered valuable tips from below while she waited for her turn. "Watch out for the protruding rock above your head," she warned, "and slow down. Remember what you told me: three limbs on the ladder at all times."

Karen wiped her sweaty palms on her pants before beginning her turn. She ran her voice over an area of rope beginning to fray, holding her breath until she passed it by. Farther up, she stopped to push an annoying hair out of her eye. Forcing herself, she moved along at a steady pace, conquering one ladder then another, until, arms trembling, she called for a break at the midpoint level before collapsing like a broken folding chair.

Jeremy nervously twisted his hands together, repeatedly inquiring about the time, since being caught and brought back to enemy territory would be tantamount to a death sentence.

Karen, in turn, forced herself to put aside her anxiety and exhaustion, knowing the danger of her surroundings required total concentration, with no room for mistakes. She signaled she was ready to continue. They moved on.

"One more ladder and we're there," yelled Randy, now waiting at the third level with Jeremy beside him. They stepped aside to allow enough space for Karen to join them in the wall's recess. "Oh my God," she said, barely believing how their luck was holding out.

Jeremy planted a kiss on his wife's face and, laughing playfully, placed one on Randy's too. The boy held out his right hand to be shaken like a man's before heading up.

As Jeremy waited below with one foot on the bottom rung for the okay to proceed, he turned toward Karen. The glint in his eyes shifted to a serious one. "I didn't know we could do this," he confessed. "To tell you the truth, I had my doubts—about me, you, Randy." Karen stared back, too dazed and stunned to speak, knowing she had had her doubts too.

Karen, clicking continuously, observed as Jeremy made his way to the very top of the last ladder and stepped onto solid, sacred ground. Having arrived at this longed-for destination, a place he wasn't sure he'd ever see again, he kissed the brown earth and called to his wife below. "Karen," he cried, tears streaming his face, "I'm sitting next to Randy. Hurry! I think I see some light."

"I'm coming," she said, her voice trembling with emotion. Randy had already yelled down about the two broken rungs, numbers eight and ten. Karen, now on heightened alert, took the necessary precautions. Flexing her biceps and quads, she grunted from the physical and mental strain as she successfully maneuvered past both problems, but as she placed her heel on rung thirteen, the step gave way without any warning, sending her foot down to twelve, which also gave way from the force of the impact. Her leg hit a jagged edge of metal, which sliced through her pants into her ankle. She shrieked in pain, but managed to hang on to the frame of the ladder and drag herself up while she felt for a new foothold. The ladder twisted in the breeze and the uneven stress loosened one of its two anchors at the top.

Still, she held on despite the shooting, knifelike sensation now running along her calf. She found the next rung and continued to climb. Then disaster hit as the final anchor gave way.

Instinctively, with no time to panic, her arms shot out, searching for a protruding rock, a tree root—anything to grab on to—but all she found was smooth earth. Yet somehow her body stuck to the wall as the ladder crashed below with a sickening boom. She remained still, hugging the flat surface for dear life, afraid to move, afraid to die. Something unfathomable was holding her up, and while grateful for this unexplained lifeline, her mind remained blank, unable to grasp what it was, until moments later, she opened her mouth in a silent scream as the truth sunk in with a knockout punch. Although she had lived underground for less than a year, her body now betrayed her with a syrupy liquid seeping from her pores, its concentrated adhesive bursting with enough strength to support her weight.

"K-Karen?" Jeremy called from above, frantic, his pitch rising to a sickening squeal.

The alarm in his voice zapped her back. "I'm here," she said, slowly moving one sticky hand, then the other, and finally her knees, the glue coming right through the material of her pants.

Like links in a chain, Jeremy seized Randy's legs while the boy reached down and grabbed Karen by the wrists. Together they hauled her the final few feet to the tippy top where she slumped, physically safe but broken in spirit.

She lay immobile, like a torn ragdoll tossed to the floor amidst broken bric-a-brac. Looking at Randy, lips pinched together in a seal, Karen suspected he knew something was amiss. In contrast, Jeremy's face lit up like Christmas lights as he scooped her in his arms, hugging her wet, sticky body, oblivious to its sweeping changes.

"We did it!" he cried, fists pumping the air. "We're free!"

Karen sat up and tried to speak, to confess her ugly transformation, but Jeremy rushed on. "Look," he said, pointing. "Can you see the light?"

She tilted her head, squinted her eyes, and, yes, she could make out a trace of sunrise down the passageway.

"Go on," she said, panting, too exhausted to move. "I'll be right there."

Jeremy protested, but barely. "You sure? I shouldn't leave you like this."

"It's okay. I just need another minute."

Seizing the sacrifice, he let go of her hand, ran a finger along her cheek before beginning to walk. Within moments, he switched to a run when just ahead lay his salvation, and now no one—not Karen, not Mary, not the devil or God himself—would stand in his way.

Rousing herself, Karen got to her knees, then stood erect, using the wall for support. She walked like a drunkard, lurching from side to side. The mud seeped into her shoes, caked her clothes, chafing like cardboard against her skin. She stumbled, caught herself, and continued. A stone's throw away, she saw Jeremy, standing tall and strong like a god, staring up at the sky before pulling himself through the hole.

"Karen," he yelled. "I'm up. Randy's up too. We did it!"

"I'm coming," she whispered, speaking so feebly she barely heard herself. The narrowness of the tunnel precluded any echoes, but the cave's silence, a sham, fought back when just a shiver away, the sound of a steady, distinctive gait—one short step followed by a longer, heavier one—increased into a crescendo and proceeded with the determination of a healthy heartbeat. Karen's eyes opened with fear and she moved on, staggering toward the light. She was almost there when a sharp pain in her lower region caused her to double over, her elbows pressing against her knees, her hands against her ears.

She had been expecting this. Mary had called it "engagement," where the baby's head drops low into its mother's pelvis a few weeks before delivery in first-time pregnancies. *Good*, she thought, eager to get the birth experience over with, but as she pressed down on her abdomen, more pasty goo seeped out. The near-term fetus kicked back in response and Karen shuddered with the sudden and overwhelming knowledge of the father's true identity. Looking down and in, with a skill similar to Mary's, one she hadn't known she possessed until this very moment, she saw the startling image of her little one, a far cry from the perfect babies pictured in magazines. Karen, horrified, bit down on her fist as tiny, budlike wings scraped the lining of the cocoon growing inside her.

"Oh, God," she moaned. "My poor little baby. My poor little baby."

"Karen," Jeremy repeated from above. "What's going on?"

Blinking through tear-streaked eyes, she looked up to see him, waiting for her in the mouth of the cave.

"Karen," she heard again, this time coming from a different person, one with a country drawl, and, as Karen surmised, the bearer of the distinctive gait. Wheeling around toward the hidden figure, standing behind a bend, she wondered, *Why isn't he coming for me? Why is he waiting so patiently?*

Then she understood. He was presenting her with a choice: the worst possible scenario. And why? Was he acknowledging he had made a mistake with the abduction or did he just realize he could no longer hold her against her will? And what was he offering? It didn't matter. She already knew—had known for some time—that she was one of life's losers, a reject, a mistake, and now her baby was too.

Protectively, she ran her hand across her swollen belly, cooing, "I'll never let anyone hurt you. Mommy loves you."

Rahm emerged from the shadows, moving closer, clicking, listening.

Karen screamed at *Him*. "You stay away! The baby's mine! *Mine!*"

"Come back with me, Karen. For the baby's sake. Our baby. You know it's for the best. Here. Take this. It's for you."

Instinctively, Karen reached out and took hold of the offering: a stone, similar to those worn by the women below. "What the …?"

"Look carefully. It's finer than all the other stones in the cave. I found it recently near the pearls you so admired on the day you let me love you; it has a slight blemish, but that's what makes it unique. And just as important, it doesn't fall apart when it's not in the water. Come back with me, Karen. I promise to treasure you and the baby, always."

Karen's lips trembled. "The baby's strange. Very strange."

"No!" said Rahm. "Not strange. Different."

"Different," she said, dragging out the syllables. As her clenched hands unfolded, she met his eyes with her own off-centered glance. Then tilting her head downwards, she studied the stone, picturing it, a one-of-a-kind gem, hanging from her neck above her suckling, one-of-a-kind infant.

Rahm pressed her hand, the pearl another link between them. "It would look lovely on you. Perfect."

She gently rubbed its blemish. "Perfectly unique."

"Perfectly different."

Karen shifted her gaze to the slice of blue above, and breathed deeply to gather her strength. She took a step forward and whispered, "*Adieu mon amour*," then looked back at the world she occupied, the underworld—her prison, her asylum, and now her aberrant child's asylum too. With fingers intertwined in supplication, she mouthed a silent blessing for Jeremy—her husband—the only man she had ever loved. Despite all they had been through, the betrayals, the lies, the hurt, she knew she would never love another. Not like this.

Concentrating, she fixed his image in her mind's eye as the rising sun framed him with a corona, a symbol of freedom in his deliverance. She would always want to think of him this way. But now she would bow to her fate, with the prehension that this moment had been sealed long ago. And though she might regret it tomorrow, she turned toward the cave—her cave. Reaching out to embrace the darkness, she didn't flinch as hands pulled her down, leading her home.

The End

Nancy Widrew was born and raised in NYC before settling in New England with her husband. She has two grown children and two four-legged furry ones, always a source of amusement. She has had short stories published in webzines and a print anthology. This is her first novel.

CPSIA information can be obtained
at www.ICGtesting.com
Printed in the USA
LVHW011537141220
674147LV00003B/585

9 780997 462197